The God Virus

- Published by Five Dimensions Press:

    - *Eye of a Fly* (Kindle edition), by Justin R. Smith.
    - *Introduction to Algebraic Geometry* (textbook), by Justin R. Smith.
    - *Abstract Algebra* (textbook), by Justin R. Smith.
    - *The God Virus* , by Indigo Voyager.

Fine Dimensions web page:
http://www.five-dimensions.org
Email: monika.sachsen.coburg@gmail.com

The God Virus

by

Indigo Voyager

Five Dimensions Press

The God Virus is a work of fiction. Any resemblance between its characters and real people (living or dead) is unintentional and purely coincidental.

Dedicated to my wonderful wife, Brigitte.

The God Virus

"Beyond our ideas of right-doing and wrong-doing, there is a field. I'll meet you there. When the soul lies down in that grass, the world is too full to talk about. Ideas, language, even the phrase 'each other' don't make sense anymore."

— Rumi

x

Part I

Inception

Chapter 1

The gentle rocking reminded him of a time, years ago, when he'd slept in the boat while his father and sister had fished for striped bass off Tumbler Island — a time he hadn't felt trapped.

A light blinded him.

It was as if someone held a flashlight against his eyes. When he opened them, he was alone again in a dark bedroom.

He tried to go back to sleep.

Light flared.

When he opened his eyes this time, he found himself in a grassy meadow filled with wildflowers under a clear blue sky. He clapped his hands over his eyes. When he opened them again, he was alone again in his dark bedroom.

What's happening? Could it be a side effect of that pill?

Plagued by suicidal thoughts, Derek had responded to an ad in the paper to participate in a clinical trial for Seshadri-Clarke Pharmaceuticals. And, a few hours ago, a man named Harry Pembroke had given him an "investigational drug" — a small red pill — to combat depression.

"What have you got to lose?" Pembroke had said. "This drug is guaranteed safe. The worst that can happen is nothing."

That's what happened. Absolutely nothing.

He drifted off to sleep again. The fluttering sensation returned, accompanied by a feeling he was bursting out of his skin like an overcooked sausage. A vivid sensation of flipping end-over-end in bed followed.

"I'm going to sue Seshadri-Clarke *and* Pembroke," he growled, leaping out of the bed.

A wonderful feeling of well-being suffused his body, a sense of being lighter than air. At the same time, he felt more awake than he'd ever been in his life.

I never had a lucid dream before. It's as if I woke up after spending my entire life in a drugged stupor. Maybe the pill really had some effect.

There was no particular reason for him to turn around, but he did. And he saw himself lying in bed.

How can I be standing here and lying in bed at the same time? Am I dead?

Then he noticed the sleeping figure's chest smoothly rising and falling.

This is the most bizarre thing that has ever happened to me.

He carefully looked around his bedroom. His sleeping body glowed slightly, flickered actually, like a candle. The glow was a color not on any palette he'd ever seen — an unnatural color, a color with no name.

Flickering with the same unnatural color, his black and white tabby, Norton, raised its head and stared at him, silently meowing.

I'm losing my mind. Will my life ever be normal again?

The bedroom looked the same as always but its walls seemed slightly transparent. Strange shadows moved through the air like ghostly presences and the air itself gave off a faint glow. He moved toward the door and tried to open it but his partially transparent hand passed through the handle.

Pembroke better be able to fix this.

✳✳✳

With no transition, Derek found himself in an ornate study, floating near the ceiling. Books lined the walls and Pembroke sat behind a large cluttered desk, apparently arguing with a heavyset man in a suit who sat across from him. Solid objects were slightly transparent, and the two men flickered with the unearthly light he'd seen earlier.

A herd of bison — transparent almost to the point of invisibility — slowly strolled through the room, the walls, and the people in it, completely unaware of them. Small transparent shapes or creatures winked in and out of existence — suspended in mid-air.

Or mid-whatever this is. It's as if I'm swimming in a ghostly ocean teeming with life.

Besides softly glowing, the "ocean" around him seemed to radiate energy or encouragement. It was as if the air itself was alive and conscious, and aware of Derek's presence.

It was so much more pleasant than the one time he'd been in the actual ocean, when his boat capsized off the Burnt Island Light, and he'd almost froze to death.

He looked at Pembroke.

I can hear them. But their lip-movements don't match their words.

"Ignorant thug," Pembroke said, without moving his lips. The ignorant thug didn't react — as if he hadn't heard Pembroke.

Derek moved toward the men and passed his arm through them.

"Cold," the heavyset man said, without moving his lips. He rubbed his hands together.

"The people I work for want their money," he continued — his lip-movements completely out of sync with his words. "They are losing patience."

"Prescription drugs cost more than *heroin or cocaine,*" Pembroke replied. "And Americans spend *billions* each year on antidepressants. I'll pay the people you work for with interest — even the rates they charge."

"Seshadri-Clarke owns you," the other man said.

With the kind of certainty found in dreams, Derek knew this man's name was Maxim Baranov.

"That's the beauty of this scheme," Pembroke replied. "I built a lab in my house and bought my own animals. I even bought my own DNA sequencer. My greatest triumph, and Seshadri-Clarke is *completely* cut out of it."

"Yes," Baranov replied, "With *our* twenty million."

"I'm barred from getting research grants," Pembroke said. "And I can't use Seshadri-Clarke facilities. I thought I explained the time-frame..."

"Excuse me," Baranov interrupted, pulling out a cell phone.

Derek hadn't heard it ring. In fact the only thing he could hear was the odd conversation.

"He's right here," Baranov said into the phone. "Of course I can speak freely in front of him. He doesn't know a word of Russian."

He's speaking Russian? I hear him speaking English.

"I think we should give him more time," Baranov said. Then, without moving his lips, added, "Not paid to think? Asshole."

"Should it look like an accident?" Baranov continued. "No? OK."

"They want to invest in your drug," Baranov said, putting the phone away. "But I must take pictures of your lab."

"Good. I tried to explain the time-frame involved in developing a new drug." "As if you apes would know lab equipment if it bit you," Pembroke replied, saying both sentences simultaneously. Derek had no trouble telling them apart, but Baranov didn't react to the second one.

"It's in the basement," Pembroke said, standing and walking to the door.

When Pembroke had his back to him, Baranov pulled out a pistol and shot him twice in the head, sending geysers of ... material against the woodwork.

Carefully sidestepping Pembroke's corpse, Baranov left, wistfully muttering, "Our own Bugsy Siegal. Or will I be the Bugsy Siegal?"

Oddly, this didn't startle Derek in the least. He'd felt the murder coming, the way one feels a storm brewing. The air's faint glow briefly intensified around Derek and radiated feelings of affection and protectiveness. A hug?

✳✳✳

Derek felt a sickening sensation of falling and found himself back in bed, awake and relieved.

He fell asleep again and had vague but intense dreams of his body changing — as if he'd begun to subtly mutate into something ... alien.

Derek got up.

He looked around his studio apartment, with its off-white walls holding the Salvador Dali poster *Persistence of Memory*, its bookcase separating the kitchen area from the table he used as a computer desk.

He made coffee, fed Norton, and cleaned the cat's litter box.

Pembroke had given him a notebook to record any "unusual experiences." Looking at the Seshadri-Clarke logo on the notebook, Derek wondered whether Mr. Pembroke *had* lied to him about the drug trial.

He thought back to when he'd signed up for the program, two days ago. He'd met Pembroke in his office at Seshadri-Clarke Pharmaceuticals — where he was the chief neurochemist, according to the secretary. That had seemed legit. Then he'd spent at least thirty minutes signing a stack of legal papers: nondisclosure forms, releases of liability, etc. Pembroke had told him this project was secret and he wasn't to discuss it with *anyone,* including other Seshadri-Clarke employees.

Derek Evans was a muscular, six-foot-four twenty-four year old with brown hair and eyes, from the lobster-fishing village of Boothbay Harbor, Maine. He'd been a A-student who loved science-fiction, science fairs, and complex, story-driven computer games like *Dreamfall, Gone Home,* and *Life is Strange.* He was so much of a nerd he'd resisted efforts to recruit him for his high school's football team. He couldn't remember the team's name.

At the age of seventeen, Derek had done the unheard-of: he won a special scholarship to New York University complete with full living expenses. The Boothbay Observer even published an article about him with his picture.

He'd reacted to the city's sensory overload like a frightened turtle: he'd pulled in his head and spent every waking moment of his time studying.

At times he yearned for the tranquility of home, the silence as he glided under sail through misty coves like a ghost, occasionally startling harbor seals, cormorants, and dolphins.

When he'd gone home on visits, though, he'd felt trapped.

8

Then, his nostalgia for New York was keener than anything he'd ever felt for home. The city was the battlefield where he'd build his future, and home was a sleepy backwater cutting him off from it. His sister's talk of getting her own lobster boat seemed parochial.

It had been the same when they'd visited him, last year. His sister, Wendy, had complained that she couldn't hear the sea, that New York even smelled "all wrong." She'd paced like a caged tiger.

His father had said his apartment was more a lair than a home, and his mother had questioned how he could ever be happy there.

He typed an account of last night's dream into a computer diary; the paperwork could wait.

"Norton," he muttered as the cat walked in front of the computer screen while he worked, blocking his view. Cynthia had given him Norton three weeks ago — just before telling him they needed a "vacation" from each other. A consolation prize?

He'd met her when she'd accosted him on the street and invited him to a party. That had struck him as odd but, perhaps, that was how things were done in the Big City. And, after a fling that had lasted a week, Cynthia had cut him off.

He shaved, showered and dressed. After spending fifteen minutes working on an inventory system for the new game, *A mind forever voyaging,* he realized he'd be late to work.

Maybe I'll be able to win Cynthia back. No — I know I'll win her back

Last night's dream was one he wished he could have a hundred times more. He'd never be trapped again.

Chapter 2

Derek briefly considered calling in sick because his nose ran, and he had a scratchy throat. Pembroke had mentioned he might experience symptoms like that and to avoid contact with others if it happened.

He rejected the idea.

The company where he worked had a new owner and today there would be a meeting with their new boss. Calling in sick was not an option.

After saying goodbye to Norton, Derek left for work. He felt sorry for the kitten, alone all day in a little Manhattan apartment, but what could he do?

Slush still covered west 76th street after the snowfall two days ago. Four story brownstone apartment buildings lined the street with snow-covered staircases up to their front entrances. Derek walked to the 72nd street subway station, bought a paper at the newsstand, and took a train downtown.

Shoved against nameless strangers more tightly than the most passionate lover's embrace, Derek spent fifteen minutes in the train.

He got off at 42nd street — near the park around the New York Public Library's main branch, with its ornate columns and concrete lions. A cart selling roasted chestnuts gave off an acrid and unpleasant aroma. He'd never understood the allure of chestnuts roasting over an open fire.

Derek entered the narrow concrete canyon of 41st street.

He fought his way through the rush-hour crush of people and arrived at 6th Avenue.

He worked at Enigmatic Adventures, a company that made games for the PC, Xbox, and recently, IOS- and Android-based cell phones. It was located on the third and fourth floors of a five-story apartment building incongruously sandwiched between high-rise office towers. An odd arrangement: since the offices had once been apartments, both floors had working kitchens and bathrooms with bathtubs.

Humming *Flight of the Bumblebee,* Derek got off the elevator on the third floor and went directly to the kitchen for some coffee. Alessandra Giancana — or Allie G, as people called her — was already there.

She was a petite blond with an olive complexion in a tweed skirt and jacket who Derek found attractive, if intimidating — a streetwise New York woman who freely used profanity and said things like, "Men are chickenshit."

Does she mean me? he'd wondered.

A jagged scar on her right jaw-line marred her otherwise-beautiful face. She was a few years older than Derek and higher up in the company: the acting head of Art and Animation.

"Don't even think about it, kid," his then-supervisor, Edwin Malloy had said. "She's light-years out of your league."

Although he'd had lunch with her a few times in the office kitchen, he'd never had had the nerve to ask her out on a date.

"Jesus H Christ, Maniac," Allie said — repeating her running joke about his being from Maine. "You're *smiling.* Something new in your life? Or some*one?* Other than … Cynthia?"

"I took an experimental new drug. An antidepressant."

"Where can I get some?"

"It's not ready for prime time," Derek said. "I had dreams that were off the end of the weirdness scale."

"Is it legal?"

"It's from Seshadri-Clarke Pharmaceuticals. And it gave me a fantastic idea for a game."

Derek launched into an animated account of his dream, and Allie agreed that it would make a good game.

Glenn Brown, the Network manager joined them. Glenn was a bald, heavyset man with a terrible cough and gravelly voice who wore a black tee shirt with "31337" on its front. Glenn imagined himself to be a super-hacker and would make mysterious references to "hacking the CIA and the NSA," saying "I can't really talk about it."

Then he'd talk about it.

Glenn had a bad smell, and Derek suspected his relationship with soap and water was tenuous at best.

They chatted about the upcoming meeting at 10.

"Maybe they'll hire a replacement for your supervisor," Allie said.

Since Roger Matthews had left, Derek had been the only person in Unreal Gameplay Programming.

Finally, they went back to their cubicles. Derek's had a framed picture of Cynthia, a potted coleus and his workstation — all under soul-sucking white fluorescent lights.

A call to Pembroke's office went to voice-mail.

Derek did a web search on Bugsy Siegal and found a Wikipedia article that detailed Bugsy's murders, rackets, and

12

how he had finally been murdered himself. None of it fit with what he'd experienced last night.

***

The first thing Derek noticed about the meeting was how empty the room was: it was just him and Allie.

Joel Mantell joined them sitting at the head of the table. He was a thirty-something, deeply tanned man in a charcoal pin-stripe suit. He had short, curly brown hair that made his head look a like a brush. He had a toothpick in his mouth.

He began by assuring Derek and Allie that their jobs were safe. As he talked, the toothpick moved around his mouth, and Derek wondered whether he'd swallow it.

"Where is everyone?" Allie asked. "Ed and Mike and the others? The Story Development team. We should wait for them."

"They won't be coming."

"How can we have a meeting without them?" Allie said.

"We're moving in a bold new direction, and I hope you can share my vision for the future."

"OK," Derek said.

"No more 'girlie games' and cell-phone puzzles. We'll be doing Galactic Marines The story-lines will write themselves: combat, combat, combat. Robots versus humans, aliens versus robots, etc. If any writing is needed, I'll do it myself."

Derek pitched his idea for a game.

"This is the opportunity to make something clear," Mantell said. "*I'm* the idea-man. Grand Theft Auto Manhattan sounds too complex storywise. And you need realistic-looking faces with facial expressions."

"Animated faces are our specialty," Allie said.

"Yeah, but how quickly?" Mantell said. "Robots are boxes

with arms and legs. You can crank them out in no time. And I'm cutting your department to the bone."

"Pardon my French, Mr. Mantell," Allie said. "But how the *fuck* can we develop games with no staff?"

"I'm hoping can understand my overriding vision for the company. This is going to be a lean mean operation. You two are going to be single-person departments."

"More mean than lean," Allie muttered.

They broke for lunch.

✱✱✱

As he headed for the elevator, Mr. Mantell stopped by the secretary, Ms. Finkel, and told her, "Anyone calls for me, tell em I went out to get laid."

"Sure about that?" Ms. Finkel replied.

"Just do it."

"OK," Ms. Finkel replied, to his back.

"What if your wife calls?" she added, but Mr. Mantell was already in the elevator.

As Derek headed toward the elevator, Ms. Finkel pointed him out to a man waiting beside her desk. He was a tired-looking, gray-haired man in a wrinkled blue suit.

"Derek Evans?" he asked.

"Yes."

"May I speak with you in private?"

"OK."

They went back to the conference room Derek had just left, and the man showed Derek his golden shield and ID.

"I'm Detective Roberts. Manhattan South."

"Detective?" Derek said with a sinking feeling.

"Are you acquainted with a man named Harry Pembroke?"

"Yes, I'm in a drug study. He ran it."

14

"We found your contact information among his papers."

"Found?" Derek said. "Did something happen to him?"

"Someone murdered him."

"*What?*" Derek gasped — almost fainting, thinking *Last night happened?*

"How well did you know him?"

"I only met him twice, in his office. I responded to an ad in the Times."

"Tell me about those meetings," Detective Roberts said.

"The first time, I filled out a bunch of legal forms. The second time, I took a pill he gave me."

"That's it?"

Derek nodded.

"Out of curiosity, what was the drug study for?" Detective Roberts said.

"An antidepressant."

"Did it work?" Detective Roberts asked, smiling.

"Yeah, I think so."

Detective Roberts shook Derek's hand, thanked him, and gave him a business card.

As he began to leave, Detective Roberts paused and said, "Oh, I have to ask. Where were you 11 PM last night?"

"I was in bed, sleeping."

✶✶✶

Now that Mr. Matthews would not be replaced, Derek decided to move into his supervisor's former office. For one thing, it was a real office and not a cubical. It even had a window.

After transferring his files to Mr. Matthews's server and his meager possessions to his new desk, Derek sat and stared out the window. A wino urinated into the gutter below, and a cop nudged him to move along.

He tried to make sense of what had happened last night. What else did he have to do? The projects he'd been working on were canceled.

He did a web-search on lucid dreams and out-of-body experiences, but nothing leaped out at him. Certain hallucinogens like ketamine, LSD and DMT could trigger them.

Their descriptions didn't match what he'd experienced, especially the feeling of being super-awake. His dream had more in common with near-death experiences, although he hadn't seen any "tunnel of light."

"Shit!" Allie said, startling him out of his seat. "Worst fucking day I've had at this chickenshit company. That suppurating pustule in a suit is running us straight into the ground."

Derek looked up at her.

"I had to fire *everyone else* in my department," she continued. "People older than me, with kids in college. Those poor bastards! They put everything they had into this shitty little company! We're going to Maxwells. Wanna come?"

"Sure."

✳✳✳

They all crowded into Maxwell's Bar and Grill, a cramped and steamy pub across the street from the office.

Derek got a beer and Allie a glass of red wine.

"The dream I was telling you about?" Derek said to Allie.

"You can kiss that game goodbye," she muttered, chugging her wine and ordering another. "I knew the company had problems, but *A mind forever voyaging* would've have been a blockbuster. We're just fucking hamsters on a wheel, running as fast as we can and getting *nowhere.*"

She threw back her second glass of wine.

"It wasn't a dream. The guy I met at Seshadri-Clarke was murdered last night."

"Huh?" Allie said.

"That guy talking to me at the office was a homicide cop."

"No *shit!* Did it happen like in your dream?"

"I didn't have the nerve to ask."

"Well that's creepy as hell," she said.

Chapter 3

That evening Derek went to bed with fear and anticipation. He smoothly slipped out of his body and floated near his apartment's ceiling. As before, Norton's eyes tracked his movements.

Maybe Pembroke's murder was a coincidence.

As he thought of Detective Roberts, he found himself in a long narrow room with Detective Roberts and others.

Faint, translucent humanoid forms strolled through the area, passing through people and tables.

It's as if another world occupies the same space as this one.

This might have unnerved Derek, but the faintly glowing air around him radiated reassurance and feelings of absolute safety.

He tried to figure out what the room was and noticed rows of bottles on shelves.

It's a bar, he realized. And, somehow, he knew Detective Roberts's first name was Ian. As he thought this, he noticed faint wisps of light floating away from him, like glowing cigarette smoke. With a dreamlike certainty, he knew that these were his thoughts as they left his mind.

It's as if thoughts have a life of their own when we're done with them, he thought. And *that* thought created another wisp of smoky light.

Detective Roberts was drinking with a fellow detective, Jose Martinez.

"Chilly," Ian Roberts muttered, rubbing his hands.

Jose nodded.

"Who do you like for this?" Jose said.

"The wife found the body," Detective Roberts said. "Said she was away on business and came back the morning after the murder."

"Her story check out?"

"Completely. She said she had no idea who would want to kill Pembroke, but I think she's lying."

"Then I suspected Evans," Roberts continued. "The Seshadri-Clarke people said there was no drug study and, if there was, Pembroke would be the *last* person to conduct it."

This sounds like my dream.

"What changed your mind?" Jose said.

"Aside from the killing being the work of a pro," Detective Roberts said. "Twenty other people showed up at Seshadri-Clarke wanting to sign up for the study. Evans must've called Pembroke the instant the paper hit the newsstands."

I'm the only one in the world who got that pill.

"So Pembroke was working solo on something?" Jose said.

"Yeah, his basement was like a Frankenstein movie," Detective Roberts said. "Rats and monkeys, weird glassware. His lab assistant said Pembroke treated the animals horribly. Tortured them even."

"There's got to be a special place in Hell for people like that."

"I still have my doubts about Evans, though," Detective

Roberts continued. "He said Pembroke *was* running the study, not *is*. Almost like he *knew* he was dead."

"Maybe it was just, you know, a slip of the tongue."

"No, Evans knows something. He's not the shooter. Probably. But my gut tells me he's holding something back."

Damn!

"What was Pembroke working on?" Jose said.

"Evans said it was an antidepressant."

They took long slow sips of their drinks.

"Happiness in a pill," Jose said, shaking his head. "So Derek really jumped on that study. Kind of pathetic, isn't it? Almost like a junkie."

"Yeah, normal people like you find happiness in a *bottle*" Derek shouted. They didn't hear him.

"You know that confidential informant I used to run out of Forsyth and Houston?" Detective Roberts said. "The one that OD'd last year?"

"Larry with the Glasses?" Jose said.

"Yeah. I was shooting the shit with him once and asked him what he thought the ultimate high was."

"What did he say?"

"He said, Man that's easy. Death. Every junkie knows the ultimate high is death."

✳✳✳

Derek wondered what Cynthia was doing at this hour and immediately found himself floating in a large room with people seated at many tables.

An elegant restaurant!

Many conversations buzzed in his mind but he focused on Cynthia and the man with her.

Cynthia sat across from a man in a suit, who he somehow knew was named Herman Berkowitz.

"When is your wife due back?" she asked Berkowitz, adding, "I wish you didn't look like a pasty, swollen toad in a suit. Can't have everything, I guess. I'll pry you loose from the crone you married."

"Next week," he replied. "How do you like this place?"

"Fantastic"

"Got rid of that cat?" Berkowitz asked.

"Yeah. I tried to kick it out the door but my nosy neighbor saw me," Cynthia said. "Bitch threatened to call the police on me for animal cruelty."

"What did you do?"

"Pawned it off on chump," Cynthia said.

"The guy you dated to make me jealous?"

"I swear I'll *never* do that again, Hermie."

"Best piece of ass I've had in ages," Berkowitz said, without moving his lips. "We can set you up in an apartment as the corporate mistress. Share you with partners and top clients. Maybe do three-ways."

With dreamlike certainty, Derek knew that the thought of sharing Cynthia with other men thrilled Berkowitz. Almost more than having sex with her himself.

And then, Derek knew — with inexplicable certainty — that this proposal would disappoint Cynthia at first, but she would ultimately accept it. The money and gifts they'd give her would excite her. And she would find the whole idea of being a 'kept woman' alluring.

"How can you do this to me?" he shouted to Cynthia. "How can you do this to *yourself?*"

Nobody reacted.

He realized that the Cynthia he'd loved had never existed, except in his own mind. This woman was a stranger and always had been.

I wish I could knock some sense into you, he thought, moving in front of Cynthia. *I wish I could see the expression on your face.*

As usual in this state, the colors he saw had a transparent, washed-out quality. Details were blurred.

When he concentrated on seeing her clearly, it seemed to work. His surroundings gradually became more distinct until — abruptly — many assorted sounds assaulted his ears: silverware clicking on plates and a roar of a hundred different voices. He fell several inches, almost collapsing to the floor.

Cynthia screamed.

I'm here? Barefoot? In pajamas?

Other patrons looked up from their dinners.

The restaurant was dimly lit by chandeliers, and every table had a candle. Out the windows to the right, Derek saw a bay with boats and flashing lights on floating buoys.

Where is this? Oyster Bay?

With a hundred pairs of eyes staring at him, Derek fought the urge to run. Where could he go? He didn't even have the faintest idea where he was.

"I don't know how I got here," he mumbled. "I was in bed sleeping, and then ... I was here."

The manager called the police.

Chapter 4

Police arrived in fifteen minutes and stuffed Derek into a car. As they drove off, Derek saw that the restaurant was City Island Steak and Seafood.

They drove him to the 45th Precinct and put him in a small interrogation room. It was twenty feet square with dark green walls, a barred window rendered almost opaque by grime, and had a table and three chairs.

Derek sat.

Two policemen joined him.

"I don't know what happened," Derek said. "I was thinking about Cynthia as I went to sleep, and then I was at that restaurant."

"Women can make you do crazy things," an officer named Pat said. "God knows, I've been there. Well, I never walked barefoot in snow. You haven't broken any laws. Maybe disorderly conduct, but that's a stretch."

"The no shoes, no service rule," another named Hernandez laughed.

They ended up dropping him off at the Bronx Calvary Hospital.

✳✳✳

In a curtained-off alcove in the Emergency Room, Derek sat on a hospital bed as a Dr. Wilfred Hendrix took his medical history and examined him.

"The surgical mask is just a precaution because you have a fever," he said. "You probably caught a cold."

"Amazingly," he continued. "For someone who sleepwalked two miles in snow, you're in remarkably good shape. Any history of sleep-walking?"

"No."

"Any changes in your life recently? Changes in diet or medications?"

"I took an experimental new drug for depression," Derek said. "From someone named Harry Pembroke."

"*The* Harry Pembroke? You *met* him?"

"You've heard of him?" Derek said.

"He's very well-known in certain circles."

"What's he known for?"

"His big idea: change brain chemistry by changing *DNA*. Wild stuff. You might actually be able to *edit* schizophrenia or alcoholism out of the human genome, permanently. Then he went off the deep end."

"How?"

"A big scandal. I don't know the details, but I heard he almost went to jail. Anyway, he wound up leaving academia and working for Seshadri-Clarke."

Dr. Hendrix stared into space and muttered, "What a tragic loss. He was *wasted* on Seshadri-Clarke Pharmaceuticals."

"What's going to happen to me?"

"Oh," he started, as though he'd forgotten Derek was there. "We'll hold you twenty-four hours for observation and release you."

✳✳✳

It took them until 3AM to find him a bed in the Psychiatric Ward. It was as private a room as possible when the door is just a curtain separating it from the nurses' station.

A nurse named Carla Mendoza adjusted Derek's bed and offered him a Tylenol for his fever. She was a forty-something Latina whose surgical mask covered her face.

"They're raping me," an elderly woman across the ward screamed. "They are so cruel. They keep burning me with hot irons."

"Severe Alzheimer's," Nurse Mendoza said, pulling the curtain aside to reveal that the screaming woman was alone in her 'room.' "You ask me, she should be kept sedated, like out cold. Hospital policy says otherwise. Are you going to give us any trouble tonight?"

"I promise I won't sleepwalk."

She chuckled and left.

When they turned out the lights, the woman's screaming died down and Derek managed to fall asleep. He slid out of his body and looked around.

Maybe I can go home the same way I landed at that restaurant.

✳✳✳

He visualized his apartment and found himself there, floating near the stove.

Maxim Baranov and another man, who he knew was Aleksandr Rabotnikov were ransacking the place.

"We've got to salvage something," Baranov said. "Or *my* neck's on the block"

"No red pills anywhere," Rabotnikov replied. "You sure you could get a chemist to reproduce the drug?"

"I'm not sure of anything. Where the *hell* is Evans?"

"Out partying?" Rabotnikov chuckled. "I wouldn't spend a *second* longer than I had to in this shithole. What do you want with him?"

As Baranov flipped Derek's bed over, Norton hissed and fled.

"I want to ask him some . . . questions," Baranov replied.

"Why did you kill Pembroke, again?"

"Ustinov ordered it."

"So tell him it's *his* fault everything went to shit."

"My dear Sasha, remember the saying about spitting up at your superiors?" Baranov said, putting his arm around Rabotnikov and kissing his cheek.

"It falls back in your face?"

Gangsters in love. Now I've seen it all.

✳✳✳

Derek returned to his hospital room — and his body. A realization struck him then: this was getting easier.

He drifted into a conventional sleep — the kind normal people do — and dreamed of Allie G.

Chapter 5

The Alzheimer woman's screams woke Derek in time for breakfast, which consisted of *quiche Lorraine* and a salt-substitute — eaten with a rubber spoon — and juice.

Derek inhaled it.

Wearing a surgical mask, a young brunette nurse came into his room, introduced herself as Kelly, and signed the whiteboard duty-roster on the wall.

Derek watched game-shows on TV and pondered Dr. Hendrix's remarks on altering DNA. Although it seemed to explain why Pembroke's drug wasn't wearing off, it didn't make sense. Profitable drugs were ones that *do* wear off and force people to buy more.

At ten, an orderly accompanied a thin, poker-faced woman to Derek's room, saying "Your sister's here."

"That's not my sister. Never saw her before in my life."

"OK, miss," the orderly said, grabbing the woman's arm. "Don't *make* me call security."

As the orderly dragged her away, she shouted, "Do you believe human evolution can achieve *transcendence?*"

"Ask me after I've had my coffee," Derek replied.

"Want some coffee?" Nurse Kelly asked through the curtain.

"That would be great."

"Never boring in a psych ward," she said, handing Derek a container of coffee. "Last week we had a woman who ate her cat whole, and vomited up fur. The doctor wrote 'woman eats pussy' on her chart."

"Quite a bedtime story."

"I've got a million of em. I should write a book. Are you a writer?"

"No."

Nurse Kelly returned to her duties, while Derek had a sneezing fit.

✳✳✳

Around noon, an orderly announced he had another visitor.

"Allie!" Derek exclaimed. A canvas bag hung from her shoulder.

"I knew you were a Maniac but this is ridiculous," she said, hugging him fiercely, as he unsuccessfully tried to suppress several powerful sneezes.

"How did you know I was here?"

"You're famous," she added, pulling a copy of the Daily News out of the bag. Its headline read **Sleepwalking Romeo stalks ex** and it had a photograph of police shoving him into a patrol car. Someone in the restaurant must've snapped it.

She handed him a business card.

"What's this for?" Derek said.

"I hate ambulance-chasers as much as the next guy but sometimes you need them. This has got to be a side effect of that drug you took."

"Thanks."

28

"How do you *feel?* I can't believed you walked barefoot all the way from 76th street to City Island — in the *fucking snow,* pardon my French. And *nobody* noticed. People in this town are *germs.*"

"I'm fine," he said wanting to explain what had really happened.

"When we broke for lunch, Mantell wanted me to have a few drinks with him," she said. "So I told him I was visiting you."

"Mantell hit on you?"

"Then he said to tell you you're fired. I said firing someone was *his* responsibility, but he said he wouldn't be alone in a room with a psycho. So *chickenshit.* He'd divorce his wife with a text."

"So you had a corner office for a whole day," she added, handing him a canvas bag containing his framed picture of Cynthia and his plant.

He pulled out the picture of Cynthia.

"I'll say it again. She's not worth it."

"I know," he said, throwing the picture into the trash. "She never was. I saw her soul."

"We're all updating our resumes. I'll give you a good recommendation, even though you don't work for me. I'll lie. Can you draw?"

"Uh, stick-figures?"

"The most expressive stick-figures I've ever seen. Their haunting eyes seem to follow you"

They laughed.

"Derek Evans?" an elderly woman said, entering the room. "I'm Ruth Horowitz, a social worker. We want to discharge you but we need to know you have someplace to go."

"I have an apartment."

"I'll take him home," Allie said.

Derek wrapped a hospital gown around himself and put on cloth booties an orderly gave him.

✳✳✳

Allie hailed a cab and they got in.

"I can't believe you sleep-walked *all that way* to Cynthia."

"That's not what happened," he said, with a sinking feeling in the pit of his stomach. "I didn't sleep-walk."

"What did you do?"

"Its hard to explain. It's a lot stranger than sleepwalking. And, if I'm not crazy, we'll find that two Russians broke into my apartment last night. I dreamed that."

"What are you telling me?" Allie said warily.

"You won't believe me, Allie. I have to *show* you."

"So show me."

"I can't do it *now*. Later this afternoon. Try to be alone in a place where no one can reach you. Lock all your doors and windows."

"Well that's officially fucking bizarre. Then what?

"I'll *prove* I didn't sleepwalk; I'll try, anyway. If it doesn't work, I'll try something else."

The cab reached Derek's building, and they went up to his apartment.

His door had been ripped off its hinges and Mrs. Cathcart, the landlady, was talking to two police officers. She was a frail white-haired lady in a bathrobe holding Norton in her arms.

"Hey Joe," one officer said, pointing to Derek. "It's the barefoot Romeo."

"They made so much noise, it woke me up," Mrs. Cathcart said. "Maybe 4AM. Then they ran out and almost knocked me down."

"Can anyone vouch for *your* whereabouts at 4AM?" Officer Joe asked Derek, laughing.

"Yeah, a lady with Alzheimer's and a healthy set of lungs."

"One of them was talking with a, you know, a Russian accent," Mrs. Cathcart continued. "Or maybe it was Greek or Hebrew. I don't know. They were foreigners."

"Maxim Baranov," Derek whispered in Allie's ear. "The one who shot Pembroke."

"OK," Allie nodded. "I'll bite. I'll take the afternoon off, and Mr. Chickenshit can fire me if he doesn't like it. Want my address?"

"No. It's better if I don't know it."

"Lock all my doors and windows?"

Derek nodded.

Shaking her head, Allie left.

✳✳✳

A carpenter had put a temporary plywood door in place, and Mrs. Cathcart said she would get a real door installed, muttering, "Nothing like this ever happened before you moved in."

Derek didn't reply. *After all, to some extent it was my fault.*

He cleaned up the apartment and fed Norton.

After showering and dressing in a loose-fitting black shirt, pants, shoes and socks, Derek unsuccessfully tried to boot his computer. He opened its case.

To his disgust, both hard drives were missing. Baranov had ripped them out so brutally the motherboard was cracked.

Luckily, he'd encrypted the drives. Enigmatic Adventures had demanded that since they had contained proprietary company software. He hoped the encryption would survive Baranov's efforts.

He'd need a new computer.

✳✳✳

Finally, he lay down and, in a few minutes, became drowsy and slipped out of his body. He desperately needed to confide in Allie and — above all — for her to know he wasn't crazy.

He thought of her.

She sat in front of an easel and appeared to be painting a picture. She held a palette that might've contained oil paints, but Derek couldn't make out any colors. The canvas looked blank.

Small translucent organisms seemed to swim through the air, looking a little like microscopic images of bacteria or amoebas.

"I belong in a psych ward myself for going along with this crazy scheme," Allie wordlessly said. "But he *was* right about the break-in."

With the dreamlike certainty he often felt in an out-of-body state, Derek knew that she had a crush on him.

"If you're going to make a move do it now, Derek," she added. "I'm getting hungry."

He materialized.

The room's translucent walls took on a serene sea-green cast, and held three oil paintings of fantasy landscapes. Two large windows made the room light and airy. In the corner, Allie had a high-end Macintosh workstation, a color laser printer, and a 3-D printer.

She wore jeans and a bright red blouse.

She stared at him for a moment, confused, as if unsure of what she was seeing. Then her mouth dropped open, her eyes widened, and she gave out a slow gasping moan. She clutched her chest and her mouth opened and closed without making a sound.

"I'm so sorry," he said, sneezing. "I couldn't think of another way."

The painting on the easel was a fantasy-landscape of an impossibly lush valley with a river running through it. A castle with many turrets surveyed it from a rocky crag.

"You ... you were a sh...shimmering heat image," she stammered. "And then the air congealed and turned opaque and ... turned into you."

"This room of yours. It's really beautiful."

"Normally, that would please me. Your timing sucks."

"Why don't we get something to eat?" Derek said. "You said you were hungry."

"I didn't *say* it, I *thought* it. And what I need is a drink or ten."

✳✳✳

They took the elevator down and stepped out of Allie's building into a bright, cold day. A nearby street-sign showed that her building sat on the corner of Kissena Boulevard, Main Street, and 41st Avenue — names that meant nothing to Derek. Densely-packed storefronts covered with Chinese characters lined Main Street, and across it was a Hong Kong Supermarket.

"I didn't know you lived in Chinatown," Derek said.

"This is Flushing, Queens. How the *hell* did you find me if you didn't know where I live?"

She led him to a restaurant named Tung Bo, two doors down from her building.

"It's not my favorite but it's close, and you didn't bring a coat. I take out from it sometimes."

"I didn't know how to bring a coat," he said, shivering. "I'm just glad I didn't show up buck naked."

"What a visual," she laughed, slowly looking him up and down.

Carved lacquered writhing wooden dragons twined around two pillars that flanked the entrance. The dimly-lit restaurant was deserted except for a tall, thin, white-haired Chinese waiter in a burgundy jacket and a similarly-dressed petite Chinese woman who tended the bar.

They took a table in the back, next to a giant green ceramic Buddha that seemed to stare at them.

"I'll have a Chianti Classico Riserva — preferably Ruffino," Allie said to the waiter. "Normally, I go to this Korean wine bar a couple blocks away. Good food and great views of the city skyline."

Derek ordered a Manhattan.

After consulting with the bartender, the waiter said they didn't have Chianti.

"OK, give me one of his."

When the drinks arrived, Allie gulped hers and asked for another.

"You're supposed to nurse these drinks," Derek said.

"Look, Maniac. I feel like I just gave birth to twins. And, on top of that, I think I caught your cold. I need my damn medicine."

"Sorry about the cold. And the twins."

"You still didn't answer my question," she said. "How did you find me?"

"I think everyone has a kind of ... essence," he began. "Something unique. When I'm in my spirit-body, I just think of a person I've met before and I'm there. My spirit is, anyway."

"Like a UUID code in a computer game?"

"Something like that I guess," he said. "So maybe the world is a little like a computer game."

"Like the Matrix? Does that make you Neo?"

"Actually it feels more like a *mind* than a computer. It's something alive, with a personality ... God, I wish you could come along with me and see for yourself."

"Commuting would be easy. No forty-five minute subway-rides fighting off pervs."

They ordered Wor Su Opp and Singapore noodles.

"Were you serious about giving me a recommendation?" Derek said.

"You have a superpower, Derek. You shouldn't be wasting your time looking for a damned job."

"I could teleport into a research lab and shock everyone," he mused.

"You'd be a sensation, a superstar."

"Or a lab rat strapped to a dissection-table."

"My grandpa would have a hundred moneymaking schemes for your superpower. All of them illegal."

She talked about her childhood in Brooklyn, going to Catholic schools, and then to the Cooper Union. He described his life in Boothbay Harbor, his sister, Wendy, and his experiences coming to New York City.

When he asked Allie whether she had brothers and sisters, her mood darkened.

"Since you can read minds, *which is creepy as fucking hell, incidentally*," she said. "I might as well tell you. You're looking at a living stereotype, Derek. Italian and related to the mafia. I might be a setup line for a bad ethnic joke if it wasn't so pathetic."

"Pathetic?"

"My father was the target and my brother, Tony, was 'collateral damage.' That's what grandpa said. At the funeral he said Tony would be avenged. And, I screamed *Why? Why papa? Why Tony?* All grandpa could think of to say was 'It's our thing'."

"Our thing?" Derek said.

"It's sure as fucking hell not *my* thing," Allie exclaimed, gulping her drink. "It never *was* and never *will* be. Mom and I didn't speak to grandpa again for ten years."

Derek tried to hug her but she pushed him away, saying, "As you may have guessed I come with baggage. A semi couldn't haul the baggage I have."

"Oh Alessandra Giancana," he murmured, relishing her name's musicality. "Sometimes you talk too much."

She laughed.

✳✳✳

They staggered back to her building.

"Where's the nearest subway?" Derek said.

"Five blocks away. You'll freeze your ass off. Come on up and let your mama take care of you."

They returned to her apartment and she mumbled, "I'm so dizzy. They should call those drinks South Bronxes."

Then she broke out in a fit of sneezing.

"Maybe you should lie down," Derek said, giving her a handful of tissues.

She gave her nose a loud, gurgling blow.

They staggered into her bedroom — a cozy room painted in cheerful tones of pale yellow with two more of her stunning oil paintings on the walls. A needlepoint cat with the caption "Man's Best Friend" hung above the head of a queen-sized bed.

"I'll loan you money if you need it," she slurred, barely able to stand. "I believe in you."

He suggested she lie down, and she did.

"I don't normally go to bed ... with a man on my first date," she mumbled and then, started snoring.

"This was a *date?*" he whispered, his spirits soaring. She was snorting and blowing bubbles out her nose, so he kissed her on her forehead.

Fully clothed, they lay there, side by side.
He tried to slide out of his body but his brain felt like mush.
He passed out.

Chapter 6

Sometime in the early morning hours, Derek found himself in an out of body state.

Allie screamed.

Derek tried to go to her and found himself standing in a grassy field with Mantell chasing Allie across it.

"It's a dream, Allie" he shouted.

She shot him a puzzled glance and mumbled, "A dream?"

The field and Mantell faded leaving Derek and Allie hovering in the air in her bedroom, both clothed as they had been on lying down.

"That's us, isn't it?" she said, pointing to the two sleeping figures.

"You've got my superpower."

Allie marveled at the soft glow that surrounded them, seemingly coming from space itself. It radiated a feeling of infinite calm. If a mountain or continent could be alive and aware, it might approximate the feeling that light radiated.

"This is the coolest thing that ever happened to me," she

said. "I feel so awake and alive. And this light … it makes me feel like I can accomplish anything."

They flew through the walls and hovered over the street below. A few cars drove past.

"I'm flying," Allie exclaimed, soaring several hundred feet into the air, then diving down to street level,

"Let's see if you can *teleport*. I'll go to my apartment and you follow."

"How?"

"Just think of me and you'll be there."

✳✳✳

Derek returned to his apartment and hovered near the ceiling. Norton looked up at him and meowed. Allie appeared, also floating near the ceiling.

"Now try to focus on the room. Or focus on Norton. Try to see him as clearly as possible."

Allie materialized and fell to the floor in a heap. Derek fell next to her.

"My God, Allie. You have *all* of my superpowers."

"Where's your bathroom? *Quick!*"

Derek showed her, and she ran to it, knelt in front of the toilet, and retched repeatedly.

"I never had so much booze at one time in my life," she said. "My head is exploding."

Derek got her Motrin.

"I've got to lie down," she said. "You know … your apartment…"

"It's a dump," Derek said, lying next to her. "The Russians who ransacked it thought so too."

She laughed.

"I like your Salvador Dali print, so there's some hope for you."

They slept for a few hours more, until Norton walked across them.

"What a cute kitty," she said, petting Norton. "Let's just relax and play with our new toys."

They slid out of their bodies, floated through the walls, and hovered over 76th street.

"That man down there," she said. "His name is Aleksandr Rabotnikov. How do I know that?"

"That's part of this ... whatever it is. You just know things for no particular reason."

Rabotnikov pulled out a phone and called someone.

"This is a *monumental* waste of time," he said. "Evans hasn't left his apartment for twenty-four hours. For all we know, he killed himself."

Fuming, he hailed a taxi.

✳✳✳

"I've got a place to show *you,*" Allie said, vanishing.

Derek thought of Allie and found himself floating beside her above odd translucent shapes.

"Are those columns?" he said. "Roman ruins?"

"*Greek* ruins. So we can visit *places* we've been to not just people we know."

"Where are we?"

"A village called Taormina, in Sicily. Last summer my grandpa tried to make nice with mom and me. He treated us to a trip to my family's ancestral home. And we took a tour of this Greek theater."

A group of Japanese tourists listened to a lecture about the place's history and snapped pictures. Apparently, an acting troupe still performed ancient Greek plays here in the summer.

"Let's find an inconspicuous place and materialize," Derek said.

"With no passport or local money?"

***

Back at Derek's apartment, the clock on the wall showed that it was eight AM.

"To Italy and back before *breakfast*," Allie said, sneezing several times. "We *better* find a way to make money with our superpowers. There's no way I'm going back to a dull job, especially working for a total ass like Mantell."

Derek handed her some tissues and she blew her nose.

Even sick, she's stunning! I can't believe this beautiful, brilliant woman is with me — in my apartment.

He'd never forget this day.

Allie called Enigmatic on Derek's phone and resigned. After listening for a few minutes, she shouted, "The 13th amendment abolished slavery" and disconnected.

"We could start a psychic detective agency," he said.

"I like it. We just *have* go somewhere and celebrate. And have an obscene breakfast ... like eggs Benedict and champagne."

"The old dilemma. I have a coat but you don't. And I don't know any place around here with eggs Benedict."

"Shit. We have to figure out how to carry stuff when we teleport."

"I can make the eggs, and I even have champagne. I was going to celebrate when we released *A mind forever voyaging*."

Derek started to make Hollandaise sauce and poach eggs as Allie looked on. Cooking had always been a hobby of his.

"A superhero who cooks," she murmured. "Mom hounded me to cook. She said I'd never find a man if I couldn't."

"You *found* a man."

She wrapped her arms around his neck and kissed him on the lips as he tried to fish eggs out of the hot water.

***

Derek put his computer on the floor in a corner and served the food.

"To the rest of our lives," Allie toasted "May they be incredible."

They drank and ate in silence.

When they were done, Derek put the glasses and dishes in the sink.

"Cooking done so beautifully is an act of love," Allie said.

"Really?" Derek breathed, wrapping his arms around her and kissing her.

They slowly moved toward his bed, ripping clothes off each other and kissing with a manic intensity, as though afraid the moment would pass.

His tongue invaded her mouth and he tasted her sweet aroma and, when her tiny tongue touched his, it sparked an electric shock that rippled though his body.

"Oh maniac," she moaned as her pupils dilated, making her eyes become black pools.

They made love with a feral intensity, the bed frame squealing in protest, dissolving their minds in sublime obliteration.

Glistening with sweat and exhausted, they lay on a bare mattress that was sliding off the bed, all the muscles in their bodies quivering. Someone knocked on the door.

"Should I call 911?" Mrs. Cathcart said. "Are those hoodlums back?"

"N...no Mrs. Cathcart," Derek stammered. "Ev...everything's f...fine."

They hauled the mattress back on the bed frame and collapsed onto it. The sheets and blankets had landed in a corner of the room.

"I ...I don't know about y...you," Derek shuddered. "B...but that was the m...most...incredible..."

"F... f...fucking ... *fucking.*"

They lay on the mattress in each other's arms, and Allie whispered, "You're the only guy I ever slept with who looks better naked."

They drifted off to sleep.

***

Some time later, they slipped out of their bodies.

"This is getting easy," Allie said. "I didn't even have to be half asleep, just relaxed."

Wisps of glowing smoke came out of her as she said this.

"Notice those things?" he said.

"What are they?"

"I think they're our *thoughts.* We give off mental energy whenever we think."

She pointed out thoughts approaching them from elsewhere. They seemed to tug at Derek.

"Thoughts *about* me but not *from* me," he said. "Let's follow them."

***

They found themselves floating near the ceiling of a warehouse. A terrified woman was tied to a chair and three others sat around her.

They both knew that she was named Sylvia Pembroke and the others were Vladimir Ustinov, Maxim Baranov and Aleksandr Rabotnikov. The three Russians sipped from glasses of liquid that Derek and Allie knew contained tea.

"That's the woman who came to my hospital room claiming to be my sister," Derek said.

How can you tell? Allie said. The partially translucent faces were impossible to see in detail.

"I just know it. Don't try to focus on the faces or you'll materialize here. Naked."

"You know how viruses infect cells?" Pembroke said.

"Pretend we don't," Ustinov said, sipping his tea.

"If Ustinov was Italian," Allie said. "He'd be called a *de facto.*"

"What's that? Oh, boss of the bosses?"

"I can't believe anyone would marry this hag," Baranov said, without moving his lips.

"It injects its DNA into the cell nucleus," Mrs. Pembroke said, "and takes over the cell's inner apparatus, causing it to make more virus particles."

"Like a computer virus," Baranov said.

"The cell dies," Mrs. Pembroke continued. "And the new virus particles infect other cells."

"Thanks for the science lesson," Ustinov said. "Why do we care?"

"Harry used this virus as a *hypodermic* needle to administer DNA to Evans. It kills some cells but just gives DNA to others."

"A custom-made virus?" Ustinov said, interested.

"Yes," Mrs. Pembroke said. "A modified, rapid-onset influenza."

"The pills gave Evans the flu?" Ustinov said.

"A mild case," she replied, nodding.

"Could someone else catch it from him?" Baranov said.

"Only if they were very close to him when he was in the sneezing phase. That phase doesn't last long, and the virus dies quickly in the open air and on surfaces."

"I caught your red pill," Allie exclaimed. "I'm not complaining, not a bit."

"So explain to me this," Ustinov said, fuming. "You husband spent a whole fucking year and twenty million dollars of our money to change Evans's DNA. Why?"

"He was an *incubator.* Harry was going to have him come in for a followup and give him a sedative. Then I would extract his pineal gland, a viral reservoir. It would contain a hundred pills worth of virus."

"Why?" Ustinov said — he must've shouted it because Mrs. Pembroke visibly flinched.

"Harry called it the *God Virus.* He wouldn't tell me more." "Be strong. Weakness is the ultimate crime. I cannot tell them about The Program or the Iron Order."

"One year seems like a short time to develop something that alters DNA," Rabotnikov said.

"We've been working on this virus for two decades," Mrs. Pembroke said. "We got most of the bugs out of it experimenting on street-people and students. This last year was to be the final push."

"Evans did sleep-walk, barefoot, two miles in the snow," Baranov said. "Something even Russians would find challenging."

"If I ever need a sleep-walking, barefoot army in Siberia, this pill will come in handy," Ustinov laughed. The other Russians laughed, but Mrs. Pembroke didn't react.

"They're probably speaking Russian," Derek observed.

"We should kill her," Rabotnikov said. "We're not getting our money back."

"We have to help this poor woman," Allie exclaimed.

"How?" Derek replied. "Our superpowers don't stop bullets. We don't even know this place's *address* or we could call the cops."

"What will happen to Evans?" Baranov asked Mrs. Pembroke.

"Over the next few months, he will change. Cells constantly die and get replaced by new cells. In his case, the new ones will express his new genes. Maybe five percent of his DNA is completely new, maybe ten."

"Doesn't sound like much," Ustinov said.

"Only four percent separates us from chimpanzees," Mrs. Pembroke said. "Evans is a new species. Probably unable to mate with human women and produce viable offspring." *"Homo sapiens superior,* a prolific species that will displace humans just as humans displaced Neanderthals. Inhumanly intelligent and telepathic."

Mrs. Pembroke decided that Derek's sleepwalking incident showed the virus had strange and disturbing side-effects. More research was clearly needed.

"Evans is turning into a sleepwalking monster?" Ustinov said.

"Most of the changes won't be visible."

Chapter 7

"We're turning into *monsters*," Allie sobbed, punching her pillow. She jumped up and ran to the bathroom.

"I don't look any different," she said, examining herself in the mirror. "And I don't feel any different."

She came out of the bathroom and started to get dressed.

"Look, Derek, I'm not blaming you," she said, filled with loathing for herself and him. "You're as much a victim as I am."

"Maybe we don't have to be victims at all."

"I need some alone-time," she said, sitting at the table. "To think about ... things."

She closed her eyes, took a deep breath, said "Please don't come after me," and vanished.

Derek sighed and picked up Norton and petted him. He'd experienced rejection often enough to know it when he saw it. He seemed fated to have a series of brief, intense flings. The one with Allie had been a shooting star, flaring brightly and fading just as quickly.

As a child, he'd often daydreamed of being a Jedi Knight

like Luke Skywalker — rescuing people, punishing evildoers, and changing the world for the better. At what price, though?

And he'd never experienced anything even remotely like sex with her. He sore muscles still twitched.

"It looks like it's just you and me, Norton," he said, his mood darkening, thinking about how his strangest and most short-lived relationship ended.

Like an automaton, he picked up the sheets and blankets and made the bed. Unmade beds depressed him.

He could not, *would* not slip into the suicidal depression that had driven him to Dr. Pembroke.

He forced himself to feed Norton and shower, and then he dressed and carried his wrecked computer to the trash cans on the street.

He went out.

The wind-whipped drizzle in his face matched his mood.

✳✳✳

Allie lay in bed crying and hugging a pillow to her chest.

"What's going to become of me?" she sobbed. "I'm turning into an alien freak! I lost my job and Derek. He was so promising, and he liked me."

She relaxed, became drowsy and slipped into an out-of-body state. Street noises vanished, and Allie mused, *The spirit-world is so peaceful. A mood permeates everything here — like the brightest, most radiant spring day imaginable — after a cruel winter.*

God, it almost makes being a freak worthwhile.

Allie felt a ghostly presence and heard a small girl's giggle. It was as if a mischievous little girl played hide-and-seek with her. The giggle returned followed by a squeal of delight.

Is my apartment haunted? No, this ghost is haunting me.

The ghostly presence gathered itself together and took on a more mature quality — of an ancient and mighty spirit — saying, *Time is a maelstrom transforming the universe with the power of consciousness itself: It turns agony into poignancy, terror into nostalgia, people into ghosts. When did I write that? I got the last part wrong, though: Now, it is turning a ghost into a person.*

I'm losing my mind, Allie moaned.

No, my dear. It is I who am losing mine, once again descending from Eternity into fluid and flesh — into the realm of seasons and years. I have seen empires rise and fall; I have been a warrior, a philosopher, a mother, and a wife.

Now I'm becoming something uncanny, something supernatural. Who ... what am I ... becoming?

I don't know, Allie replied.

We'll figure it out together, beloved mother.

Mother? At that moment, a flicker of wonder and joy radiated from within her — a sensation like a child's first dawn, magnified a million-fold. In her mind's eye, she saw a human ovum, wheeling like a tiny galaxy and — with a white-hot flash of energy — it expanded and divided. The spirit turned back into a spirit-child and giggled again, darting around the room.

God damn it, I'm pregnant! she realized, with absolute certainty — although it would be a while before a pregnancy test registered, if ever. Perhaps her alien hormones wouldn't even trigger one.

"I'm a freak giving birth to a freak!" she muttered, getting out of bed and pacing.

Derek has a right to know, but I can't tell him yet.

***

Derek purchased a new computer and cheap laptop at Best Bargains near Times Square. After lugging his purchases on the subway, he dropped them off in his apartment. He unpacked the laptop and took it with him.

He couldn't bear to be alone.

On Amsterdam Avenue he went to the *Beans 'n Cream Cafe*, a coffee shop with free Wifi. He bought some coffee, and turned on the laptop.

A quick scan of the news brought up typically depressing fare: President Eakins battling news outlets over negative editorials, trying to abolish the two-term limit on the presidency, and calling the Pentagon's Joint Chiefs of Staff "a bunch of pussies."

A search on 'Harry Pembroke' brought up a flood of information. His experiments at Arkham University were legendary. He'd restored the sight of congenitally blind mice by infecting them with custom-made viruses that altered their DNA. He'd been widely regarded as a leading candidate for a Nobel Prize in Biology.

Then came the scandal. A graduate student with a mild cold died of liver failure. Friends of the student claimed Pembroke had given him a pill — something Pembroke denied. Pembroke's research notebooks and computer files conveniently disappeared.

"Even if I *was* responsible — which I deny," Pembroke said. "Great discoveries require great sacrifices. One cannot create a garden without pulling out weeds."

Derek recalled Mrs. Pembroke's statement about working on the virus for decades.

Arkham University fired him, and he was barred from ever receiving Federal research grants. They briefly arrested him and charged him with criminal negligence but they couldn't make the charges stick.

He went to work for Seshadri-Clarke, where he developed two wildly expensive and successful antidepressants. Pembroke had even translated his research on mice to *humans:* A virus that cured congenital blindness in humans was in a "third stage clinical trial" — whatever that was — and the results were stunning.

A Wikipedia search on 'transhumanism' took him to a web pages with vast amounts of information. Many transhumanists believed humans could get implants that would enhance human abilities. Computer implants in the brain could enhance memory and computing ability, and other implants that could grant super-strength and speed.

A search on 'transhumanism' *and* 'Pembroke' brought up a web page that asked, "Where will human evolution go in the next 100,000 years? The next million years?" It appeared to be a sort of cult. Derek stumbled across a video on the site of Harry Pembroke making a rousing speech before a small group:

> "There is a glorious *music of the spheres* that *wills to be heard!* And only the genetically enhanced of the coming age shall experience it."

He seemed so mild-mannered when I met him.

A search on "Iron Order" raised nothing significant: a motorcycle gang probably not involved in genetic engineering.

A pretty pathetic cult, borrowing from the Russian mob.

A web search on 'pineal gland' brought up a Wikipedia page that showed that it was at the *base* of the brain. Further searches on pineal tumors revealed that surgery on it was possible but was the most difficult and exacting form of neurosurgery known — requiring special training and equipment. And it was *always* dangerous.

A search on 'Sylvia Pembroke' revealed that she was a surgeon at Columbia Presbyterian Hospital. She was probably a good surgeon — but she specialized in *knee replacements,* not neurosurgery.

"They planned to *kill* me," he exclaimed, startling a middle-aged man hunched over his laptop at the next table.

And he became aware of the ultimate irony: he owed his life to Maxim Baranov.

He brought up web pages on becoming a private detective. Unfortunately, to get a license, one had to work in a detective's office for three years, take a test, submit fingerprints and — as of this year — a *DNA sample.* That last requirement was a deal-breaker, if the others weren't.

Derek sat quietly and let his eyes go blurry. As if someone flipped a switch, the street noise and the clattering of dishes in the cafe ceased. In its place he heard a dozen people speaking. His surroundings took on the transparent cast they normally did when he floated out of his body.

I must be slightly out of my body, a millimeter or less.

"I hope that creep isn't dangerous," thought the man he'd startled earlier — Derek realized that his name was Wilfred Goode. "Lunatics everywhere in this goddamn city."

Sharon Porter, a young brunette in the corner, mentally re-hearsed an upcoming job-interview at James Hall, a Wall Street hedge fund.

If I hung out in a Wall Street coffee shop, I could probably pick up insider stock tips.

Unfortunately Derek lacked the prerequisite for making a small fortune in the market: a large fortune.

He realized he could teleport now, probably giving Goode a heart attack.

Everything I can do now violates the laws of physics. How's it possible?

Then, as though the universe answered his question, a thought popped into his head. He remembered a computer game, *Grand Theft Auto.* Despite its disgusting glorification of rape and mayhem, it vividly simulated a medium-sized city with streets, stores, traffic, and people. If a game-character dropped something, it fell to the ground — because that behavior was programmed into the game.

Then an enterprising hacker altered the game's underlying program-code to devise the *car-gun:* a machine gun that fired full-sized automobiles instead of bullets. He'd posted it to Youtube.

After cars left the gun, they obeyed the game's "laws of physics," wreaking havoc the way one would expect two-ton automobiles hurled at high speeds to do. In seconds, one could litter a "city street" with "piles of burning auto-carcasses," or "knock down buildings."

Scientists are characters in a computer game, painstakingly mapping the streets of a simulated city. And, when my spirit floats free, I'm that hacker, operating in Creation's womb — where all stories, dreams ... and realities are born.

One other person on Earth would understand.

✳✳✳

He spent the afternoon installing Linux on his new computer, trying not to think of Allie — and wondering why he needed a high-end computer now that he was unemployed. A strange craving came over him. He went out and bought a chilled bottle of cheap champagne and a box of microwave popcorn.

He came home, popped the corn, melted butter, opened the champagne — and indulged. The odd combination of flavors had an extraordinary effect, invigorating him and lifting his spirits.

He went to bed and dreamed of Allie and an odd little girl who called him dad.

Chapter 8

As he shaved, Derek noticed that his face looked different some-how. It took several minutes to identify what had changed: His brown eyes had become steel-gray. Not necessarily a bad look — indeed, his eyes had taken on an eerie, almost haunting quality.

"Let's play," Norton said, biting his fingers. As he played with Norton, his fingertips began to itch. When he put his socks on, he was shocked to learn that he had *no toenails.* They must've fallen off in bed.

***

He took his laptop to *Beans 'n Cream* and had coffee. At the food-counter, an irresistible smell caressed his senses. It took him several moments to determine the source of this aroma: lox. He'd only eaten it once before, in Maine, and had hated it.

He ordered a bagel with lox, took it to a table, and booted his laptop.

His fingertips itched worse than ever and he tried scratching. This didn't help because the itch came from *beneath* his finger-nails. After trying to scratch some more, all of his fingernails dropped off — painlessly — revealing pink skin underneath. There was no bleeding.

Derek numbly stared at the pile of fingernails on the table, wondering what further surprises awaited him.

Maybe Allie is right and we're turning into monsters. He thought of the movie, *The Fly,* and how Jeff Goldblum's body slowly mutated until it became unrecognizable — and the only way he could eat was by vomiting acid on people and drinking their melted bodies.

He focused on his laptop.

Derek pondered how to make money *legally* using his new abilities. The irony of it was that there were a thousand ways to make it *illegally:* Teleport into a bank vault, stuff his pockets, and teleport out.

In his childhood fantasies of being a Jedi Knight, he'd been pretty sure they didn't steal or lie. When his friends had hounded him into shoplifting a piece of candy, he'd been haunted by guilt days afterwards — feeling he'd betrayed his ideals.

If he became a criminal, he'd be as bad as Allie's grandfather, and she'd never forgive him.

His heart ached for her.

Finished with his bagel, he bought three more pieces of lox and grabbed a handful of sugar-packets. He poured five packets of sugar onto the lox and ate it with a fork, deciding that his latest craving made nutritional sense at least: lox was rich in protein and fish oils.

A man at the next table stared and grimaced at his culinary choices.

He detached, and the street noise ceased — and his surroundings became colorless and translucent. A woman seemed to appear out of nowhere.

Did she teleport here?

He rewound the scene and the woman walked backwards and ducked behind a panel in the wall. A hidden pantry for various supplies.

She's not One of Us. Wait a minute; I can rewind time? That's like the Life is Strange game.

He tried to push time *forward* with bizarre results: a man paying his check split in two. One copy went to the men's room and the other went out the door. A woman carrying dishes tripped and dropped them on the floor.

The further he tried to see into the future, the more confusing the view became. People split into thousands of copies doing different things until everything became a blur. The only things he could see clearly were some of the inanimate objects in the room, like the counters and door-frames.

He returned to the familiar *Beans 'n Cream*. The man he'd seen earlier paid his check, briefly paused at the mens' room door without going in, and left. A loud crash nearly startled Derek out of his seat. One of the two waitresses had dropped a pile of dishes.

An idea was forming in his mind.

He left the cafe and bought a deck of playing cards.

✳✳✳

Back at home, he dealt out the cards on the table and went into an out-of-body state.

To his disgust, he couldn't read the playing cards: They all looked blank.

So much for becoming a card-counter.

Still, he mused, gambling was the only way one could make large amounts of money with no questions asked.

"It's Vegas, baby," he said, cuddling Norton. As he petted Norton, the cat said, "I love it when you lick me, mama."

***

Vegas was a bit of a stretch, Derek decided. Atlantic City was closer and there were buses one could take. Unfortunately, a computer search of their schedules showed that he'd just missed today's bus.

He decided to fly.

Derek plotted a route to Atlantic City on his cell phone: cross the Hudson River, take route 95 south to New Brunswick, and then switch to the Garden State Parkway until it reached the Atlantic City Expressway. Simple

And it *was* simple: Derek was delighted to discover that he *could* read road-signs in an out of body state. They were embossed.

He glided over the roads, zipping past cars that seemed to crawl. He materialized in an alley in a small city. Questioning a passer-by revealed that this was New Brunswick.

He went out of body again, located the Garden State Parkway and zoomed on over what looked like an endless line of parked cars.

He ended up at the Hotshots Casino on Boardwalk and South Carolina Avenue.

He floated into a stall in a men's room and materialized. His trip had taken a grand total of fifteen minutes. A simple calculation showed that he'd averaged almost five hundred miles per hour.

***

The casino floor was a dizzying array of slot machines making noises and playing music. The cacophonous shreds of music, bells, and cartoon-sounds blended into a tuneless din.

Derek wandered the floor between depressing rows of lost souls feeding their retirement checks to slot machines — some in wheelchairs with oxygen tanks beside them — running out the clocks of their lives.

He picked one named *Blackbeard's Treasure*. He went out-of-body and ran time forward — and saw the machine settle into a bonus round or jackpot. Although he couldn't see the numbers displayed, he saw that its lights flashed. He put a dollar into the slot, pushed the button, and went out of body again — mostly to tune out the mind-numbing noise.

The silence was surprising — the other players weren't thinking much of anything.

Not today, chump!

Derek traced that stray thought to a man named Daryl Antonio who sat in an office and watched him on a monitor from one of the floor's surveillance cameras. He'd pushed an override button, changing the numbers at the last minute — and taking Derek out of the bonus round or jackpot.

"Goddamn it!" Daryl's supervisor snapped. "More smoothly! Once the numbers come to a complete stop you *have* to let them ride."

"They never notice," Daryl said.

Derek returned to his senses, stood, and wandered the floor until he found blackjack tables in a far corner.

The cards there were as unreadable as the ones in his apartment.

✳✳✳

Allie staggered through her morning. Not having to go to work was a relief, but she knew money would be short soon; maybe grandpa would spot her.

Fat chance!

She tried to work on a painting, but she couldn't concentrate and kept coming back to the idea of being pregnant.

Maybe I just imagined it.
She dressed, went down to a drugstore and bought a pregnancy test kit. As expected, the test was negative.
Derek's honoring my request to not come after me. Damn him! What's he up to?
She lay in bed and slipped out of body.
He's in a casino, peeking into the future! Can I do that too?
A cyclone of images roared through Allie's mind, images of a playful little girl, a young lady, and images of their lives together.
Allie's daughter had black hair, a high forehead, and high cheekbones. The most distinctive aspect of her face were her eyes: almond shaped and slightly oriental, with irises that sparkled like diamonds. Sometimes, she wore brown contacts to hide their glitter.
Her natural charm and charisma affected everyone around her.
She's so beautiful!
The images became more varied as Allie saw a thousand possible futures: images of woolly mammoths and sabertooth cats roaming a bizarre land they *owned* — and of another, an impossibly opulent Victorian world where men in black tuxedos covered with medals bowed and kissed Allie's and her daughter's hands.
Where the hell will these things happen? They're not like anyplace on Earth!
In almost all of the images, Derek stood by their side.
I'm better at looking into the future than Derek.

✳✳✳

Derek found the casino's roulette machines. They were in a cordoned-off section of the floor, quieter than the rest — as though the casino regarded roulette as a dignified gentleman's game and tried to create that illusion. Smoking was allowed.

Derek went out of body.

Winding time forward showed the ball sometimes ending up as copies in *many* slots, and other times, only one or two. Some of the ball-images were sharper than the others, too. He decided that these intensities indicated the *probabilities* that the ball would end up in these slots.

Unfortunately, in an out-of-body state, he couldn't read the numbers on the wheel any better than he'd been able to read cards. He sighed and started to leave.

Then he realized something: the roulette wheel was divided into eight lacquered, burled wood sections by brass dividers. And the dividers showed up clearly when he was out-of-body. Two of those dividers intersected the number-wheel squarely in the center of the numbers 3 and 4. The other six dividers intersected the wheel to *one side* of the numbers.

He bought $200 worth of chips — all the money he had left.

He went out of body, and the world went silent.

When he rolled time forward, he noticed that the ball mainly fell on *one* of those choice spaces — and only *faint* images elsewhere. He returned to reality and bet $100 on 3 and 4, each.

The operator spun the wheel, tossed the ball, and it eventually came to rest on number 4. Derek won $3500 — more than seventeen times what he'd bet.

In the next few hours, Derek bet cautiously — only betting when the outcome was definite and was numbers 3 or 4. He won each bet and his pile of chips accumulated, along with a crowd that cheered his every win.

At one point, a man jostled him out of his out-of-body state and almost knocked him down.

"Sorry!" the man said, pointing. "My wife won!"

An obese woman in a pink "Winey bitch" tee-shirt and shorts had won the big jackpot at a progressive slot machine and rolled on the floor screaming ... and then vomiting. She rolled into it. The machine flashed colored lights in time with a loud honking car-horn: honk, honk, honk...

They must be staying at the casino.

Derek resumed playing.

Impressions of Allie haunted him from time to time, but he ignored them.

At noon, he bribed someone with a $100 chip to bring him a ham and cheese sandwich on rye.

At times, he felt like a thief, stealing the other players' money. Each time this happened, he remembered Daryl Antonio's comment and reminded himself he was stealing the casino's money. Legally.

At four in the afternoon, they shut down the table.

✳✳✳

A fifty-something heavyset man in a black pinstripe suit introduced himself as Dan Amato, the casino manager.

"Quite a run you've had today," he said, shaking Derek's hand. "Congratulations."

"Thank you," Derek replied. "I've never been so lucky in my entire life. Is there any way I can get a check for my winnings?"

"Of course. Why don't you come to my office?"

A casino employee produced a cloth pouch and filled it with Derek's chips and handed it to him.

Derek followed Mr. Amato to his office where he was introduced to Tom Dohrn of the Internal Revenue Service and Richard Coombs of the New Jersey Gaming Commission.

Casino employees tallied up Derek's winnings, arriving at a total of $623,480. The IRS employee filled out forms for estimated tax, and the Gaming Commission representative took a call and reported that the roulette wheel had checked out.

Derek signed a affidavit. It declared, under penalty of perjury, that he was not working for the Hotshots Casino in any capacity.

At the end of the meeting, Derek left Mr. Amato's office with $10,000 in cash and a certified check for $401,127.

He went into a restroom and teleported home.

Chapter 9

After feeding Norton, Derek realized it was too late to deposit the check.

He took a cab to the Plaza Hotel and went up to the Champagne Bar, a beautiful expanse of white marble under a coffered ceiling with recessed blue lighting. It overlooked Fifth Avenue and the Pulitzer Fountain.

Derek sat at the bar and ordered a bottle of Veuve Clicquot 'La Grande Dame' for $500.

"Any way I can get a bowl of buttered popcorn with that?"

"This isn't a movie theater."

"I'll give you a thousand dollars if you get me a bowl of heavily-buttered popcorn," he said, fanning out ten hundred-dollar bills. "Real butter."

The bartender made a call.

"It will take a few minutes, sir."

"No rush," Derek said, picking up a glass of champagne.

"Here's to you Allie G," he softly toasted.

"I'm done thinking, maniac," a familiar voice said. "And feeling sorry for myself. I mean I'm finished with that too."

The bartender stared at her as if she had two heads.

"My gray-eyed beauty," Derek whispered, hugging and kissing her. "I was so afraid I'd lost you."

"You're the classiest celebrator I ever met. You know, I peeked a few time, in the casino. I didn't want to distract you."

"We'll need another glass for the lady," Derek told the bartender.

They sipped champagne, and a waiter brought a large bowl of buttered popcorn. Derek paid the bartender.

"Oh my God," Allie moaned, scooping up popcorn and washing it down with champagne. "You *really* know how to show a girl a good time."

"I don't want to lose you," she added. "I can't bear it. And we have to stick together more than ever, now."

"More than ever?"

"We're two of a kind, Derek. Who else could understand either of us? And I'm pregnant."

"Pregnant?" he said. "You must've been when we..."

"Nope," she interrupted. "The fertilized egg is up to eight cells now. Isn't it *creepy* that I know that?"

"Maybe you shouldn't be drinking."

"A little champagne is OK, I think. And the popcorn helps. I don't know why it would, but I have the feeling it does."

"A baby that can teleport," Derek sighed, shaking his head.

"She'll be beautiful," Allie said. "I've seen flashes of her ... grown up. It made me feel so much better about what we're becoming."

"It did?"

"I know, it's shallow of me. I was afraid of us turning into pointy-eared, furry hunchbacks. But, we are *amazing"*

They relaxed and allowed their spirits to drift.

"I feel so close to you," Derek said. "And we've only really known each other for a few days."

"Then let's know each other."

Their spirits drew close and merged. Each felt a blinding flood of images and impressions from the other, as though their very consciousnesses were being burned away. They parted, overwhelmed and numb.

For several minutes, they closed their eyes and tried to assimilate their experiences.

Derek finally said, "You thought I was a nerdy, handsome, well-hung lumberjack from the Maine woods you could take under your wing."

"It sounds shallow when you say it like that," she laughed. "You had something I can't put into words. There was an instant chemistry."

That was true, Derek realized: she'd obsessed about him after they first met at Enigmatic Adventures, mystified by it herself.

"And you thought I was a sexy, streetwise New York woman you wanted in the worst way. But I was so sophisticated you didn't stand a chance with me."

"Sophisticated doesn't *begin* to describe you, Allie. Saving up to fly to Amsterdam just to see a painting? Rembrandt's *Jeremiah mourning the destruction of Jerusalem*."

"I love the Dutch Masters," Allie said. "My bucket list is to see the four great art museums on the planet. One down, three to go."

"Seeing that painting through your eyes, just now, blew me away. The grieving man lit by a diagonal light like a lightning bolt. It made his grief cosmic, a force of nature."

"You were so wrong about not having a chance with me," she said. "I was on the verge of asking *you* out on a date."

"You fantasized me *raping* you?" he exclaimed.

"Shit!" she muttered, blushing. "Our mind-meld was a big dose of — *too much information.* Those fantasies *don't mean I want to be raped.*"

"I know," he said. "When that guy grabbed your crotch on the subway stairs you whacked his face with a wine bottle."

"I heard something crack and it wasn't my wine bottle. I wonder what he told his wife."

"Rape is sex without guilt?" he said. "Women feel *that* guilty about sex?"

She shrugged. "Horny men are studs; horny women are whores. Especially in certain Italian-American circles. You're really hung up on my dumb fantasies."

"I'm really hung up on you."

"They're no big deal," she said. "They were never violent. In my fantasy, I want you but — since I don't want you to think I'm a slut — never, *ever* do anything to show it. But I'm just so totally sexy, you're overwhelmed. My awesomeness drives you insane, you can't help yourself. You quietly, even tenderly, wrestle me into submission."

"You never protest?"

"Like a good girl, I struggle valiantly but I'm paralyzed by *your* awesomeness," she said, eating some popcorn and washing it down with champagne. "I manage to softly squeak 'help'."

"I'm awesome?" he sighed, turning red as a traffic light.

"You had fantasies about submissive girl *robots*," she said. "Your fantasies about me are creative. I like the one where we do it in a zero-G environment in a space ship."

"You do?" he chuckled.

"I've met men who live in their own dream worlds and think I'm coming on to them," she said. "They won't even listen to subtle hints, like 'no' or 'fuck off' or 'eat shit and die'."

"Those are pretty subtle," he said, grabbing some popcorn. "When I came on to *you,*" she said. "And I *did,* you seemed to ignore me. You were so afraid of rejection."

"What did you learn from me?" he sighed.

"The nerdiness is strong with you, young Jedi," Allie said, sipping champagne. "I never had any interest in *Star Wars* but, after our mind-meld, I know every moment of every movie. And every moment of ever *Star Trek* episode. Brain cells I'll *never* get back."

"Sorry about the brain-cells," he said sipping champagne.

"There's something charming about the *Star Trek* universe. A world where racism, poverty and war have been eliminated. We humans finally get our collective shit together and stop clubbing each other over the head."

"We move on to clubbing aliens over the head."

They laughed.

"That game that'll never get made, *A mind forever voyaging,*" she said. "That's you, Derek. Yearning to explore the universe and understand unsolved mysteries. It's beautiful."

Thoughts about them drifted over to them.

"Most bizarre couple I've ever seen," the bartender thought. "I turn away for a second and she's standing there in the middle of my bar. It's like they're having a conversation but they don't make a sound. And they're not even using sign-language."

"I love your people," Allie said. "Your parents and your sister, Wendy. She's a child of nature."

"I've called her a lot of things but ... yeah, I guess she really is that. Your brother Tony was such a sweet kid. And your grandpa is terrifying."

"Poor, poor Tony," she sobbed, as Derek hugged her. "Papa wanted to leave, you know, the mob life but was afraid of his father."

"He wanted to start a restaurant," Derek said.

"Your father is such a *homebody,*" Allie said.

"I know," Derek said.

"He turned down a job in Wiscasset that was fifteen minutes away?" she said.

"Boothbay Harbor is home for him, a little slice of Heaven. The other job was a lot more money but it wasn't home."

"I love Boothbay Harbor too," she nodded. "I always thought it was, you know ... the middle of nowhere. I didn't know it has artist colonies and Edgewood Pottery. Like a gallery in the Museum of Modern Art."

"I love you so much," he said. "I feel its our destiny to be together. As though the universe itself wants it."

"I know."

"We should get married," Derek said.

"We will."

"Their eyes drill holes in you," the bartender thought. "They pay $1000 for *popcorn?* I wish all my customers were like that."

Other thoughts drifted toward them.

"Evans raped the Hotshots Casino," Baranov said. "At roulette."

He sat in a car in front of the hotel with Alexei Rabotnikov.

"You can't cheat at *roulette,*" Rabotnikov said. "The casino can but the player can't. How'd he do that?"

"Maybe there's something to this God virus thing. Put your gun away. You don't go into the Plaza with guns blazing. We'll pick him up when he comes out. He'll be easier to handle drunk."

Derek looked up briefly to put $5000 on the counter, telling the bartender to keep the change. When the bartender turned to put money into the register, Derek and Allie vanished like forgotten dreams.

✳✳✳

"They'll come here once they realize you're not at the Plaza."

"You like cats, right?" Derek said.

"You *know* I do."

"Is it OK if I bring Norton to your place?"

"Sure. I have stuff left over from poor Mittens."

Mittens was Allie's little brown kitten that had died of feline infectious peritonitis.

Derek put his coat on, wrapped Norton into it with a few shirts, and teleported to Allie's bedroom. She followed.

Chapter 10

While Allie slept, Derek made coffee and fed Norton. After eating, Norton said, "Everything smells different."

Derek sat at the kitchen table scanned Allie's memories, recalling a thousand moments of triumph and disappointment. She'd placed fourth in the National Latin Exam when she was a senior at Sacred Heart High School, and they'd celebrated at a restaurant.

Studying art at the Cooper Union had thrilled her, presenting her with an infinite array of possibilities.

He focused on her relationships: Losing her virginity to tiger-tattooed Vinny Barbarino in the back of his battered blue chevy. A few unsatisfying pick-ups in bars.

She'd dated a plastic surgeon who was his own favorite patient — writing prescriptions for himself and fictitious people for Oxycontin — flirting with loss of his license and even prison. He'd turned violent when Allie confronted him. And Allie — the one and only time in her life — had invoked her grandpa with threats of broken limbs or death.

Then, she'd had two seeming chance encounters with handsome Sicilian-American men who asked her for dates. They'd both been arrogant, expecting her to jump at their every command. Something her mother assured her all men did. The second such relationship had ended when he'd called her art bullshit and her a dog. "I don't care if you're Don Giancana's granddaughter, you're still a dog, and I won't be seen with you in public." Allie realized that her grandpa had tried to play matchmaker.

Her most promising experience had been with an older divorced man named Wilson Straik. He'd seemed to love Allie, admired her art and treated her like a queen. Unfortunately, she found he had a bad drinking problem, and later, an even worse gambling problem. That relationship ended when he'd tearfully talked of committing suicide and begged her to "loan" him money for gambling debts.

The scar on Allie's face — the result of a childhood playground accident — had cast a shadow over her entire life. She'd always felt things would have turned out better were it not for that scar. The man who'd called her a dog had mentioned it.

For God's sake, it's not that bad! It gives your face character!

When Allie had first chatted with Derek in the Break Room at Enigmatic, he'd been a knight in shining armor. And, in the Champagne Bar at the Plaza, he'd become a prince.

She joined him, carrying a bowl of sugar with a spoon in it. He poured her some coffee.

"I was looking through your memories," he said.

"Oh shit," she sighed.

"We're *made* for each other. Even without gray eyes, I'm sure we'd wind up together. And you had a *lot* more sex than I did."

"Women have more opportunities to do stupid shit. And, after my dad and brother died ... I went a little crazy."

They wandered into the apartment's second bedroom, which Allie used as a studio.

The easel held a sketch of a young woman whose face radiated intelligence and a sardonic sense of humor. Their daughter.

And it hit him like a punch in the gut: He had a beautiful and brilliant future wife and child — and perhaps more children, later. They would be the strangest and most wonderful family on the planet.

"I just started on her," Allie said.

"I can't wait to see her in the flesh."

"She can't wait to *be* in the flesh," Allie said.

"Poor, sweet, naïve kid," he said, tears welling up in his eyes. "Does she have the *faintest* idea what she's letting herself in for?"

"Would any of us do anything if we knew what we were letting ourselves in for?"

✳✳✳

It was cold, gray, and drizzling.

At 8:30, when the Continental Bank branch near Allie's apartment opened, they went in, opened a joint checking account, and deposited Derek's check. The bank manager balked at accepting the deposit until she called the Hotshots Casino to verify that Derek had won the money.

They had breakfast at Lew's Diner across the street, a cozy, stainless-steel 1950's style place with booths and paper placemats covered with advertisements.

At Derek's recommendation, they had fried eggs on strips of lox and drenched in Hollandaise sauce. Allie approved. They poured several sugar-packets down their throats and washed it down with coffee.

"I can't believe how talented you are," Derek said. "That quick sketch captured a real personality."

"I used to have to use charcoal and erase and smudge a *lot* to get that good an image. Watch what I can do now."

She turned over a place-mat, grabbed the ballpoint pen from Derek's shirt pocket, and her hand darted across the paper in a frenzy of motion.

After a few minutes, she held up her sketch — an almost photo-realistic image of Derek and the people in the diner behind him.

"I'm not just a camera," she said. "Gimmie another piece of paper."

Derek grabbed a placemat from the next table, and Allie did another blindingly fast sketch.

"My arm's cramping up," she said, shaking her arm out and massaging it.

It was another amazingly detailed and accurate drawing of the diner, except that the waitresses wore togas and the owner looked like a Roman gladiator.

"My artistic style hasn't changed a bit," Allie said. "Just the basic mechanics of drawing and painting."

"Hey boss," a waitress said. "Look at this."

Lew himself came over and Allie handed him her sketches after signing them "Allie G."

"Your breakfast is on the house," he said, showing her sketches to the staff.

"We're where human evolution is going?" Allie said.

"According to that monster."

"We have to take Baranov out," Derek said, his mood darkening.

"Marrying me might stop him. He *knows* who my grandpa is. He's probably even met him."

"If not, we go full mafia on his ass. *Nobody* threatens our family."

"*Full mafia?*" she laughed. "Did you actually *say* that?"

After breakfast, they went to Allie's favorite clothing store in Flushing and bought Derek a coat, several shirts and pairs of pants. Allie got a sky-blue dress with a golden brooch. Then they went home and changed into their new clothes.

✳✳✳

They flew to Times Square, and then two avenues east, to fifth avenue. Five streets north of there brought them to 47th street, where they entered a restaurant and materialized in its restrooms.

The restaurant turned out to be Corned Beef East, a frenetic deli with people running around and shouting orders — in the heart of New York's Diamond District.

Delivery boys awaited phone-orders on a staircase to the basement, directly under a griddle. Cooking fat occasionally dripped on them.

Derek and Allie left.

The International Diamond Exchange was a gemological supermarket — a vast open space with rows of booths operated by independent jewelers. They looked over an endless array of engagement rings, none of which impressed Allie.

"Remember when I said I didn't feel any different?" she said. "As a result of what's happening to us?"

He nodded.

"A month ago, I would've swooned over these rings, squealed like a schoolgirl. And your marriage proposal felt like..."

"I was stating the obvious?" he said.

"*Exactly* like stating the obvious. You know I love you, Derek, but our marriage seems *inevitable.* Every future I see

74

has us together. I don't *feel* different but I must *be* different. We're turning into cold-blooded aliens like Mr. Spock."

"You're the most passionate person I ever met, Allie," he said *"After* your eyes turned gray."

"You're just saying that 'cause we fuck like rabid rabbits."

"All the teleporting we do," he said. "We need the exercise, and sex is like running five miles."

They kissed and, with their faces almost touching, she whispered, "Five miles in ten seconds? You belong in the Olympics."

They sensed a bald man standing next to one of the booths snapping pictures of them with his phone.

"Ustinov put out a mob-APB on you," Allie wordlessly said. "We should get married soon."

"Vegas, baby," he said.

"I'd love that, but it would kill mom, and grandpa would go ballistic."

"OK."

"Getting married in a *Catholic* church might be complicated," Allie said. "You're not Catholic and they have their rules. Mom should be satisfied if it's *Christian*. I used to taunt her by saying I'd get married by an Orthodox Druid Priestess."

"We'll figure something out," Derek said.

"People expect me to have an engagement ring, so could you just pick something out? Something inexpensive."

He found a ring with a solitaire surrounded by a star-burst of small diamonds for $20,000, paid, and the jeweler sized it for Allie on the spot.

"I said *inexpensive*. But my friends and mom will be impressed."

"It has good luminescence, too," the jeweler said, switching on a light fixture.

"Watch where you point that," Derek said, covering his eyes. Allie covered hers too.

"It's *black* light," the jeweler said. "Just a faint purple glow."

"It's a *lot* brighter than you think," Allie said. "You probably shouldn't look at it yourself."

The jeweler turned off the UV light.

Then they bought plain gold wedding bands and had them fitted.

***

"OK," Derek said, as they left the jewelry exchange. "We see ultraviolet, now."

"Pathetic superpower," Allie said. "Like being able to make food go bad."

"It's time we found out how deep our rabbit-hole goes."

"I noticed my color-sense changing," Allie said. "I named the new color *indigo.* I know that's the name for a shade of blue, but 'indigo' sounds way cooler than 'ultraviolet'."

Derek led them into a drugstore around the corner and searched the racks and shelves. The pharmacist was a twenty-something oriental man wearing a antiseptic-looking white uniform. His name tag said "Spencer Wong."

"This is a request you've probably never gotten before," Derek shyly told Spencer. "Is there any way we can get . . . um . . . DNA sample kits?"

"We might have to go to a forensic lab . . . and bribe some-body," Allie said.

Spencer smiled and produced a box labeled *Who's Your Daddy?* — a paternity test kit.

"That's a *thing?*" Allie laughed. "There's that much . . . fooling around?"

"A bestseller around here and Wall street," Spencer said.

76

Derek laughed, paying for the kit.

The box contained two DNA cheek-swabs with test-tubes, and a pre-addressed padded mailer to the company. It promised an answer within six to eight weeks.

Derek handed a swab to Allie and they both swabbed their cheeks and put the swabs into the test-tubes.

"That's not how you use them," Spencer said.

"Thank you," Derek said, as they left.

"I'm guessing we're not mailing these to the *Who's Your Daddy* people," Allie said.

Derek laughed.

Allie put the kit into her purse.

They returned to Corned Beef East.

✳✳✳

They ordered corned beef sandwiches and sodas and sat at a small table in the back.

"This is a monster sandwich," Derek said. "I don't know if I can finish it."

"I've been thinking about our teleporting," Allie said. "And how it could possibly work."

"We go somewhere in our spirit-bodies and then bring our physical bodies along — *somehow,*" Derek said. "I don't have a clue how that happens."

"If we summon our physical body, couldn't we summon an *earlier* version of it? I mean, we can *travel* into the past in our spirit bodies..."

"Interesting," Derek said. "You're really asking whether we could avoid growing old?"

"When we're ninety and super rich," Allie said. "Could we teleport across the room and become twenty-six again?"

"Wouldn't we lose sixty-four years of memories?"

"That would suck," Allie said.

"One way to find out."

They stood and walked to the men's room.

"I'll teleport from one end of the restroom to the other, and try to imagine myself as I was after I got dressed this morning. I may come out of here confused."

"I'll be waiting."

Derek entered the restroom and, moments later, staggered out.

"Allie! You're here. You won't believe what just happened to me."

"Let's sit down, honey," she said, hugging him. "I'll explain everything."

They sat.

"I'd just finished putting my shoes on and suddenly, I'm ... here. Wherever here is."

"You don't remember anything else?" she said.

"No. Wait! It's coming back to me. We deposited the check and went shopping for your engagement ring. The last thing I remember is ordering these monster sandwiches."

Allie explained their theory of rolling back time.

"So we could be young and healthy *forever,*" Derek said.

"I wouldn't want to live forever," Allie said. "At some point, we'd have a 'been there, done that' feeling about *everything.*"

"We could even go back to pre-Pembroke times," Derek mused. "We could be *normal* again."

"Why *would we?* That would be insane. And we'd still have the Russian mafia chasing us. With no superpowers to protect us."

"My theory," Derek said. "Short-term memory is stored in the brain, and long-term memory is stored in the soul. The brain transcribes memories into the soul."

"That's why you can't remember the last few minutes before our experiment."

They finished their sandwiches.

"Maybe we could even teleport *into* the past," Derek said. "Go the the 1950's or something."

"Why?"

"I don't know. Just a thought."

✳✳✳

They teleported to restrooms near the NYU Biology department office.

Years ago, Derek had been here. In college, he'd toyed with the idea of going into medicine, and mainly learned that pre-med is not something one toys with.

He'd taken a course in Comparative Anatomy. It was a difficult but fascinating subject that entailed dissecting cats and tiny dogfish sharks — and writing a term paper. His subject was "Fish of the Devonian Era" — a period some 370 million years ago. That paper had been the bane of his existence.

Writing it might have been fun if Derek hadn't been under so much pressure. After all, the Devonian seas were populated by nightmares like the *Dunkleosteous* — a whale-sized fish covered in thick, black, bony armor with a beak powerful enough to puncture any submarine hapless enough to time-travel to that era.

Derek barely made it.

At the day and hour of the deadline, he'd slipped his term paper into Professor Whittemore's mailbox.

The place hadn't changed. One whole wall held mailboxes for faculty and graduate students, and a coffee machine. There was a department secretary and several assistants — even the same people as before. One door led to the department Chairman's office, and another led to a room with a copy machine.

They explained what they wanted to the department secretary.

"We don't do that kind of work," said Mrs. Wu.

Derek offered $1000 to any secretary who could find someone willing to do the job and $10,000 to the person who did it.

A frenzy of phone calls ensued.

Finally, a woman named Birgit Fischer introduced herself. She was heavyset, middle-aged, blond, and wore jeans and a pink sweatshirt with the logo "I ♥ New York."

"Please come with me," she said with a faint German accent. She led them through a serpentine array of offices and labs until they ended up in a tiny office with barely enough room for a small desk and two chairs.

They sat in the chairs and Professor Fischer disappeared behind foot-high stacks of papers covering her desk.

She pushed two stacks aside to create a big enough gap that they could see her.

"I'm visiting for a year from Ludwig-Maximillian University in Munich," she said. "I have access to all of the Gen-Core gene sequencing machines here. Are you serious about the $10,000?"

Derek wrote her a check and handed it to her.

"The tissue samples?" Dr. Fischer said.

Allie rummaged in her purse and handed them to her.

"These are *cheek swabs*. Are they from humans?"

"You tell us," he said.

"*Absonderlich,*" she muttered, shaking her head.

"That's why we're paying so much," Allie said.

Dr. Fischer said the tests would take several weeks, and Derek gave her their contact-information.

After leaving her tiny office and asking people for directions twice, they eventually reached west 4th street, bordering a bleak-looking Washington Square Park.

"I didn't know I understood German," Allie said.

"Reading minds is so easy, you don't even know you're doing it."

"Suppose it turns out we *are* a new species," Allie said. "What will we call ourselves?"

"Mrs. Pembroke calls us *homo sapiens superior.*"

"Fuck her and the horse she rode in on," Allie muttered. "Let's call ourselves *Indigo* people. *Homo sapiens indicus.*"

"Indigo people. I've heard that phrase before."

She did a search on her cell phone and said, "Oh, it's a new age thing. Indigo is the color of their auras or something. We'll be our own flavor of indigo. *Biologically* indigo."

✳✳✳

They took a cab to 141 Worth street, a massive gray art-deco building that was the home of the New York City Clerk. Unfortunately, there was a block-long line in the hall leading to the Marriage Bureau. At least a hundred couples stood there: Hasidic Jews, Latinos, whites, blacks — people of every imaginable description.

"There's a place with no waiting," Derek said. They went to their respective restrooms and teleported.

Chapter 11

The Boothbay Town Hall was a large single-story white clapboard building that could have been a private home. When Derek was fifteen, he'd gotten a license here for his dog, Bourbon. As he expected, the Business Office was practically deserted.

"Hi, Derek," Joan Miley, the town clerk said. "Didn't know you were in town." She was the same person who had processed Bourbon's dog-license, but time had turned her auburn hair gray.

Derek introduced her to Allie and asked for Marriage License forms.

As they filled out the forms, Ms. Miley made several calls, beginning each with, "Guess who's getting married!"

Derek also applied for a birth certificate so he could get a passport someday.

Derek recognized Ed Brocklesby, a friend of the family.

"I'm getting a license for my *boat*," Ed explained. "You know, the one I've been working on for a whole year."

Derek introduced him to Allie and told him they were getting married.

"I didn't know you were dating anyone."

"It was a whirlwind romance," Allie said. "He swept me off my feet."

"Wow! Let us know when the wedding is. We'll be there! I wish I could stay and chat, but I promised Heidi I'd pick her up."

Ed left.

After the forms were filled out and fees paid, they said good-bye to Ms. Miley, and went out the arched doorway.

It was a clear, crisp day, the sun cruel in its brilliance.

Wiscasset Road flanked the town hall's front entrance, and a small parking lot with two cars lay at its side entrance. A snowy field, now deserted, stood across the road.

In summer, concerts and flea markets were held there. When he'd been ten, Derek had picked up a broken short wave radio at one of those flea markets and managed to repair it, opening up a strange and fascinating world for him. It was like the Internet.

A small statue stood where Wiscasset Road intersected another — a Civil War monument.

"Downtown is a few miles in that direction," pointing down Wiscasset Road.

"Ah, the mean streets of Boothbay Harbor," Allie laughed.

"And Edgewood Pottery is about ten miles in the opposite direction."

"*That,* I'd *love* to see."

When they satisfied themselves no one could see them, they teleported to the St. Faith Episcopal church.

✳✳✳

They arrived on a deserted two-lane road running through a dense pine forest. Like a paleolithic monument, massive stones composed the facade and steeple of the the church across the street.

"It's a church primeval," Allie exclaimed. "I can't wait to paint this in summer."

Derek briefly shut his eyes and said, "Dad's teaching a class on *Hamlet,* and mom's giving piano lessons to a really bad student named June Connor. Wendy's mending lobster traps."

"I've only been here once, for my grandmother's funeral," Derek added, as they entered the building.

The interior consisted of darkly stained wooden timbers that didn't match the exterior. It appeared to be deserted.

"I was raised Catholic but wasn't devout," Allie said crossing herself. "I was even an atheist for a long time. I got into such fights with mom over religion."

"I can't be an atheist anymore," she continued. "The soul exists. That's a direct experience for us, not an article of faith."

"And physical laws don't apply to them," Derek said. "Our souls are *more real* than physical matter."

"And that beautiful, knowing light that comforts and sustains us. What can that be but God?"

"I've wondered that myself," Derek replied. "If our bodies died while we were out of them, we wouldn't even notice."

"We would," Allie said, her mood darkening. "They bind us to this world. Our bodies. Everything looks so pale when we're in our spirit bodies because this world is meant to be seen with physical eyes. If our bodies died, we'd be free."

"Free?"

"I *tried* to tear free, the other day, and glimpsed ... stunning ... spirit-worlds. Cities of light. Souls the size of galaxies. There are artists there, too. They create entire worlds as art. Entire universes, even."

"Sounds like you have some incredible subjects for your paintings."

"I didn't want to come *back,* Derek," Allie said, tears running down her cheeks. "My body would've gone into a coma and died. I would've left you and our daughter."

Tears welled up in Derek's eyes.

"Then something happened," she said. "The light around me flickered and plunged me into a memory. One of *yours*. I was *you*, sixteen years old, standing in your parents' living room. Reciting a poem. The woods are lovely, dark, and deep. But I have *promises* to keep."

"And miles to go before I sleep," Derek continued. "Miles to go before I sleep."

"And then I *remembered*," Allie said. "I remembered that I *chose* to be born here. I chose *this world*. Just like our daughter chose it and *us*. This where we *find* ourselves … we learn who we really are."

"And I'll *never* leave you," she sobbed, hugging him. "Those worlds of light will be waiting for *both* of us someday."

A woman stepped out of the shadows.

"I … I didn't mean to eavesdrop," she stammered. "I … I just couldn't bring myself to … interrupt you. I'm the Reverend Chloe Teague." *The strangest couple I ever met.*

The Reverend Teague was a short, thirty-something woman with light brown hair, wearing a large silver cross on a chain — over a radiant white cassock

"You have *no idea* how strange we are," Allie chuckled.

The Reverend Teague registered shock.

"Forgive us. Sometimes we can't help overhearing people's thoughts. We're very pleased to meet you. I'm Derek Evans."

"I'm Alessandra Giancana. We'd like to get married in your lovely church."

Reverend Teague mulled this over and asked them to accompany her into her office, a spare room with a walnut desk and two chairs.

Before Reverend Teague could say anything, Allie said, "Do you guys do confessions? I mean the Episcopal Church."

"Yes, we observe the sacrament of confession. Our motto is All may. None must. Some should."

"So they're confidential, like in the Catholic Church?"

"Absolutely."

"We should *both* tell our stories since we share the same memories up to a day or so ago," Allie said.

Reverend Teague looked perplexed.

And for the next forty-five minutes, Derek and Allie did that, occasionally demonstrating teleportation and mind-reading.

Oh, what I could learn from you two, Reverend Teague wordlessly said, staring at them. *Glorious messengers of God.*

Derek and Allie cringed.

"When do you want to have the wedding?" Reverend Teague finally said.

"As soon as possible," Allie said.

After settling on a date and time, Derek called his parents.

✳✳✳

At five, they all gathered in Derek's parents' living room and repeated the presentation they'd made to Reverend Teague, with a few minor changes.

"Our wedding is Saturday at one at St. Faith church," Derek concluded.

"Giancana," Thomas — Derek's father — murmured. "That name sounds familiar."

"My grandpa is Carlo Giancana," Allie frowned. "You've probably seen him on TV. He's testified before Senate Committees on Organized Crime."

"The Mafia?" Wendy said. "Cool. Have you ever *killed* anyone?"

"I've never broken a law in my life. *This* is who I am," Allie grabbed a sheet of paper and Derek's pen and did a lightning sketch of the Evans family.

"It's a little known fact that most Italian-Americans actually came from Sicily," Thomas said.

"Huh?" Allie said. "Yes, my family came from Sicily."

"That picture's amazing," Wendy said.

Allie wordlessly told Derek, *It's so easy to impress people with this so-called artwork. What's up with your papa?*

He thinks he's at the Happy Cormorant Pub, where he regales people with his words of wisdom, Derek replied in kind.

Allie passed her cell phone around showed them pictures of her other material.

"I also do three dimensional modeling using Blender and the Unreal Engine," she said. "I did Dyna-girl in the *Wakeman Procession.*"

"A video game?" Thomas said. "I'm not familiar with it."

"Not many people are," Derek said. "Unfortunately."

"Here's sketches for the Haunted Forest in *A mind forever voyaging,*" Allie said, scrolling to other pictures on her phone. "I was going to create blender models for Orcs."

"It's a 3-D modeling program," she added. "You were wondering what blender is."

"You answered a question I didn't have the nerve to ask," Thomas said.

"When we accumulate some money," Derek continued. "Allie's going to open an art gallery in Manhattan. We might also start our own game company."

"Accumulate money?" Liz — Derek's mother — said. "You were fired from your job and Allie quit hers..."

"Derek won almost a half million in Atlantic City," Allie interrupted. "After taxes."

"You're *gambling?*" Thomas said. "Mathematically speaking, the odds always favor the house. The house advantage is called vigorish. A little known fact."

"It isn't really gambling when we do it," Allie said.

"Well, that's our big announcement," Derek said. "Now we've got to go home and feed Norton."

"We'll come back after we feed the cat," Allie said.

"You brought your cat?" Liz said. "Where are you staying?"

"At home," Allie replied.

"Won't you have dinner with us?" Liz said. "We want to get to know Allie better."

"We'll be right back," Derek said.

✳✳✳

The Evans family and the Reverend Teague were seated at a round table at Taylors, a restaurant on a pier. Lobster boats unloaded at the pier's end and men carried buckets of live lobsters into the kitchen.

The Reverend Teague had changed out of her cassock into a navy-blue dress.

Derek and Allie emerged from restrooms, dressed as before, minus their coats.

"Restrooms," Allie laughed. "Our stinky portals to the universe."

Derek and Allie sat.

"I wanted to go to the Happy Cormorant, but got overruled," Thomas muttered.

"I ... I asked to come along," Chloe Teague said. "I hope you don't mind."

"That's fine," Derek said.

"Do you have a big family, Allie?" Liz said.

"Not really," Allie said. "In the US, it's just my mom and grandpa. I have an aunt Rita who lives in Rome. She's a graphic designer at an advertising firm. I also have an uncle Luigi in Palermo."

"Is he an artist, too?" Liz said.

"No, he has a violin shop."

"Art and music are in your blood," Thomas said.

Allie smiled.

"How do you explain what you can do?" Liz said. "You must have some ideas."

Allie explained Derek's theory of the world-as-computer-simulation.

"We leave our bodies and cease to be *players* of the game," Allie said. "That's our basic superpower. We can go into the underlying game-code and *hack* it somehow."

"We send our spirit-bodies somewhere," Derek said. "And then summon our physical bodies. Luckily our clothing seems to come along — and other stuff."

"Maybe we can move bigger things," Allie said. "We have a *lot* of experimenting to do."

"When our lives settle down," Derek said.

A waiter appeared, and they all ordered twin lobsters, except for Reverend Teague who ordered lobster and chips.

"How did you win at the casino?" Wendy said.

Derek explained about winding time forward and seeing all of the possible outcomes of an event.

"Sometimes, the play of the roulette wheel is not as random as others. Maybe it has to do with how the operator throws the ball. Anyway, sometimes I only see copies of the ball in a *few* spots so the odds favor me."

"Which one is the future?" Thomas said.

"There is no *the* future," Allie said. "Like the many-worlds form of quantum mechanics."

"You studied physics?" Liz said.

"No, but Derek did, and I have all of his . . . it's a long story."

"Whenever an event has more than one outcome," Derek said. "The universe splits into different time lines. When you roll a die, it comes up 1, 2, 3, 4, 5, *and* 6."

"The whole universe, from here to the most distant galaxy," Thomas said. "That's crazy There's not enough room for all that"

"Remember the game, *L. A. Noire,* you used to play, dad?" Derek said.

"*That's* the game your company *should've* developed."

"It contains two hundred and fifty square miles of Los Angeles, yet the game fits on a laptop. Hell, it fits into magnetized dots on a hard drive."

"That's not *real space,*" Thomas said.

"What's not real about it? You can drive around for hours, passing stores, buildings, people."

"A masterpiece of design," Allie said. "They researched 1950's L. A. so extensively."

"So our universe could be a simulation that doesn't take up *any space at all,*" Derek said. "The *concept* of space is just a premise of the simulation."

"An *idea* in the mind of God," Chloe Teague breathed, shutting her eyes. "And God pursues *every* possibility."

"If every possibility occurs," Thomas said. "There must be worlds where Pembroke succeeded."

"Worlds with people like us," Allie said.

"Nightmare-worlds," Derek said. "Either his mutant army was annihilated."

"The most likely outcome," Allie said.

"Or it succeeded in murdering and enslaving billions of innocent people."

Their food arrived.

"The lobsters I had in Sicily were pacifists," Allie laughed. "They had no claws."

"You said you knew physics because Derek studied it?" Liz said.

"Uh . . . yes," Allie mumbled. "When we were talking about getting married."

"We merged our souls briefly," Derek said. "I have all his memories up to then, and he has all of mine. It was wild impulse. Maybe not the best idea I ever had . . . but it's done."

"That's *so romantic,*" Chloe exclaimed.

"You're an artist now?" Wendy asked Derek.

"No. I feel like I memorized a hundred books on artistic technique, but I can still only draw stick-figures."

Allie laughed.

"And Allie knows a lot of math and physics," Derek said.

Chapter 12

After breakfast, Allie called her mother and her grandpa. During the conversation, she told her grandpa Derek's date of birth and his parents' address in Boothbay Harbor.

"What was that all about?" he said.

"Typical Don Giancana — looking for skeletons in your closet. You don't have any. Just the great big one that we'll tell him."

Then she called her four best friends.

"OK, we're having lunch with my friends at Tavern in the Park," she said. "Our treat."

"I always wondered what that place was like."

"Me too. And at five, grandpa's car will pick us and mom up."

She booted her workstation and scanned his fingertips.

"I'm going to make us clip-on fingernails with my 3-D printer. While I'm doing that, why don't you clear out your apartment?"

✳✳✳

Derek returned to his old apartment to discover that it has

been ransacked again and his new computer and laptop had been trashed.

He packed the few clothes left into a small suitcase and told Mrs. Cathcart he was moving out. Then he took a cab to Allie's apartment.

She was out, so he unpacked his suitcase and folded his clothes. In one pants pocket, he found a metal ball, like a ball-bearing but larger.

"I took our clip-ons to the nail salon to get them colored," Allie said, coming through the door. "Try them on."

They were plastic thimbles with normal-looking fingernails that fit his fingers perfectly.

"I'm guessing you didn't want Midnight Passion on yours."

"What about mid-morning passion?" he said hugging and kissing her.

"Lucky for you The Change made me hornier," Allie said.

"Yeah, we've had the best sex ever," he said. "I thought it was just because we were great together."

"We *are* great together."

"Maybe it's the God Virus," he said, his erection fading. "Maybe we're just trained monkeys, dancing to Pembroke's tune. Mrs. Pembroke thought we'd be *prolific,* be *fruitful* and *multiply.*"

"What are you saying?" she said, eyes tearing up. "Can't we just say we're great together and leave it at that?"

"I know we'd end up together even without the Indigo thing," he said, hugging her. "We *are* great together, the *greatest.*"

"I guess we have to talk to Professor Fischer," she said.

"My God," he said. "Comparative Anatomy: A modern perspective."

"One of your textbooks when you were pre-med," she said.
"What about it?"

"Picture it in your mind. You have my memories."

"OK."

"Now look at page 327, bottom of the page"

"OK, I see it," she said, closing her eyes. "The most sexually active members of the animal kingdom are *humans* and *dolphins.*"

"And if we're *super*-humans?"

"We're horny because of our awesomeness," she exclaimed.
"I love it."

She unbuckled his belt and pulled down his pants and underpants.

He kissed her. Then he undid her slacks and pulled them to the floor, and she stepped out of them. The magic aroma rose on her breath, making his eyes go blurry — and she turned beet-red and moaned, her eyes becoming black pools.

They ran to her bedroom. Allie's panties dropped to her ankles, tripping her. Derek caught her before she hit the floor, stumbled and almost fell, scraping his knee. They collapsed into her bed.

"W...w...what d...did the *B...B...Belgian* judge give you?"

They made love.

"Your knee," Allie eventually mumbled. "You're bleeding like a stuck pig. Heal yourself. Do what you did in Corned Beef East, honey."

"I'd rather bleed."

Derek got up, staggered into the kitchen, and returned with a dishrag tied around his knee.

***

They found her friends at *Tavern in the Park,* floated into restrooms and materialized.

The restaurant was a sprawling open place with white interior walls, white tables and chairs, and glass exterior walls that looked out on the sunlit snowy fields of Central Park. Its monochromatic whiteness gave it an otherworldly quality — like a hospital ward in Heaven.

From Allie, Derek knew their guests well. Dolores was a willowy woman in a long, floral-patterned skirt and peasant blouse. Megan was a heavyset redhead in a black pantsuit. Alicia was a thin Latina in jeans and a pale blue silk blouse. They were artists and animation specialists — Allie's former co-workers.

Linda was a thirty-something petite woman in a navy-blue pantsuit with short-cropped hair. She'd had a crush on Allie in college. After Allie let her down gently, they remained friends. Now, Linda was married to a woman named Marcia, and they had two adopted children.

For the sake of appearances, Allie went through the motions of introducing them.

"You've already met Dolores, Megan, and Alicia. And this is Linda, an old college friend."

"What's with the dark glasses," Alicia thought. "Trying to look like secret agents?"

"Flushed and disheveled much? Like you 'did it' five minutes ago." "You're positively glowing, Allie," Dolores said.

Derek and Allie both blushed.

"I'm pregnant," Allie said, showing them her engagement ring. "And engaged"

The ladies admired Allie's ring.

It's always the quiet ones, Dolores thought, looking Derek up and down. "Did you get some fantastic new job, Derek?"

"He won a bundle at a casino," Allie said.

"Must've been a big bundle," Megan said.

"The wedding's this coming Saturday," Derek said. "And we'd love it if you could make it."

"My schedule's wide open," Megan said. "It's not like I have a job or anything."

Dolores and Alicia murmured their agreement.

"That bastard's turning Enigmatic into a *money-laundry,*" Allie said. "And he's keeping you all on the books and pocketing your salaries."

The ladies registered shock.

"Guess who he works for?" Allie asked Derek.

"Ustinov?" Derek said.

"Damn right"

"My God, Allie," Alicia said. "You should call the police."

Allie became flustered and mumbled, "I ...uh just heard some rumors..."

"Yeah, I heard those rumors too," Derek said. "It's too bad the police won't investigate rumors."

They ordered appetizers and drinks.

"Show Linda what you found, Derek," Allie said.

He handed Linda the metal sphere and she examined it carefully.

"It's a GPS tracker," she said. "Expensive one."

"*What?*" Allie exclaimed, nearly choking on her food.

"Someone's keeping tabs on you, Derek," Linda added. "Someone with *beaucoup* bucks."

This revelation put a damper on the luncheon.

"They burgled Derek's apartment *twice,* and now they know where *I* live," Allie said.

Linda offered to put the device in a long-haul truck to Albuquerque.

They ordered entrées and discussed travel arrangements for the wedding. Derek would get them first-class tickets and have a limo pick them up from the airport in Portland, Maine.

***

That afternoon, Allie worked on her painting of their daughter, as Derek used her computer to book first-class tickets for her friends. Booking them hotel rooms was more challenging because most of Boothbay Harbor's hotels were only open during the tourist season.

He eventually found them a bed-and-breakfast.

Part II

War

Chapter 13

Under a molten-lead sky that threatened snow, a frigid wind whipped Allie's hair as she and Derek waited in front of her building.

A black limousine pulled up.

A husky six-foot five man in a dark green suit with a military crew-cut stepped out of the driver's seat.

"I'm Brian," he said, shaking their hands, and opening the car's rear door. "I'll be your driver tonight."

A frail, thin fifty-something woman in a brown dress came out and hugged Allie.

Allie introduced her to Derek.

"My name is Renata, but I'd like you to call me mom," Allie's mother said, with a noticeable Italian accent. "You remind me of my dear Tony."

"Come on, mom," Allie said, hugging her. "Let's go."

The car's back seat easily accommodated all three of them.

As the car pulled away from the curb, Brian chuckled, "Marrying the Don's granddaughter. Suweet. You've got it made in the shade."

Allie and her mother glared at him.

"I was afraid my baby would *never* get married," Renata said. "Living alone, like an *animal,* in this ... evil city."

"Mom!"

"What do you do, Derek?"

"I'm a video-game programmer, but I'm thinking of investing in stocks."

The car left the New York city limits and merged onto the Long Island Expressway.

Renata talked about living in Palermo and moving to New York so her husband, Alberto, could work in his father's business. She spat that word like an epithet.

"Allie was my miracle baby," Renata continued. "Born in a *taxi.* A *policeman* delivered her."

Allie frowned.

"I guess nobody likes to hear about when they were a baby," Derek chuckled.

"That policeman had a scary snake tattoo on his arm," Allie said. "But he flashed me a smile like sunshine. I knew everything would be alright."

Allie's mom gave her a puzzled stare, and she remained silent for the rest of the drive.

The scenery become more rural, and in twenty minutes, the car took the Syosset exit.

Finally breaking her silence, Renata said, "Yes, the policeman who delivered you *did* have a snake tattoo. I remember now."

The car reached a walled compound and passed through iron gates guarded by several burly men, finally pulling up in front of an ivy-covered mansion.

✳✳✳

Full bookshelves lined Carlo Giancana's study and an antique globe sat in front of a massive oak desk. Two men awaited Derek, Allie, and Renata.

White haired Carlo was a massive bear of a man with a weathered, scarred face. He hugged Allie and shook the hands of Renata and Derek.

"I love my only granddaughter deeply and have asked my *consigliere*, Robert Accardo, to look into your background."

"An interesting resume, Mr. Evans," Mr. Accardo began, staring at Allie and Derek. "A good family in Maine. Parents who are school teachers. A special scholarship to NYU where you graduated with honors."

"Allie wouldn't hook up with a moron," Carlo said. "At least she wouldn't *marry* one. She's *taken home* a couple of real beauts."

Allie glared at him, and Derek wordlessly told Allie, *I'm guessing your grandpa's idea of a beaut is different from yours.*

She smiled and nodded.

"Now things get interesting," Mr. Accardo continued, and he recounted recent events in Derek's life, ending with his win at the Hotshots Casino.

"The surveillance video is fascinating," Mr. Accardo said. "You never go near the wheel and only bet on 3 and 4. And *always* win."

"You were able to get the surveillance video?" Derek said.

"Every casino in the country is studying it," Mr. Accardo said. "How did you do it?"

"That's part of our announcement," Allie said. "But it's for *family only.*"

"I think of Rob as family," Carlo said.

"This will be the," Derek said.

"Strangest story either of you ever heard," Allie continued.

***

Toward the end of their presentation, Derek said, "No!"

"I see it too," Allie said.

"Four of Ustinov's men are kidnapping my family in Maine," Derek said. "Putting them in a truck."

Allie vanished.

"What happened to Allie?" Renata said, shocked.

"She went to Maine for a minute," Derek said. "We told you we can do that."

Allie reappeared and said, "They're using a Thompson Rental truck, and I got the license number."

"We'll give the cops an anonymous tip," Derek said.

"No cops," Carlo said. "There's a better way to handle this. Get Ustinov on speaker phone."

"You are marrying into a powerful family, Mr. Evans," Mr. Accardo intoned, typing something into the land-line phone on the desk. "You are about to see a display of that power."

"Greetings, Vladimir," Carlo said. "I have a request to make of you."

"Anything, my dear Don Carlo," the Russian accented voice replied.

"My granddaughter is about to marry a man named Derek Evans, and he claims that your men are kidnapping his family in Maine."

"I'm impressed," Ustinov murmured.

"Impressed? What do you mean you're impressed?"

"I told you Evans would develop telepathy," a woman's voice said on the line. "Whenever Harry *thought* about torturing the animals, they became agitated. They calmed down whenever he changed his mind."

"And I didn't believe you, Mrs. Pembroke," Ustinov continued. "Here's a message for Evans. Turn yourself over to my men by morning or your family dies."

Mrs. Pembroke came on the line and she said, "You will be under deep anesthesia when you die, Mr. Evans. Absolutely zero pain."

"And if Derek doesn't show up," Ustinov said. "Your granddaughter will know her fiancée is a coward who would not lift a finger to save his loved ones."

"Wait a minute," Derek said. "You plan to kill them anyway."

"Can't lie to a telepath," Ustinov laughed. "If you turn yourself over to us, their deaths will be as painless as yours. Otherwise, ask Don Carlo what I know of pain — I'm a connoisseur of it. And don't even *think* of calling the police. The truck is rigged with a bomb I can set off if they are stopped for any reason. Just hope they don't get a speeding ticket."

"You fucking bastard," Allie screamed.

"Look, we can work something out," Carlo said.

"No, Giancana," Ustinov said. "Not this time."

"You fuck us and we'll fuck you," Carlo bellowed.

"As you Italians say, *che sera sera*."

Chapter 14

"The bomb is wired to a cell-phone and Ustinov has the number on speed-dial," Derek said.

"He doesn't know it himself," Allie said. "Someone named Marvin Pinkowitz rigged the bomb and programmed the phone for him."

"Pinkowitz?" Mr. Accardo said. "That little prick has done work for us before."

"Mrs. Pembroke told Ustinov that he had to act *soon*. The virus will only last a week or two in Derek's pineal gland," Allie said. "She's afraid it's already too late."

"I need a weapon," Derek said. "A quiet one like a taser."

"I respect your spirit, kid," Carlo said, clapping Derek on the shoulder. "But he has a hundred men guarding his compound."

"There's no place on *Earth* we can't reach," Allie growled.

She shut her eyes and added, "He's got a lot of men around him, a wife, a nanny, two kids, and two mistresses."

"One big happy family," Derek said. "We just have to get him alone."

Carlo nodded to his *consigliere*, and Mr. Accardo left.

Five minutes later, Mr. Accardo returned and handed Derek what looked like a mobile phone and a pistol.

"The phone is a stun-gun with two electrodes on the top," he said. "Just push the red button. 200,000 volts."

"And the pistol," Derek continued. "Was stolen from a military shipment fifteen years ago in an unsolved crime. And all identifying information was filed off by someone named Jack Macintosh, also called Apples. It's treated not to carry fingerprints."

"Jesus," Carlo laughed. "If you weren't marrying into the family, I'd have to kill you."

"If the stun-gun doesn't work, shoot him, drop the gun, and haul ass," Mr. Accardo said. "You know how to use that?"

"Yeah, we have guns at home. Every Thanksgiving we go out and shoot a bunch of bottles after dinner."

Allie hugged and kissed Derek, whispering, "We both need you, sweety."

"Ustinov is heading for the bathroom," Allie said. "He's been constipated all day and told people he'll be a while."

"He's locking the door," Derek said.

With the stun-gun in his hand and the pistol in his pocket, Derek sat down and went out-of-body.

✳✳✳

Derek floated near the ceiling of Ustinov's cavernous bathroom, watching Ustinov lower his pants and sit on the toilet.

"A draft," Ustinov muttered, looking around. Unable to find the draft's source, he took a cell-phone out of his pocket and set it on the sink next to him.

Then he opened his magazine and read.

Derek floated to an open space to Ustinov's left and materialized.

As soon as possible, he activated the stun-gun and pressed it against Ustinov's neck. Ustinov fell to the floor, convulsing and flopping around like an enormous beached fish.

Ustinov looked up at Derek and moaned in shocked horror.

Derek pocketed the cell-phone and said, "Don't *ever* threaten me and my family again"

Ustinov began to stir, and Derek stunned him a second time.

There were voices outside, and someone knocked on the bathroom door.

Ustinov didn't see me materialize. The less he knows about my abilities the better.

Derek threw a bath towel over Ustinov's face, took the magazine, and returned to Carlo's study.

✳✳✳

"Jesus!" Carlo sputtered. "I'll never get used to people popping in and out"

"I think I cured Ustinov's constipation," Derek said, removing the cell phone's battery and dropping Ustinov's magazine on the desk.

Carlo laughed and said, "He always has that dumb magazine. The American word snob in Russian letters."

"Now I give the police an anonymous tip," Allie said and vanished.

"When Allie hugged you," Renata said. "She said *we both* need you."

"She's going to have our baby," Derek said. "A girl."

"She always said she'd never bring a child into this insane world," Renata sighed, hugging Derek. "You must make her very happy."

"I give you and Allie my blessing, Derek," Carlo said, patting him on the back. "Anyone who can attack Ustinov in the middle of his fortress is OK by me."

"On his porcelain throne, yet," Mr. Accardo added.

"Actually it's solid gold," Derek said. "Like all the other fixtures."

Allie returned.

✳✳✳

Derek's spirit-body floated in Ustinov's spacious but crowded living room.

In the adjoining dining room, a servant served Ustinov's wife, Irina, food she didn't like. With a sweep of her arm, she sent the plates crashing into the wall. She hurled a water-goblet against the wall hard enough to make a deep dent.

This terrified Ustinov's children and their nanny.

"Evans was here," Ustinov howled. "In the bathroom with me."

"Do something about our cook," Irina said. "Have someone beat the shit out of him. I'm tired of his sloppy presentation."

"Shut the fuck up, Irina," Ustinov responded. *I'd kill Allie's mother if I could be sure Carlo would retaliate by killing you.*

"In the *bathroom?*" Baranov said, pulling out a pistol and heading to the bathroom. *You've finally lost it completely.*

"Search the house," Ustinov said. "And find that Pinkowitz asshole. I want the Evans family *dead*. Evans will pay for dissing me."

✳✳✳

Derek and Allie floated near the truck's roof, their translucent spirit-bodies seemingly clothed in what they had worn in Carlo's study.

The two thugs guarding the Evans family were named Marko and Nikolai. The other two were in the front cab.

I'm scared, Allie said.

People who never saw us teleport before tend to be stunned when we appear, Derek said. *They can't believe their eyes. Even hardened criminals.*

Derek materialized next to Marko and stunned him in the neck, dropping him. Then he pointed his gun at Nikolai and said, "Kick your gun across the floor."

Nikolai looked down at his gun on the floor, hesitated, and then sent it sliding over to Derek.

To Nikolai's astonishment, Allie materialized next to the gun and picked it up. Then she slung it over her shoulder and untied Thomas, Liz, and Wendy.

Derek picked up the Marko's gun.

"Wendy's bleeding from the chest," Allie said. "That can't be good."

"Nikolai," Derek said. "Can you talk to the driver?

Nikolai nodded as Marko began to stir.

"Tell him there's a bomb on this truck and we have to get out," Derek said. "It'll go off any minute."

"That's the truth," Allie said. "Pinkowitz installed it on Ustinov's orders."

"Pinkowitz!" Nikolai said, dialing his phone.

Derek's father called 911.

After a short discussion between Nikolai and the driver, the truck pulled over.

One man from the truck's cab rolled up the door.

"Drop your gun," Derek and Allie said with one voice, waving their machine guns. "This truck is going to blow!"

He complied and they climbed out of the truck, helping Wendy.

The other truck driver fired a shot at them, and Derek fired back. The man slumped to the ground, shot in the leg.

Allie also slumped to the ground, a wide bloodstain spreading on her dress.

Derek hugged her quivering body.

"I ... I c...c can't feel my legs," she stuttered.

"Teleport over there," he said, pointing to a spot a few feet away. "And picture yourself as you were in your grandpa's study."

"H...huh?"

"Just *do it.*"

Allie vanished, reappearing a few feet away, standing.

"How the *hell* did I get here," she shouted. "I was in..."

"What the *fuck*," Nikolai exclaimed, looking at Allie.

"You did my experiment, Allie," Derek said. "Corned Beef East. Remember?"

"Yes, but why would I do that?

"You were *dying*," Derek said, hugging her fiercely. "Your *spine* was severed."

Police sirens sounded in the distance.

"I was *shot?*"

"Let's get away from the truck," Derek shouted.

Thomas and Derek half-carried Wendy as they all distanced themselves from the truck.

"You had a huge bloodstain soaking through your dress," Liz said, pointing to Allie's belly. "It looked like a major artery was involved."

As the sirens got closer, the truck exploded, knocking them all to the ground. Showers of debris hit the ground feet away from them.

Two cars on the highway swerved to avoid burning truck parts, almost colliding with each other.

Nikolai and Marko disappeared into the forest that bordered

the highway. The other two were next to the truck when it exploded and probably dead.

"Allie and I have to leave before the police get here," Derek said. "Mom, dad, Wendy."

Wendy slumped into unconsciousness.

"God, I wish we could heal her," Allie said, with tears running down her face. "I wish we could teleport her to a hospital. I feel so helpless."

Derek and Allie kissed Wendy and returned to Carlo's study.

Chapter 15

They found Carlo, Renata, and Mr. Accardo glued to the TV, watching a special news report.

"You two have had a busy evening," Carlo said. "You should get some sleep. I have several empty bedrooms upstairs."

"My sister's evening is just beginning," Derek said.

"They're airlifting her to Portland General," Allie said, shutting her eyes. "They're prepping an operating room for her."

"You guys don't need any Internet," Mr. Accardo exclaimed. "You're wired into the world."

"Want something to eat?" Renata said. "There's some ham in the fridge, and I can make a sandwich."

"No thanks, mom."

"You should keep up your strength, Allie."

"OK, mom."

"I'll get you one too," she said to Derek and left.

Allie shut her eyes and started sobbing.

"What's wrong?" Derek said, putting his arm around her.

"I rolled time back and saw myself," she said. "I was *really dying* there. Ten seconds and I would've bled out *completely.*"

110

"What?" Carlo said. "Should I call a doctor?"

"No, grandpa," Allie said. "I'm fine now. I was able to … reset my body."

"Reset?" Mr. Accardo murmured.

Carlo was silent for a moment and then he glared at Derek.

"You put your *fiancée* and *child* in harm's way?" Carlo howled. "You're not a man. You're a worm."

"He didn't *put* me in harm's way," Allie said. "*I* did. And he couldn't have stopped me. And I'm fine now."

"I forbid you to marry this spineless asshole," Carlo said.

"You should have forbidden papa from taking *Tony* with him," Allie said. "Apologize to Derek."

"One more word," Carlo murmured. "And I will kill him."

OK, Derek, Allie beamed to Derek. *Time to go.*

They teleported to the kitchen to say goodbye to Renata and then to Allie's apartment.

***

Baranov and Rabotnikov watched the apartment from a car across the street, so Derek and Allie didn't turn on any lights.

Their spirits floated above the Russians' car.

"I put a key-logger on Giancana's computer," Baranov said. "Every keystroke she types will show up on my laptop. We also have listening devices behind her paintings. She'll lead us to Evans."

"Why not just grab her and sweat it out of her?" Rabotnikov said.

"Giancana family members are off limits. Ustinov's kids would become targets."

"Amazing he has kids," Derek said.

"I scanned them briefly," Allie said. "Alex and Marina. They seemed nice."

112

"Why does Ustinov want Evans?" Rabotnikov said.

"He think it'll make him a superman, and he'll wipe the Giancana family off the map."

"Did Evans really attack him on the can?" Rabotnikov said.

"Of course not. The surveillance video didn't show him entering the house anywhere. We tore the whole fucking place apart. Ustinov had a brain fart. Maybe a stroke."

"He won't go to the toilet without an armed escort," Rabotnikov said. "We all have to smell his shit."

"Tell me about it. His mistresses don't want to fuck him with a bunch of armed men watching."

"Speaking of fucking, I think Irina was coming on to me," Rabotnikov said.

"She comes on to all the guys," Baranov said. "If you want to stay above ground, you'll pretend you don't notice."

"If Ustinov is losing it, his days are numbered."

"As fascinating as this is, we should find a place to crash for the night," Derek said.

"We can't go to my place," Allie said.

"Go to my parents' house in Boothbay Harbor. I'll get Norton and meet you there."

✳✳✳

The Evans house was empty and — as far as Derek could tell — no one surveilled it. Derek managed to bring a few cans of cat food with Norton.

They went to the kitchen — a large, cheerful, powder-blue room that had always been the center of the Evans household. Derek remembered countless meals eaten here and occasional Game Nights — when friends came over for cards and boardgames.

Allie eyed the Swear Jar on the counter.

"If we had one, most of our income would've gone into it," she said.

Derek fed Norton, and they sat at the kitchen table, eating the ham sandwiches Renata made.

"Seeing you dying was the most horrible moment of my life," Derek said, his eyes tearing up. "Your grandpa had a point."

"Don't you *dare* say that, Derek!" Allie said. "He browbeat papa to the point of tears. I can't *stand* him doing that to you. I expected him to explode at some point. It was a question of *when* not *whether*."

He kissed her.

"I admit we were cocky and *stupid*," she murmured. "Grandpa always said *'La donna e la gaddina si perdi si troppu cammina'*."

"Women and hens get lost if they wander?"

"Very good, maniac," she smiled, stroking his face. "It means women are helpless and need to be protected. Old school."

"We still have to avoid physical confrontations. We're not fighters."

"Did we have *any choice?* If there was *any other way* we could have handled things, I'd love to hear it."

After they ate, Norton started scratching the floor and said, *Where's the poop-place?*

"Hang on Norton," Allie said.

Derek teleported to a Hanneford Market a few miles away, bought a bag of cat-litter, and teleported back. Only half of the bag came through, the missing bottom spilling litter all over the kitchen floor. Allie swept it into a low sided cardboard box, and Derek introduced Norton to it.

They went upstairs.

Derek's room was exactly as he'd left it, years ago. A big poster graced one wall: the Milky Way galaxy with a pointer to a spot on one arm and the caption "You are here." Another wall had a big photo of the North America in partial daylight from space. On the night-portion of the poster, one could see many cities glowing in yellow.

A reflecting telescope on a tripod stood in the corner.

Allie examined the objects on the dresser.

"Your science fair trophy for a game-playing computer," she said. "And your Google-NYU STEM award that got you through college. This room is swimming with memories. You lost your virginity to Madeline Ames in this bed. She followed you upstairs after a evening playing Monopoly."

"She visited me a few times in New York, too."

"Whatever happened to her? Oh yes, she joined the army. Wow."

"She wanted to get out of Boothbay Harbor in the worst way. I guess the army was easier than living in New York."

They tried to create new memories on his old bed but it collapsed and dumped them onto the floor.

As they surveyed the wreckage, Allie murmured, "Sorry I smashed your ... childhood."

"That's OK. I was done with it."

Chapter 16

In the morning, a light snow was falling. In their spirit-bodies, they checked on Wendy. She was recovering from her surgery and would have to remain in the hospital for a few days.

After eating breakfast and getting dressed, they teleported to their Continental Bank branch and withdrew $100,000 in cash — ten bundles of $100 bills. Bank employees begged them to not carry around so much cash, but they insisted.

✳✳✳

They teleported to Macy's. The last time Derek had been here was Christmas shopping for Wendy and his parents. There had been an insane throng of tired, frantic people battling to purchase the last remaining Clownies — creepy clown dolls with lopsided smiles that were all the rage. Incredibly, some people had even flown in from Europe to buy them.

The store was relatively deserted today, just beginning to gear up for Valentines Day.

It didn't help.

People's thoughts buzzed through Derek's and Allie's minds like a swarm of angry bees: worries about cheating spouses, potential job losses, health concerns, unwanted pregnancies, and a sweet woman whose beloved had just proposed.

"It's Internet shopping from now on," Allie said.

"Why are we here?" Derek said.

"You need a place to keep your shit. Especially when said shit includes $50,000 cash."

At Men's Accessories they bought Derek a rectangular black leather man-purse with a strap long enough to loop over his opposite shoulder. It had a pocket for a phone. Now, he and Allie could each carry five bundles of bills.

They passed a man who drew caricatures of people in colored markers for $20. And Allie and Derek knew his name was Patrick O'Donnell and he was from Ireland on a tourist visa, and that his wife had recently died of breast cancer. He was trying to raise his two-year-old daughter, Kara, and avoid deportation.

They posed for him.

His caricatures of Derek and Allie were uncanny, depicting them as elves with pointy ears, mischievous grins, and shiny gray eyes.

"How did you know, Patrick?" Derek said.

"We really are elves," Allie chimed in, adding in a stage-whisper, "In disguise."

Patrick nervously laughed, wondering how these odd strangers knew his name.

"You're very talented," Allie said, handing him a $1000 bundle of bills. "If we ever need an artist, we'll be in touch."

"I can't accept this money," Patrick said. "Who are you?"

"We're friends," Derek said. "Buy something for yourself and Kara."

✳✳✳

Then they went up to the the top floor cafe and got coffees.

"They say everyone's fighting a battle you know nothing about," Derek said.

"Except we know all of them," Allie said. "If we get rich, we have to start a foundation to help people like Patrick."

"Absolutely."

"I can't believe we're supposed to get married *tomorrow*."

"Maybe we should postpone it."

"I thought marrying me would make grandpa protect you," Allie said. "I overestimated him. And now he probably doesn't want to protect you. I'd still like to get married ... if you do."

"I love you more than ever. It's us against the world."

"No kidding. My baggage just got a few tons heavier."

"I guess this is something we can't do over the Internet," he sighed. They bought clothes for their wedding: an elegant brown dress for Allie and a gray suit for Derek.

They made the odd request that the store hold onto their purchases until they picked them up tomorrow.

✳✳✳

They teleported to the St. Faith church. As before, the place was almost deserted.

A haggard Reverend Teague almost collided with them as she left her office.

"I can't *believe* what happened to your folks, Derek," she exclaimed. "I've been praying for them and for you two. I was glued to the TV all night."

"Thank you," Allie said.

"They're OK, except for Wendy," Derek said. "She's in Portland General and it looks as though she'll make a complete recovery."

"We wonder if it would still be possible to have the wedding in that hospital," Allie said. "Since Wendy can't travel."

"Portland General has a beautiful chapel," the Reverend Teague said. "Come with me."

Then went into her office and she made a call.

After talking a few minutes, she hung up.

"Father Podsiadlo would *love* to have a wedding in his chapel," she said. "They mostly have funerals there. In fact, there's a funeral that morning, so we'll have to move the time to 2PM, but it's a go. I'll officiate, of course, since it won't be a catholic wedding."

"We'd like to make a donation to your church," Allie said. "Do you need anything?"

"We could use a new roof," the Reverend Teague said.

Derek wrote her a check for $50,000.

"What I would really like," the Reverend Teague said, eying the check. "Is to just ... chat with you two, to hear what you have to say about ... things."

"You're our dear friend, Chloe, and always will be," Allie said, hugging her. "You can't get rid of us." *She keeps expecting words of wisdom from me. I've got nothing.*

"Once our lives settle down," Derek said. "We'll have a lot of long talks."

***

They spent the rest of the day in Manhattan, making count-less calls and arrangements at Worldwide Wired, an Internet cafe that served assorted coffees and offered privacy-booths one could rent.

They had dinner at Captain Nemo's — a restaurant on west 72nd street decorated to look like the interior of an elegant Victorian-era submarine. It had an ornate brass pipe-organ in the back that played the dreamy tones of Debussy's *Reverie*. The portals on its walls held fish tanks.

Dressed in a red silk Victorian smoking jacket with steampunk goggles on his head, Captain Nemo himself asked them how they'd liked their Dover sole.

They slept in Derek's parents' house in Maine.

Chapter 17

It was snowing hard in the morning, and a blizzard was forecast. A quick check on the Reverend Teague revealed that she was already on her way to Portland — before the roads closed. She had hitched a ride with Ed and Heidi Brocklesby.

Allie called the Portland Host hotel and reserved rooms for Chloe Teague and the Brocklesbys. It appeared likely that they would have to spend the night there before the road were clear.

They teleported to Portland General Hospital and visited Wendy.

When they entered her room, she waved to them so hard it threatened to rip the IV line from her arm. She had a private room with a window that looked out onto a snowy bay. It was more pleasant than the room Derek had had at the Psych Ward in the Bronx Calvary Hospital — almost cheerful, even.

Thomas and Liz were already there and hugged them.

"How are you feeling?" Allie said. "Up to coming to our wedding today?"

"Yeah."

"She can't travel," Thomas said. "I don't know when she'll be able to."

"We're holding it here," Derek said. "Maybe even in this room. The Reverend Teague is on her way."

"Your eyes are so sparkly," Wendy said.

"Huh?" Derek said. He and Allie looked into each other's eyes.

"The gray in your irises has turned to silver," Allie said. "Tiny silvery facets."

"Like fish-scales," he said. "Part of the experience of being ... us."

"It's like the images I saw of our daughter," Allie said. "She looked like she had diamonds in her eyes."

"My mom and friends are arriving right now," Allie added, shutting her eyes briefly. "In the nick of time. They're talking about closing the airport."

"We spent the whole night talking to the FBI and the police," Thomas said. "We told them Wendy slipped out of her ropes and grabbed one of the kidnapper's guns."

"They think I'm a hero," Wendy said. "They even want to put me on TV."

"You are a hero, sis."

Liz hugged Allie saying, "I just can't get that ghastly image out of my mind. You almost died there."

"Thank God I don't remember," Allie said. "Resetting wipes out the last few minutes of memories."

"Resetting?" Thomas said.

"We can survive practically anything," Derek said. "And we were lucky that shot didn't hit your head, Allie."

✳✳✳

Derek, Allie and his parents had coffee in the hospital cafeteria.

"I sensed our daughter's spirit the other day," Allie said.

"She has a deep psychic link with our daughter," Derek said. "I'm kind of jealous."

"Most of the time, her spirit's like a very playful little girl but sometimes I see … more of her soul," Allie said. "Like an ancient and powerful being. She loves the name Victoria. Because it means the one who will win."

"You guys believe in reincarnation?" Liz said.

"We remember being born," Derek said. "And have images of things that happened before."

"So we should name our daughter Victoria," Allie said.

"Everyone will call her Vicky," Liz said.

"OK," Allie said. "We go Italian and name her *Vittoria.* Her nickname will be Tori. There's even a cute little Sicilian town named Vittoria."

"I like it," Derek said.

"Derek has an aunt Abigail, Allie," Thomas said. "Did you even consider naming her that?"

"Dad," Wendy said. "Vittoria is *much* better. And it's what *she* wants."

"It just sounds kind of foreign," Thomas said.

✱✱✱

By noon, the snow was two feet deep and the airport had closed. All of their wedding guests were checked into the Portland Host hotel across the street from the hospital.

Allie and Derek and his parents had lunch in Wendy's room. The Reverend Teague joined them, saying "I'm going to be stranded here."

"We got you a room in the hotel across the street," Derek said.

As she thanked them, Allie's mother and Robert Accardo

came into the room. Allie introduced her mother to Thomas and Liz. Mr. Accardo pulled Derek aside and congratulated him.

"I hate to cast a pall on this happy occasion," he said. "But I spotted four of Ustinov's men on the plane with us. Some frightened woman was with them."

"Mrs. Pembroke," Derek said. "The wife of the man responsible for . . . us."

Derek flashed this information to Allie, who shot him an apprehensive glance.

He closed his eyes and scanned Mrs. Pembroke.

"They've gotten firearms and checked into the Portland Host across the street," Derek said. "I wish I had a burner phone."

"Take one of mine," Mr. Accardo said, handing him a cell phone. "Keep it. It's untraceable."

Derek made a few calls.

"Portland's Finest is busy with weather-related problems but will look into this," Derek said.

Mr. Accardo shook his head.

∗∗∗

At one-thirty, Derek and Allie teleported to Macy's, changed into their wedding clothes and threw out the clothes they'd been wearing.

"One of these days," Allie said. "We have to figure out how to carry stuff that we're not wearing."

Chapter 18

At two, Derek and Allie were married.

A white-haired man in a priest's collar played the organ as they walked down the spacious chapel's aisle, past family, friends, and clouds of beautiful white flowers. Nurses had wheeled Wendy's hospital bed to the chapel, complete with its IV bags. Medical personnel also attended, techs in lab coats and doctors and nurses.

With glistening eyes, the Reverend Teague administered their vows and said they may kiss.

They sobbed as they did.

Then Allie waved enthusiastically to the assembly, and people applauded.

The organ-player introduced himself to Derek and Allie as Father Podsiadlo. When Derek offered a donation to his chapel, he replied, "Just be happy. That's all you owe me."

"How much for the flowers?" Derek said.

"Left over from this morning's funeral. We would've just thrown them out."

125

"We're having a little reception at the restaurant in Portland Host Hotel," Derek announced. "Across the street."

Allie's friends came over and congratulated them.

"Those glittery *contacts* you're both wearing," Dolores said. *"Love them!* I'll get myself a pair if it's the last thing I do."

Alicia presented Allie with a book saying, "It's a *little risqué,* but it really spiced things up for Carl and me. I didn't have time to wrap it."

It was a copy of the Kama Sutra.

"Thank you," Allie said, hugging her. "That's so *sweet.*"

"Very thoughtful," Derek said. "I'm sure we, uh, will put this to ... good use."

Alicia blushed.

Alicia and Carl are very sweet but are going through a rough patch, Allie wordlessly replied.

Linda presented them with a taser and electronic bug detector.

"Unfortunately, these things will probably come in handy," Derek said, hugging her.

"You don't want to know," Allie said. "You wouldn't believe us anyway."

"Intriguing," Linda said. "I'll take it as a challenge."

Renata gave Allie a diamond ring that had been in the family for generations. She hugged Derek, murmuring, "Welcome to the family," in Sicilian. With Allie's memories, he understood her.

"Happy to be in this family, mom," he replied.

"You speak *Sicilian?*" Renata exclaimed.

"Allie taught me."

Derek shut his eyes and checked on Ustinov's men. Two had been arrested and Mrs. Pembroke had escaped in the ensuing confusion. The other two were hiding out in another hotel across town.

Derek phoned the police with another anonymous tip.

✳✳✳

The restaurant seated the fifteen-person wedding party in the back at three tables pushed together. Chloe and Allie flanked Derek and his parents sat on her other side. Poor Wendy was still stuck in her hospital room.

"Let me pick up the tab for this dinner, at least," Robert Accardo said.

"We can pay our own way," Allie said.

"This is not from Carlo, it's from me," he said. "And I'm sure Carlo regrets the things he said to Derek."

"That's very kind of you," Allie replied. "But I'm hearing those words from *you,* not from grandpa."

In the end, she agreed to let Mr. Accardo pay for the dinner and hotel bills for the guests if they had to stay extra days.

"This has been the cheapest wedding I've ever seen in my life," Mr. Accardo said. "If Carlo had done this right, you would have been married in St. Patrick cathedral and had a huge reception with music and dancing. Like the opening scene in *The Godfather.*"

"With the FBI taking down license numbers?" Derek said.

Mr. Accardo laughed.

"I've been to fancy weddings that lasted longer than the marriages," Allie said.

Mr. Accardo chuckled again.

"This was the most beautiful wedding I ever saw," said the Reverend Teague. "A true meeting of souls in the sight of God."

Father Podsiadlo agreed.

"I have a story for you, Chloe," Allie said. "It involves an artist."

"Everything with her begins and ends with art," Renata said.

"This artist," she continued. "Has no studio, no canvases, and no paints. He has nothing."

"He's poor?" Renata said.

"He sees nothing and hears nothing," Allie continued. "His mind is all that exists."

"How can he be an artist then?" Mr. Accardo said.

"His mind is his studio and his thoughts are his paints. They are so powerful they come alive and think their own thoughts. And they are eternal. They don't fade as our thoughts do. He quickly learns that controlling this infinite array of living thoughts will lead to madness. And true creation implies a lack of control. So he takes the terrifying leap of splitting his ego from his creations."

"Interesting take on cosmology," Father Podsiadlo said.

"He allows them to develop their own egos," Allie continued. "And the Great Experiment begins: creating all forms of consciousnesses, personalities, and experiences possible. Limited only by *logic*."

"Wow," Chloe breathed.

"His earliest creations live in intimate contact with him, and he realizes that this limits them. To create all possible experience, he needs creatures that live with the illusion of separation and death. They live all the more intensely."

"I never knew you were so spiritual, Allie," Renata said. Allie's friends murmured their agreement.

"Our universe is one his more recent creations. He imagined it as a mathematical exercise in particles and force-fields. He didn't know sunsets were beautiful until viewing them though the eyes of his people."

"That's where you part from Catholic theology," Father Podsiadlo said. "We believe that God is *separate* from His creations.

You seem to be implying that God's creations are *part* of him. That's an idea that goes back to Spinoza."

"He's trying to find new forms of beauty," Derek said. "All forms of beauty possible."

"Where does he get the energy?" Dolores said. "Will it run out?"

"It's mental energy," Derek said. *"Engagement,* or the sense of being *interested.* Every time his creations surprise him, his engagement increases. These surprises happen all the time. So the energy is self-generating. And always increasing."

"That's all I got," Allie said. "Let's eat."

***

Most of the guests had various forms of lobster. Allie, Derek, and Dolores had Lobster Thermidor. The others had lobster pie or lobster tails.

"I'll have a glass of *pinot noir,* please," Alicia said.

"It's pronounced p*inyo noir,"* Thomas said.

"Are you thinking of the Spanish n with a curly line over it?" Alicia said.

"Absolutely not," Thomas replied.

"Oh, come on, Tom," Liz said.

"Dad, I'm pretty sure it's *pinot,"* Derek said.

"You flunked French, as I recall," Thomas replied. "I just want words to be pronounced accurately."

"Ask the waiter," Allie said.

The waiter confirmed that the wine was called *pinot,* not *pinyo.*

"Does the waiter know French?" Thomas said.

"He's black and he's gay," Allie exclaimed. "Of course he knows French."

As you know, dad can be a pompous ass, Derek wordlessly

told Allie. *He thinks he knows everything about everything. His friends at the Happy Cormorant hang on his every word.*

Allie laughed and replied, *Will this be a problem while we're all on the lam?*

I hope not.

✱✱✱

As the dinner wound up at seven, the newlyweds said good-bye to their guests.

"I'm sorry I didn't write down what you said," the Reverend Teague. "You two are prophets. If Father Podsiadlo knew what I know about you, he'd agree."

"Oh dear," Allie sighed.

"We'll have plenty of chances to talk," Derek said, hugging her.

"What are your plans?" Mr. Accardo said.

"Ustinov's men have been arrested. Allie and I will spend our wedding night ... somewhere. When the airport opens tomorrow, we'll return and send my folks and Allie's mom to a safe place."

"Renata? If Ustinov harms her, Carlo will target Irina."

"Ustinov's counting on that."

Mr. Accardo raised his eyebrows.

"I'll hurt Ustinov and his organization any way I can," Derek continued. "The NYPD will get an avalanche of anonymous tips."

"This will interest Don Carlo," Mr. Accardo said, shaking his hand. "Good hunting."

Chapter 19

They flew to the Evans home in Boothbay Harbor and fed Norton. Derek chatted with someone on the computer.

"Where are we going to spend our wedding night?" Allie said.

"It's all set up. Let's lie in my parents' bed."

"You've got to be kidding!" she said. "That's our *honeymoon?*"

"Just a place to park our bodies."

✳✳✳

They hovered over their prone bodies and Derek said, *Follow me.*

They shot through the roof up into the spirit-world's vastness, caressed by its loving, knowing light.

Someday I want to spend a lot of time in the spirit-world, studying it, Derek said. *In any case — we're here!*

Creation's womb around them flickered and pulsated with a thousand earthly and unearthly colors. Incipient life-forms appeared in their midst and faded from view — perhaps manifesting in different dimensions.

Where is here?

Space — the final frontier, he said.

Enough with the Star Trek crap.

There's the Earth, he said, pointing.

What Earth? I don't see any Earth.

That transparent disk, he said. Amid the riot of color, it was as if someone had lightly etched a globe-image into a sheet of clear glass — except that it also flickered and shimmered.

OK, I sort of see it.

I'm just guessing, he said. *But it looks like we're about 15 to 20 thousand miles away. If distance makes any sense in the spirit-world.*

The continents look wrong, she said.

It's upside-down.

As he said this, the globe-image rotated until they could recognize North America.

There's the west coast and that blank area is the Pacific Ocean, he said. *Let's focus on that.*

At this, the Earth image rotated until the Pacific Ocean occupied its center.

Now look at my map, he said, and a full color map of the Hawaiian Islands appeared in front of them, floating in space.

How did you do that?

I just visualized a map I saw once, Allie. Your spiel on how creation is imagination inspired me. Solid matter has a ghostly appearance here, but ideas look real.

Allie sang *Fly Me to the Moon,* and her voice smoothly morphed into the perfectly rendered sound of Sinatra.

My God, Derek. The possibilities are incredible. I could create paintings here and render them on canvas later.

Isn't that what you already do? he said.

Yes, but I can see them here in brilliant color.

They moved toward the large blank space in the Earth-image until a diagonal streak of dots appeared near the center.

The Hawaiian islands, he said, summoning the map again. *We'll head for Oahu.*

The dots resolved into blotches and they headed for the one shaped like Oahu. The bottom edge glowed with life-force and they headed for it.

At street-level, they searched for a place to materialize. Unfortunately, this area was like Manhattan — high rises, many pedestrians, and endless traffic.

They flew up the mountain slope until the streets became smaller. Gliding along a side-street, they finally came upon a building with an embossed sign they could read: *Sayako Matsumoto's Real Italian Pizza.*

They found its restrooms and materialized.

✳✳✳

They walked out into a dimly-lit bar and pizza parlor. People played pool in the back, and music blared from a jukebox — guitars and drums accompanying a golden-tongued man singing in Hawaiian.

They stepped outside, slamming into a wall of heat, humidity, and blinding sunlight.

"It was nighttime at home," Allie said, covering her eyes.

"It's five hours earlier here."

"A steambath," she said. "The air's like thick hot scented oil."

A bracing wind carried the sweet perfume of wild orchids mixed with hints of onions and mushrooms.

"The humidity's probably always a hundred percent," he said. "You saw how these islands are pinpricks in the Pacific."

As their eyes adjusted to the light, they saw that they were in a quiet neighborhood on a street lined with palms and plumerias in front of tiny homes. A mango tree to the right littered the sidewalk with fermenting fruit that smelled like beer.

"I never dared to explore other dimensions," she said. "Afraid of getting lost."

"Me too."

"Our own world has such contrasts, such magnificence. In a hundred years, I couldn't scratch its surface."

He kissed her.

"We need a taxi," he said. "And we're not going to get one standing here."

They headed back into the pizza parlor.

"I'm famished!" Allie said.

"Me too."

"I noticed I've eating more than usual and I'm not gaining weight," she said. "If anything, I'm losing it."

"Excuse me, ma'am," Derek said to the bartender, an elderly Oriental woman whose face was as weathered as an old catcher's mitt. "Can we order a small pepperoni pizza and beers?"

"We never get tourists here," the bartender said. "You must be the first. I'm Sayako by the way."

"We're on our honeymoon," Allie said. "This is the first place we stopped."

"Congratulations!"

Derek and Allie introduced themselves.

"You know a local cab company? We need a cab to the Piikoi Palace."

"You mean the Pee-ee-koy Palace," Sayako replied. "Aloha Taxi is good."

Sayako deftly tossed their pizza and put it into the oven.

Allie did a lightning sketch of Sayako Matsumoto on a paper placemat and handed it to her.

"You're an artist!" Sayako said.

Derek and Allie sipped their beers as they waited for the pizza to be done.

Then Sayako sliced and served it.

"Speaking as a real Italian from New York City," Allie said, holding a slice. "This pizza is fantastic."

Sayako beamed.

***

They checked into the Piikoi Palace's Honeymoon Suite. The desk clerk asked for a credit card, but Derek paid them $5000 to cover possible room-charges.

The room was huge, decorated in pale green with a private balcony, its wallpaper making it look as though it sat in a bamboo grove. The tub in its center was big enough to easily accommodate both of them. The tiled area around the tub had drains set into it to catch spilled water.

A wood-framed sepia photo of a hula dancer on a beach hung over a large bed in one corner. The dancer wore a circular crown of Ti leaves, a white blouse, and a skirt of palm fronds.

"I love that photo's mood," Allie said. "So elegant and serene. When we get a house, we have to put one like it over our bed. I'll paint it from memory."

They stepped out onto the balcony. An infinite expanse of blue greeted them, the hotels lining Waikiki beach looking like an unbroken cliff. The Honolulu Yacht Harbor spread out below and to the right. Dark clouds roiled overhead.

"You did good, maniac," Allie murmured, hugging him. *"Husband.* God, I never thought I'd call anyone that."

"Being married doesn't suck as much as you thought it would?"

"Not half as much."

It started to rain.

They went back inside as the rain intensified, the droplets sounding like gravel hitting the glass doors.

"The room comes with complimentary champagne and massages," he said.

"Oh, Mr. Masseuse Man, Sir, I have some kinks in my groin. Whatever shall I do?"

"I'll be happy to smooth out the wrinkles, Ma'am. We aim to please."

✳✳✳

An hour later, Derek limped over to the tub and turned on the water.

"I pulled a muscle," he said.

"Poor *baby.* I can hardly walk."

"Then I'll carry you," he said, lifting her up.

"You *better* carry me," she whispered, kissing him. "It's all your fault."

He carefully laid her down in the swirling water, and joined her, and they spent the next hour there, each washing and kissing every inch of the other's body.

They went to bed.

Serenaded by rain against the balcony doors, they fell asleep.

Chapter 20

Derek had a dream.

A beautiful woman lay on a raised wooden pallet in a small room lit by four blazing torches. A bronze dagger pierced her left breast just below a wide gold and turquoise necklace covering her upper chest.

Her dead almond eyes sparkled in the torch light, which also flickered off the gold headband holding her long braided black hair in place, its crest's golden cobra and vulture heads peering into the gloom.

Her white linen gown reached to her ankles.

Two men wearing white linen skullcaps and naked above the waist entered the room and prostrated themselves before the pallet, chanting,

> We play the tambourine for Your Ka,
> We dance for Your Majesty,
> We exalt You
> To the height of Heaven.

You are the Lady of Sekhem,
The Menat and the Sistrum,
The Lady of Music,
For whose Ka one plays.

Then they stood, closed her eyes, and removed the dagger from her chest, setting it beside her body. Murmuring prayers, they reverently removed the woman's jewelry and clothes.

They began to wash her body with what Derek knew was palm wine. They stopped, one man spoke to the other, and then they both left through the room's other door.

A large, haggard man in an Egyptian headdress staggered into the room sobbing, *"Why,* Sit-Hathor? *Why did you leave me?"*

It was the beloved mentor, Sinhue. Derek wanted to answer that life had not seemed worth living at the time.

Sinuhe snatched the dagger from the table and pressed its point against his heart, saying, "I'll join you, my love."

When the embalmers returned, though, he fled.

"Why did you *leave* me?" Allie screamed. It was three in the morning.

Derek woke and shook her.

"It's a nightmare, honey. Tell me your dream."

"It was bizarre," she began. "I was a man and you were a woman, and you had killed yourself. They were washing your body in preparation for embalming."

"Do you remember any other details?" he said.

"My name was . . . Sinuhe and yours was Sit-Hathor."

"I had that dream too."

"I was an advisor to the Living God. Your father, Amenemhat the first."

"Sit-Hathor. . ." he said. "I've heard that name before . . ."

"Your father commanded me to tutor you," she said. "In preparation for your marriage to . . . your younger brother."

"I would become Queen of the Two Lands," he said, his eyes glazing over. "It's like remembering a story I read . . . long ago. So long ago."

"Your brother was weak-willed and slightly retarded, so you would rule the nation," Allie said. "Pharaoh counted on that. Your *brother* counted on it."

"And you and I fell in love," he said.

"We didn't just fall in love," Allie exclaimed. "We *held hands* and *kissed*. Something that would get us *both executed*. Then you left me, you stabbed yourself. Was your brother so horrible?"

"He wasn't you, that's all. He worshiped me."

"We were so *vehement*, then," she said. "Anything worthwhile was worth dying or killing for."

"We were such . . . savage children, in a world of savage children," he murmured.

"I guess our marriage triggered this memory, somehow," Allie said. "And our bath. It reminded me of them washing your body. When I met you at Enigmatic, I felt a . . . shock of recognition. When we shared our souls. It was as if my mind acquired a new filing cabinet named Derek. And now I have one named Sinuhe."

"I have a one named Sit-Hathor," he said. "There's no way I'm going back to sleep."

"We're still on New York time, anyway" she said. "Let's get some breakfast."

"Everything's closed here."

***

Still wearing their wedding clothes, they fed Norton and cleaned his litter-box. After playing with him for a while, they wandered into the Portland Host Hotel's dining room.

Their friends were eating from a breakfast buffet.

"Wow," Dolores exclaimed. "I thought you two would be someplace warm, sipping drinks with umbrellas in them."

"The airport's still closed," Ed Brocklesby volunteered

"So I heard you're a graphic designer," Heidi said.

"I quit my job," Allie said, doing one of her lightning portraits of Ed and Heidi.

"That's quite amazing," Heidi said.

They got scrambled eggs and sausages from the steam tables.

When Chloe showed up with a plate of pancakes, they waved her over.

"Inquiring minds have to know," Derek said. "What became of you, dear Sinuhe?"

"Sinuhe?" Dolores said.

"A past-life memory I had on our wedding night," Allie said, recounting her impressions of Sinuhe and Sit-Hathor.

"You believe in that stuff?" Ed said.

"You always sneered at ideas like that!" Renata said.

"Derek and I have gone through a few changes, mom."

"Our *book* must've really rocked your world" Alicia said. "Carl and I never did that…"

"Egyptians did incest?" Megan said.

"In the royal family, it was common," Derek said. "Royals could only marry other royals. And there was only one royal family. So again, Sinuhe, what happened?"

"After?" Allie said. "I tried to kill myself with your dagger."

"Yes," Derek said. "That was in my dream."

"I didn't have the guts," Allie said. "So I ran away. I wandered the deserts, a brokenhearted coward, hoping to die."

"How could I have done that to you and my brother?" Derek said.

"Incredibly, it worked out," Allie said. "Really well. As an educated Egyptian and advisor to a Pharaoh, I was an honored guest. Everywhere. The Bedouin chieftains prized my counsel, and rewarded me. I became rich; I even married and had children. But I never forgot Sit-Hathor."

"You had a wonderful life," Derek said.

"When I was old, Pharaoh Senusret — your brother — invited me back to Egypt. He even ordered his soldiers to meet me at the border and give me safe passage to his palace. I ended my days there. I entertained him with tales of my adventures. Of course, he never knew my reason for leaving. He wouldn't have been so welcoming if he did."

"Sinuhe," Chloe said. "The name sounds familiar. I'm sure you'll find something if you Google it."

"You know about ancient Egypt?" Allie said.

"At the Berkeley Divinity School, I studied the World of the Old Testament," the Reverend Teague said. "We had to learn Hebrew and Aramaic and read the Book of Moses. I even spent a year in Jerusalem. My dissertation was *The Pharaoh Akhenaten's Influence on Moses.*"

"I'm impressed," Derek said.

"I'm a doctor of theology," Chloe said. "After I got my degree, I drove all over the country, searching. And this place called to me. A holy place, of peace and beauty."

"They're lucky to have you," Allie said.

Derek web-surfed on his phone.

"Here it is," he said, looking at his phone. *"The Tale of Sinuhe.* A classic of ancient Egyptian literature."

"I'm famous," Allie said. "At least Sinuhe was. Your brother's scribes must've written down my stories."

He passed the phone around to the others.

Chapter 21

After breakfast, they hugged Chloe, and the Brocklesbys and the three of them started their drive back to Boothbay Harbor.

They met Derek's parents and Renata and explained their plans: they would each take planes to different random airports and Derek or Allie would meet them there and give them tickets to their final destination, where they would lie low for a week. Derek's parents both had one week leaves of absence from their jobs.

"What about Wendy?" Liz said.

"When she's released from the hospital, she does the same thing," Derek said.

An airport shuttle picked up Allie's four friends.

"Something's wrong here," Allie said. "I feel it. We should go back inside."

"Yeah," Derek said. "I can't put my finger on it, but something's coming, like a storm. We need to check on our old friends."

"Nonsense," Thomas said. "The airport is just opening. Those Russians can't get to us yet."

"Is he always like this?" Mr. Accardo said.

"Unfortunately, yes," Derek said.

"We should *listen* to them, Tom" Liz said. "Wendy almost got killed"

"OK," Derek said. "Ustinov chartered a jet to fly here with several of his men."

"Then he contacted four men here," Allie said. "Former Army Rangers. And offered them ten million dollars each if they could capture us."

"That's insane," Mr. Accardo said. "He wouldn't spend that kind of money."

"He has no intention of paying them," Derek said. "He promised them a flight to Vegas in the chartered jet, but his men will actually kill them. I know the local men's names: Daryl Maugham, Joseph Brown, Leroy Watkins, and Ron Michaels. I can't scan them because I haven't met them."

"Time to give the cops an anonymous tip," Allie said, pulling out Mr. Accardo's burner phone.

Before she could dial, a rifle appeared in front of her face.

"He said you'd try to mess with our heads," Ron said.

Teleport out, Derek silently shouted at her.

They'll kill the others, she silently replied.

***

The four thugs drove them in one of the hotel's airport shuttle vans to the General Aviation part of the airport, arriving at an empty hangar.

They tied everyone except Allie up and dialed a cell phone, putting it on speaker.

Thomas was pale looked as though he would vomit. Liz and Renata wept.

"Greetings, Evans," Ustinov said. "We'll find Mrs. Pembroke eventually, but we don't really need her to do

144

your surgery. I might do it myself. I might even use anesthesia. Before we bring you back to New York, I want you to watch your new wife slowly die."

"No!" Renata sobbed. "She's all I've got"

"You'll get your turn, bitch," Ron sneered. "We'll put you all out of your misery."

Allie struggled and Daryl and Leroy grabbed her while Joseph wrapped his hands around his neck.

The cat litter! Allie wordlessly said. *Imagine their hands are clothing.*

Allie's face turned red as the man squeezed her neck. Then she and Derek teleported a few feet from where they stood.

The men's hands and some of the rope restraining Derek went with them. The rest did not.

The three men who'd tried to kill Allie stared numbly at the arterial blood gushing from their stumps. Ron lowered his gun in shock.

Allie shrieked as she shook off the amputated hands clinging to her like six-inch cockroaches.

Derek shook off the severed ropes around him and charged at Ron. The man fired, hitting him in the chest and knocking him back. Derek reset and, after momentary confusion, charged Ron again. He fired and hit him again and the cycle repeated. This time, Derek reached Ron and pummeled him into unconsciousness.

"Stop," Allie said. "You're going to kill him."

"Do we have a problem with that?" Mr. Accardo said.

Derek and Allie untied the others as a private jet slowly taxied toward the hangar.

"After you," Derek said, pointing to a door in the back. They ran out and spotted the passenger terminal half a mile away. They walked.

"Those men will bleed out if they don't get tourniquets," Allie said.

"Let 'em use the rope they tied us up with," Derek said. "Actually, Ustinov's men are just getting out of their plane now. They're shocked at ... what's there. They intend to fly the four over the Atlantic and dump them. Which is what they planned to do anyway."

"I'm shocked myself," Mr. Accardo said. "You two are a wrecking crew. You took two shots to the chest and just shrugged them off."

"Two?" Derek said. "I knew I took at least one."

"The first one was to your heart," Mr. Accardo said. "And both were through and through."

"Time to call Portland's Finest," Allie sighed, pulling out a phone.

Police sirens sounded in the distance.

"No," said Derek. "Someone already called them. I guess gunshots in an airport get noticed."

✳✳✳

In the main terminal, Mr. Accardo boarded a flight to New York.

At the gate he hugged Allie and shook Derek's hand, saying, "Congratulations again. And good hunting."

Allie and Derek demanded the other's cell phones, to which Thomas said, "Is this really necessary?"

"Don't you dare argue with them," Liz shouted.

"Only the government can trace our cell phones," Thomas said. "And we're not running from *them,* are we?"

"Just *do it,*" Liz said snatching the phone from his hand.

"We're running from corrupt government officials on Ustinov's payroll," Derek said. "Or private hackers who are even better."

"I want to go home," Thomas mumbled. "I need to go home. This isn't right, this isn't what's supposed to happen."

"We're going on *vacation,* honey," Liz said.

"Hawaii," Allie said.

"See," Liz said. "A *Hawaiian* vacation."

***

Allie took the phones, teleported to the Evans home in Boothbay Harbor, and put them on the kitchen table.

She also fed Norton and petted him, sobbing, "You saved my life."

"I can't believe people tried to kill me," she sobbed as Derek appeared and hugged her.

"Your dad is losing it," she added. "I feel his mind on the verge of coming apart."

"I've got to calm him down somehow," he said.

Derek searched the medicine cabinet in the upstairs bathroom and found a bottle of Ativan.

"Maybe I'm also crying because of a horrible thought I had," Allie said. "You, me and Vittoria were never in any real danger. We're practically invulnerable."

"Yes, if things really turn to shit, save yourself and our daughter," Derek said.

"I feel like a monster even thinking that."

***

Back in the main terminal, they put Renata on a flight to Cincinnati and Liz on one to Kansas City, Missouri.

Thomas was a problem. Strolling down Concourse C, they found a restaurant called Winston's Tavern and took a table. They finally persuaded Thomas to take two Ativans with a glass of red wine.

"I could use a stiff drink too," Allie said. "And not just wine."

"Allie," Derek said.

"I know, I know, we've got a lot of teleporting to do."

Breaking news interrupted the game show on the TV that hung over the bar, something in this very airport. A police car drove in front of a private jet on the runway, blocking it from taking off. After a SWAT team surrounded the plane, the cabin door opened, a staircase unfolded, and the occupants came out with their hands up.

"See dad," Derek said. "The men who kidnapped us are under arrest."

"One is dead, two are in critical condition, and the rifle man is babbling incoherently," Allie said. "The thugs on the plane are under arrest."

"I just want to go home," Thomas said, less insistently than before. "I need to make up my lesson plans."

"You should go with dad on the next leg of the trip," Allie said. "I'll check on Wendy and find an Internet cafe."

✳✳✳

Derek and his father got first class tickets to "anywhere" — the next plane taking off. After lowering his eyebrows, the agent booked them on a one way flight to Chicago.

About an hour into it, Derek told his dad, "Allie is renting us a house on the north shore of Oahu. A place called Kawela Bay. It'll be quiet and peaceful. Right on a beach."

Thomas numbly nodded.

"We have to meet Mrs. Murakami this afternoon and finalize everything."

Chapter 22

They finally all assembled in the Piikoi Palace's honeymoon suite.

"Wendy will be discharged tomorrow," Derek said. "We'll take her to the airport."

Allie called Mrs. Murakami on a burner phone she'd just purchased.

"OK," she said. "We meet her in an hour."

In the hotel gift shop, Derek bought a spiral-bound booklet of Oahu road maps. He and Allie flipped through the pages, memorizing them.

The hotel desk clerk helped them to rent a van big enough for all of them, and they asked Thomas to drive.

The white van sported a bumper-sticker that said, "Ho hum. Another shitty day in Paradise."

"Mom and me can't drive to save our lives," Allie said. "We're New Yorkers."

Although Derek also could drive, they had decided that having him drive would take his mind off other things.

They headed out.

"OK, dad," Allie told Thomas. "This should be Atkinson coming up. Make a left and we can merge onto the H1 interstate."

Sweet of you to call him dad, Derek wordlessly told her.

For better or worse, honey, she wordlessly replied. *Besides, I feel sorry for him. He's barely hanging on by his fingernails.*

Thomas followed Allie's directions, and on the H1 freeway, Allie said, "Now we want to go on the Pali highway, route 61, north."

They eventually followed a steep upgrade through dense forests on either side of the road. They passed an elegant white house on the right, and Allie said, "The map says it's The Queen Emma Summer Palace."

"What map?" Renata said.

"The one in my head, mom," Allie said, handing Renata the booklet. "At the top, there's a scenic lookout. The Nu'Uanu Pali State Wayside. I've got to learn how to pronounce these *names.* We should stop there for a few minutes."

They took the turnoff and pulled into a small parking lot.

The lookout was a fenced-off area that opened out onto the island's windward side. Kaneohe bay and the town of Kailua lay before them a thousand feet below. To the left and right, the near-vertical Koolau mountain range stretched into the distance like a green velvet curtain — blasted by a misty gale bearing the sublimed essence of the Pacific Northwest, and five thousand miles of ocean.

"The Trade Winds, dad," Derek said, bracing himself against the steady roar. "The mountains act like a funnel and channel them through here."

Thomas numbly stared into the distance.

"The map says there's supposed to be an upside-down waterfall," Allie said. "But I don't see it."

They got back into the car and continued on their way, passing through the town of Kaneohe and up Oahu's Eastern coast. Most of the ride was on a two-lane road with a small beach on the right and a sheer, foliage-covered cliff on the left.

"There are little waterfalls on top," Allie exclaimed, looking up the cliff.

They passed a wagon selling "Shave Ice" and another with the sign, "Mary's plant."

Eventually, the land flattened, spread out and they passed the graceful arc of Turtle Bay.

✳✳✳

Jessie Murakami was a sweet, white-haired woman of Japanese descent wearing a floral-print cotton muu-muu that looked like an ankle-length nightgown. Her sister in Tokyo had passed away, and she needed money to attend the funeral and spend a week in Japan with relatives.

"We will take good care of your *lovely* home," Allie said, giving her $20,000 in cash.

The house *was* lovely: a single-level home with a master bedroom and two others, a koi pond in front with a dozen swimming carp. There was a small algae-choked swimming pool in back, and the home's front faced the road and the beach.

"I have to put this in the bank," Mrs. Murakami said, waving to them. "Aloha."

They all said Aloha to her as she drove off in her rusted Toyota.

Derek brought little Norton to the house and the cat did somersaults and dashed around.

"He likes it here," Allie said.

They let him into the yard — the first time the cat had ever been outside.

A quick scan of Ustinov revealed that he had no idea of where the Evans family or Renata were. One of his men had traced her to Cincinnati but lost the trail there.

∗∗∗

They went to a nearby strip mall and bought stuff for Norton and had dinner from a truck named Giuseppe's Shrimp Shack. They got food on paper plates and every plate included two scoops of rice.

"Can I get this without the rice?" Thomas said.

"That cost extra, brah," the Hawaiian man serving food replied.

They sat at nearby picnic tables and ate.

"What I don't get is why the mob is after us," Liz said. "Gangsters usually only threaten each other."

"True most of the time," Allie said. "It's rare for the mob to go after innocent citizens, but it happens. For instance, if a citizen witnesses a mob murder, they go after them. Pembroke got the mob involved and they want something from Derek's brain."

"My second favorite organ," Derek said as Allie dug him in the ribs.

"Isn't the correct parlance 'a mob *hit*'?" Thomas said. "For a mob killing?"

"Thanks dad for clearing that up," Allie said, adding wordlessly. *I don't know which is worse: him as a zombie or a know-it-all.*

"My Alberto always wanted leave that life and open an Italian restaurant," Renata said. "He loved northern Italian cuisine even though we were from Sicily."

"I never knew what to say when kids asked what my papa did for a living," Allie said. "I wished I could've said he owned the

best Italian restaurant in Brooklyn. I daydreamed about helping
out, operating the register or waiting tables."

"I was a waitress for a while," Liz said. "It's not half as fun
as it sounds."

"Oh my God," Allie exclaimed.

"What?" everyone shouted.

"Images are flowing through my mind," Allie said. "So
vivid."

"What images?" Derek said.

"OK," Allie said. "It's like a little movie. Papa and Tony
don't get killed. Papa starts a restaurant with grandpa's help. I
skip art school and work at the restaurant and take bookkeeping
classes. A year later, papa has a fatal heart attack, and we run
his restaurant without him. Grueling work. Over the years, I
regret I never pursued my art and do paintings of fruit in the
little free time I have. I'm kind of bitter and wonder where my
life went. Then one rainy Tuesday evening, the place is empty.
I'm thinking of closing early. Then you, Derek, wander in and
ask me what's good. I recommend the veal *Francese* and we
wind up joking and chatting. We have dinner together and start
dating."

"Quite a story," Derek said.

"It feels so *real,*" Allie said. "Like something that happened."

"It *did,*" Derek said. "*Somewhere.* I see those images too.
I'd just moved into the neighborhood and was overjoyed to find
a friendly face. We eventually get married."

"Yes," Allie said. "But we have a much stormier relationship
than we have *now.* Or *here.* I don't know how to say it."

"Allie has become so serene since she met you," Renata said.

"Serene?" Derek said.

"You wouldn't believe the fights we used to have," Renata said. "She was so full of anger."

"Mom!"

"There's something so sweet about them," Derek said. "That Allie and Derek. You, know, with the restaurant."

"Really?" Allie said.

"They're us but not us," Derek said. "Or other versions of us. They need each other so much but they're so insecure. They have silly fights and make up. They struggle with making ends meet from day to day. In one future, we move to Boothbay Harbor and start a web-development firm with Ed's wife, Heidi. In another, they send that Derek to the Culinary Institute of America, and he becomes a master chef."

"I see that version too," Allie said. "We almost get a divorce, there. It's such a struggle to pay the tuition and keep the restaurant going. And that pastry chef tries to get her hooks in you. Monica. What a bitch."

"You want to just go there, grab them by the lapels, and shake some sense into them," Derek said.

"We could, you know," Allie said. "Teleport into their timeline and meet them in the flesh."

"Are these people real or imaginary?" Thomas said.

"They're as real as we are," Derek said. "Hell, *we're* more imaginary than them. Superpowers? Teleportation? You can't get more unreal than us."

"We shouldn't interfere," Allie said. "Just love them to death and hope they muddle through. Looking at the other Allie, I realize I *am* more serene. Maybe we *are* becoming like Mr. Spock."

"Is that good or bad?" Liz said.

"I don't know," Derek said. "It's not like we can change."

✳✳✳

Escorting Wendy to the airport was easy and uneventful. Although, neither Derek nor Allie detected any surveillance, they decided to play it safe and put her on a flight to Rochester, Minnesota. After meeting her at the airport there, they put her on a flight to Hawaii.

With her safely in Hawaii, it was time to begin the attack on Ustinov.

Chapter 23

Derek and Allie spent the night in the Piikoi Palace. After a morning of lovemaking, they bathed and ordered room-service.

"I want to send you into battle with a smile on your face," Allie said. "Hon, could you put the mattress back on the bed? Before room service gets here?"

"Oh, of course. Sorry about that."

"Don't bother with the sheets and bedspread," Allie said. "The maid's going to make the bed anyway. And give 'em hell, Maniac."

She vanished.

When room service arrived, he tipped generously, and ate breakfast.

Then Derek gathered his stun-gun, Don Carlo's pistol, and Linda's wedding present and placed them in his pockets. He lay on the bare mattress and went out-of-body.

***

He floated above a meeting between Ustinov and his top lieutenants.

155

156

"Allie's a hundred and twenty pounds *dripping wet*," Baranov said. "They're full of shit."

"Nope," a man named Dmitri said. "Ron clearly saw her move with incredible speed and rip their hands off. She was a blur."

Teleporting short distances looks like darting around. Especially for people who don't know we can teleport.

"Why didn't she just kill them?" Baranov said.

"She was sending a message," Dmitri Teplov replied. "Brilliantly. The two who survived will never forget her. They're also living warnings to anyone else who'd fuck with her or Evans."

"Where are these rocket scientists?" Ustinov said.

"The safe house at 53 Surf Avenue in Brighton Beach," Dmitri said.

"Anyone guarding them?" Ustinov said.

"They're not going anywhere," Dmitri said. "They think we'll reward them."

"Disappear them," Ustinov said. "*Carefully.* I don't want their bodies ever turning up."

"Sure boss," Dmitri said, pulling out a phone. "We'll process them at Beneficial."

Derek realized that Beneficial Pet Foods was one of Ustinov's few legitimate businesses, manufacturing dog and cat food.

"I can't believe they shot Evans *twice* and he didn't have a *scratch*," Baranov said.

"That moron missed," Baranov said. "*I* can't believe he fired a gun in an airport. What an idiot."

"Our police contacts said they pried bullets out of the hangar wall," Dmitri said. "With blood on them."

"Super strength, super speed, and instant healing?" Ustinov said. "And *telepathy*. That virus really *does* make men into superior creatures." He resolved that he alone would take the virus if they managed to acquire it — him and, possibly, his children. He couldn't trust anyone else.

"Any lead on Mrs. Pembroke?" Baranov said.

"No," Ustinov replied. "But we located her daughter, a senior at Binghamton University. We snatch her in broad daylight, it gets reported on the news, and Pembroke comes to us."

"Good," Ustinov said. "She can work off her father's debt in one of our brothels."

Their discussions turned to their various criminal plans.

Derek teleported to Grand Central Station in New York, where he bought a burner phone.

He pulled a business card from his wallet and made a call.

"Detective Roberts?"

"Speaking."

"Call me Ultraviolet," Derek said. "I'm highly-placed in Ustinov's organization."

He told him how Baranov had murdered Pembroke, how Mrs. Pembroke's daughter would soon be kidnapped in Binghamton, how an illegal gun shipment would arrive at the Port of Bayonne, New Jersey, and how a shipment of cocaine would arrive on Universal Air, flight 1553 at Kennedy Airport.

"Who are you? Your voice sounds familiar."

He cut the connection. He made calls to the Binghamton police and Campus Security at Binghamton University, and then threw away the phone.

He briefly considered going to Binghamton University and trying to track down Pembroke's daughter but he didn't even know her name.

***

He located Mrs. Pembroke alone in a small bedroom. It was on the second floor of a mansion with several other people on the first floor. He materialized in the hallway outside the bedroom. The place had clearly seen better days — the walls featured cracked plaster and peeling greenish wallpaper.

He knocked on the door.

"Mrs. Pembroke" he said, knocking on the door. "It's about your daughter."

She opened the door and said, *"You!* What did you do to my daughter?"

"I didn't know you had one. The Russian mob is going to kidnap her and put her in one of their brothels unless we stop them."

"She was my weakness," Mrs. Pembroke mumbled. "My shame. I set my husband's research back ten years."

"What's her name?"

"Eugenia," she said.

"Of course it is."

"Her name was supposed to be Subject Two, but I was weak," she said. "After Harry euthanized Subject One, I cracked and gave her a name. I couldn't bear to lose her too."

"He murdered his own child?" Derek said.

"Neurons grow fastest in newborns," she said. "They're ideal test subjects. *Here he is!"*

A stocky, bushy-haired man with a mustache held a gun to Derek's head, and Derek teleported to his parents' home in Boothbay Harbor.

✳✳✳

Then he drifted to a restaurant on Wall Street. After coming out of the restroom, he learned that it was called The Boardroom Grille. It was an elegant place, with darkly-stained walnut walls and white linen-covered tables. A portrait of Theodore Roosevelt hung on the back wall.

He took a table and called Binghamton University again with the news that an attempt would be made to kidnap *Eugenia* Pembroke. When they asked when, he said soon.

It was all he could do.

He relaxed and took in the place's atmosphere. The air seethed with baffling thoughts of quants, the Greeks, and merger arbitrage.

He let his spirit drift into the future. The world became a bewildering array of random movements as he saw thousands, perhaps even millions, of alternate futures superimposed on each other. One thought echoed from many minds: the wish that they had bought Energistics stock when it was cheap.

A waitress tapped him on the shoulder, bringing him back to the present. He ordered a Boardroom Burger.

He let his mind drift again and heard a heavyset, bald middle aged man in a black pinstripe suit named Martin Rothstein planning to flee to Paraguay with his mistress, a stripper named Cashmere Jones. He was chief accountant at a startup named Blink Reality Tools. They'd just raised $200 million in venture capital which Mr. Rothstein had diverted to an offshore bank account.

The scandal will break in two days tops, Mr. Rothstein thought. *I'll be Asunción by tomorrow.*

Derek's burger arrived — an obscene concoction of ground filet covered with blue cheese, sliced onions, with truffled French fries — all dusted with specks of gold leaf.

He bit into the burger.

It tastes good. And I'll be shitting gold by morning

A young man named James Clabel ate a burger two tables away from Derek. He was sandy-haired, in his early twenties, and wore thick glasses and an ill-fitting blue suit. He was mentally preparing for an exam at a brokerage firm named Baker,

Beans, and Richards — apparently part of their interview process.

Derek eavesdropped on James for a while and got an idea.

He paid his bill, left the restaurant and strolled down Wall Street. It was sunny but cold so he ducked into the first brokerage firm he passed: Jacobson and Morse.

Chapter 24

It was still early afternoon in Hawaii when Derek rejoined the others. They all sat around the kitchen table staring glumly at the torrential rain outside.

"This isn't the way Hawaii's supposed to be," Wendy said. "I might not get a chance to go swimming."

"It's the rainy season," Derek said. "We should come back another time of year."

Derek explained to them what he'd done.

"How can you make money on a stock that's going down?" Thomas said.

"You short it," Derek said. "You borrow shares of stock and sell them at today's prices. Then you buy them back at tomorrow's prices and repay the loan."

"You can *do* that?" Allie said.

"Jacobson and Morse had 2.7 million dollars worth of Blink Reality Tools stock in their inventory and I borrowed all of it and sold it."

"We have 2.7 million dollars?" Allie exclaimed.

"In theory," Derek said. "Normally, I'd be able to spend

161

it, but they don't know me. So I have to keep the money at their company — in an escrow account. I can claim it when the transaction is finished."

"What if the stock goes up?" Allie said.

"If it goes up a little, they can cover it from our bank account. If it goes up a lot, we make another gambling run."

"Monaco's nice this time of year," Allie sighed. "Hell, Monaco's nice *any* time of year. I've always wanted to see the Casino Royale."

"Let's hope we don't have to."

"Aren't you profiting from other peoples' misery?" Thomas said.

"It's *gambling,* dad," Derek said. "The stock market as a whole bet the stock would go up, and I bet it would go down. I won. If the stock had gone up, we'd have been screwed."

"It just seems wrong somehow."

"The real scandal is that it's a solid company," Derek said. "Brokers encouraged their clients to panic and dump its stock. Whether people buy or sell, they make their fees. They like their accounts *active.*"

"A dirty business," Thomas muttered, shaking his head.

"I feel like cooking," Derek said. To get my mind off ... things."

Derek and Allie went to the local supermarket and shopped. Back at the house, Derek fried bacon in a large pot, browned cubes of beef and carrots in the bacon fat, and put them in a casserole with red wine and herbs. He made a mahogany roux from flour and bacon fat, put it into the casserole, and put that in the oven for several hours.

✳✳✳

Derek and Allie served the casserole over mashed potatoes

and sprinkled pearl onions simmered in beef broth and thyme on top.

"This is incredible" Liz said.

"It's like *candy,*" Wendy said. "What is it?"

"Beef *Bourguignon*," Derek said.

"Did you find a recipe online?"Liz said.

"He got it from Culinary Derek," Allie said. "In that other timeline we discussed."

"It's as if I spent years at that cooking school. I know all about how a professional kitchen works."

"These timelines are real?" Thomas said.

"Of course they are," Derek said. "It's quantum mechanics. Everyone has millions of time lines. Even inanimate objects have them. That's the reason for the Heisenberg Uncertainty Principle. On an atomic scale the timelines are so close together you see multiple ones at the same time. The particle is in a slightly different position in each one."

"The only difference with us is we can *see* these timelines," Allie said. "I think I learned to play the piano in one of mine."

"I tried to get you to take piano lessons," Renata said. "But you hated them."

"In one timeline, I loved them and got really good. I wonder what talents Vittoria will have. Besides being one of us."

"In every timeline with us together," Derek said. "We have at least one child. In most of them we have two. So that has nothing to do with Pembroke."

"That's a relief," Allie said. "I think we'll have three kids, and then both of us will get fixed. Maybe four."

"You're planning on that?" Wendy said.

"Let's face it," Allie said. "I'll be pregnant five minutes after Vittoria's born."

"TMI!" Wendy said.

∗∗∗

"I put food out for Norton, but he's nowhere to be seen," Liz said.

"He went outside earlier today," Wendy said.

"He's never been outside in his entire life," Derek said. "He's probably lost. I'll find him."

"In the pouring rain?" Liz said.

"It's only water. I'll located him in my spirit-body."

Derek found Norton meowing beneath a bush.

He materialized, picked the cat up, and carried him home.

"He was almost a hundred feet from the house," Derek said.

Liz wrapped Norton in a towel and dried him off.

∗∗∗

After dinner, they turned on the TV.

The evening news featured stories about the seizure of three tons of cocaine at Kennedy airport with a street value of 90 million dollars, and a huge illegal arms shipment in New Jersey.

"You're pissing them off," Thomas said.

"They tried to kill you before they were pissed off," Derek said. "It's not like things could get any worse."

"But what did you gain by tipping off the police?" Thomas said.

"I figure the mob runs on money."

"Yes," Renata said. "It's like a business. They pay their people $20,000 a week or more."

"Derek is cutting off their air supply," Allie said. "The *soldati* will get restless when their paychecks dry up."

The news anchor said an unnamed source in the New York Police Department attributed the anonymous tips to 'Ultraviolet,' a lieutenant in the Ustinov syndicate.

"Ultraviolet?" Allie chuckled, digging Derek in the ribs.

"That's a dangerous leak," Derek said. "Or would be if Ultraviolet wasn't me."

"The Pembroke's had two kids just to experiment on them?" Liz exclaimed.

"Not your typical Disney family," Derek said. "Subject One was a boy. Pembroke gave birth at home so there was no record or birth certificate. Then they experimented on him and put him down like a dog."

"Mrs. Pembroke got maternal with Subject Two and tried to give her a life," Allie said. "She sent Eugenia to live with her aunt Maris, in Binghamton. She was afraid her husband and his followers would kill her."

"That's the saddest story I ever heard," Liz said.

***

Derek let his mind drift and found himself floating near the ceiling in a conference room with several detectives.

"I want the son of a bitch," Detective Roberts growled. "He may have gotten ultraviolet killed."

"Yeah," Detective Martinez said. "Let's check all the phones in the station."

Unfortunately for Detective Roberts, his partner was the son of a bitch. Detective Martinez had called his contact at the TV news on a burner-phone he kept in his pocket — right after he'd called Ustinov.

An idea formed in Derek's head. He carefully scanned everyone in the entire police station and teleported to Grand Central Station, where he bought a burner phone. It was midnight, and the place was nearly empty.

He called Detective Roberts.

"Ultraviolet here," Derek said.

"I have to apologize for the leak to the press," Detective Roberts said.

"Never mind. Here's list of police department employees working with Ustinov." Then he gave a list of five names, ending with Detective Martinez.

"That's my partner," Detective Roberts said. "I can't arrest people based on what you've given me."

"Of course not. Just investigate. You're a good cop."

Derek returned to the Murakami house.

Chapter 25

The next morning, Derek teleported to the offices of Jacobson and Morse. The firm's main floor was a huge area with rows of men and women making phone calls and typing at workstations, each with multiple monitors.

He approached the receptionist and asked to speak to Finnbar Burke, the broker he'd dealt with.

Mr. Burke was a gray-haired short thin man in a tweed suit who spoke with a faint Irish brogue. He had a large office paneled with darkly stained wood and an oriental rug on the floor. A large walnut desk sat in front of the window and a flat screen TV covered one whole wall. The office also had an area with several fluffy brown leather chairs arranged around a coffee table.

From scanning him earlier, Derek knew he had a wife named Siobhán and daughters named Alice and Fiona. He'd grown up in Dublin and had a masters degree in Financial Mathematics from Trinity College.

"I'd like to conclude our business," Derek said, shaking Mr. Burke's hand.

"I thought you might. You clear 2.1 million dollars. You

know, the company's fundamentals are good, despite having a crooked accountant. Many investors stampede when a scandal breaks. Not that it matters to us. We collect our fees whether they buy or sell."

A quick scan showed that Mr. Burke believed every word of that.

"I agree," Derek smiled. "I'll buy a thousand shares. And could you wire a million dollars to our Continental Bank account?"

"Sure."

"Oh, one last thing. Could you research a company called Energistics? I'd like to buy stock in it if possible."

"No problem What kind of company are they?"

"I have no idea," Derek said.

Mr. Burke's eyebrows went up but he said, "We'll see what we can do."

✳✳✳

Derek hovered over Detective Roberts and his partner, who were having a sort of confrontation.

"We've got a tip on a large drug deal on Forsyth and Houston," Detective Roberts said, after laying his service revolver on a nearby table.

"I've got to make a call," Detective Martinez said.

"No time for that This is going down *now*."

Detective Martinez picked up Detective Roberts's gun and pointed it at him, saying, "No, Ian. I don't think so."

"The last Ultraviolet message said you were dirty," Detective Roberts said. "I didn't believe him."

"Once you start taking money from Ustinov, he has you by the balls," Detective Martinez said. "They keep records of everything and can send you to prison in a heartbeat."

"So what happens now?"

"You were despondent after your wife died," Detective Martinez said. "Everyone knows that. You decided you couldn't go on. You can't imagine how much it pains me to do this."

"You're not going to shoot me. We've had each other's back for twenty years."

Detective Martinez pulled the trigger and nothing happened.

Detective Roberts pulled out a gun and said, "I can't believe you did that."

"Oh, shit," Detective Martinez sighed, his shoulders falling. Then he launched himself at Detective Roberts, knocking him down. They struggled and Detective Martinez took the gun away from the other man.

"I could always take you any day of the week, old man," Detective Martinez said as he held the other detective at gunpoint.

"Holy Mother of God!" Detective Roberts whispered, as Derek materialized behind Detective Martinez.

"Nice try," Detective Martinez said, before Derek shocked him with a stun gun. Martinez fell to the floor, convulsing.

Detective Roberts gaped at Derek, until Detective Martinez began to come to. Derek shocked him a second time.

Detective Roberts finally came to his senses and handcuffed Detective Martinez.

"We'll have a long talk," Derek said. "And I'll explain everything. But not right now. You have to book this guy."

"You saved my life," Detective Roberts said. "I have to put you in my report."

"Don't. Five minutes from now, I'll be several thousand miles away, waving at a surveillance camera. You'll have to explain that."

"How is that possible?"

"The pill Pembroke gave me had some side-effects."

Derek teleported to Honolulu International Airport and waved to a surveillance camera.

***

Derek checked on Ustinov.

He was in a strange place, naked except for a towel around his waist and sitting on a bench of some kind. Three similarly-clothed men stood around him.

Maybe it's a steam bath or sauna.

"We're being butt-fucked by an elephant's dick," Dmitri said. "Two hundred million in drugs and arms lost. Our upcoming deals are all on hold because of this Ultraviolet asshole. They don't trust us."

"Ultraviolet is Evans," Ustinov said.

"What do we tell them?" Rabotnikov said. "We're being stalked by an angry telepath?"

"Maybe we should make our peace with him," Dmitri said. "He can fuck us at his leisure and there's nothing we can do about it."

"No," Ustinov said. "We locate his family and he'll be eating out of our hand. That Grigory guy at Universal Airlines. Tell him we'll free his sister if he can locate them."

"Are you kidding?" Dmitri said. "Our women bring in eight hundred grand a year. They're practically the only source of income we have left."

Your woman are about to get a vacation. If I can only locate them.

"We tried getting Evans's family twice," Rabotnikov said. "And it blew up in our faces both times. Your decisions have sabotaged our operations all along. Beginning with the decision to kill Pembroke."

Ustinov reached into a canvas sack on the bench beside him, pulled out a gun, and shot Rabotnikov three times.

"Anyone else want to question my judgment?" Ustinov said.

The others shook their heads.

Derek materialized in a toilet stall in a nearby restroom. The air stank of sweat, steam, and shit. He pulled out a smart phone and called Detective Roberts.

"Ustinov just murdered a man named Aleksandr Rabotnikov," he said.

"Where are you?" Detective Roberts said.

"I don't know the address but it's some kind of sauna," Derek said.

"Ustinov has a private club with a Russian-style *banya*," Detective Roberts said. "Councilman Harare is giving us hell for investigating without probable cause. We're persecuting a fine upstanding citizen on the word of a nobody."

"Here's probable cause. This phone has a GPS locator in it. Trace it. It's near the crime scene."

He wiped the phone down with toilet paper and laid it face-down on the floor.

Derek teleported to the Hanneford Market in Boothbay Harbor and purchased a decongestant at the Pharmacy that required him to show his driver's license.

Then teleported to his parents' home and raided the refrigerator.

It was snowing.

We could use some more money, Allie said in Derek's mind.

On it.

✳✳✳

In an out of body state, he drifted to the Continental Bank branch in Flushing. Dmitri's girlfriend, Valentina Panova, loitered in the hallway keeping an eye out for Derek or Allie. Her right hand rested on a pistol in her purse.

Derek materialized in the men's room at Lew's Diner, peeked out the front door, and looked across the street at the bank.

Valentina turned out to be a platinum blond in her mid-twenties wearing a long red leather coat with a large black patent leather purse slung over her right shoulder, and white high-heeled patent leather boots.

She wore dark glasses to be inconspicuous.

Derek ducked back into the restaurant and called 911.

"There's a woman hanging around in the Continental Bank lobby flashing a gun," he said. "I think she wants to rob the place. Maybe she's waiting to meet up with partners." He followed this with a description of Valentina.

Fifteen minutes later, a police car pulled up and two policemen stepped out and asked to inspect Valentina's purse. She shook her head and started to walk away. One of the policemen grabbed her purse and a scuffle ensued. When her gun fell out of the purse, both policemen drew their weapons, and Valentina raised her hands. They handcuffed her and put her in their patrol car.

After they left, Derek walked into the bank and asked to speak to the manager, Gloria Smith.

"You have a very active account, Mr. Evans," Ms. Smith said. "We just received a wire transfer for a million dollars."

Derek asked to draw two hundred thousand dollars from the account. After resisting Ms. Smith's sales pitch about the bank's "Wealth Management" services, he shoved the bundles of bills into his purse.

It was all that would fit.

***

He parked his body in the Boothbay Harbor home and checked on Mrs. Pembroke. She was still in the run down mansion, joined by her sister, Maris, and her daughter, Eugenia. She was worried that the Iron Order would throw them into the streets because they could no longer help the cause.

***

At 5:30 in the evening, Derek drifted in his spirit-body and thought of Detective Roberts. The detective was in a bar — perhaps the same bar he'd been in when Derek first saw him. Derek materialized in a restroom.

The bar was a dimly lit hallway paneled in wood stained dark brown. To the right was the bar with stools and glowing glass shelves to the right covered with liquor bottles — the place's main source of light. To the left were booths. Derek strolled down the bar until he reached Detective Roberts sitting alone in a booth.

"Want to have that talk now?" he said.

"How the hell did you find me?" Detective Roberts said, almost jumping out of his seat.

"The same way I found you when your partner tried to kill you. Once I've met someone, I can always find them. Anywhere on Earth."

"Lucky me," Detective Roberts muttered. "Look, I'm not ungrateful but I've had a long day. Someone I trusted with my life — for years — pulled a trigger on me."

Derek ordered a beer.

"My day hasn't exactly been great either," Derek said. "Ustinov keeps trying to kill me and my family."

"Why is that?"

Derek sat and explained.

"The Pembroke murder was to be my last case," Detective Roberts said. "Before I retire."

Derek knew but said nothing.

"If I believe *half* of what you told me, it's the most bizarre case of my career. If I was twenty years old, I might've jumped at it."

"Everything I said is true," Derek said. "We even have a professor at NYU studying our DNA."

Why the hell did I mention that?

"Ustinov's crew tried to kidnap your family twice? How did those men in Portland lose their hands?"

"They were trying to strangle my wife," Derek said. "So she defended herself."

"Your wife? I know she's Don Carlo's granddaughter, but those guys are built like King Kong."

"She caught the virus from me," Derek said. "I sneezed in her face."

"Jesus."

"We've never harmed anyone except in self-defense. And we never will."

"You know," Detective Roberts said. "Ustinov will probably beat that murder rap. He's claiming he was cleaning his gun and it went off by accident."

"Cleaning a gun in a steam bath?" Derek said. "And it went off three times?"

"We surprised him and his men as they were hauling away the body. They didn't have time to come up with a better story. Unfortunately, it doesn't have to be believable. It just has to give his supporters talking points."

"He has *supporters?*" Derek said.

"Maybe that's too strong a word. It's rumored he has blackmail-material on half of the city council and the mayor."

"At least it will keep him occupied for a while," Derek said. "And I plan to reduce his income. I'll go after his brothels next."

"That's going to be tough," Detective Roberts said. "Most

of those girls are illegals and will be deported. And they never testify against their traffickers. Even when they do it's hard to get convictions."

"Why?"

"We had a case where a girl was forced into prostitution when she thought she was taking an *au pair* job. She testified. In excruciating detail, for hours. Everything they did to her. And the jury acquitted. They said her tormentor was too good-looking and soft-spoken to be a criminal. And she was a whore."

"They disregarded her testimony?" Derek said. "She didn't start out a whore."

"A lot of people don't think; they have knee-jerk reactions. You remember the trial of Timothy McVeigh?".

"No, but I see it in your mind," Derek said.

"God, that's creepy," Detective Roberts said, shaking his head. "At the end of the trial, they spent hours showing photographs of the one hundred and sixty-eight victims. They interviewed their families too. You know why they wasted so much court-time?"

"Because the bailiff overheard some jurors saying one hundred and sixty-eight is just a number. And McVeigh's such a good-looking man. They didn't have the heart to convict."

"Damn right," Detective Roberts snarled. "They actually had to convince the jury that what he did was *bad*."

"That's so depressing," Derek said. "Do you know where Ustinov's brothels are?"

"No."

"Who was Bugsy Siegal?" Derek said.

"What about him?"

"Baranov mentioned him after he shot Pembroke," Derek said. "I looked him up but I can't figure out his significance."

"Bugsy Siegal is the gangster who discovered Las Vegas," Detective Roberts said. "He realized how the mob could move into legitimate businesses. Casinos. He was right too, but the money didn't roll in fast enough for the New York people. They had him killed."

"So that was Baranov's game. He wanted to invest in prescription drugs."

"Makes sense. Except Pembroke was lying to him all along. You think his people could've taken over the world?"

"A hundred ruthless people with my abilities? They could give the world a run for its money. Especially if they were smart."

"Ustinov gaining your powers would be a nightmare."

"It was nice talking with you, Detective," Derek said, shaking the other's hand. "I'll be in touch. I'll feed you tips that would put Sherlock Holmes to shame."

Chapter 26

In an out of body state, Derek found Wendy driving Allie and Renata down a two lane road through an open field. He materialized in the back seat next to Renata, who shrieked in shock. The car almost swerved off the road.

They pulled over to a shoulder.

"You almost got us killed, you idiot," Allie yelled. "Don't ever do that again!"

"Let's take a deep breath and calm down," Renata said.

"I'm sorry. I had a depressing conversation with Detective Roberts and just had to see you. I should've landed alongside the road up ahead."

"That would've been better," Allie said. "And I see your depressing conversation and it's making me depressed."

"Sorry about that."

"We're in this together, honey. And ignorance is never bliss."

"I have an idea that might solve our problems," Derek said.

"I know and I'm against it."

"Will someone tell *me* what's going on?" Wendy said.

"My idea is to find a *competent* brain surgeon," Derek said.

177

"And get my pineal gland removed. Then we give the God Virus to you, mom and dad, and Allie's mom."

"Cool," Wendy said. "We get your super-powers"

"You'll be immune to the mob, and just about anything else. We could get our lives back."

"Unfortunately this surgery is always dangerous," Allie said. "They can nick your carotid and you bleed out in seconds. They can cut your spinal cord and you're paralyzed from the neck down."

"I can reset from that."

"Can you reset from death? Even doing this surgery on a healthy person is considered malpractice. I made a few calls."

"Well it was a thought," Derek sighed.

Derek looked around, shielding his eyes from the sunlight. The car was in the middle of a pineapple field in a wide sun-drenched valley between two green mountain ranges.

"Where are we?" Derek said.

"We're driving up the middle of the island," Allie said, pointing to the right. "Those mountains over there are the backside of the mountains we passed the other day."

"Less than a minute ago, I was in New York and it was night," Derek said. "And snowing."

The change in time and scenery was mind-numbing — as though he'd awakened from a mid-afternoon nap, unable to get his bearings.

"Teleport-lag sucks," Allie said. "You look like hell, honey. You should turn in early."

"Travis says the few sunny days in the rainy season are the best weather Hawaii has," Wendy said.

"Wendy made a friend," Allie said. "Cute kid named Travis Howland."

"He's going to teach me to body surf. If we have another sunny day."

✳✳✳

They continued along the highway until they came to a small town of immaculate lawns, Japanese gardens, and palm tree lined streets.

They stopped at a shopping mall called the Town Center of Mililani.

"An Italian restaurant," Renata said, pointing. "Let's have lunch there."

They shrugged off the glare and steamy heat of Hawaii in its air-conditioned silence. The walls held murals of Roman gardens and fountains, and one had a mosaic of gladiators in combat, all lit by blue recessed lights set into the ceiling. Potted ferns and bamboo plants dotted the room, and the tables had starched white tablecloths and sculpted napkins.

A palace of crystalline perfection.

They sat.

"You should've heard Allie play the piano," Renata said. "What was that piece?"

"It's Beethoven. *Für Elise,*" Allie replied. "My hands got completely numb. I'm just beginning to get the feeling back."

"We stopped at a music store in Pearl City," Renata said.

"Is that musical ability from your past life?" Wendy said.

They ordered food: Antipasti, Sicilian chicken, veal *Francese,* and *ossobucco alla Romana.*

"Not a past life," Allie said. "A *current* life. I have two albums out in that timeline. Bach's Goldberg Variations, and one of New Age music. Stuff musical Allie wrote herself. She joined an online dating site, and Derek is one of her matches."

"You need an online dating service?" Derek said.

"I had a bad breakup with a violinist and still had to run into him almost every day. I decided I wanted a man who likes classical music but isn't a musician."

"Yes," Derek said. "I would've checked off liking that."

"So you're leaching off the other Allie?" Wendy said. "Sucking up some of her talent?"

"Talent can't be sucked away. It affects her, though. She has intense dreams of Derek and me. Some of them are down and dirty. When she wakes up, she wants to jump the first man she sees."

"Wow," Wendy said.

"When Derek's name and picture appeared on her dating site, it blew her mind," Allie said. "And part of her is afraid of her feelings for Derek."

"When did the split happen?" Derek said.

"Split?" Renata said.

"When musical Allie's timeline split from mine. I think it happened when papa and Tony died. I became bitter and rebelled. The other Allie plunged into Catholicism and her piano lessons, fleeing from her grief. Her musical talent is remarkable. It's the ultimate example of turning lemons into lemonade."

Their food arrived.

"Derek's food tasted a lot better than this," Wendy said.

"That's because our restaurant has two Michelin stars," Derek said. "And we're working on a third."

"Don't all these different timelines confuse you?" Renata said.

"No," Derek said. "Strangely, they don't."

"I don't have any problem either," Allie said. "Sometimes I feel like teleporting into these other timelines and meeting the other versions of me and Derek. Probably a bad idea."

"Veal *Francese* shouldn't be breaded," Renata said.

"Look, mom. This isn't New York and sure as hell isn't Italy. We should've eaten at the Hawaiian Barbecue. Or the Shrimp Shack."

"Isn't there any good Italian restaurant in Hawaii?" Renata said.

"I know a really good pizza place," Allie said.

"My God!" Derek said. "There's a timeline where I shoot Ustinov while he's sitting on the toilet."

"That would've solved all your problems," Wendy said.

"I see it too," Allie said. "You *die* in that timeline."

"Somehow, killing someone in cold blood wipes out my superpowers. I can't teleport out of the bathroom, and Ustinov's men break down the door and kill me."

"*Why?*" Renata said.

"It scars the soul somehow," Derek said. "Killing someone."

"It's a lonely life," Allie said. "I raise our daughter as a single mom, without anyone else in the entire world like me. I become a billionaire eventually and marry a nice man, but he'd not Derek."

"When you amputated those men's hands, did your superpowers weaken?"

"No," Allie said. "I guess self-defense is OK."

Chapter 27

At four in the afternoon, Derek and Allie returned to their honeymoon suite and bathed together.

After, they threw towels on spilled water and went to bed.

At 3AM, Derek crept out of bed without disturbing Allie and kissed her cheek.

She stirred and mumbled, "Don't get yourself killed, baby. Tori and I would be very pissed off."

He picked up clothes and teleported to the Boothbay Harbor house, where he showered, shaved and got dressed.

✳✳✳

His first stop was the Boardroom Grill, where he materialized in the Men's Room. He stepped outside and found a newsstand where he bought a New York Times.

He returned to the restaurant and took a table. A waitress whose name tag said "Carol" poured him coffee and took his order for eggs over easy with toast.

He sipped his coffee and read the paper. President Eakins pushed for a constitutional amendment restricting freedom of speech, saying "Freedom of speech is not freedom to utter bullshit." Thousands of his supporters demonstrated in front of the Capital building.

Ustinov was out on five million dollars bail. Several city councilmen decried the "witch hunt" against him, calling Robotnikov's shooting a "tragic accident."

He thought of the timeline where he'd shot Ustinov. *Maybe Pembroke's evil plans in other timelines came to nothing.*

He thought of the infinity of timelines that had him and Allie together, with every possible variation of their lives pursued and explored. They were like the facets of a vast gem, as if their love was a multidimensional event transcending space and time, one that could only be understood — if at all — by being split into tiny fragments.

Even the timelines with him and Musical Allie occurred in a mind-boggling array. From the ones with them together to ones where Allie — overwhelmed by her feelings for him — fled and became a nun. In those, Derek was her never-forgotten One That Got Away. In some, they reunited in their 60's.

And what happens when we die? Is there a Grand Reunion where we come together and remember all the things we did — and might have done? Or are some timelines so divergent they spawn new, independent souls?

Carol served his breakfast.

Back to reality, he thought, thanking her.

He scanned Mrs. Pembroke. Afraid of losing her job, she'd come out of hiding to perform knee replacement surgery that had been scheduled six weeks ago. With two nurses, a surgical assistant, and an anesthesiologist, she reamed and drilled the bones of her patient's right leg.

More carpentry than surgery.

✳✳✳

He paid his bill and visited the offices of Jacobson and Morse.

"I wanted to contact you," Mr. Burke said. "You didn't give me any contact information."

"That's OK. I travel a lot. I'll keep in touch with you."

"I located Energistics Corporation. It's a small startup incorporated in New York State. They don't have any stock listed but are looking for investors."

"Good. I'm looking to invest."

"I can set up a meeting with their founder in our conference room. If you negotiate any deals, we have lawyers who can draw up contracts."

"Fantastic."

"If you have a minute, I can try now."

"Sure."

Derek sat in one of the comfortable leather chairs in Mr. Quirk's office while the latter made a call.

"It's set for noon," Mr. Burke finally said, hanging up the phone. "We can order food from the Boardroom Grill."

"Lately, it's the only place I eat."

"Oh dear," Mr. Burke laughed. "We'll have to remedy that."

***

With two hours to kill, Derek teleported back to the Boothbay Harbor house and lay on his parents' bed.

In an out of body state, he checked on Ustinov.

He sat in his house's dining room, conferring with his lawyer, Henry Vandermonde. Derek guessed that the many indistinct objects covering the dining room table were file folders and papers.

"A forty-four magnum never accidentally goes off," Mr. Vandermonde said. "Certainly not three times. An indictment is guaranteed, and you will be remanded at that point. Regardless of how many politicians speak up for you."

"I'm not in jail yet," Ustinov said.

"Bill Jennings will be prosecuting, and he told me he'll ask for the death penalty."

"It won't come to that," Ustinov said.

"If worst comes to worst, he'll take death off the table on one condition."

"What?"

"You testify against all your former associates. Your entire... organization."

"I'll keep that in mind. I wish we could implicate Evans. I know he made that phone call."

"Stop flogging that dead horse. There's nothing to suggest he was anywhere near there."

Irina sobbed in the living room, heartbroken at the prospect of losing their palatial house. They'd owned it free and clear until Ustinov had taken out a huge mortgage on it to raise bail — as well as several sketchy loans. It looked as though Ustinov would have to jump bail and flee to Europe, probably Russia.

She didn't want to move.

Of course Ustinov had no intention of taking her and the kids with him if he fled.

✳✳✳

Derek checked on the Hawaii people, but they were still asleep.

Dmitri Teplov and a man named Yevgeny Gorchkov held a meeting without Ustinov or the others.

"I told her to just keep an eye on the bank," Teplov said. "She wants to be a hot-shit gangster."

"Now she gets to do time in gangster-school," Gorchkov said. "I wonder if she'll come out gay."

"Her brains never were her best assets," Teplov said. "The bottom line is I'll support you if Ustinov goes. Your idea of going legitimate is the right one."

"Baranov is broken up about Rabotnikov's death," Gorchkov said. "He wants to kill Ustinov."

"So the rumors were true."

"And Ustinov still thinks catching Evans will make his problems go away."

Chapter 28

"I'm not going to kiss some *vulture* capitalist's *fat hairy ass!*" a voice echoed in the corridor as Derek approached the conference room at Jacobson and Morse.

"We need the money," a woman's voice said.

Derek entered the conference room. It was a windowless room lit by harsh fluorescent lights. A large oval table filled surrounded by a eight office chairs dominated the room.

Mr. Burke introduced Derek to to the others: Reginald Pincus and his wife Joyce. Reginald was a heavyset man with ragged gray hair wearing a weathered brown suede jacket over blue jeans. His wife was a thin nervous, blue-eyed woman who looked older than him. Her white hair was in a ponytail and she wore a green wool sweater over a blue denim skirt.

"I'm the vulture," Derek said, shaking their hands. "Please don't kiss my ass. I'm ticklish."

Mrs. Pincus laughed nervously.

"Why don't you explain the nature of your business, Mr. Pincus," Mr. Burke said.

"You want to invest in it and you don't know what we do?"

Derek nodded.

"What I want to know is what the hell is with your eyes?" Mr. Pincus said. "You're not wearing contacts. Your irises expand and contract naturally."

"My God, Reg," his wife sighed, tearing up. "What do his eyes have to do with anything?"

Derek realized that Reginald had been hospitalized twice for psychotic episodes. Although he wasn't dangerous, his wife lived in constant fear of him saying or doing something irrational or inappropriate. He'd sabotaged three other attempts to raise venture capital.

"I'm not going to answer any questions until he explains his eyes."

"I'm sorry we wasted your time, Mr. Evans," Joyce Pincus said, tugging on her husband's arm. "Once he obsesses over something, he won't budge."

They started to leave.

"It's a genetic mutation," Derek said.

"Really?" Mr. Burke said. "I always thought you were wearing artistic contacts. I didn't have the nerve to ask. I wondered where I could get some for my wife."

"You could probably get contacts made that look like my eyes. I've often thought of getting brown contacts to make my eyes look normal."

"Energistics has had a breakthrough in cold fusion," Mr. Pincus said. "The original Fleischmann–Pons experiments turned out to be a low quality battery. Over the years, some researchers claim to have positive results in cold fusion but they can't be reproduced."

Derek knew what Mr. Pincus would say next, but simply nodded.

"I discovered the common denominator in the rare success stories and a catalyst, which I will *not tell you.*"

Derek knew it was vanadium pentoxide and palladium — used to modify a Farnsworth fusor to produce muons rather than neutrons.

He just nodded.

"My experiments succeeded," Mr. Pincus concluded. "They skip the step of producing heat and turning it into electricity. They produce electricity directly."

Derek saw that he was telling the truth. Indeed an early prototype he built on his kitchen table had nearly electrocuted him.

"How much money do your need?" Derek said.

"$200,000, for twenty-five percent of the company."

"I'll give you $500,000 for fifty-one percent of the company," Derek said.

"I'm not giving up control of my company," Mr. Pincus shouted.

"We can't pay our *rent,* Reg," Mrs. Pincus said.

"Thanks for destroying our bargaining position, miss!"

✳✳✳

Reginald finally agreed to Derek's terms and two Jacobson and Morse lawyers drew up contracts while they all ate lunch from the Boardroom Grill.

Derek scanned the lawyers and satisfied himself that they were honestly representing his interests. Most of the material was boilerplate.

"What kind of mutation?" Mr. Pincus said.

"Huh?"

"Please," Mrs. Pincus said. "Let it go."

"If it affected your eyes, it must've affected your brain too. The eyes are a tract of the brain."

"It probably did," Derek said.

"No probably about it. You're being evasive."

Pincus is a true genius. Instantly zeroing in on what makes me unique. He naturally thinks outside the box. Probably couldn't find the box if he tried.

The exchange fascinated Mr. Burke who resisted the temptation to get involved.

They spent the next hour signing and initialing a six inch stack of documents, as the lawyers notarized them.

Mr. Burke produced two black leather monogrammed attache cases and packed the Pincus's copies of the notarized documents into one of them, presenting it to Mr. Pincus.

As the Pincus's were about to leave, Reginald said, "I will learn your secret!"

"We're in business together, so I guess you'll get more shots at it."

When the two of them were alone in the conference room, Mr. Burke said to Derek, "Simply amazing."

"You didn't mean that in a good way," Derek chuckled. "Half a million for an energy product like that is a bargain. The ITER fusion reactor is costing tens of billions."

"You have a lot of faith in the less-than-nothing he gave you. Normally, companies seeking capital investments make elaborate presentations. With printed documentation. Mountains of it."

"I have a unique ability to spot ... deception. He believed every word he said."

"Oh, I hope it all works out for you, Mr. Evans."

"That's why I demanded fifty-one percent. So I can replace Reginald if he has a psychotic episode ... or something."

Mr. Burke packed Derek's copies of the legal documents in the remaining attache case and handed it to him.

They shook hands and Derek left.

***

Derek left Jacobson and Morse and strolled down Wall street with his attache case of documents. Sleet fell from the leaden sky.

When he spotted a Continental Bank branch, he went in and opened a safe-deposit box in his and Allie's names. He left the attache case there.

He went to the Boothbay Harbor home and relaxed for a few minutes. It was two in the afternoon, and the Hawaii people were just stirring.

A check on Mrs. Pembroke revealed that she was bound and gagged in a van driven by two men. They had abducted her from the Columbia-Presbyterian Hospital garage.

They were taking her to one of Ustinov's brothels.

"I've got you now," Derek said.

Although he could have rescued her, Derek followed the van in an out-of-body state, wanting to learn the brothel's location.

***

The van entered a warehouse filled with small enclosures. Each had a curtained off area with a bed where the prostitutes performed their services.

Waves of fear and despair assaulted Derek's soul as he hovered over the arrayed enclosures, paralyzing him.

In back was a separate, smaller room where the girls were broken by a man everyone called "Ivan the Terrible." This was a running joke among the Russians because he was the only one there who was not Russian. His real name was Angus McTavish — a former world wrestling champion.

He job was to torture women into submission, to break them so completely they would do anything they were told.

He loved his work.

Suicide-attempts were punished so severely women wouldn't dare further attempts, fearing they might not succeed. Two men carried a squirming Mrs. Pembroke down the warehouse's main aisle. When one of the prostitutes' "customers" asked what was going on, one of the men said, "None of your business," and displayed a pistol. The man returned to his prostitute.

They took Mrs. Pembroke into the back room and slammed its soundproof door. There, they tied her hands and ankles to the corners of a table and cut her clothes off with a pair of shears.

They left.

McTavish entered the room and said, "Soon, you will tell us where your daughter is and we will get her. We'll bring her here and make her watch while we kill you. Then she will spend the rest of her life here, working twenty hours a day. When she becomes too sick to work, we'll turn her into dog food."

McTavish always maximized the stakes, making his victims resist him with every fiber of their being. When they broke under these conditions — as they always did in the end — they became whimpering zombies without a shred of will or personality left.

Mrs. Pembroke sobbed and shook her head.

"We'll start with this," he said, holding a metal rod trailing an electric cord plugged into the wall. "I can do things to you I couldn't do to the others because you won't be working here. Ever have sex with a red hot soldering iron?"

She screamed and thrashed in her bonds.

Derek materialized and shot McTavish with a taser. The mountain of a man fell and convulsed, the soldering iron falling on some papers that started to smolder. He was bald, ruddy, and had a bushy red mustache.

Derek tried to untie Mrs. Pembroke but it was slow going. Allie appeared and said, "I'll do that. You concentrate on him."

He tried tying McTavish's hands behind his back with the soldering iron's power cord; no other rope was in sight.

Allie had untied Mrs. Pembroke but her clothes were in shreds. Allie vanished and reappeared moments later with one of Murakami's muu-muus.

"Put this on," she said. Mrs. Pembroke was in a daze but she complied.

The smoldering papers began to burn.

Derek opened the door to the "work area" and went out.

McTavish came to and snapped the wires binding his hands — with sheer brute force. He chased Derek out into the "work area" and grabbed him.

"Not out here!" a man shouted, but McTavish ignored him.

"The next sound you hear will be your your back breaking," McTavish said.

Derek teleported a foot to the right and McTavish exploded into blood and tissue. His arms fell in one pile, his head and upper torso in another, and his pelvis and legs in a third.

Derek wiped stinging blood from his eyes. It drenched him from head to toe.

The prostitutes and their clients nearest to him screamed. Other prostitutes and clients came out of their curtained enclosures and screamed upon seeing Derek and what was left of McTavish.

In short order, all the curtains fell to the floor exposing a a city-block sized array of filthy beds with naked women and, in some cases, naked men.

The man who'd shouted "Not out here" fired a shotgun at Derek's stomach, knocking him down. Derek reset and ran at the man, who dropped his gun and fled.

Derek picked it up.

Smoke poured out of the back room.

Two burly men with pistols ran up, glanced at Derek and McTavish's body, and fled without firing.

"OK, ladies," he said. "You all have to leave."

Smoke pouring out of the back room punctuated his demand.

"We don't have any clothes," one woman said.

"Take your customers' coats and shoes," Derek said. "Hell, take their cash too."

"This is a Cole Haan coat," one of the men said. "I'm not giving it to a whore."

"Is it worth dying for?" Derek said, pointing the shotgun at him.

Incredibly, the man still balked before giving up the coat.

Allie handed out small bundles of cash to the women, saying, "It's not much but it'll buy some clothes and transportation."

"What do we have to do for it?"

"Leave and don't come back," Derek said.

"I can do that," one woman said.

"What do we do without coats or shoes?" one of the men said.

"Call your wives to pick you up," Allie snarled.

They helped Mrs. Pembroke out the door to the street. Flames gushed out of the warehouse's upper windows. Multiple sirens — police and fire — echoed in the distance.

"Help is on the way," Allie said. "If you care about us at all, you'll say you don't know who rescued you."

"You better reset, Derek," she added. "You look like a nightmare."

He did.

Chapter 29

At the Murakami house, it was still late morning. Derek and Allie arrived in the master bedroom and strolled out into the back yard, the bright light and humidity stunning Derek.

Wendy, Liz and Thomas sat around the now-spotless swimming pool. The sky was crystal blue, although the Trade Winds blowing against palm trees made the sound of rain.

"You know the Turtle Bay resort, just down the road?" Allie said. "We paid some of their pool guys to clean the pool and put chlorine in it. When we leave, we'll have four chambermaids clean the whole house."

"What have you two been up to all morning?" Liz chuckled.

"I've been in Manhattan since three," Derek yawned.

"He signed a deal that could make us billionaires," Allie said. "Then he freed about fifty sex slaves from a brothel and killed the man who tortured them. I helped with the last part. Not the killing but the other part."

"If you don't want to tell me just say so."

"You killed someone?" Wendy said. "Cool."

"It wasn't cool," Derek sighed. "Though he deserved it more

195

than anyone I ever met. I took a bath in his blood, an image I wish I could erase."

"I have a *lot* of images I wish I could erase," Allie said, patting him on the leg. "It's all good now, honey."

"What?" Derek said, scanning her. "Oh! I was almost cut in half by a shotgun?"

"Travis and his folks are coming over for lunch," Wendy said. "His mom will make barbecue sausages on the hibachi. They're called *lap cheong*. Ever have *lap cheong* before?"

"Can't say that I have," Derek smiled. "I can't wait."

"We got you swim trunks, Derek," Wendy said.

"No way. The ocean's for boating and fishing."

"Stop talking like a maniac," Allie said. "Put the bathing suit on or I'll belt you."

✳✳✳

The party had moved a hundred yards to the beach where hauled a set of beach chairs and Thomas set up a hibachi grill and lit charcoal briquettes.

"Now to get you into the water," Allie said, removing her white terry-cloth robe to reveal a stunning black string-bikini underneath. Derek's Indigo body responded to the visual.

"Don't be a chicken!" Allie said. "It's only water!"

He turned his back on the others and hobbled to the water line as Allie laughed and clapped. For the second time in his life, he went into the ocean.

The sea was a living thing, surging, stirring, and caressing him — reminding him of the spirit-world. The morning's horrors seemed to fade with each ebb and flow. He swam out past the coral reef that paralleled the shore, to where the ocean floor dropped off, and he floated on his back.

A young man and older couple joined the others on the shore.

That must be Travis and his parents.
Derek surveyed the shore line. To the left, the mist-shrouded Koolau mountain range loomed green and foreboding in the distance. To the right, an impossibly rugged, brown mountain range stretched off to the horizon.
That must be the Waianae Range and the Napali coast.
The Murakami house and Turtle Bay lay in a cleft between the two ranges.
Derek headed back toward the beach.
A wave caught him. When he shut his eyes and made his body rigid, it lifted him and surged forward, its wild turbulence pumping sea water up his nose and rumbling in his ears.
Sand finally scraped his belly.

***

"Hey brah, howzit?" Travis said, shaking Derek's hand.
Travis was about six foot three with a husky build, and a golden complexion and dark brown hair. He wore a green bathing suit with a floral pattern.
"Aloha," Travis's mother said, shaking Derek's hand. "Call me Grace."
Grace Howland was a petite, forty-something Oriental woman with a kind face. She stoked the hibachi's charcoals and put sausages on the grill.
Her husband, Kurt, was a thin, wiry tanned man in a torn aloha shirt, shorts and flip-flops. With thinning white hair, he looked at least twenty years older than Grace.
Derek shook Kurt's hand and sat.
"I'm living the dream," Kurt thought, smiling.
Without making any effort to scan him, Derek realized Kurt sixty-seven years old, and that Grace was an "outer island Japanese," for whom he'd traded in his older first wife, a

198

"loudmouth *haole*." The "outer islands" were the rural areas on small islands like Lanai or Maui — far from the cities like Honolulu — where people were old-fashioned. *Haoles* were white people from the mainland, and *haole* women were regarded as "excessively liberated."

Derek sighed.

"Been living here long?" Thomas asked Kurt.

"I'm a *kama'aina*," Kurt replied. "My family has been here since the nineteenth century. They were missionaries."

"Wow!" Thomas uttered.

"This is almost beginning to feel like a vacation," Derek finally said, yawning.

"You came to Hawaii but not for a vacation?" Grace said.

"It's a working vacation."

"Get me a beer, dear," Kurt said, thinking, *You clueless workaholics.*

Grace handed him a beer.

"A working honeymoon, actually," Allie added. "Someday, I hope we can have a real one. Without a care in the world."

The sausages on the grill sizzled and dripped fat onto the hot coals making flames shoot up and producing clouds of sweet smoke that smelled like incense.

"A honeymoon with your parents?" Grace said. "You are very devoted children."

"Very bizarre children," Kurt laughed.

"I wanted to take my parents on our honeymoon but Kurt wouldn't allow it," Grace sighed.

"We have a room in the Piikoi Palace where we can get away."

"And I just had an idea," Derek said. "For later."

"I'm game," Allie replied. "It looks interesting at least."

✳✳✳

Lying against a dune, Derek and Allie lounged in the sand, wordlessly chatted, and ate.

With their crisp fat and rose scent, the cooked *lap cheong* were candy.

Travis seems like a nice kid, Allie beamed to Derek. *And he finds us all utterly fascinating.*

He's right about that, Derek wordlessly replied. *We are fascinating.*

Allie laughed.

"See!" Wendy said, pointing at Derek and Allie. "They're doing it again, talking without words. I bet they're talking about us."

"Not!" Travis said. "Talk story without words? Some ono!"

"They can!"

"Wendy said you believe in past lives," Travis said.

"It's hard not to," Derek said. "When you remember them easily."

And not just past lives.

"What was Sit-Hathor like?" Wendy said.

"She had the heart of a warrior," Allie sighed, closing her eyes. "The mind of a philosopher, and a form ... like mortal sin."

"You knew each other thousands of years ago," Wendy said. "And waited until *now* to get together again?"

"No," Allie said, her eyes misting over. "We've known each other countless times in different forms. We were brothers, sisters, friends. It's like we were circling each other warily. That's why we felt kind of desperate to get married now."

"Do you remember the life you lived right before this one?" Wendy said.

"We were American soldiers in the great war," Allie said.

"The great war?" Wendy said.

"World war one. Our unit was shredded in the Argonne Forest. Machine-gun fire hit you, Derek. Your name wasn't Derek, of course."

"I *remember* that! I felt so cold and thirsty ... and tired. I asked if you believed in life after death."

"I lied and said I did," Allie said. "You died in my arms."

"What happened to you afterward?"

"I went home to my fiancée. I found her with another man, living on the military paycheck I'd signed over to her."

"Did you *kill* him?" Wendy exclaimed. "I'd have killed them both!"

"No," Allie said. "I punched a hole in the wall. And went to a bar and drank myself into oblivion. Then I staggered through the streets and got run over by a trolley."

"What's a trolley?" Wendy said.

"Like a bus," Renata said.

"After all that *shit?* You must've been one of the few people in our *unit* to make it home."

"Never underestimate New York trolleys. The Kaiser's army had nothing on them."

"I saw a past life once," Kurt said. "In a mirror, I had *Chinese* eyes. Of course it could've been I was stoned out of my gourd."

"I wish you wouldn't joke about drugs in front of guests," Grace said. "Or Travis."

"To change the subject, what do you do?" Kurt asked Derek. "In *this* life. When you're not dodging bullets. If Grace doesn't object to *that* too."

"I used to develop computer games, but now I deal in investments."

"Quite a change!"

"What do you do?" Derek asked. "To answer a question with a question."

"I tan and surf," Kurt replied. "In my foolish youth, I did a little work for the defense department. I had a lunatic idea I should work for my living."

"Oh?" Allie said.

"I monitored those little islands where we used to test atomic bombs in the 1950's and 60's. Melted buildings and a trillion buzzing roaches. Set you beer down, and the roaches'll drink it for you."

"They couldn't pay me enough," Allie said.

"They didn't. It cured me of working real quick."

***

Travis Howland's parents went home and the others moved the party indoors.

Derek had never been in the living room before. It had white walls and two potted palm trees flanking wide French doors to the back yard. The sofa and chairs had identical floral print patterns of plumerias.

Renata turned on the large flat-screen TV that occupied one wall.

The evening news had a report of a big warehouse fire in Brooklyn. The building had contained a human trafficking ring and someone had robbed the johns and given their money to the prostitutes, who'd melted away into the city.

"You?" Renata said, pointing to Derek.

He nodded.

"Caspita!" she said, shaking her head.

***

That evening, Derek and Allie returned to their honeymoon suite.

They stripped naked, put on water-wings, and lay on the bed. In their spirit-bodies, they flew over Waikiki Beach and people dancing around a bonfire, and Honolulu Harbor with its dinner-cruises and many yachts. They flew south over the open ocean.

They might have flown a hundred miles or a thousand — distances were vague in the spirit world. For all they knew, they'd flown halfway to Tahiti.

They reached a place and scanned the area carefully for potential danger. The only animals around were a pod of dolphins a hundred yards away, a school of several thousand tiny fish, and two whales about a mile away. A lamprey eel lurked in a sea cave, waiting to spring on prey that swam past it.

It was safe.

They materialized, naked, into the water.

The sea sparkled like jewels in the full moon's light, and the Milky Way crossed the sky like a glowing highway to heaven.

Derek and Allie hugged and made out, licking tongues and tasting each other. She wrapped her legs around him as they made love and howled their passion to the moon and the billion stars piercing the ink-black sky.

Then they floated on their backs.

As gentle waves caressed their exhausted bodies, the dolphins approached, calling to each other and singing.

"Land-ones so far from land," one dolphin said. "Did their boat sink?"

"No," another replied. "They fell from the sky. And I think they were mating."

"They hear and understand us," another dolphin said. "Land-ones never understand us. How strange."

"They smell different from other land-ones," another dolphin said. "I never saw land-ones mate before."

They circled Derek and Allie.

"Back on topic!" another dolphin said. "The Society of Tremlyka. And how they'll never let you in."

Derek and Allie realized that membership in the Society of Tremlyka involved reciting the names of ten thousand generations of one's ancestors.

"You'll never recite the Nievuees clan," the dolphin added.

"Already did," the first sneered. "All of them. Officially recorded!"

"Best wishes," Derek said, trying to project thoughts into their minds.

"I hope you make it into the Society of Tremlyka," Allie added.

"I hear them in my head," one dolphin said. "They can *talk* to us too. I *love* it."

The dolphins squealed in delight and did somersaults in the air around them, their massive wet bodies flashing silver in the moonlight. They churned up the water so much Derek and Allie had to tread water.

"Best wishes, land-ones-who-hear-us," the dolphins each said, playfully nudging the two before swimming away.

Derek and Allie resumed floating on their backs, listening to the whales' songs in the distance.

"The stars are so close you can almost touch them," Derek said.

"You know, in life there are a few perfect moments that make up for all the shit. You did good, maniac."

They returned to their hotel room, rinsed off in the tub, and went to bed.

Chapter 30

At nine in the morning, New York time, Derek sipped coffee and ate a danish in the Boardroom Grill. A quick check on the Russians didn't disclose anything interesting. A check on Detective Roberts showed that he'd met Professor Fischer, discussed Derek and Allie, and had even *dated* her.

Good going, Ian!

A check on Mrs. Pembroke showed that she'd returned to her hiding place with her daughter and sister, and a check on the Pincus's showed them to be in the throes of a major crisis. Tomorrow, Reginald Pincus was due to demonstrate his technology before a group of businessmen and representatives of the Navy.

Unfortunately, hallucinated voices urged him to kill himself.

Joyce Pincus sobbed and tried to calm him down. He had anti-psychotic drugs that would banish the voices, but they turned him into a barely-functioning zombie.

Anything I do to intervene will come off as creepy. Oh well.

He decided to call.

"This is Derek Evans, Mrs. Pincus," he said.

"This is a bad time. An *incredibly* bad time."

"I know, and I'm sorry to intrude, but you should give your husband his meds. You and I can do the demonstration tomorrow."

"How do you know about the demo? Who gave your our number?"

"Your husband is right, I have a massive secret. It explains how I know these things, and why I can do the demonstration. May I meet with you two and tell you my secret?"

"I don't know," Mrs. Pincus said.

"Look, Mrs. Pincus, when I said my eyes were different because of a genetic mutation, it was an understatement. Strictly speaking, I'm not human."

"What?"

"Give your husband his meds and pick a restaurant where we can meet for lunch. My treat."

"OK. How do I contact you? To tell you where it is?"

"This is going to sound creepy but I'll find you two. Anywhere on the planet."

"Oh God," she sobbed. "What have we gotten ourselves into?"

"I think… I hope, someday, you'll be grateful I became involved in your business. Pick a public place. A nice restaurant. And I'll see if I can get my wife to come along. You'll like her."

"Oh, what the hell. What've we got to lose?"

"Nothing. You have a lot to gain. See you at noon."

Of course I'll be there, Allie said in his mind. *Those poor bastards. Poor sweet bastards.*

✳✳✳

He returned to Allie's apartment in Flushing, which was no longer under surveillance. Among the mail, he found his birth certificate from Boothbay Harbor. He went out, had a passport

206

photo taken, filled out an application for a passport, and sent it off.

✳✳✳

Derek and Allie walked out of their respective restrooms into a large room lit by recessed lighting. Gold mirrors, and paintings from the Baroque age covered the walls. The mirrors gave the space an insubstantial quality — one couldn't distinguish between walls and their reflections — and highlighted the many elegant floral displays.

It's as if they sensed the spirit-world and longed to recreate it.

Joyce and Reginald Pincus occupied a table in the center.

"Thanks for picking the *Le Petit Trianon!*" Derek said. "French cuisine is my second favorite."

He introduced Allie to them.

Reginald looked half-asleep and limply shook their hands.

"Your eyes," Joyce said, looking at Allie. "They're like his."

"Indigo eyes, darling," Allie said. "We're *homo sapiens indicus.* And did you *have* to tell her we're not human?"

"I needed to get her attention."

"It did that," Joyce said. "Is it true?"

"We have a biologist analyzing our DNA," Derek said. "I scanned her this morning."

"Yes?" Allie said. "Inquiring minds want to know."

"She's decided the DNA is from an unidentified species of ape. Except that we have sixty chromosomes, which is more than apes generally have."

"Humans have forty-six," Reginald mumbled.

"Yeah, so we're not human."

"Wow!" Allie muttered, shaking her head. "I suspected... What a kick in the head."

As they examined menus, Derek began his prepared remarks and the Pincus's listened.

"You can *teleport?*" Joyce said.

"Demonstrating that here would probably be awkward," Allie said. "You had your eyes glued to the front door, waiting for us to arrive. We didn't come through the front door. We teleported to the restrooms."

They all ordered lobster bisque to start. For their main entrées, Derek ordered Châteaubriand, Allie ordered Dover sole and the Pincus's both ordered the caramelized duck breast.

"Why is the Russian mob after you?" Joyce said.

"They paid for Pembroke's research and feel they own it," Derek said. "The only way they can get it is by scooping out my brain like a cantaloupe."

"They can't really hurt us," Allie said. "But they've gone after our non-indigo families."

"Are we in danger now?" Joyce said.

"They don't know about you two," Derek said. "And we're going to keep it that way."

Then Derek recited everything he knew about Reginald's research.

"You stole the ideas right out of my mind," Reginald muttered.

"If I wanted to steal your ideas, I could've just built our own machine and claimed I discovered it independently."

"We didn't do that," Allie said. "We invested in your business instead. We're not thieves. If we play our cards right, we could all be billionaires in a few months."

"Billionaires?" Joyce said, adding wordlessly, *Mindless optimism.*

"Allie's good at seeing the future," Derek said.

The lobster bisque arrived.

"Delicious!" Allie said. "Almost as good as what we serve at our restaurant."

"You have a restaurant?" Joyce said.

"In another timeline," Allie said.

"Timeline?" Joyce said. "I don't understand."

"The many-worlds form of quantum mechanics," Reginald muttered.

"You have to forgive my husband," Joyce said. "He's obsessed with that insane theory. Especially in his troubled state."

"It's true," Derek said. "In fact his invention wouldn't work if that theory weren't true."

"So he's always claimed," Joyce said. "It's just a theory, isn't it?"

"It's absolutely true," Derek said. "One of our superpowers is seeing other timelines."

"I'm looking at the presentation tomorrow," Allie said, shutting her eyes. "Thousands of timelines."

"How do we do? Derek said.

"The ones Joyce and Reginald do are failures," Allie said. "The ones you and Joyce do are fifty-fifty. These are shallow people who judge you by appearances."

"I should get my hair colored," Joyce said, adding wordlessly, *Seeing future timelines? That's insane.*

"No, your white hair gives you gravitas. Derek's youth is a big problem and you counterbalance it somewhat. See that woman over there?"

She pointed to an impeccably dressed, severe-looking woman at a table in the corner with two men sitting across from her. They seemed to be having a heated discussion.

"She's the CEO of Avipro corporation," Allie said. "They make medical test equipment. She's negotiating contracts with Mainline Health. A hospital chain in Pennsylvania."

She's making this shit up, Joyce wordlessly said. *What's their game?*

"That's the look you want," Derek said. "She went to Manhattan Executive Image Consultants. They do clothes, makeup, hair. Everything."

"Here's twenty thousand dollars," Allie said, handing her a wad of bills. "They're not cheap."

"I can't accept this," Joyce said. *Maybe they arranged this in advance and tailed Reginald and me to this restaurant.*

"It's not a gift," Derek said. "It's a business expense. An investment."

"And you," Allie said, pointing to Derek. "Have to get a nice suit. Maybe you should go to those people too."

Their main courses arrived.

✳✳✳

They ended the luncheon with champagne.

"I don't suppose you could bribe someone to get us popcorn with this," Allie said. "I don't know whether it's an Indigo thing or just an us thing. The combination of buttered popcorn and champagne is ... heavenly."

"We are the only indigos, so it's an Indigo thing," Derek said.

"Baby Vittoria will make three," Allie said.

"You're pregnant?" Joyce said.

"Yeah," Allie replied. "She's more than half a billion cells now. And counting. Her spirit hovers around me, urging it on."

"Oh, uh... that's nice," Joyce said, wordlessly adding, *She's crazier than uncle Herman.*

"Derek, she's saying I'm crazier than someone who bicycled through Central Park wearing nothing but boxer shorts! In winter!"

"Oh my God," Joyce blushed. "You really *can* read minds."

"It's what we've been saying," Allie muttered.

"That's what your uncle Herman *did?*" Reginald said.

"Yeah," Allie replied. "After exposing himself to a bunch of nuns. Then cops on horseback chased him as he rode off almost naked on a bicycle. I would've loved to be there with a camera!"

Joyce slammed the wad of bills Allie had given her on the table and stood, saying, "This was a lovely lunch, but we're leaving."

She yanked her husband to his feet and they made for the door. Derek ran after them, saying, "You need this money for your makeover."

"Keep it! I feel *violated* and I'm *not* doing the presentation. You own half the company, so *you* do it with your ... bizarre wife. I'm sure you know where and when it is."

They left.

When Derek rejoined Allie, she said, "I'm sorry I pushed so hard, but I just couldn't take any more of her crap."

"What are our chances?"

"Fifty-fifty," Allie said. "Some people will pleased the Pincus's aren't doing the presentation because they are flakes. They've been no-shows at two previous demonstrations. Tomorrow will be their absolute last chance."

"No pressure there."

Chapter 31

Allie and Derek took a taxi to the address of the Pincus's workshop in Brooklyn. This is where the demonstration would take place.

It was an old warehouse filled with machine lathes and electronic equipment.

The company's only employee, Vaughn Williams met them. He was an African-American machinist who manufactured most of the device's large components.

"Mrs. Pincus called and said you'd be doing the demo tomorrow," he said, shaking their hands as they introduced themselves. "She said you owned the company now." *Weird eyes! Are they wearing contacts?*

"A little more than half of it," Derek replied.

"She sounded upset," Vaughn said. "Did you have a fight with her?"

"Unfortunately, yes," Allie said.

"Here it is," Vaughn said, pointing to a rectangular piece of machinery about two feet by two feet by one foot with two large electrodes protruding from its front. Then he laughed, "Know how it works?"

"I hope so," Derek said. "Mr. Pincus briefed me."

"*What?*" Vaughn exclaimed. "Whenever I asked him anything, he'd bite my head off and accuse me of stealing his ideas. He's crazier than a soup sandwich."

Derek connected a huge power-meter to the electrodes and switched on the Farnsworth fusor. He adjusted main machine's bias to its nonlinear cutoff point and then turned the knob on the hydrogen tank, sending gas into the device.

The power meters jumped, indicating six hundred volts and one hundred amps.

"That's it," Vaughn said. "Sixty kilowatts from a little box. It'll change the world someday."

Derek shut off the machine.

"Do we have security guards or an alarm system?" Derek said.

"Never needed one," Vaughn said. "Who'd break into this dump?"

"We will after tomorrow. Now we have to get properly suited up."

"Ah, yes," Allie laughed. "The monkey suits."

Derek handed Vaughn $5000 to buy a suit.

After Vaughn left, Derek and Allie locked up the warehouse and flew to Manhattan in their spirit-bodies.

✳✳✳

Derek picked out a Brioni suit and had to be fitted for it so it would be ready tomorrow morning.

He spent an hour being measured in every way imaginable, and some he'd never dreamed of.

"On which side do you dress, sir?" the tailor asked.

"Dress on a *side?*" Derek said. "Um ... usually I dress in my bedroom. Sometimes in the bathroom. Oh, that's not what you mean." By now, he'd read the tailor's mind, and he blushed.

"No, sir, you don't understand. On which side does your penis normally hang?"

"I ... um ... never gave it any thought."

He grabbed his crotch and said, "I suppose ... on the right?"

"Very good, sir."

Did I give the correct answer? Derek wondered. *Will people look at me and think, This idiot doesn't even know which side he dresses on for Christ's sake!*

✳✳✳

After that surrealistic experience, Derek checked in with the Ustinov gang.

They had decided to beef up security at their other brothel and sent Dmitri to oversee it.

Derek teleported to an alley outside the brothel. It was also a warehouse in a grimy industrial area. After wandering around, he figured out its address and teleported to Grand Central Station. There, he bought a burner phone and called Detective Roberts.

"Jesus, Evans!" Detective Roberts said. "Did you have to burn the place down?"

"It was an accident. McTavish was about to shove a hot soldering iron into Mrs. Pembroke's ... um hoohah, and it fell on some papers. Any casualties from the fire?"

"*Hoohah?*" Detective Roberts laughed. "I'm not sure what that is. Can you be more specific?"

"You know what I mean. And I repeat my question."

"Only McTavish died. Pembroke said you killed him before the fire. One witness said you turned him into fucking hamburger."

"He was trying to kill me. Look, I have a lead on another human trafficking center. If you're interested."

He gave Detective Roberts the address.

"Mrs. Pembroke said she has no idea who rescued her," Detective Roberts said. "She's lying."

"No comment. Any other eyewitness descriptions?"

"Some kind of monster covered in blood," Detective Roberts said. "Most of those people refused to talk to us. The few who did couldn't give our police artists any more of a description than that. Hell, most of the women melted away into the city. You gave them money for that. You know, among the coatless, shoeless johns there was a city council member."

"Why would someone like that go to a sketchy brothel like that? He could afford a high-priced call girl."

Like Cynthia.

"Maybe he gets off on it, I don't know. I'll follow up on your lead."

"I wish I'd turned *him* into hamburger."

✳✳✳

Derek rejoined Allie in at the Murakami house.

"I rented office-space in Flushing," Allie said. "It'll be the Energistics *worldwide* headquarters."

"Couldn't we use your apartment?" Derek said.

"Our apartment's not zoned as a business, and I still have this vain, *wistful* hope we can actually *live* there someday. Like *people.* The place I rented is on Kissena Boulevard, a couple blocks away. It gives our company a mailing address."

"Hey, Derek's home," Wendy shouted. "Let's have hamburgers for lunch! The hibachi's ready."

Hamburgers! What an image!

"I'm sure Culinary Derek knows how to do hamburgers," Liz said. "We'll do the work."

"Yes," Derek said. "There are people who come into a high-end restaurant demanding burgers and fries. But *fancy* ones. *Le burger et fries.* Or *La burgera e fries.* So he came up with something and charged twenty-nine dollars for it."

"That's pretty steep," Liz said.

"They said it wasn't fancy enough when he charged ten dollars. Customers like that want to impress people with how much money they spend. Get five pounds of filet mignons — with *zero* fat — and have the butcher grind it."

"You need fat to make a burger!" Liz said.

"Suit yourself then."

"No," Liz said. "Go ahead."

"Oh," Allie said. "Butter-burgers!"

"Get some unsalted butter, onions, eggs, and thyme. Finely chop two onions and mix it, two egg yolks, the thyme, and half a pound of butter with the meat and blend it. Lightly dust the patties with flour before you put them on the grill."

"You forgot the bread crumbs," Liz said. "You can't mix eggs with ground beef without bread crumbs."

"No bread crumbs," Derek and Allie both said.

***

Derek lay against a sand dune with Allie in the crook of his right arm.

"Worried about the presentation?" she said.

"A bit. I guess we just read their minds and tell them what we know they want to hear."

"I'm sorry I pissed off Mrs. Pincus," Allie said. "She just pushed my buttons. They started the company and they should be involved."

"Oh, shit," Derek said. "Speaking of Mrs. Pincus. Her husband is catatonic now — in the Bellevue Psych ward. He did this once before."

"I did a deep scan of both of them," Allie said. "And it scared the *shit* out of me."

"Yeah, it's scary."

"What's scary?" Liz said. "The burgers are on the grill. I forgot what I was supposed to do with the flour."

"Lightly dust the patties before you grill them."

"Oh," Liz said. "I mixed two cups of flour *with* the meat. Who knows? Maybe I discovered a wonderful new dish."

She hadn't.

Luckily, Grace Howland brought over more sausages to grill. Her husband didn't accompany her.

Chapter 32

At one in the afternoon, New York time, Derek and Allie met Vaughn in the Pincus workshop.

"You both look stunning," she said.

Vaughn Williams had bought a blue pinstripe Armani suit.

"You look fantastic yourself," Derek said to Allie. She wore a black skirt that went slightly below the knees, sheer black stockings, a dark blue satin blouse with a black beaded jacket with gold accents that matched her hair, and a necklace of large gold beads.

She radiated sex-appeal, sophistication — and money.

The roar of a motorcade escorted by six motorcycle cops echoed through the warehouse.

The lead car, a black Lincoln MKZ with government plates, pulled up and the driver opened the door for a stocky white-haired man in a naval dress uniform with gold bars on its sleeves. He and introduced himself as Admiral Horatio Pike.

Derek introduced himself as the CEO, Allie as the President, and Vaughn as the Chief of Manufacturing.

A man in a less ornate naval uniform stepped out of the second car, a white Ford, and introduced himself as David Scott, the Nuclear Officer of the USS Massachusetts, currently docked at pier 92 on the Hudson River.

A blue Hyundai pulled with two women and a man. One woman looked to be in her early 20's and introduced herself as Ruth Melendez, from CNN. The other woman was middle-aged and introduced herself as Jessica Grey, from the New York Times. The man was a shaggy twenty-year-old who didn't introduce himself and pulled video equipment from the car's trunk.

Derek and Allie knew who all of them were — indeed they knew everything about them.

Finally, a silver Mercedes-Maybach limousine pulled up and the chauffeur opened the door for a man in an elegant black pinstripe suit, who introduced himself as "Whitney North Seymour." The woman with him had blond hair and dazzling blue eyes and wore a plain blue dress. He introduced her as his secretary, Alice Collins.

How devious, Derek mused, and Allie chuckled.

Two other men introduced themselves as engineers, one hired by Seymour and the other by the Navy.

A large flatbed truck pulled up and several men unloaded equipment from it.

Derek, Allie, and Vaughn watched silently as the engineers attached equipment to the cold-fusion device. This equipment included a power meter, magnetometers, a mass-spectrographic device to test the exhaust gasses from the reactor, and radiation detectors.

Several MP's stood guard outside.

Derek began his presentation, calling the device a Pincus Generator.

"Anyone need background on nuclear fusion?" he said.

Alice Collins and the reporters raised her hand.

"She's just a secretary," Admiral Pike muttered. "And they're the press.

"No," Derek said. "Ms. Collins is the investor. Whitney North Seymour is window dressing. Or should I call you by the name your parents gave you? Regina Maas."

"I pay people very well to keep me out of the public eye," Alice Collins said with a faint German accent and laughed.

"We pride ourselves on being well-informed," Allie said.

"You may wait for me in the car, Mr. Seymour," Regina added.

"As you wish, ma'am."

A taxi pulled up to the warehouse and Mrs. Pincus stepped out.

"Let her in," Derek told the MP's. "She belongs her. She's the wife of the genius who invented this technology."

✳✳✳

"There are two methods for extracting energy from nuclear processes, fission and fusion," Derek began. "Fission occurs spontaneously in the proper materials and can't be shut off. Fusion only occurs *naturally* in the core of a star like the sun. And it generates more energy than fission, without radiation or radioactive wastes."

"Is that a Farnsworth fusor?" one of the engineer asked, pointing to a device at the end of generator.

"Yes," Derek said. "A miniature, custom made one."

"What's that?" Ms. Maas said.

"Farnsworth invented the picture tube that made television possible," Derek replied. "Before LED's. How many people had a TV with a picture tube."

Admiral Pike and Mrs. Pincus raised their hands and smiled.

"Then, Farnsworth went a step further. He found a clever

modification of it that does nuclear fusion. It uses energy, does fusion, and doesn't give off any energy."

"What good is it then?" Ms. Maas said.

"It is normally used as a neutron source," Derek said. "For atomic research. Pincus found an ingenious modification that makes it produces particles called muons instead of neutrons."

"What is cold fusion?" Ms. Maas said.

"Well," Derek said. "Hot fusion is what the sun does. And other things that simulate conditions in the sun, like a hydrogen bomb, or the Farnsworth fusor, which does it on a microscopic scale. It takes a lot of energy to create those conditions. You have to extract more energy than you put in for it to break even."

"In the 1950's," Admiral Pike said. "They seriously considered using hydrogen bombs as a power source. Detonate them underground."

"Really?" Monika said.

"Create pockets of magma and run pipes through them, boiling water and using the steam to run generators," Admiral Pike said.

"Man-made geothermal?" Allie said. "Sounds dangerous."

Admiral Pike nodded.

"So cold fusion tries to get hydrogen atoms to fuse *without* enormous heat and pressure," Derek continued.

"And all earlier attempts have been mistaken or fraudulent," the engineer from the Navy said.

"Fine!" Derek said. "Let's cut to the chase and *light this candle.*"

"A car battery supplies the power before the generator starts," Derek said, turning on the Farnsworth Fusor. Then he started the flow of hydrogen.

The power-meters jumped.

"I know you're seeing what I'm seeing," Admiral Pike said. "That sure looks like sixty kilowatts."

"Impossible!" the engineer scoffed. "You need a boiler, steam turbines, and a huge generator to produce that much power."

"Oh," Derek said. "Did I forget to mention? We generate electricity *directly*. We skip the primitive, inefficient step of boiling water."

"You're good," the engineer said. "I'll give you that. But I'll find out how you're faking this."

"Knock yourself out," Derek said.

The engineers moved equipment around and under the table containing the Pincus Generator.

"They're trying to figure out where the power is coming from," Derek explained to Mrs. Pincus. "Looking for hidden cables or electromagnetic sources."

✳✳✳

Derek used this break to scan Detective Roberts and Dmitri. Roberts was organizing a raid on the second Ustinov brothel, and Dmitri and his men were emptying it — herding the women at gunpoint into a semi-trailer. A clerk named Greg Polhamus in Roberts's police station had called him.

"I have to use the restroom," he said.

"Oh," Allie said. "That stomach flu again?" *The gun is on the kitchen table in Boothbay.*

Derek entered the warehouse's filthy restroom and locked the door.

He teleported to the Boothbay Harbor house and picked up the gun.

A scan of Dmitry showed that the semi was locked and had started to roll. By the time Detective Roberts and his raiding party arrived, they'd be long gone.

Derek teleported to the moving semi's roof and clung to it for his life. Then he crawled to its edge and spotted a police car in the traffic. He fired two shots into the street. The police car ignored it, so he fired another shot in its general direction. That got its attention, and its siren sounded.

Derek teleported back to the restroom. He straightened his tie and brushed off some dirt he'd picked up from the semi's roof. Luckily, his expensive pants hadn't ripped.

✳✳✳

"Feeling better, honey?" Allie said.

The others registered surprise.

"We're married," Derek said, adding, "A bit better."

"Is that really a car battery?" the engineer said. "Or something else?"

"Swap it with one of yours," Derek said, turning off the generator. "You have several cars out there."

Admiral Pike nodded.

The engineer and one of the MP's opened the truck's hood, removed its battery, and swapped it with the battery on the generator.

When they restarted the generator, the power-meter still registered sixty kilowatts.

"Can you scale this up by a factor of ten thousand?" Admiral Pike said.

"To power a Virginia-class submarine?" Derek said. "I don't know. We have to study this issue."

"We do our homework," Allie said, as the admiral's eyebrows shot up. "And we don't make promises we can't keep."

You two are young but have integrity and reek competence, the admiral thought, looking Derek and Allie up and down.

"I actually envision a Pincus generator in every American home and car," Derek said. "Unlimited cheap, clean power."

Really? Allie beamed to Derek. *We'll have to make it fool-proof and totally safe. Do we want to become industrialists?*

"I understand Mr. Pincus is insane," Ruth Melendez said. "And in a Bellevue psych ward."

"I will not comment on our founder's medical issues," Derek growled.

Loyalty! the admiral thought. *I admire that.*

***

The demo ended with the reporters interviewing Derek and Allie.

Admiral Pike shook their hands and said," You'll be hearing from us. Sooner rather than later."

Allie gave him their "corporate address."

After the audience left, Derek said, "Do those offices have a security system?"

"Yes," Allie said. "The building has a security guard and the offices have their own security system."

"Then let's move the generator there."

They loaded the generator on a pickup truck.

"We'd like it if you came with us," Allie said to Mrs. Pincus.

"OK," she replied. "How do you think we did?"

"Women's intuition tells me we did *wonderfully*," Allie said, winking at Mrs Pincus. "We're going to be receiving several interesting offers."

"Could you drive Joyce Pincus?" Derek asked Vaughn. "We won't all fit in the truck."

They left.

Derek locked up the warehouse and Allie teleported to the offices she'd rented. Derek followed.

Chapter 33

Allie had rented a suite of five large bare rooms with white walls and hardwood floors. The front entrance opened on the largest of them with a hallway in back leading to three other rooms and a powder room, and ending at a room in back.

Their footsteps echoed in the empty space.

The front room and three of the others had windows that opened onto busy Kissena Boulevard. The back windows opened on a concrete courtyard behind the building.

Derek and Allie went down to the security desk and introduced themselves to the first shift guard, explaining that some equipment would be arriving. He showed them the freight elevator.

In a half hour, Vaughn and Joyce Pincus pulled up.

Derek and Allie introduced Vaughn and Joyce to the security guard, who would get them photo-ids.

Then they took the Pincus Generator up on the freight elevator and hauled it to the room at the end of the hallway.

"Would make a nice apartment," Vaughn Williams said.

"No kitchen or full bathroom," Allie said.

"Kitchen's not a problem," Vaughn laughed. "Rosa's best dish is reservations. She's my wife."

"Speaking of reservations," Derek said. "We should go out and celebrate. Our treat."

"Do we have anything to celebrate?" Vaughn said.

"Allie's intuition is always accurate," Derek said. "Scary-accurate sometimes."

"Can't tonight," Vaughn groaned. "Gotta have dinner with the in-laws."

"Some other time then," Derek said. "Joyce, would you celebrate with us? We'd love it."

"OK."

✳✳✳

On Allie's recommendation, they went to the Han Joo Chik Wine Bar — located in what was once a greenhouse on the roof of a five-story building.

The view was spectacular.

In the dark, Manhattan rose in the distance like a glittering, jewel-encrusted cliff.

Tiny white lights strung across the glass ceiling and walls cast a warm glow over the twenty tables in the room. Four tiny barbecue grills sat in the room's center, giving off a rich aroma of crisping pork fat and garlic. A well-stocked bar filled one entire wall.

They took a table in a corner.

"If I can only have one glass of wine, I want it to be good," Allie said, ordering a Ruffino Chianti Classico Riserva.

Derek and Joyce had the same.

"You people did a *lot* better than Reginald and I could have," Joyce Pincus said. "You looked so *professional*. Like you really knew what you were doing. I *loved* the way you honored Reginald."

226

"He deserves the credit for his invention," Derek said. "The admiral, the reporters, and Regina Maas were impressed with our outfits, and the engineers sneered at them."

"Speaking of her," Allie said. "Her men are breaking into our workshop this very moment."

"*What?*" Joyce Pincus said.

"It's a good thing we moved it," Derek said.

"Who is this Regina?" Joyce said.

"Her family owns several steel mills in Germany and Sweden," Derek said. "And a big chunk of Daimler. She thinks she can steal our generator because it isn't patented."

"Oh God," Joyce moaned. "Reginald is so paranoid. He doesn't trust the government."

"He's right for the wrong reasons," Derek said. "The patent system works fine if you invent a fancy new toothbrush or toaster. If you invent something that impacts national security, all countries have escape clauses in their patent laws. Even England and France wouldn't honor a patent for this technology. Our only option is to keep it secret."

"As I *didn't* say earlier," Allie said. "Admiral Pike wants to give us a seed-grant of fifty million dollars to develop a power plant for a submarine and maybe surface ships. It will be non refundable, so we keep it even if we don't succeed in scaling up the Pincus generator."

"He's giving us that much?" Joyce said.

"He doesn't have the final say," Derek said. "But it's likely he'll get it approved. And it's cheap compared to what they usually spend on power plants."

On Allie's advice, they ordered kang poong saewoo shrimp, donkatsu, and beef tang soo yook.

Joyce started to sob.

Allie hugged her, saying, "I'm so sorry I blurted out your family secrets. It was very bitchy of me."

Joyce's sobbing turned into full on crying.

"Help us!" she moaned. "Please read our minds and for *God's sake help us."*

A couple at the next table stared.

"I wondered when this would come up," Allie sighed. "I can tell you things, but I don't know whether it'll help. OK. Here goes. You and Reginald were once a single person."

"What?"

"The human body is made of billions of cells. The human soul is far more complex, composed of trillions of threads of consciousness. Like soul-atoms. They unite to form mini-personalities. And those combine to form larger personalities. A whole human soul is like a nation, composed of billions of mini-people."

"OK?" Joyce said.

"When you have mixed feeling about something, they disagree. Their belief in being Joyce Pincus overrides their differences. In the life you lived immediately before this one, your name was Nathan Lewinsky."

"Nathan...Lewinsky," Joyce mumbled, giving a thousand-mile stare. "That name sounds so familiar."

"Reginald had nightmares as a child," Allie said. "In which he screamed that name, for hours. And, in the morning, his parents couldn't wake him ...for half a day, sometimes. They just couldn't snap him out of it."

"I don't know much about his childhood," Joyce said. "His parents institutionalized him when he was eight and basically abandoned him. I never met them. I always blamed them for his problems."

"Nathan was talented mathematically," Allie continued.

"But his soul was at war with itself. One portion of it was focused on mathematics and violently opposed to emotions and any form of human interaction. This war consumed most of his energy, making him listless — even suicidal. Then his soul split into yours and Reginald's."

"Is this possible?" Joyce said.

"I deep-scanned you and Reginald, and it horrified me," Allie said. "What it taught me about souls in general was very unnerving. I'm sorry I did it without your consent. When Nathan's soul split, it was nowhere near an even split. You got most of what made up Nathan, and Reginald was the small part that split off. The immediate effect was that Nathan felt more energized than ever, now that the war was over. He also felt a sense of loss."

Joyce nodded, tears running down her face.

"You reincarnated as Joyce Swanson," Allie said. "Still haunted by this sense of loss."

"I always felt that way!" Joyce said. "Since I was a little girl. I married and had children but that feeling never went away. And after my husband passed away..."

"You ran into Reginald when you volunteered at a halfway house," Allie said. "He reincarnated too soon, and was not ready to be a fully-functioning human being."

"Will he ever be?"

"Yes, eventually," Allie said. "Souls constantly grow and develop. He'll regrow his missing limb and so will you. Your being together is part of the healing process. There will come a time when his psychotic episodes fade away forever. I don't know if what I've said helps."

"It's the most bizarre story I ever heard," Joyce said. "But it makes perverted sense ... somehow. More than what his psychiatrists told me. It explains why I need him so much. My friends and my children keep telling me to leave him, but I just can't."

"That's one way new souls come into existence," Allie said. "There are healthier ways, but nature isn't always tidy."

***

Their food arrived.

The kang poong saewoo shrimp was batter coated and served in a spicy orange sauce with peas and carrots. The donkatsu were panko-breaded deep-fried pork cutlets with shredded cabbage and a brown sauce. The beef tang soo yook was batter-fried pieces of beef in a brown sauce with vegetables.

Allie explained how to eat it.

"To change the subject from the spiritual to the mundane," Derek said, serving himself a bit of each entrée. "You need money."

Joyce nodded.

"Your forty nine percent of the company won't bring in any money until we make a profit. And that could be a while."

"So we want to hire you," Allie said. "For a salary of two hundred thousand a year with full medical benefits. Including psych benefits, for Reginald."

"What do I have to do?"

"Run our office," Derek said. "You saw what it's like. Go online and order office furniture, computers, etc. Maybe some plants. Hire a receptionist and secretary. You'll have a budget for that. Tomorrow, we'll get together and make the arrangements."

"I've never done anything like this before," Joyce said.

"Well, we're merciless bosses," Allie said. "In the next few weeks, we're going to be getting important mail at that address and need someone to accept it. Stuff from the navy. Requests for interviews."

"Whatever you do will be good enough," Derek said. Keep the back room empty. You know, where the generator is now. We'll use it as a teleport-room."

"It'll be nice not to have to teleport into stinky restrooms all the time," Allie said.

Joyce laughed.

"Wait a minute!" Allie said. "Are you forgetting we had a demo with members of the press present? There will be a newspaper article about it and our company, probably tomorrow. With your name plastered *all* over it, Derek. Won't that attract Ustinov's attention?"

"Shit," Derek muttered. "It probably won't be front-page news but we can't count on them missing it. OK, I'll move the generator again. And, in the beginning, you should stay away from the office, Joyce. I'll check the mail and hand it off to you. You could take it home and sort through it. Tomorrow, I'll give you your first half-year salary in cash. When our problems with the Russians are over, we can go back to our original plans."

"Will they end?" Joyce said.

"Yes," Derek said. "Ustinov is about to be indicted for murder. If he flees, his influence with his gang evaporates. If he stays and is indicted, he goes to jail and his influence disappears. His gang regards him as a liability. Most of his top lieutenants are in jail or worried about how to stay out of jail. If he's jailed and *convicted,* he'll testify against his entire gang to get a life sentence."

"He'll betray his own people?" Joyce said.

"There's zero loyalty in the mob," Derek said. "It's all about money. Or avoiding a death sentence."

"Anyway — when we get back on track, and when Reginald's ready, he's got a job as Director of Research," Allie said. "For the time being he should concentrate on getting well."

"You two are a team," Derek said. "He can't function without you."

"I should visit him and give him the good news!" Joyce said. "I hope he recognizes me."

She stood and dashed out.

Derek and Allie sat quietly, staring into each other's eyes, their noses touching.

"Ah, my glorious Sinuhe," he murmured to her. "Forever the healer and wise counselor."

"My fierce shadow-warrior," she replied, caressing his face. "Ka of Sit-Hathor, mistress of fire — fated ruler of Kemet — unto the very Horizon."

Startled, they realized they'd both spoken Twelfth-Dynasty Egyptian.

Derek threw three hundred dollars on the table and — the moment they felt people weren't looking — they vanished.

Chapter 34

Although was early afternoon Hawaiian time, their honeymoon suite hadn't been made up. They ripped off their elegant clothes, put on water-wings and, just as the maid cracked their door, teleported to their "ocean getaway."

It looked different in the light of day — with blinding sunlight sparkling off gentle two-foot swells. Although their dolphin friends were long gone, a quick scan revealed no danger.

They made love.

Afterward, they floated on their backs, arm in arm.

"This the way to go when I'm as big as a house," she said.

"I won't be scaling Mount Allie."

"You better not. We should try the Caribbean sometime."

"The water would be warmer. I've heard it's like a bath. The trouble is there are so many cruise ships and yachts going through there."

"Yeah. We could get 'rescued'," Allie said. "You know, honey, we took on quite a burden with the Pincuses. I kind of like them, though."

"Their invention will change the world. And we'll be part of it."

"Do we really want to be captains of industry? Running a company can be a lot of work."

"I know and it scares me, too. Think *they* could run their company?"

"*No!*"

"You'll get your art gallery, honey. You'll get everything you want."

"I already have that," she said, kissing him.

"Yeah, but your artistic talent is so incredible..."

"Just take the damn compliment, maniac."

They returned to their hotel room. They flew into space on their way back and saw that their playground was squarely on the equator.

***

After a nap, they returned to the Murakami house.

"You two have quite a sunburn!" Liz said. "Hanging out on Waikiki beach?"

"No," Derek said. "Floating in the ocean at the equator."

"Why do I have the feeling you didn't make that up?" Liz said.

"The equator's fourteen hundred miles from here." Thomas said. "I looked it up."

"That far?" Derek said. "I had no idea."

"A great place to get away from it all," Allie said. "As long as sharks don't show up."

"Where's Wendy?" Derek said.

"She's on a date with Travis," Thomas said. "Something at the University of Hawaii. I didn't know Hawaii had a university. Although land-grant colleges are found in almost every state, I didn't think Hawaii had enough land for one. What are your thoughts?"

"We need to catch up with Wendy," Allie said. "There's something important I have to tell her."

✳✳✳

Derek and Allie arrived in the bushes on the edge of a mob, a few feet behind Wendy and Travis who were kissing.

"What did you have to tell Wendy?" Derek said.

"I had to say *hey!*"

Derek laughed.

"Where *you* guys come from?" Travis said, turning.

"It's like I told you, Travis," Wendy said. "You know they call this a *Kanikapila,* Derek!"

"Like you *told Travis?*" Derek said.

"Oh boy," Allie said.

"We need to talk, Wendy," Derek said. "After the concert."

The concert crowd occupied a courtyard in front of a Japanese garden with the greenest grass Derek had ever seen, and ferns hung over a pond with foot-long orange carp that swam between lichen-covered rocks .

A golden pagoda stood at the edge, and a stage had been set up on the steps of a wide white building behind it bearing the logo, "The East-West Center."

Clouds rolled in, misting the crowd.

"Now for someone who needs no introduction, Bla Pahinui," the MC said.

The crowd went wild as a bearded middle-aged Hawaiian took the stage and said, "I'll begin with one of my father's favorites and one of mine, *Moonlight Lady.*"

He played an acoustic guitar and sang in a golden voice about a woman of singular beauty, more a force of nature or goddess than a mortal — and the work she did in haunting moonlit fields.

"You're my moonlight lady," Derek said, hugging Allie and sobbing.

"Good fun, ya?" Travis said.

✳✳✳

The mist that had rolled in earlier had become torrential rain, turning streets into rivers.

Soaked, the four of them ran the two blocks to Sayako Matsumoto's Real Italian Pizza, and took a table in the back.

It appeared to be a student hangout.

"So what did she tell you about us?" Derek asked Travis.

"Pretty much everything," Allie sighed before Travis could reply,

"It just came out," Wendy said. "One thing led to another. I had to explain how you could talk to each other without saying a word."

"At least we can trust you, Travis," Allie said, patting his arm.

"I *love* her," Travis said, putting his arm around Wendy. "I would never harm *any* of you."

Wendy kissed his cheek and snuggled him.

Sayako came by to take their orders.

"Did you guys ever find the Piikoi Palace?" she said.

Derek replied and introduced her to Wendy and Travis.

"I know Travis," Sayako said. "He come here a lot. So your sistah's dating a local boy?"

She pronounced "local" as "loco".

"I'll be going to the U of Hawaii!" Wendy said. "I'll be coming here all the time."

"If Travis gets her to go to college, that's a plus," Derek thought.

Allie laughed.

"The UH is good in some subjects," Sayako said. "Oceanography, astronomy."

***

At the Murakami house, Travis asked Derek if he'd really lived in ancient Egypt.

"We both did," he said, as Allie nuzzled him. "I always wondered how things turned out afterward."

"There's a lot of material online," Allie said. "Gotta love Egyptologists! They spend their entire lives studying a dead civilization. I'd like to meet one and give him a big hug."

"So what happened?" Wendy said.

"The twelfth dynasty faded and the thirteenth was weak. Then all Hell broke loose. The Bedouin tribes in the deserts overran most of Egypt, and the era of the Shepherd Kings began."

"You screwed things up by killing yourself, Derek," Wendy said.

"I'm not going to feel guilty about something I did almost four thousand years ago."

"Depends on what you mean by screwing up," Allie said. "The best thing for Egypt would have been if Sit-Hathor had been born the oldest son. Second best would have been if she stayed alive and helped her brother."

"Was there any silver lining at all?" Derek said.

"After you died, your brother and I discovered reservoirs of strength we never knew we had," Allie said. "It broke my heart but I developed an inner toughness I have to this day. And you have to be tough as nails to be your wife."

Wendy and Travis registered shock.

"That came out the wrong way," Allie laughed. "I mean all the crap we have to deal with, the mafia, getting shot and almost killed. Hell, I bet some people would freak out at out-of-body travel or even telepathy. I have girlfriends who have nervous breakdowns if their mother-in-law says catty things about them."

"So what happened to Egypt afterward?" Derek said. "Was that the end?"

"No! Two hundred years later, in the eighteenth dynasty, the warrior-Pharaohs of Thebes came roaring back. They retook Egypt and drove out the barbarians."

"Upper Egypt saved the day?" Derek said. "Tough bastards. They always were."

"And ancient Egypt's most prosperous period began. They built monstrous, gaudy temples at Karnak and Amarna. No creativity. They even stooped so low as to cut out names of Pharaohs from *our* temples and substitute their own. They'd regained their land and become powerful — but something in their souls had dried up."

Chapter 35

At nine in the morning, New York Time, Derek planned to report the break-in at the Pincus workshop. Still on Hawaii time, he couldn't function without coffee.

His throat felt scratchy.

He went to the Boardroom Grill and took a table near the front, by the windows. It was raining outside and the slush that filled the gutters clogged drains, making little ponds in the street.

Derek sipped coffee and scanned the Times. The main story involved President Eakins and his endless battles with the Pentagon. He wanted the military to swear allegiance to him, personally, rather than the constitution.

"The American army should be loyal to today's America, not a yellowing scrap of paper."

Thousands of the president's heavily-armed supporters demonstrated on the Washington Mall.

Finnbar Burke approached Derek and said good morning.

"Mind if I join you?"

"No, go ahead."

Derek realized that he fascinated Finnbar who had come by hoping to run into him.

"I understand you quite impressed members of our armed forces yesterday," Finnbar said.

Derek registered surprise.

"I'm not as well-informed as you, perhaps, but I try to keep my finger on the pulse of things," Finnbar said. "I have contacts in the Defense Department."

"There were reporters at the demonstration," Derek said. "I'm curious to see what they wrote."

Derek searched the paper for an account of the demonstration, and found it on the tenth page. The article seemed to be tongue-in-cheek and didn't list their "corporate address." It barely mentioned Derek's name.

"That's a relief," Derek sighed. "They think we're crackpots."

"You don't want publicity?"

You have a great secret, Burke thought. *And I'll make it my business to learn it.*

"We impressed the people we needed to impress," Derek said. "The navy and Regina Maas."

"*Maas?* You met her? More to the point, you recognized her?"

"Yes to both. She invited herself to the presentation, posing as someone's secretary."

"Maybe there's more to Energistics than I thought," Finnbar said, standing. "If you ever contemplate an IPO, please keep us in mind."

"You are a remarkably astute businessman, especially for someone so young. I sense there's something else behind your success, though."

Derek realized Finnbar had *thought* his last statement, so he didn't respond to it. He knew the term "IPO" referred to an Initial Public Offering, when a company's stock is put up for sale to the public and made available to stock exchanges. This would be a time when Derek and Allie could make billions in a single day. If the company was highly-regarded.

"I wouldn't dream of going anywhere else," Derek yawned.

"You look like you could use a vacation, Mr. Evans."

✳✳✳

Derek teleported to the Pincus workshop. Luckily, the street outside was deserted so no one saw him arrive — the warehouse's door had been ripped off its hinges.

He called 911 and Vaughn Williams.

When the police arrived, he gave them a statement. While they inspected the premises, Vaughn Williams arrived in his pickup truck and inventoried the equipment. Nothing appeared to be missing.

The police canvassed the neighborhood for eyewitnesses and looked for surveillance video.

Derek said goodbye to Vaughn and flagged a taxi.

✳✳✳

Derek took the cab to a car-rental agency on Astoria Boulevard and rented a full-sized car.

Then he drove to their empty corporate offices. The security guard found him a dolly and Derek loaded the Pincus generator into the trunk. Driving down Astoria, Derek saw a sign advertising ZZ-Storage Lockers with a nearby address. He rented a locker there and put the generator into it.

After returning the rented truck, he teleported to a Westside Market on Broadway, where Mrs. Pincus was grocery-shopping. He materialized in a restroom and ran into her in the produce aisle.

She jumped when she saw him.

"Sorry to pop out at you like this," Derek said, yawning. "I hope this isn't a bad time. I'd like to give you some money."

"I guess there are no bad times for that."

She paid and he carried her groceries to her place around the corner, an ancient art-deco building covered in a hundred years of grime.

Probably the height of elegance in the early 1900's, he thought.

They took a creaky elevator up to the seventh floor, walked down a dim hallway, and Mrs. Pincus opened her purse and pulled out a ring of keys worthy of a night watchman.

"You can't be too careful in the city," she said, unlocking four deadbolts. The door opened to a short hall with a kitchen on the left and a living room on the right.

"Come on it."

"Big apartment," he said. "My old place would fit in your living room."

"It's been rent-controlled since 1970. That's the only way we could afford it."

"I hope you'll be able to afford your own island soon."

He didn't ask what she and her husband had done with the five hundred thousand dollars he'd paid for his share of the company. That had been sucked up by a long list of creditors, including Vaughn Williams.

Derek set her groceries on the kitchen counter.

"What would we do with our own island?" she said, putting groceries away. "We're too old to enjoy being rich. I am, anyway. And Reginald ... well, you know."

"You could get an apartment with only *three* deadbolts instead of four."

She laughed.

The living room was spotless, a threadbare oriental rug covering its parquet floor. The sofa and chairs had worn-out patches in their fabric. Many framed photographs covered an old cherry end-table to the sofa's right.

A black spinet piano sat against one wall and an elegant brass menorah rested on top of it.

"My daughters from my first marriage. Marjorie and Joanne."

"Attractive ladies."

"So what's the drill? What do you want me to do?"

"Oh, right. Go to your bank around the corner and wait for me. I'll come and give you cash. Do you want me to teleport from another room?"

"No," she laughed. "I'd love to see you vanish before my eyes!"

He obliged.

✳✳✳

Mrs. Pincus's bank was a massive stone building on 73rd street and Broadway. Its cavernous lobby looked like an ancient Roman temple's interior or a gallery in an art museum.

Derek exited its restroom.

"There you are," Joyce Pincus said. "Watching you disappear was so amazing. I didn't believe the crazy stories you told us, but I guess they were all true."

The teller they approached balked at depositing $100,000 in Mrs. Pincus's savings account.

They finally had to talk to a bank officer and Derek explained that he'd drawn the money out of his Continental Bank account on Wall street.

The deposit was approved.

"My goodness," Mrs. Pincus said. I don't think I've ever had this much money in the bank."

"You should probably set aside thirty grand or so for income taxes."

They agreed to meet in her living room at noon each day, when he would turn over the corporate mail.

As Derek headed for the restroom, she said, "Reginald and me! Does your wife really think we're good for each other?"

"She thinks your being together is part of the healing process."

"What do you think?"

"She was the most extraordinary person I ever met, *before* she was indigo. And now, she's ... she's a bona-fide goddess. In times past, they would've built temples in her honor. I hope to build her one someday."

"Can't argue with a goddess."

"You can, but it wouldn't be wise."

"Hug your goddess for me," she murmured, fiercely embracing him.

∗∗∗

Derek teleported to the Boothbay Harbor home and went out-of-body.

A check on their corporate offices revealed that the mail had not yet arrived, and a check on Ustinov revealed that he had arranged for a receipt of a large shipment of cocaine into Patterson New Jersey.

Ustinov also considered fleeing.

Derek teleported to Grand Central Station and bought a burner phone. Since the train station was noisy at this hour, he teleported to their corporate office's back room.

He called Detective Roberts and relayed the time and place where the cocaine shipment would arrive.

"I suppose you can account for your whereabouts yesterday," Detective Roberts said.

"It's on page ten of the Times," Derek said, explaining the demonstration and who attended it, suppressing a sneeze.

"I see. A man on a moving semi's roof fired a shot at a police car. Witnesses said he looked like James Bond. One of them even thought they were filming a movie."

"Was anyone hurt?"

"No. Even stranger, the truck turned out to be full of handcuffed naked women. Packed in like cattle."

"How did the drivers explain that?"

"They refused to say *anything*. One big fat no comment. Including the women. They were packed so tightly one of them suffocated and *died*."

"Can't you arrest them for that?" Derek said.

"Their lawyers concocted a story they didn't have the imagination to do. They say it was a kinky sex game, completely consensual. The death was a tragic accident. What the hell happened? If we'd caught them at the brothel, we could've easily arrested everyone."

"Ask Greg Polhamus in your precinct. He was on that list of dirty cops I gave you earlier."

"Can't arrest people on your say-so."

"He called Ustinov, I think using the land-line at his desk. Ustinov yelled at him to use a burner-phone."

Derek almost asked what happened to the women, but a scan of Detective Roberts revealed they were in protective custody, and most would be deported.

He heard a commotion in the hallway and said, "Four of Ustinov's men are breaking into the building where I am."

He gave Detective Roberts the address and teleported to Hawaii.

Chapter 36

"You look like hell!" Allie said as Derek materialized in the Murakami house's living room. It was raining hard outside.

He sneezed.

"The changes in time and temperature," he said, blowing his nose with a wad of tissues. "Getting up at four AM."

"Take a rest. You've earned it. I can handle things with Mrs. Pincus and the office."

"I could reset and get rid of it," Derek said. "But I think never getting sick might weaken my immune system."

Derek went to one of the house's three bedrooms. The small room had a queen sized bed covered with a thick comforter and a window over the bed facing the back yard. The walls were a cool aquamarine and a white bushy throw rug covered the hardwood floor.

He closed the blinds, making the room as dark as possible, and collapsed into the bed.

***

Allie lay on the sofa and said, "Time to get your ass in gear, Allie."

She teleported to their corporate offices, went down to the lobby, and checked the mail. Just some junk and bills.

"This wouldn't fit in the mailbox," the security guard said, handing her a huge packet from the Department of Defense. She returned to her empty office.

Then she scanned Joyce Pincus and learned she was visiting her husband in the Bellevue Psych ward. She teleported to a nearby restroom and went into Mr. Pincus's room.

"You!" Mrs. Pincus said.

Allie hugged her.

"Poor Derek's sick as a fucking dog, pardon my French. So I'm handling things."

Mrs. Pincus laughed and said, "You people can get sick?"

"Derek thinks never getting sick harms his immune system, so he allowed it. And he really needs a rest. So my vacation's over."

"Vacation?"

"We stashed Derek's family and my mom in Hawaii, and I've been living it up. How's Reginald doing?"

"You tell me," Mrs. Pincus said.

"He's in there and he's aware of us, but he can't react. It's like he's mentally paralyzed."

Allie told Reginald the story of Nathan Lewinsky and his relationship to the Pincuses. Reginald turned his head and stared at her.

"My god!" Mrs. Pincus said. "That's the biggest response he's had in *days.*"

Joyce called in a nurse who called in a doctor named Hans Fenichel.

Dr. Fenichel examined Reginald who mumbled, "Nathan Lewinsky" over and over again.

"Do you know the significance of this name?" Dr. Fenichel said.

"No," Joyce lied.

Reginald became agitated and screamed "Nathan Lewinsky," and Dr. Fenichel sedated him.

Joyce and Allie went to the hospital cafeteria, an Au Bon Pain.

"Oddly enough, I think Reginald's improving," Allie said. "He's drawing energy from Nathan Lewinsky."

Joyce Pincus smiled.

They bought croissants and coffee, and Allie opened the packet from the Defense Department. As she'd expected, it awarded them fifty million dollars towards their developing a power-plant for a Virginia-class nuclear submarine. They could keep the money even if they failed. The only condition is that they had to qualify for a security clearance.

"Any problems there?" Allie asked Joyce.

"No, I've never even jaywalked!"

"I'd probably say 'pardon my Russian'. You wondered what I'd say to a *French* person when I use dirty language."

Joyce Pincus laughed.

✳✳✳

Derek stirred and shielded his eyes from the light.

"He's waking up," Wendy said. "You've been sleeping for hours."

Derek realized he was still fully clothed.

"My mom made made this for you," Travis said, handing him a small bowl and spoon. "It's *chawanmushi*. It cure any*ting*, bruddah."

The bowl contained egg-custard with embedded shiitake mushrooms, noodles, and scallions in a clear broth.

Derek sneezed uncontrollably several times.

"Sorry!" he said, taking the bowl. "Thank your mother for me."

Travis offered him a bottle of soy sauce.

"It's *delicious,*" he said, pouring a few drops of soy sauce on the custard and tasting it. "I mean *ono-licious!* If this doesn't cure me, nothing will."

They left him alone.

After he ate, he stripped to his shorts, got under the covers, and fell asleep again.

✳✳✳

After lunch, Allie handed the mail to Joyce and teleported to her apartment. She lay on her bed and scanned Ustinov.

He was arranging to receive a shipment of cocaine in the suitcase of someone named Martin Rozhkov, when the SS Holiday Spirit docked at pier 32 at 4PM.

Grigory at Universal Airlines had finally figured out that they'd all flown to Hawaii and passed that information on to Ustinov.

Son of a bitch!

She scanned Detective Roberts and found him at his desk. She teleported to a ladies' room at the precinct and walked up to him.

"May I help you, miss?" Detective Roberts said. "Oh...your eyes!"

"Yes, I'm Derek's wife. He's under the weather, so I'm taking over for him."

"Maybe we should talk someplace less ... public."

They left the police station and went to a coffee shop across the street.

Allie told Roberts about the cocaine shipment and he wrote down her information.

"Are you really Carlo Giancana's granddaughter?" he said.

"Guilty as charged, unfortunately."

"You don't get along?"

"No, we don't. I'll leave it at that."

"And you and Derek aren't human?" Detective Roberts said.

"Apparently. Professor Fischer concluded that, though she doesn't know she's working with *our* DNA samples."

"You didn't tell her?" he said.

"She loves detective novels, you know. You remind her of her favorite detective, Franz Hoffman, of the Frankfurt PD. You were wondering what a world famous professor would see in an old detective. And she loves New York. You know, the way only someone who didn't grow up here can."

Detective Roberts smiled.

"I wish I'd scanned her sooner. It would've saved a lot of time."

"Huh?"

"She knew Dr. Pembroke."

They chatted for a while. He advised her on a good security firm to secure their warehouse.

"Well, got to get back to Hawaii," Allie said, standing. "Ustinov knows our families are there."

"I better get back too. Leaving the office with a beautiful woman will start tongues wagging."

He stood, and she startled him by hugging him.

"You're not what I expected," Ian Roberts said.

"I know."

"Derek's a very lucky man."

She smiled.

✳✳✳

"Are you among the living, honey?" Allie said. "You slept more than twelve hours."

"I think so," Derek said. "I'm feeling a bit better."

"Glad somebody is. Wendy, Travis and your parents are sneezing their brains out. Travis is even sleeping on the sofa so he doesn't give it to his parents."

She filled him in on current events.

"Greg Polhamus is under arrest and feeling sorry for himself," Allie said.

"What?"

"Amazing how self-centered some people are. Even after they told him about that woman's death, he just feels he broke some silly rules to make extra money. Whenever you try to get the goodies you *deserve* in life, the system slaps you down. Also..."

"Ustinov knows we're in *Hawaii?*" Derek exclaimed.

She nodded.

"Oahu has a million people," Derek said. "Finding us won't be easy."

"His gang doesn't want anything to do with us, so he contacted locals and made them outrageous promises."

"Portland all over again," Derek said. "Sounds like we should return to New York."

Derek got up, put his stinky, wrinkled clothes back on, and they joined the others in the living room.

✳✳✳

"Detective Roberts recommended Praetorian Security Services," Allie said. "So I hired them to install a state-of-the-art security system in the workshop. So we can actually *work* there. They're sweeping our apartment too, and they'll put in a security system. So we can live there like people."

"I can't wait to get home," Thomas said. "It's beautiful here, but it's not home."

Derek and Allie sat on the sofa.

"I had the weirdest dream last night," Wendy said. "I was floating in the air and could see myself in bed, sleeping."

"Yeah," Travis said. "I had a dream like that too. I saw you floating in the air *and* in bed. At the same time."

"Oh my *god!*" Allie and Derek said with one voice.

"What?" Thomas said.

"That's no common cold you have," Derek said. "It's the God Virus. You're becoming *indigos.*"

"*Not even!*" Travis said. "Fo real?"

"There must've been a little of the virus left in my system," Derek said. "Going home's going to be a *lot* easier than coming here was."

"I had a dream like that," Thomas said. "It was so awful. I wanted to get back to my body."

"You guys are in for a wild ride!" Derek said.

They spent the afternoon discussing what to expect and what they'd be able to do. Derek and Allie talked Wendy out of flying to Las Vegas and plundering a casino.

❋❋❋

That night, they all floated floated in the living room above Travis's sleeping body.

"This is horrible," Thomas said. "I don't like it a bit."

"It's not so bad," Liz said. "This light all around us... It's encouraging, somehow. Joyful, even."

"No it isn't!"

"Now we go to Boothbay Harbor," Derek said. "I'll go there and you guys think of me."

Without any transition, he was floating in the Boothbay Harbor kitchen. Moments later, the others appeared.

"Now try to see this room as clearly as possible," Derek said.

"Everything's a ghost image," Travis said.

"Focus on details!"

They all fell to the kitchen floor in a heap.

"Well, Travis," Allie said. "You just traveled five thousand miles in a few seconds."

"Some *ono!*" Travis said.

"Home!" Thomas said. "I was counting the days until we could come home."

"Keep indoors until you're over the virus," Derek said. "We've got to go back to Hawaii in a bit. Loose ends."

Travis opened the kitchen door to the back yard.

"Cold!" he exclaimed. "Shave-ice on the ground?"

"We call it snow," Wendy chuckled.

"I know all about snow!" Travis said. "I saw it on TV. On the Big Island, they got snow on Mauna Kea."

"It's great to be here!" Wendy said, teleported to a corner of the room.

"But it's good being *here* too," she added, teleporting to room's center.

Liz laughed.

"And over *here* wasn't so bad," she said teleporting to the door.

"*Stop that!*" Thomas shouted. "You're making me sick."

"Come on, Travis," she said, taking his hand. "I'll show you the rest of the house."

They left.

"I wonder how long it will take her to become pregnant by him?" Allie said. "Just sayin..."

"Don't even think that!" Derek muttered.

"What?" Liz said.

"Indigos tend to be," Allie said.

"Horny?" Liz said. "You said that with your mouth closed!"

"Telepathy, mom," Derek said. "It's that easy."

Wendy and Travis returned to the kitchen.

"What happened to your bed?" Wendy asked Derek. "You were *doing it* so hard it *fell apart? Eew!*"

"One thing about being indigos," Allie said, her face incandescent. "We have *zero* privacy. When it was just Derek and me, that was OK."

"We have to come up with some rules of etiquette," Derek said.

"We're an *ohana*, bruddah," Travis said. "We indigos, we got to stick together."

"I remember that word from the Disney movie Lilo and Stitch," Allie said. "Mom took me to it. *'Ohana* means family. Nobody gets left behind. Or forgotten'."

✳✳✳

All but Derek's parents returned to the Murakami house and went back to bed.

Chapter 37

After leaving five hundred dollars in the maid's tip-envelope, Derek and Allie took the elevator down to the Piikoi Palace lobby.

"Oh shit," Allie muttered.

Derek realized that the entire hotel staff awaited them in the lobby.

"I guess we're kind of noisy," he said.

"We never were before."

***

When they reached the lobby, at least thirty people stood next to the front desk. Some applauded, others shook their hands and others simply stared, shaking their heads ruefully.

Derek paid their room charges of $1023 in cash.

"Enjoy your marriage," the desk clerk said. "As much as you seem to have enjoyed your honeymoon."

"Thanks!"

They went to rest rooms and teleported to the Murakami house.

Four maids from the nearby resort were cleaning the place from top to bottom and laundering all of the sheets and towels.

"I told my folks we're feeling better," Travis said. "They invited us to lunch."

The Howland home was a ten minute walk along the beach from the Murakami house.

"You *told* them about Derek and Allie?" Wendy said.

"They didn't believe a word of it," Travis said. "I just sort of blurted it out. I'm sorry."

"I say we tell them the absolute minimum," Allie said. "We don't lie but we don't put it out there either."

✳✳✳

Derek teleported to Boothbay Harbor to invite his parents to the luncheon.

"I'm never performing that ... *abomination* again as long as I live," his father snapped.

"Come on, Tom," Liz said.

"It's not normal! I want our lives to be normal again! I want to go to the Happy Cormorant with my friends."

"Teleporting means you're *never* far from home, dad. Anywhere on Earth."

"I forbid you from using that word in my house!"

"I'll go with you, Derek," Liz said. "We'll make excuses for you. Calm down, honey. Go to the Happy Cormorant."

"While you were frolicking on the beach, it was *snowing* here. It'll take me forever to dig out."

Derek suppressed the urge to remind him he could teleport.

✳✳✳

The Howland home was a two story white Mediterranean style villa with a balcony over its patio. Four palm trees adorned its circular driveway, and a concrete wall surrounded it.

Kurt showed up.

"Fantastic house you have here!" Liz said.

"It doesn't belong to me," Kurt said. "The Howland Family Trust owns it."

"The Howland Family Trust?" Liz said.

"A sweet deal. I live in it for free and my wives never get it in divorce settlements."

Derek scanned Kurt and learned that the Howlands were one of the wealthiest families in Hawaii. During the monarchy, there was no private ownership of land — it all belonged to the king. When the missionaries arrived, they befriended the king who rewarded them with huge tracts of land.

They came to do good and did very well.

Over the decades, the Howland Trust had sold off or leased most of its land in small parcels to cover expenses — like everyday living expenses. Many of the Howlands never worked a day in their lives. Kurt was one of more enterprising family members. The trust still owned this house and eight other properties on Oahu as well as a thousand acres of pristine land on Kauai.

"Where's Tom?" Kurt said.

"I'm sorry," Liz said. "Tom had to fly back a day early. An emergency at work."

"I thought he was a school teacher," Grace said.

"They had a curricular problem. The curriculum and budget have to be planned by a certain deadline. It's state law in Maine."

Grace took them on a tour of the house. The front door opened to a two story atrium ringed by a balcony with a staircase and hardwood floors. A powder room flanked the entrance.

A spacious living room lay to the right with a brick fireplace. All of the house's walls were white with dark brown koa wood door and window frames.

"You ever use the fireplace?" Liz said.

"Yes," Grace said. "We have to turn up the air-conditioning." The kitchen lay to the atrium's left — with stainless steel appliances and a Subzero refrigerator. It would've suited a small restaurant.

Grace led them up the staircase, saying, "We can't redecorate anything without the family trust's permission. And they usually say no."

Three bedrooms lay off the balcony that circled the atrium, decorated in the same theme. The koa wood beds matched the door and window frames. Travis's room was a refreshing change from the rest of the house's antiseptic look: an unmade bed, a cluttered desk, and posters of swimsuit models on the walls.

"What a mess," Grace muttered, slamming the door.

They returned to the patio.

"I can't believe we're leaving soon and we never went to the Hawaiian Cultural Center," Wendy said.

"Wendy," Allie said. "You can come back anytime you want. Remember?"

"Oh ... yeah," Wendy smiled.

"Watching Hawaiians crack coconuts is a *rare experience*," Kurt Howland chuckled. "Top of my bucket list."

"Sit down everyone," Grace said. "Travis! What's different about you? Your eyes. They're gray."

"Remember what Travis told you about Derek and me?" Allie said. "As a result of our illness, it has spread to all of us."

"Those contacts are *tres* cool," Kurt said. "Are they difficult to put in?"

"No, dad," Travis said. "They're not really contacts."

"I'm sorry you had to spend your last days here sick," Grace said.

258

"It wasn't so bad," Renata said.

"I have some Maui-wowie," Kurt said. "Pure buds. Who's going to join me?"

Grace frowned.

"I'm allergic to marijuana," Derek said. "I had some in college and was puking for a week."

"You smoked *marijuana?*" Liz said.

"Just one cigarette, at a concert."

Everyone else declined Kurt's offer.

Derek munched on macadamia nuts from a huge bowl.

Grace served the first dish: spam musubi.

"Spam?" Kurt muttered, puffing clouds of marijuana smoke. "Nobody on the mainland eats that crap."

Grace offered her guests knives and forks, but Allie insisted on trying to eat with chopsticks, like Travis and his parents.

"It's delicious," Liz said.

Fried *ono* followed — a kind of fish with a sauce made of teriyaki with chopped scallions.

Kurt stood and ran to powder room. His repeated toilet-flushes couldn't cover up the sound of him retching over and over again.

"Well that's a charming sound while we eat," Grace muttered, turning on the stereo system and playing Hawaiian music.

When they'd finished the ono, Grace served lomi-lomi salmon.

"This salmon is like candy," Allie said, wordlessly adding, "It could use sugar, though."

Dessert consisted of *malasadas*, which were sugar-coated jelly donuts filled with *haupia,* a white pudding made from coconut milk.

✳✳✳

On their walk back to the Murakami house, Liz exclaimed, "Oh!"

"Huh?" Derek said.

"Your mother just learned she's pregnant," Allie said.

"It's amazing," Liz said. "I just felt it divide. You know there's one thing about being Indigo that your father doesn't mind a bit."

"*TMI!*" Wendy said.

"Wait!" Derek said. "Three guys are waiting for us at the house. Kimo Makeloa, Joe Toledo, and Gabby Bosco. They tied up three of the maids and put them in a truck. The fourth maid tipped them off. Janet Suzuki."

Derek dialed 911 and passed the information along.

"Mom," Allie said. "Go home."

"We should all go," Renata said.

"They're going to kill those maids!" Allie said. "And we owe them money. Except for that Suzuki bitch."

✳✳✳

A battered white panel truck with many rust-holes stood in front of the Murakami house. Derek trotted up to it and shouted, "Here I am. Come and get me!"

"It's one trick kine, brah," Kimo said. "Ustinov said to get your whole family!"

Liz, Allie, and Wendy appeared.

Sirens sounded in the distance.

"Five-oh is on the way," Allie said. "You rocket scientists better do something quick."

Three enormously fat gun-toting men emerged from the house. They wore flowery aloha shirts, flip-flops, and shorts, with waist-length black hair and heavily-tattooed arms.

"Get in da kine truck!" Kimo said, waving his pistol.

They climbed into the truck's cabin. Three bound and gagged maids lay on the floor in the back sobbing.

"Why they giving themselves up?" Joe said. "Too easy."

"Who cares?" Kimo said. "Make our job easier."

Joe pulled out a cell phone and made a call.

"Yeah, tell Ustinov we got them all," he said, then he listened and added, "We sure we've got them. They're right in da kine truck."

He snapped a photo of the truck's interior and messaged it to the person on the other end of the connection. Then he listened again and added, "Bystanders. No huhu. We get rid of dem."

The maids tried to scream through their gags and writhed in the ropes binding them.

"We promise Suzuki they no get hurt," Kimo said.

"She cry all da way to da bank."

Kimo jumped into the truck and carefully tied up the Indigos.

Then he closed the truck's metal sliding door and the truck lurched into motion.

The four Indigos teleported, shredding the ropes binding them. Then Derek lay on the floor beside the three bound maids, trying to put his arm around them.

"Just once," Allie muttered. "I wish we could test our powers in a *non-combat* situation!"

Derek went out of body and visualized his spirit-body expanding to include the three maids — a strange experience. Their life-force pulsated through his being, and he felt their hearts beating and sending blood through their bodies, and he felt their terror and sorrow at lives cut off too soon.

It stunned him.

"Wow," Allie said, in her spirit-body. "You've engulfed them completely."

"You and the others go first."

They vanished.

Derek teleported to the beach in front of the Murakami house.

Sunshine blinded him and he saw the three maids lying next to him with blissful red faces and closed eyes. Their brief time in the spirit-world seemed to have calmed them.

He stood and untied them.

As they stood, they braced themselves against him, dazed, with eyes half closed.

"I feel terrible about what you've been through, ladies. As you see, we have certain ... abilities. There are criminals who want to steal them."

"No problem," Maria said.

They leaned and put their arms around him as they stepped over part of the truck's floor and walls that had come with them and staggered back to the house.

"When are you coming back?" Maria said.

"We were hiding out, here, but I'm sure my *wife* and I will be back. We'll pay you ten thousand each for the trouble you've experienced."

When they reached the house, a squad car had arrived. The kidnappers' truck had crashed into a tree and the three were running away.

"Just tell them the truck fell apart," Derek said. "I can't believe it was drivable."

Maria talked to the police officers. They got into their car and drove down the road in pursuit of the kidnappers, returning a few minutes later with Kimo in handcuffs.

"He joked about killing us!" Maria sobbed, raining punches on his chest.

Janet Suzuki ran from the Murakami house sporting a black eye.

"She punched me," she screamed, pointing at Allie.

"You bitch!" Maria said, running at Janet and forcing a policeman to pull her away.

"And what is your part in all this?" a policeman asked Derek.

"They rescued us," Maria said. "Saved our lives!"

As the police made notes, Derek reached into his purse and slipped each of the three maids ten thousand dollars.

The police took the maids in for questioning and told Derek and Allie to make themselves available in the future.

"We're going home," Derek said, picking up Norton.

Chapter 38

Derek and Allie teleported to the empty hallway outside their apartment in Flushing.

"Let me out!" Norton said, squirming. "I want to play."

"So we can transport large objects," Derek said. "Someday I'll build us a house on Mars."

"Those maids really enjoyed being teleported," Allie said. "One of these days, you have to take *me* as a passenger."

"No wonder Norton's so playful when we take him somewhere," Derek blushed.

Derek handed Norton to Allie and called Detective Roberts.

"Ustinov is on flight 5823, nonstop from New York to Honolulu," he said. "Due to land in about an hour."

"I'll contact Honolulu's finest," Roberts replied and hung up. Ustinov had boarded the flight minutes after Kimo had told him he had Derek and Allie. He'd intended to return before anyone knew he'd left.

As they approached their apartment, an forty-something black man in a long black leather coat came out the door.

263

264

"Perfect timing!" he said. "I was just about to call you, Ms. Giancana."

Anne introduced him to Derek. He was Royce Watkins from Praetorian Security.

Allie set Norton down, and the cat ran into the bedroom.

"We've wired the windows and doors and the system calls the police automatically," he said. "We've replaced your locks with electronic ones that can only be opened with these."

He handed them small black plastic pods.

"In the event of a power failure, they have a battery-backup that lasts a week. If you have the time, I can go over what we did at the workshop."

"I'm afraid not," Derek said. "There's a little crisis we have to deal with."

They shook hands and Mr.Watkins left.

Derek and Allie went into their apartment and teleported to Boothbay Harbor.

✳✳✳

They arrived in the living room and went to the kitchen.

Thomas held a loaded pistol to his head.

"I can't live like this!" he shouted, tears streaming down his face as Liz and Wendy tried to comfort him. Ed Brocklesby had cleared their driveway with his snow plow, and Thomas had driven to the Happy Cormorant.

It hadn't been so happy.

"My best friend, Mullins, wondered what little-known facts I'd *lecture* him about," Thomas sobbed. "He used to hang on my every word."

"Come on, dad," Derek said. "It can't be that bad."

"You're thinking I was living in a fool's paradise," Thomas said.

"Yes, I was thinking that. But they are your true friends. They listen to you even when they think you're lecturing them."

"I'm sure they'd *love* to hear about Hawaii," Liz said. "None of them have ever been there."

Unfortunately, Thomas had fled the Happy Cormorant as soon as he'd picked up Mullins's negative thoughts.

"Why don't we all go there for dinner?" Allie said. "We'll invite Mullins to join us and you'll tell him about Hawaii."

Thomas allowed Derek to take the gun from him.

They squeezed into the family car and went to the Happy Cormorant, a two story wood-shingled building on the shore of Adams Pond. The pond was a dark void in the night, but Derek had happy memories of ice-skating on it.

The pub was warm and steamy, heated by a massive stone fireplace in the back and a wood-fired brick pizza oven by the bar.

Wooden pillars as thick as tree-trunks supported wooden beams that crisscrossed the ceiling. Carvings adorned each of them: mythic animals, people, and cryptic comments.

The family took a table. Mullins waved to them and Derek invited him to join them.

Mullins was a retired lobster-fisherman with a weathered face and short white hair, who'd taught Wendy how to repair lobster traps.

"We're just back from Hawaii," Thomas said.

"Wow!" Mullins said, meaning it.

They ordered a lobster pizza, handcrafted beers called Starlight Ale, and Cormorant burgers, which — despite their names — were beef.

"I'll go to college in Hawaii!" Wendy announced.

"A long way from home," Mullins said.

"She met a boy there," Liz said.

Mullins chuckled.

Then Thomas enthralled Mullins with descriptions of Hawaii: the Koolau mountains, the trade winds, the roaches, the rainy season and how close to the equator they'd been.

"I can't wait to visit Travis," Wendy exclaimed.

***

On the drive home, Derek said, "If you ever get used to teleporting, you can visit the most exotic places in the world and talk about them."

"Teleporting? Oh, God. I don't know..."

"It'll be easy to visit Wendy at the U of Hawaii," Liz said. "Are you really serious about going there?"

"I am!"

"If you can't stand being an Indigo," Allie said. "There's probably a way to reverse it. You'll develop amnesia, though."

"That's good to know," Thomas said. "I guess I'll stick with it a while longer."

"If I did that, if I de-indigoed myself, would I lose Thomas Junior?" Liz said.

"Thomas *Junior?*" Thomas said. "I'd *hate* to go though life named junior. You know it'll be a boy?"

"Yes. What do you want to name him?"

"Kyle," Thomas said. "Kyle Evans. It's a manly name."

"Kyle it is then."

"Mom," Allie said. "If you reset, you'd lose Kyle. He wouldn't die, but his soul would go elsewhere. He'd be born to someone else."

"I have the strangest feeling he *wants* to be an Indigo. And I can't *believe* I got pregnant at my age!"

"We Indigo women seem to be fertile," Allie said. "Does Kyle talk to you sometimes."

"Yeah," she said. "It's like a tiny ghost is running around, playing hide-and-seek with me. Sometimes he becomes an adult. Once, he said he'd been a corrupt stockbroker who lost everything in 1929 and jumped out a window. Maybe he'll be good at math."

"Vittoria does that too. Sometimes she becomes an ancient soul who saw empires rise and fall."

"We're ancient souls, too," Derek said. "We've seen empires rise and fall."

"Hell, you *caused* an empire to fall, Sit-Hathor. Gave it a swift kick anyway."

"You're not going to let me forget that, are you?"

"We're Indigos; we never forget anything."

✳✳✳

Back in their own bed, Derek said, "Dad considered suicide just because people had negative thoughts about him?"

"Cut him some slack, honey. He doesn't have a mean bone in his body, and he was always a good father to you. Hell, *I* lost it when Mrs. Pincus had negative thoughts about me."

Part III

Peace

Chapter 39

At ten in the morning, Derek and Allie teleported to the NYU Biology department and ran into Professor Fischer.

"I just finished my report and wondered how to contact you two," she said.

"It's lucky we happened by then," Derek said.

She showed them to her office, invited them to sit, and handed Derek a thick manila envelope..

"Those DNA samples you gave me were quite remarkable," she said. "Did you find bigfeet or something?"

"Are they human?" Derek said.

"Absolutely not! They appear to be from primates of some kind, but definitely not human."

"Ah, the sixty chromosomes!" Derek said.

"How did you know?"

"I read you mind the other day."

"You *what?*"

"The DNA samples came from us," Allie said.

"*Unmöglich!*" Professor Fischer muttered. "Is this some sort of joke?"

"Ever heard of Harry Pembroke?" Derek said.

"Of course I have. A monster! I met him in Paris at a conference on Post-Transcriptional Gene Regulation. He invited me to have drinks with him after one of the talks."

"What?" Derek said.

"The talk was on Regulating Translation Through Internal Ribosome Entry Sites."

"I mean, did you go out with him?"

"*Natürlich.* I was very flattered but it turned out not to be a social occasion. He wanted to *recruit* me. For an insane project to create a master race that would rule the world. I refused and he *threatened* me."

"He *what?*" said Allie.

"He said my refusal to join him would not be forgotten or forgiven. And now, I think, it is your turn for explanations."

Derek told her everything.

"So what *are* your plans?" Professor Fischer said.

"We sure as *hell* don't plan to take over the world," Allie said.

Professor Fischer laughed.

"We couldn't, anyway," Derek said. "We have evidence that murdering someone in cold blood destroys our super-powers. We haven't done it but ... there's evidence. We can effectively defend ourselves though."

"*Very* effectively!" Allie said.

"Why?" Professor Fischer said. "It does not make sense."

"A gun fires for whoever pulls its trigger," Derek said. "It's a machine. Modern civilization is machine-oriented, so we think of everything as a machine."

"Well yes."

"The soul and the spirit-world are *not* machines. They're *alive* and have... attitudes. Or maybe a sense of morality? I don't know. There's so much we don't know about the spirit-universe. We haven't scratched its surface."

"We just want to live our lives," Allie said. "And raise our children."

"You are pregnant?"

"Yes. We don't even know my due-date. Do you have any idea how long it will take for my daughter to be born?"

"That does not show up in DNA. Hominids have a gestation period of eight to ten months. Your DNA differs from the human more than any hominid, including chimpanzees."

"Wow!" Allie said.

"It is thought Neanderthals had a gestation-period of *twelve* months. I cannot imagine how anyone could *possibly* know that."

"I guess she'll come out when she's good and ready," Allie said.

"I think we're a force for good," Derek said. "We've been working with Detective Roberts to put a mafia gang out of business. Incidentally, that's how he met you."

Professor Fischer smiled.

"Are more chromosomes better?" Allie said.

"It depends on what you mean by better," Professor Fischer said. "Some caterpillars have four hundred chromosomes. That's because they undergo elaborate transformations in their lives. Humans have one big adaptation that makes many small ones unnecessary. When we're cold, we turn up the heat instead of growing more fur."

"What do *our* extra chromosomes do?" Allie said.

"Since you appear human, I would guess they involve something internal, like your brain or nervous system. It would take *years* of research to determine what."

They broke for lunch.

***

It turned out to be a sunny and unusually warm day. At Professor Fischer's suggestion, they crossed tree-lined West 4th street and strolled through Washington Square park. Students were taking advantage of the unusual weather to sunbathe at the dry fountain in the park's center. Their stroll through the park took Derek back to his student days. He'd attended concerts in the park every summer and even smoked marijuana for the first and last time at one of them. A policeman had pointed to a sign that said "Keep off the grass" and asked Derek "Can't you read?"

He should've obeyed the sign.

Near its Arch of Triumph, they passed a black man dressed as an ancient Egyptian pulling a little wagon with two cats that also wore Egyptian headdresses.

"I'm the Pharaoh Akhenaton."

At eighth street they went to Katz's Deli, a bright airy establishment with four white-marble topped tables in the back. It had a white marble slab topped glass display case containing cold-cuts, flavored cream-cheeses, bagels, and lox.

They took a table.

Professor Fischer ordered a corned beef on rye, and Derek and Allie ordered plates of lox — raising the waiter's eyebrows.

When the food arrived, Derek grabbed a handful of sugar-packets and he and Allie poured sugar over the lox, raising Professor Fischer's eyebrows.

"We've developed some odd tastes in food," Allie said.

"I would say so," the professor grimaced.

"You want to study us," Derek said.

"Of course I do! It is not every day one discovers a new species of human. Nobel prizes have been won for less."

"I officially named us *Homo sapiens indicus,*" Allie said. "We're *Indigo* people."

"Really? If I made some calls, could you travel to the Ludwig-Maximillian university in Munich?"

"Travel is easy for us," Allie said. "Even international travel."

"We teleport," Derek said. "We're not opposed to being studied. We'd like to understand what Pembroke did to us."

"I'm beginning to like us," Allie said.

"You didn't *like* us?" Derek said.

"Indigos, I mean," she said. "I like being one, and I like ... our species, I like what we bring to the table. To me survival used to mean the two of us and our loved ones. But now I want our species to survive, too. Maybe our descendants will be evil assholes, but all the indigos in the world, now, are decent, honorable people."

"There's a limit to how much evil our descendants could do," Derek said.

"There are others?" Professor Fischer said.

"A few," Derek said. "I had a relapse and some...people caught the virus from me."

"Ah, professor," Allie said. "You'd like to catch it from us!"

"I would. Travel between Germany and the US would be so easy."

"You wouldn't have to go through airport security," said Derek.

Suddenly, Derek sensed doubts forming in Professor Fischer's mind.

No one can lie to them, but they can lie to others, she thought. Derek and Allie's Indigo powers would arouse deep suspicions in authority figures, already paranoid because of terrorism.

"I guess you can't research us in secret, can you?" Derek said.

Professor Fischer shook her head. Articles in research journals had to be peer-reviewed, and any claims had to reproduced by other researchers.

"If you keep our secret, and it comes out anyway," Derek said.

"You get the first shot at researching us," Allie continued. "Exclusive access."

"Thank you," she said, thinking, *It's as if these two are parts of a single person. Unnerving.*

Professor Fischer decided that becoming an Indigo might not be a good idea after all.

The human race has never played well with others, she thought. *Just ask the Neanderthals and the other extinct branches of the human family-tree.*

"Shit," Allie muttered. "You think people will attack us."

"Ask Ian Roberts about my work with him," Derek said. "He doesn't need to keep it secret from you."

"It is not your intentions or even your actions that matter," Professor Fischer said.

"It's our abilities," Allie continued her thought.

"Yes. If your numbers increase, you will eventually compete with humans."

"We'll try to avoid that," Allie said.

"And do things that benefit everyone," Derek added. "We have a company that will provide unlimited energy to all. Imagine a car that can go fifty years on one fueling. And its fuel is almost free."

"Really?"

"The Energistics corporation," Derek said. "We didn't invent its technology, but it wouldn't survive without us."

"I think the next few years will be interesting," Professor Fischer said. "For all of us."

"Good luck!" Professor Fischer said, as they parted company.

✱✱✱

After checking that it was empty, they teleported to an alley around the corner from the Energistics workshop. The workshop's door had been replaced by a massive steel one and a small office with a security guard had been constructed just inside the door.

"Surveillance cameras everywhere," Derek growled. "Teleporting here will be challenging."

He called Praetorian Security and, fifteen minutes later, Royce Watkins pulled up in black Range Rover. He issued them ID cards and spoke to the security guard.

Derek and Vaughn Williams moved the Pincus Generator to their secure workshop — the old fashioned way, using a pickup truck. It was stowed in a locked back room that only Derek and Allie could access.

Allie went to the corporate offices.

Derek and Allie found Joyce Pincus sitting at a desk directing technicians installing a telephone system and unpacking boxes with computers.

Derek called a lawyer Finnbar had recommended to get copies of standard contracts and nondisclosure agreements.

Reginald Pincus came out of one of the side-rooms.

"I'm so glad you're up and about!" Allie exclaimed, hugging him. "How do you feel?"

Derek shook his hand.

"He's on his meds," Joyce said. "So he won't be very talkative. I have interviews set up for some office staff. I assume you will want to ... screen them."

"Good idea!" Derek said.

The first job applicant was an attractive thirty-something woman named Claire Eakins. She sat across from Derek and handed him her resume.

"You realize that this is a very sensitive job," Derek said. "With proprietary corporate technology. Do you consent to a thorough background check?"

"Of course." She signed a consent-form.

Derek handed it to Allie and said, "This shouldn't take long. She's a genius on the Internet. Want a cup of coffee?"

"Love one."

Derek poured two cups and handed one to Claire.

Allie returned and said, "Her real name is Klara Bentner and she's a division-head at Valhalla, a German security firm owned by Regina Maas."

Claire shook her head, smiling.

"Normally I'd wish you luck in finding employment," Derek said. "But you've already got a job."

"Impressive!" Claire laughed. "I thought I'd built a bullet-proof legend. If *you're* ever looking for a job, I'll hire you in a heartbeat at Valhalla."

The next four interviews were similar, except that the last applicant, a man named Joe Chen, applied for the job of tech support.

Derek looked over the sheaf of papers Allie handed him — a bunch of purchase orders — and pretended to scrutinize them.

"OK, your real name is Lee-Kuan Yu and you were a corporal in the Peoples' Liberation Army until you were recruited by Colonel Tan Huizhong for espionage work."

Joe laughed nervously and said, "Is this some kind of joke?"

"You were top of your class at the Espionage School Number Seven in Xian."

Suddenly, Derek felt his mind reaching out to many others, people acquainted with Lee-Kuan Yu and people acquainted with them. It was as though an Internet of thoughts spanned the globe and he had linked to it somehow.

"Colonel Tan is not concerned with our little startup," Derek continued. "He sent you here mainly to get you away from your wife, Guan-Yin, with whom he's having an affair. They're together in Hong Kong's Winter Garden Hotel. Room 2250."

"*What?*"

"I feel for you, man. Of course, you're not exactly lonely. You have a mistress named Huilang in Bejing, one named Mary Choi in Hong Kong, and another named Lucy Blake in New York. When it comes to the ladies, James Bond has *nothing* on you."

Mrs. Pincus laughed.

Joe's eyes darted around the room, like a lion about to pounce.

"Relax, Lee-Kuan," Derek said. "You haven't broken any laws ... yet. We're not hiring you though."

Joe/Lee-Kuan stood and ran from the room.

"How did you do that?" Allie said.

"I honestly don't know."

"So that's how a spy reacts when his cover is *vaporized*," Mrs. Pincus laughed. "Working here will be fun."

Derek pondered this strange expansion of his telepathic powers, wondering how far it would go. Something about the exchange he'd had with Lee-Kuan Yu disturbed Derek.

Chapter 40

The next few days were a blur of interviews for engineers and machinists. Derek purchased enough brown-colored contact lenses for the whole family, and wore them for interviews and presentations.

They performed a demonstration of the Pincus Generator for several auto companies, including Daimler, Ford, and Joule Motors — who all offered them electric cars to prototype their generators.

It was a strange transition for Derek and Allie both: trading the tension and excitement of waging war for the mundane details of operating a business.

Two days later, Derek learned that the Navy contract was canceled: his association through marriage with the Giancana crime family caused him to be denied security clearance. A scan of Carlo Giancana showed that FBI agents had tried to question him about Derek and Allie, and he'd just thrown them out of his house.

"I'm changing my name to Evans, honey," Allie said.

"That wouldn't have gotten us the clearance."

"I know. Grandpa hates the FBI, but he could've at least tried. He decided we're not worth the effort."

They took their marriage license to the Continental Bank branch near their apartment and changed her name on their account. She would change her social security card online.

Renata accompanied them to the Boardroom Grille where they ran into Finnbar Burke.

He joined them.

"My condolences," Finnbar said. "On the loss of that navy contract."

"It's my grandpa's fault," Allie said. "It's fashionable for women to keep their maiden names, but mine carries too much baggage."

"Don Carlo threatened Derek's life, too," Renata said. "We haven't spoken to him since. If he doesn't apologize, we may never speak to him again."

This raised Finnbar's eyebrows and he said, "What was that line in *The Lion in Winter?*"

"*The Lion in Winter?*" Allie said.

"A wonderful old movie! Based on a Broadway play, I believe. Katherine Hepburn plays the queen and tells the king how wonderful sleeping with his father had been. He howls, rolls around, and vomits, and she murmurs 'ah, every family has its ups and downs'."

Allie and Renata laughed.

"Several auto companies are interested," Derek said. "We'll still build the power plant the navy wanted. It could power a small town."

"Your stocks are doing well," Finnbar said. "You have an uncanny knack."

At they talked, Derek picked up despairing thoughts of a biologist named Ramos Azmitia who had discovered that one of his colleague's data on the success of a highly touted diabetes drug had been faked. The news would break soon, and Ramos wanted to unload his stock in the company — which was *Seshadri-Clarke.* Derek couldn't resist!

After lunch, Derek walked Finnbar back to Jacobson and Morse and discussed what he wanted to do.

✳✳✳

After the transaction was completed — involving a half billion dollars of Seshadri-Clarke stock, borrowed from multiple brokerage firms — Finnbar produced a bottle of champagne.

This time, Finnbar and his company had also participated in the stock-short.

Roald Morse himself joined them.

"May the master of disaster strike again!" Mr. Morse toasted.

"What's the time-frame?" Finnbar said.

"I have no idea. Maybe a week?"

"Fantastic!" Mr. Morse said.

"What will you do?" Finnbar said. "When it's concluded. I mean, if it's successful."

"I'd like to start a foundation and a scholarship fund. The Indigo Foundation."

"I know a good lawyer," Finnbar said.

✳✳✳

Derek returned to the workshop where Vaughn Williams and Reginald Pincus were studying schematics of a Joule auto on their workstation. They wanted to remodel the Pincus Generator so it could be a drop-in replacement for the car's battery-pack. The generator was cubical, and the battery pack was long and flat. Derek couldn't contribute anything, so he teleported home and lay in bed.

There, he went out of body and checked on Ustinov's gang. They felt that Ustinov's story about accidentally shooting Rabotnikov was so implausible they ran the risk of prosecution. They contacted Bill Jennings's office and got an agreement in writing to avoid charging them as accessories if they testified against Ustinov. They didn't realize that Ustinov would then gleefully testify against all of them for the many crimes they'd committed over the years.

Bill Jennings would eliminate the entire gang in one stroke.

Chapter 41

Allie got her art gallery.

Derek and Allie leased a six thousand square foot space in the Chelsea District, on 25th street, near Broadway. She named it Indigo East.

She contracted with a web development firm named The Spider and the Fly. They spent a day going over the site's design, and the company promised to have it up within two days — including three email addresses. One would be for artists' submissions.

Next, she contacted her alma mater, The Cooper Union, and asked for two interns who would be paid minimum wage. An hour later, two twenty-somethings named Maureen Richards and Beth Cohen showed up, and Allie hired them on the spot. Her scans of them were their interviews.

Decorating was easy: white walls, hardwood floors, a ceiling that is either white or black, and many well-placed spotlights. She placed movable white walls in such a way that one had to follow a serpentine path through the studio, and constructed a teleport booth near the front door. It was situated in a way you

282

283

could disappear in it and others in the studio would think you had gone outside.

She advertised the gallery's Grand Opening in the Village Voice, the New York Times, ArtForum magazine, and NY Arts. The opening would take place in two weeks.

She also announced the opening on three social media sites and an online art forum. Artists were required to submit emails with a bio and images of their art — initially screened by the interns. This brought surprisingly quick results: by the end of that day, ten submissions had landed in their email account.

The two interns laughed loudly at the first one. It contained an image of colored feathers scotch-taped to a cardboard toilet paper roll and was entitled "Dispair."

"Ah yes," Allie said. "Let's try to be respectful. Thank her for her submission and say it isn't for us."

Another email featured a video of a iridescent holographic dragon taking flight, apparently simulated by hundreds of lasers controlled by computerized motors. Allie replied to it, asking for the studio's physical address.

It turned out to be a place in Sackets Harbor, New York. Allie Mapquested driving directions to Sackets Harbor — a trip that would take more than five hours by car. Then she Mapquested a map of Sackets Harbor, located the address, and memorized that.

"I've got to take care of some business," she said to the interns. "Just keep going over emails, and try not to burn the place down."

She stepped into the teleport booth and teleported to her apartment. There, she lay on her bed and went out of body. Her memorized maps floated in front of her in the spirit-world and she flew along Interstate 81 so fast the cars below seemed to be parked. The entire trip took ten minutes.

She didn't even want to think of how fast she'd flown.

***

Sackets Harbor turned out to be a cute village of red brick buildings on Lake Ontario, which was so vast no opposite shore was visible. A damp, icy wind blew off the lake, chilling Allie to her bones. She spotted a man coming out a door.

"Mark Korzipsky?" she said.

"Who wants to know?"

"I'm Allie Evans from the Indigo East Gallery. We were impressed with your submission. I happened to be in the area, and they told me to check it out in person."

"Happened to be in the area? Nobody ever *happens* to be in this area. It's the putrid anus of the world. Well, come on in."

"I don't smell anything," Allie volunteered, hesitant about defending this town. "This place is probably nice in the summer."

"It wafts the stench of small, provincial minds. Middle America at its materialistic worst."

"Oh."

Allie went into a warehouse. Mark flipped a switch and his installation sprung to life.

Beams of red, green, and blue laser light intersected and crossed each other in moire patterns that evoked a large beast taking flight. Where the beams crossed, their colors flared, forming new colors. The effect was breathtaking.

"We'd like to display your work," she said, pulling out a contract. "When can you get it there? Our grand opening is in two weeks."

"Wonderful!" Mark said. "I can get it there in a couple days."

He signed the contract and shook her hand.

"Let us know when you're coming, and we'll arrange a hotel room."

✳✳✳

Back at the gallery, the interns stared at one of Allie's paintings. Allie's artwork had taken off, and she'd dashed off two eerie oil-paintings of the spirit-world. One showed its radiant colors with its incipient life-forms — objects that looked like paramecia or amoebas swimming between objects that looked like galaxies. The other showed the pale Earth, from twenty-thousand miles away. She'd hung these — still wet — in her gallery.

"It's the spirit-world," Allie said. "The colors aren't right, of course. The colors there don't correspond to any Earthly spectrum."

"It's like you've seen it," Beth said.

"Isn't it?" Allie smiled. One thing she loved about the art-world is that you could be openly eccentric and people didn't think you were crazy.

"It's beautiful," Beth said. "But weird."

"Weird and beautiful are what we're aiming for, remember?"

Allie sensed Wendy's presence and mentally told her to use the teleport-booth.

Wendy stepped out of it.

"My God, you're pregnant!" Allie said.

"Twins. A boy and a girl. Travis used a condom but it kind of ripped."

"That would be funny if it wasn't so serious. What will you do?"

"We're getting married. I know — we're too young to get married, and I'm too young to have babies but what can we do?"

"As Travis said, we indigos are an *ohana*. Derek and I will support you."

"Think my folks know?"

"Of course they do," Allie said. "You should tell them in person as a courtesy. And Travis shouldn't tell his parents you're pregnant."

"Why?"

"They'd insist on you going to a doctor. I know I would if my son said he got a girl pregnant."

"Oh!"

Wendy shut her eyes for a minute and then said, "OK, he won't tell them."

Allie introduced Wendy to the interns and showed her around the gallery.

***

That evening, they all met in The Happy Cormorant for dinner, including Renata and Travis.

"Running an art gallery is so exciting," Allie said. "It's like sitting at the hub of the universe and seeing what everyone's doing."

"You're like an agent for artists?" Thomas said.

"Exactly."

"We're ignoring the elephant in the room," Thomas said.

"We're getting married," Wendy said, putting her arm around Travis. "We shared our souls and there's no one else in the world either of us could marry. And I want Chloe Teague to do it."

"I need it to happen in Hawaii so my friends and relatives can go," Travis said. "You guys can teleport."

"Thomas teleported from home to here," Liz said, patting his arm. "I'm so proud."

"Let's not make a big deal of it," Thomas said.

"I'm sure Chloe would love a Hawaiian vacation," Derek

said. "We'll fly her out there and put her in the Piikoi Palace for a week."

"You *shared your souls?*" Allie said. "So it's not just us. Maybe it's an Indigo thing."

Wendy and Travis blushed deeply.

Their food arrived.

Derek became aware of people staring at them.

"We're holding a conversation without making sounds, and it's creeping people out," he said. "We should talk *out loud.*"

"Funny!" Liz said. "I hadn't realized! Talking with words is work."

"I have some friends we have to fly out for the wedding," Wendy said. "Annmarie and Jewel."

"There's also my sister, Abigail," Thomas said. "And Ed and Heidi Brocklesby."

"No problem," Derek said.

"When do you want to do it?" Allie said.

"I don't know why," Travis said. "But I have a feeling it should be soon."

"I feel it too," Allie said. "There's something ... forming on the horizon. I can't tell what. Let's aim for next week. Before my gallery opening."

"We have a *lot* of calls to make, Wendy," Liz said. "And we'll need money, Derek."

"Of course."

Chapter 42

The next morning, Derek wired a half million dollars to his parents' bank account.

Then he went to the Energistics workshop — strictly speaking, to the restroom in Joey's Diner down the block.

In the workshop, he encountered a new face, a middle-aged, short bird-like woman who introduced herself as Judith Buckley, an electrical engineer from Joule Motors.

He shook her hand.

"We managed to shoehorn the generator into the battery-slot," Vaughn Williams said. "Now it's a matter of matching voltages and power-profiles."

"A standard power-converter will do it," Ms. Buckley said. "We'll be able to drive this pup by morning."

"Impressive," Derek said. "What happens then?"

"I report on it," Ms. Buckley said. "Very positively! Then corporate will contact you. It'll be a long time before it's ready for prime time. We'll safety test it, see that it follows all regulations, etc. They'll probably want to drive it around for a year before going into production."

They all went to Joey's and had breakfast.

"I can't wait to take this sucker on the road!" Vaughn Williams said.

"It's not a hot-rod, Mr. Williams," Ms. Buckley said. "We'll instrument it up and have a chase-car recording telemetry-streams. And we'll follow it with a tow truck."

"Tow truck?"

"This thing will be gerry-rigged at best," Ms. Buckley said. "A wire could come loose. Sixty kilowatts continuous is a hell of a lot more power than batteries provide. If you open it up, you could burn out a motor or start a fire."

Vaughn groaned.

"Mr. Trask will probably want to build a formula one race car and enter the Indy 500," she added.

"Great publicity!" Derek said. "For all of us."

***

Derek checked on Finnbar to learn that the scandal hadn't yet broken — and Seshadri-Clarke stock had even gone up slightly.

He teleported to Indigo East, and found Allie in the throes setting up a stunning ten by twenty foot square mural called *The Mote in God's Eye* — an image of stylized city buildings scanned by an enormous green eye whose pupil was a galaxy.

She didn't need his help.

He teleported home.

He lay in bed and clenched his jaw. It was the first time in a week no one threatened his life. If there ever was a time to relax and explore, it was now.

He drifted out of his body and tried to take a mental snapshot of this place, this bedroom with Allie's magnificent artwork, and little Norton. He'd mentally scanned Culinary Derek several times before, so that timeline was an easy target.

He focused and found himself in a restaurant before opening time. Culinary Derek directed two prep-cooks who were chopping vegetables and cutting meats.

Derek materialized in a restroom and noted, with some pride, that it was spotless. He sneaked out into the empty, dark restaurant. Colorful murals of Italian cliffside villages covered the walls — one looked like Positano.

Must be Allie's work.

He unlocked the door and stepped outside.

It was a neighborhood of two-story buildings, and the street sign said Astoria Boulevard. He looked at the restaurant he'd just left: *Ristorante Alberto.*

"Derek?" a familiar voice said. "I thought you were prepping for this evening."

He turned to see an older non-indigo Allie — very pregnant. "What happened to your eyes?" she said. "You lost weight. I'm sorry — I'm mistaken. You just look so much like..."

"Oh, Allie!" he muttered. "It's... it's... it's hard to explain. Your husband *is* in the restaurant, prepping. In a sense, I'm related to him."

"I thought I met all his relatives. The family resemblance is uncanny. Come on in."

I stepped in it now!

He returned to the restaurant with her and met his alter ego.

Culinary Derek was visibly older and heavier than Derek, and he looked tired.

Derek spent an hour explaining things as best he could, as Allie became increasing furious.

"Tell your story walking!" she said, pulling out her phone. "I'm calling a *cop.*"

"It was wonderful meeting you two," Derek said, standing and bowing. "I hope we meet again."

Then, before their eyes, he teleported home.

✳✳✳

Derek lay in bed. A glance at the clock showed that he'd returned to the *exact moment* he'd left. It was as if the mental snapshot he'd taken marked the time as well as the place. He went out of body again and checked his surroundings. Allie had mounted the mural on the wall and was arguing with her interns about the proper placement of spotlights.

In an out of body state, he returned to the Derek and Allie he'd just visited.

They were in shock.

"Could his batshit story be true?" Culinary Derek muttered, knocking back a shot of scotch.

"You never went in a drug study," she said.

"Yes I did, honey. About a year before I met you. I was supposed to get a red pill but couldn't make it. Pembroke rescheduled for the next day but turned up dead."

They went into their office and watched surveillance video.

"He fucking vanishes on the *video* too!" Allie said. "We didn't just imagine it. We have documentary proof, right?"

"You know," Culinary Derek said. "I hope we meet him again."

"Really?"

"There's more to life than ... pounding veal and chopping vegetables. There's a universe out there. A vast and strange universe."

"I love you so much," Allie said, hugging him. "It's like when we met. You were such a dreamer, then."

"Dreams..." he said. "Remember those off-the-wall dreams we used to have? Hawaii. Having sex in the ocean with dolphins circling us."

"Yeah. It was like we were living another life, a really *exciting* life. Will he ever come back? He came *this* time so maybe he'll come back, right? It's like a creature from another planet visited us. Or ... an angel."

"I don't know," Derek sighed. "Shit! I lost an hour of prep time for this evening."

Allie made a call.

"Mom, can you watch the kids a while longer? You won't *believe* what just happened..."

She listened, hung up, and said, "I'll help, honey. Just tell me what to do. "

***

Derek teleported to Indigo East.

"That is stunning," he said, of *The Mote in God's Eye*.

Allie stared at him a moment and said, "I can't believe you *did* that!"

"Very sloppy of me."

Allie shut her eyes, sighed, and said, "Your screwup did some good. They were depressed and feeling beaten down by life's bullshit, and now they're energized. They'd love to meet you again. I'll go along next time. We could have dinner there."

"It's strange," Derek said. "The way time got shifted several years."

"Maybe the timelines are out of sync with each other," Allie said.

"I'm going to do more exploring," Derek said.

"Try to avoid timelines with us in them."

***

He lay in bed again. Out of his body, he took a mental snapshot of his surroundings and then floated down to the street.

He hovered in the air by Main street, watching traffic and pedestrians and allowed his mind to go blank.

I'll drift with the flows of the spirit-world's energy.

Ghostly bison wandered through the scene, faint almost to the point of invisibility, and he focused on them.

The bison are exactly like the ones I saw that first night, in Pembroke's study. It's as I have some strange affinity for them — or the timeline where they live.

The bison grew clearer and more well-defined as the images of cars and people grew fainter.

He materialized on a meadow with a herd of bison ambling by, not in the least startled by his sudden appearance.

The cloudless sky was blue, and sweat formed on his brow from the heat and humidity. A dense forest ringed the meadow and there was no sign of New York City.

So this timeline is in summer. At least six months out of sync with ours.

He returned home. Again, no time had passed since he'd left.

In an out-of-body state, he returned to Bison World — easy to locate now that he'd visited it in the flesh. He soared high enough to see the whole region — all of Queens, Brooklyn, and Manhattan. Then he flew to Manhattan, which appeared to be a wilderness. As he flew to the southern portion of the island, he encountered what appeared to be a swamp. He recalled that Canal Street had originally covered a canal dug to drain a swamp.

He flew some 20,000 miles into space and descended on the Hawaiian Islands — as he'd done with Allie over what seemed like a lifetime ago. Geographically, the islands looked the same as in his world, so he descended to Oahu.

It appeared to be deserted.

Derek flew to Waikiki beach and scanned for potential danger, learning that the only animal life consisted of birds in the trees and vast schools of tiny fish in the water. Two dolphins swam parallel to the beach.

He materialized.

He found himself standing on a gracefully curved beach with Diamond Head in the distance and a dense wall of palm trees to the left. No trace of any human habitation existed.

He ripped his clothes off and waded into the water up to his waist. The fish were so dense they brushed against his legs, showing no fear of him.

He pitched a mental greeting to the dolphins.

"No creatures live on the land!" one dolphin said. "Not in these islands."

"It's one we've never seen before," the other said. "It speaks in my mind."

"Even on the mainland there aren't any creatures like this," the first dolphin replied.

"This world is a paradise," Derek said to himself. "As if it was made for us."

He went back to the beach and sunned himself on the warm sand until he was dry. A brilliant blue bird with iridescent violet rectangles on its wings flew overhead — it was like nothing he'd ever seen before.

"I wonder what we'll name you, pretty bird," he said. "Stands to reason there are species here unique to this place."

A scan showed that the pretty bird was thinking typical pretty-bird thoughts — looking for bugs to eat.

He dressed and teleported home.

At Indigo East, he told Allie what he'd discovered.

"What will we name it?" Allie said. "Bison-world just doesn't do it for me."

"Oz!" Derek replied. "Like all the Oz books."

"I loved those Oz books," Beth Cohen exclaimed. *The Wonderful Wizard of Oz, The Road to Oz, Princess Ozma of Oz.* I read em all."

"It's as good a name as any," Allie said.

***

At five, Derek teleported to Oahu's north shore, where Travis and Wendy were arguing with Travis's parents and Luther Howland, the sole trustee of the Howland Family Trust.

Luther was a white-haired man in a weathered aloha-shirt, shorts and flip-flops.

"I thought I'd put in my two cents," he said, strolling toward them.

"I thought you'd gone back to the mainland," Kurt said.

"I travel a *lot!*"

Wendy and Travis laughed.

"Please try to talk some sense into these two," Grace said. "They should wait until they graduate from college at least."

"She's not marrying into the Howland family money," Luther muttered. "She'll have to sign a prenup."

"That's fine," Derek said. "Our family has resources, too. One — I'll pay for their wedding. Two — as a wedding present, I'll pay their way through college and graduate school. Tuition and living expenses."

"Dorm fees too?" Grace said.

"A married couple should live together," Derek said. "I'll spring for an apartment near the UH campus. I assume that's where you'll be going."

"Yes," they both said.

"Grad school?" Kurt said. "I never figured you for grad school."

"I want to be a doctor," Travis said.

"And I want to study astronomy," Wendy said.

"Doctor?" Kurt said. "I'll believe that when I see it."

Derek shut his eyes and scanned Finnbar to learn that the Seshadri-Clarke scandal was breaking. He mentally told Liz not to book any plane tickets; he'd charter a plane.

Good, because I can't find any, Liz replied. *Hundreds of flights are canceled. Half the airports in the Midwest are socked in from snowstorms.*

"We can get the chapel Wednesday," Travis said. "It's a great place on the Punahou School campus."

Derek passed the information on to Liz who would contact the others.

"The wedding party will arrive the day before," Derek said. "I'll put them up at the Piikoi Palace for a week.

"Quite the wheeler-dealer, Mr. Evans," Luther said. "We investigated your family, you know. You're the only one who amounted to anything."

Kurt frowned at Luther. Travis and Wendy glared at him.

"Depends on your definition of amounting to anything," Derek growled. "My parents are hard-working, respected educators. Pillars of their community. They never had a trust fund to bail them out."

"Yes but we are the latter-day *alii* of these islands," Luther said. "You probably don't know what *alii* are."

"I know *alii* are Hawaiian nobility," Derek said. "But I didn't see anything especially noble about you."

✳✳✳

Derek strolled down the beach with Wendy and Travis.

When they reached the Murakami house, they saw a Gold Coast Realty For-Sale sign.

They waved to Mrs. Murakami.

"Aloha," she said. "I appreciate how you cleaned the pool and left the house spotless. But I thought you went mainland."

"I'm back on business," Derek said. "As for the house and pool, it was the least we could do. You're selling it?"

"When I was in Japan, I realized I'm getting too old for this big house. My sister in Sapporo invited me to move in with her family."

"How much you want for it?" Derek said.

"I hope to get one and a half million, but the Realtor said that might be too much."

"I'll pay it," Derek said. "Depending on how a certain business deal goes tomorrow. You and Travis can live here while you're in college."

"It's not close to campus!" Wendy said.

"And that matters, why?"

"Oh. Wait a minute! It'll be hard to throw parties here. Our classmates will have drive an hour."

"My mom would be over every day," Travis said.

Wendy groaned.

✳✳✳

Derek, Allie, Wendy and Travis had dinner in a restaurant around the corner from Indigo East, an Indian place called The Monsoon Palace. Large oil paintings of rural India covered the walls, and it smelled of incense. One painting showed a young couple staggering home after a grueling day in the fields.

The paintings were for sale.

An musician in a red velvet waistcoat and pants and a white turban played soft sitar music that drifted through the air like a ghostly essence, asking unanswerable questions.

Travis had never tasted Indian food.

He ripped open a hollow, football-shaped *puri* bread and dipped it into the chilled cucumber-yogurt sauce named *raita*, and then sampled *lamb saagwala*.

"New York has every*ting*," he said, shaking his head.

Derek told them about his visits to Culinary Derek and Oz.

✳✳✳

After dinner, they all returned to the now-empty gallery.

They lay on the floor and went out-of-body.

"Take a mental snapshot of this place," Derek said. "Then follow me!"

He teleported to Waikiki Bay in Oz, and the others followed.

"Oh wow!" Travis said. "This is what Hawaii looked like before they built hotels."

"It's really beautiful here, maniac," Allie said, kissing him.

"We can be ourselves," Derek said. "Teleport in broad daylight. As far as I can tell, there's very little intelligent life here. Except for dolphins."

"We always always got along with dolphins," Allie said.

"The local ones seem friendly," Derek said.

"Look at those beautiful birds!" Wendy said, pointing to a flock of blue birds with violet rectangles on their wings. She snapped a picture with her phone.

Another flock of bright red birds with long curved beaks flew by.

"We can build houses here," Travis said.

"Or build them at home and teleport them here," Derek said.

They wandered into the rain forest that lined the beach.

"We need machetes or chain-saws," Derek said.

"I figured out what I don't like about this place," Allie said. "It's boring as shit! It's more like a *picture* of a place than a place."

They laughed.

A rich array of colorful fruit hung from what looked like a banyan tree. Derek picked a purple fruit and something that looked like a mango.

"Let's see if it's safe to live here," he said.

"You brought us here but it might not be safe?" Allie said. "Thank you very much!"

Nevertheless, they hung around for another hour.

After an hour, they teleported back to the gallery.

Travis returned to Hawaii, where it was still late afternoon, and Wendy went to Boothbay Harbor.

Derek and Allie went home.

Derek returned to Oz with a glass jar with a lid and wandered through the rain-forest until he came across a stream. He took a sample of the water and returned home.

Chapter 43

The nest morning, Derek teleported to a restroom near Professor Fischer's office with his samples from Oz.

He collided with her in the hallway.

"I wonder if you would be willing to do more analysis for me," he said. "Ten thousand dollars like before."

"Natürlich!" she said. "I'm honored that you come to me. You don't need to pay me."

They went into her office.

"We have found a new world," he began.

"Another planet?"

"Let's just leave it at 'new world' for the time being. We call it Oz. My question is: Are there any snakes in our Garden of Eden?"

He handed her the two fruits and water-sample.

"Where is this world?" Birgit Fischer said. "It's *very dangerous* to transport biological materials from one ecosystem to another. Even bringing them to my office might be dangerous."

"I know," he said. "I should've worn a space suit and sterilized it afterward. But I didn't have one."

Derek decided not to mention that several of them had visited Oz and returned.

He tried to explain the Many-Worlds form of Quantum Mechanics and the nature of different timelines.

"If this world is *related* to the Earth," she said. "Life on it should have DNA and the same general structure as here."

"Geographically, Oz is this world's twin. Wait, it's possible for life to *not* have DNA?"

"DNA is one way to record genetic information. All life here uses it, including you indigos. But on another planet it might be different."

"I must say, Hawaii is very beautiful without hotels and honky-tonks."

"You visited that world's version of Hawaii?"

"Yes."

"That might not be so bad. As I recall, Hawaii had no native animal life except for birds and very little bacteria. When Captain Cook landed there, natives started dying in huge numbers from the bacteria his men brought."

"So we just have to avoid the mainland?"

"Especially Europe and Africa. North America was almost as bacteria free as Hawaii."

"If Oz is inhabitable, it could be our Indigo homeland. We don't *ever* have to ever compete with the human race. Incidentally, that water's in an old jelly-jar so it might have traces of raspberry jelly."

She smiled.

"Have you wondered why humans don't exist in your Oz?" Professor Fischer said.

"There's something that kills humans?"

"Be *careful*, Derek! I don't want to miss my chance to study you people."

***

Next, Derek went to the Energistics workshop.

As he checked in with the security guard, the Joule Roadster pulled in with Ms. Buckley at the wheel and Vaughn Williams beside her.

"I never should've let you talk me into this," she muttered.

"You *loved* it! Admit it!"

"OK, I admit it," she laughed. "Driving a Joule is better than sex. Can you believe Marketing wouldn't accept that as a advertising slogan?"

"You're bad!" Vaughn laughed, wagging his finger at her.

"We'll be able to sell these cars with a *lifetime* fuel supply — *built in.*"

She parked the car and they stepped out.

"If you love her, give her a Joule," she said. "They didn't like that one either."

Vaughn laughed.

"Would you be available to speak with our head of R and D?" Ms. Buckley asked Derek. "Maybe Trask himself?"

"I'm looking forward to it. Just contact our corporate office."

***

At Jacobson and Morse, Derek said he wanted to cash out of his short-sale.

"You don't think the stock will drop any further?" Finnbar said.

"I have no idea," he said. "Seshadri-Clarke is a solid company, so I don't see how the panic can last much longer. I'm cashing out because I need money now. My sister's getting married, and I may be meeting Trask of Joule Motors."

"Joule?" Finnbar said. "Then congratulations are in order! On both accounts."

Derek's take turned out to be seventy million dollars. He wired it to their Continental Bank account and set aside thirty million for taxes.

He went home and spent the rest of the afternoon playing with Norton and making arrangements for the wedding. He chartered a jet with Eagle Air Charters to take the wedding party to Hawaii and booked them rooms in the Piikoi Palace.

At two in the afternoon it was nine in the morning in Honolulu. Derek called Gold Coast Realty, made an offer on the Murakami house, and wired $1,501,907 to an escrow account in Honolulu. Closing could happen within days.

Then he joined Allie at her gallery.

✳✳✳

The next morning, employees of Joule Motors swarmed over the Pincus workshop. Five large men with submachine guns slung over their shoulders confronted Derek.

"Hello," Derek said to them.

"He owns Energistics," Judith Buckley said, waving them away. "Derek Evans."

"I'm Henry Delacroix," stocky, middle aged red-haired man said, shaking Derek's hand. "Director of Research and Development at Joule."

"Preparing to hit the road?"

"We plan to drive to Los Angeles and back," Henry said. "Several times, if possible."

"Two attempts have been made to steal this technology," Derek said. "The second time it was men with machine guns."

"The chase-car will have Judith and these three former Navy Seals," Henry said, pointing to three men.

"Those two will drive the tow truck," he added. "When they stop for meals or for the night, someone will stay with the cars."

"That's reassuring."

"Right now, we're checking for obvious defects, like loose wires," Judith said. "We don't want to break down for stupid reasons. We'll take a basic repair kit in the trunks. Spools of wire, two spare motors, etc. We're also installing radiation detectors on your generator."

An hour later, the convoy pulled out.

"Drive safely," Derek said, waving.

✳✳✳

"Now that they're gone," Derek told Vaughn. "I'd like to watch you build a generator from scratch. Maybe we can figure out how to do it on an assembly line."

"Our generators are a lot simpler than cars," Vaughn said. "Hell — they're simpler than car *engines*."

For the next hour, Derek watched and took mental notes as Vaughn assembled another Pincus generator.

Then he scanned Finnbar at Jacobson and Morse. It turned out that he'd pulled out of the short-sale too soon. Ten patients had died from the defective drug and hundreds had fallen sick, causing a team of attorneys to file a twenty-billion-dollar class-action lawsuit against Seshadri-Clarke.

Its stock was in free-fall.

Jacobson and Morse had made two hundred million more since yesterday. Finnbar and Morse were sharing a celebratory drink.

"The lawyers will make millions in fees," Mr. Morse said.

"There might even be some left over for the patients," Finnbar said. "I don't know where Evans gets his tips."

"We don't *want* to know," Mr. Morse said.

Derek focused on the workshop.

"We make everything from scratch except for these," Vaughn said, pointing to odd glass tubes with a bulge in the middle. "We order these from a company in the Czech Republic."

By lunchtime, the generator was almost finished, and Derek was intimately familiar with every step in its construction.

After lunch, Derek spent the two hours building a second generator with Vaughn Williams supervising.

At two, Derek called Gold Coast Realty and said he'd like to close on the Murakami house tomorrow, if possible. They'd contact Mrs. Murakami and would have the closing at ten Honolulu time.

Both generators tested out perfectly.

"You're hired!" Vaughn said.

They couldn't build any more generators because they had no more glass tubes. Derek told Vaughn to order a thousand more.

✳✳✳

Derek, Annie, Joyce and Reginald ate dinner at the Han Joo Chik Wine Bar in Flushing.

"Setting up an assembly line shouldn't be difficult," Derek said. "I built a working generator from scratch by myself."

"How are the Joule people doing?" Joyce said.

"They're in Youngstown, Ohio," Derek said. "They've stopped several times for gas for the tow truck and recharges for the chase car. Our car keeps chugging along."

"Two people in a green Ford sedan have been tailing them the whole way," Allie said.

"Can't they lose them?" Joyce said.

"A convoy of two cars and a tow truck?" Derek said. "Headquarters told them not to even try. They'll get the car's license plate and figure out who it is."

"They call headquarters a lot?" Joyce said.

"Every time they stop," Allie said. "When they passed a broken-down car, headquarters told them to tow it to a service station. For free."

"The Pincus Generator isn't producing any detectable radiation," Derek said.

"I could've told them that," Reginald said.

✳✳✳

Derek spent the next day flying over parts of Oz and comparing land masses with a memorized map of our world. The correspondence was extremely close.

Nowhere did he see any sign of organized intelligent life — cities or even villages — except for pods of dolphins. They were uniformly friendly. None of them had ever run across anything remotely like a boat or ship.

The other islands in Oz's version of Hawaii appeared to be deserted, and the Big Island had an active volcano.

He materialized on a black landscape as barren as the moon, its rocks so sharp and jagged they would've shredded his feet if he hadn't worn shoes.

The ground shuddered as a fountain hurled glowing lava hundreds of feet into the air, and it came crashing back.

Sulfur fumes choked him.

A river of lava rumbled past him, its heat singing his eyebrows.

He backed away until the heat and stench were bearable and followed its path to the sea.

At the shoreline, the lava hit the water in explosions of steam and lava-sprays that roared like never-ending thunder. One droplet landed on his sleeve and started to burn its way through, but he brushed it off.

"What a fierce and beautiful world you are," he said, musing that it was nothing like his childhood's bubblegum-colored Oz.

He took photos with his phone.

He returned to Oz's Waikiki Beach, knelt, and kissed the sand.

"We'll do right by you," he murmured, tears filling his eyes. "You magnificent world."

I'm talking to a planet as if it were a woman! What do I say if she answers me?

***

"You went *back* there?" Allie said.

"I scanned Professor Fischer," Derek said. "She decided the bacteria in the water were harmless Earth bacteria. Either they came from the stream or the jelly-jar. Look at these pictures!"

Allie gasped.

"I'll blow these up, get them framed, and hang them!" she said. "The one with lava going into the ocean is incredible."

"Oz is not such a boring place after all."

She smiled.

Derek beamed a suggestion at all of the Indigos. They agreed.

***

Dinner for all of them was a cookout at Waikiki beach on Oz. Luckily, it wasn't raining.

Derek brought steaks, and lap cheong from the Hong Kong Market in Flushing. Travis brought an iPod and Wendy managed to bring an amplifier and speaker — although parts of the table they'd been sitting on came with them.

Allie brought a hibachi and charcoal.

"Let's give this beach a name," Derek said, lighting the charcoal. "I'm sick of calling it 'Waikiki in Oz'."

"Destiny Beach!" Liz said. "And that is Destiny Bay."

They liked it.

308

"Let's call this Travis Island," Wendy said.

"No, *Wendy* Island!" Travis said.

"Arrival Island," Derek said. "The first place we came to in this world. Or First Island."

"What about the ocean?" Wendy said.

"Just call it 'the ocean'," Derek said. "There's really only one. In our world, oceans have different names because European explorers didn't know they were connected. Or call it 'Oz Ocean'."

They sat in the sand, cooked on the hibachi, played music, and ate — all the while making up names for different parts of Oz.

"It's weird," Wendy said. "That funny song we sang at Bass Lake Farm."

"Your summer camp, five years ago," Liz said.

"I forgot it, but now I remember all the words and the melody!"

They read it from her mind and sang:

> One morning in a fit of pique,
> Sing rickety-tickety-tin,
> One morning in a fit of pique,
> She drowned her father in the creek,
> The water tasted bad for a *week,*
> And we had to make do with gin, with gin.
> We had to make do with gin.

After four more stanzas of a woman murdering family members in gruesome and imaginative ways, the song ended with

> And when at last the police came by,
> Rickety-tickety-tin,
> And when at last the police came by,

Her little pranks she did not deny,
To do so she would have to *lie,*
And lying she knew was a sin, a sin.
Lying she knew was a sin.

Allie jumped up.

"An image flashed through my mind," she said. "Millions of Indigos, cities full of them."

"On this island?" Thomas said.

"All over this world. The strangest cities you can imagine. With high rises but not a single street or road. The closest thing they have to roads are hiking and jogging trails and sports arenas."

Chapter 44

The next morning, the Energistics corporate offices received a call from Eldon Trask himself.

"Our Joule has driven three thousand miles using your generator," he said. "Without a hiccup. We should talk."

"I'm going to my sister's wedding tomorrow in Hawaii. I can swing by Los Angeles on Thursday."

"I have a better idea. Suppose I have my jet pick you up in Honolulu, Thursday?"

"Thank you!" Derek said. "That's very kind of you."

Damn! I'll have to spend hours staring at clouds. Oh well ... that's why I get the big bucks.

Derek flashed the experience to Allie and told the Pincuses what had happened.

❋❋❋

Wendy decided to accompany her girlfriends on the flight to Honolulu. Annmarie and Jewel were both nineteen and had never been outside Boothbay Harbor before. Chloe had agreed be an informal chaperon for them. The Brocklesbys drove everyone to the airport.

"What's the flight number?" Ed asked.

"There isn't any," Wendy said. "We go to the General Aviation part of the airport and find our charter."

"A charter?"

"Yeah, Derek's been doing well in the stock market lately."

"I'd say so," Heidi said.

"There's a reason for that." Wendy sighed.

"Money is the root of all evil," Abigail said.

"Your eyes?" Chloe said to Wendy.

"Yes."

A pert lady in an Eagle Air Charter uniform whose name tag said "Odette" waited in the lobby. She held up a sign for the *Wendy and Travis Wedding Flight,* greeted them, and led them onto the tarmac to a short staircase attached to a jet bearing the Eagle logo.

They boarded.

The interior was like an elegant conference room, with a sofa, flat-screen TVs, a bar, a kitchen and a full bathroom where one could shower. An area in the back had a bedroom.

"Are we all here?" Odette said.

"I think so," Wendy said.

"Wow!" Annmarie said. "So this is what traveling by plane is like. Cool!"

"No!" Ed laughed. "Traveling by plane is like being packed like sardines."

"What about Thomas and Liz?" Heidi said.

"They traveled on ... their own. I'll explain."

"I guess we can take off then," Odette said. "I'll tell Captain Vollmer."

She went forward to the cockpit.

Captain Vollmer came on the speaker system and greeted the passengers, thanking them for using Eagle Air Charters and giving technical information about the flight: altitude, cruising speed, and duration.

It would take eight hours.

"Extravagance is the road to Hell," Abigail said. "The Reverend Felcher always says that."

"Thanks for noticing, aunty," Wendy said.

Annmarie and Jewel sat side by side, texting each other.

***

Derek teleported to NYU and ran into Professor Fischer.

"I wanted to tell you the fruits and water samples are harmless," she said.

"Fantastic!"

"I've talked to Professor Koppel, down the hall," she said. "He's a botanist. It turns out very few plants and animals are native to Hawaii. Most of the interesting ones were brought in by Polynesians or Europeans."

"I see."

"I asked him to compile a list of plants and animals to bring there if they would want to create a perfect ecology. He and his students debated this at great length. Here it is."

She handed him a list and he examined it.

"*Mangoes* and *papayas* aren't native to Hawaii?"he said.

She smiled and shook her head.

"*Grass?* Hawaii, *here,* has incredibly lush grassy meadows."

"We remade those islands in our image," Professor Fischer said. "Not always the best. I hope this list is a much better way."

"Thanks you *so much,* Professor Fischer!" he said. "And thank Professor Koppel."

"Of course, we cannot tell him the real reason for our interest."

"Someday, would you like to visit Oz?"

"*Es wäre fantastisch!*"

These ... *non-tropical* ... vegetables and fruits. Like carrots and potatoes. Will they grow in Hawaii?"

"Professor Koppel said Hawaiian soil is the best in the world. Things should grow *twice* as fast as elsewhere."

***

Derek had lunch with Allie in a diner near the gallery and he mentally summoned Wendy and Travis. Wendy came out of the ladies' room, and Travis staggered out of the mens' room, yawning.

"I was in the airplane restroom. It's really nice with a real shower!"

"It's five AM back home," Travis said. "You're lucky I'm not in pajamas."

"You're barefoot," Wendy observed.

"*Auwe!*" Travis moaned.

"You can go back to bed in a few minutes," Derek said, showing them all Professor Koppel's list. "Just memorize this."

"Roaches and termites came from *outside?*" Travis said.

"Brought in on ships," Derek said.

"I can get half of this stuff at the Hanneford Market in Boothbay," Wendy said. "Even mangoes and papayas. We need to get a tractor."

"See if it's possible to find an *electric* one," Derek said.

The soon-to-be wed couple left: Wendy to the restroom in her wedding flight, and Travis to his bedroom.

"I think those two will be *very* involved with Oz," Allie said. "They're pioneers at heart. It's their new toy."

"What about you?"

"I'm a city girl. It's hard to get excited about a wilderness, even one as beautiful as Oz."

"What about that future Indigo civilization?"

"I'd *love* to visit *that*. It won't be built unless somebody gives Oz some love."

✳✳✳

At one in the afternoon, Derek and Allie teleported to restrooms in the Gold Coast Realty office in Honolulu. The Realtor, Alvin Speer, shook their hands.

They hugged Jesse Murakami and spent the next half hour signing and initialing a tall stack of documents: title insurance, termite inspections, disclosures, etc.

As Derek did this, a strange feeling came over him, the sensation that a spirit eavesdropped on him, astounded. To this spirit, the Murakami house was smaller than a doll house, as insignificant as a speck of dust. The spirit marveled that *anyone* would expend time and effort to own something so unimportant.

The feeling passed.

Do my growing psychic powers mean I'm aware of the spirit-world even when I'm wide awake? Do spirits often look through our eyes, and I'm just becoming aware of it?

Allie flashed a look at him, sensing what had happened.

The house may be insignificant to you, Derek mentally addressed the spirit. *But to specks of dust like us, it's worthwhile.*

With affection and humor, a voice in his mind said he and Allie wouldn't always be specks of dust.

He focused on the real estate office.

"What does this term 'leasehold' mean?" Derek said.

"The house is on leased land," Mr. Speer said.

"We don't own the land?"

"Of *course* not. The house would've been *much* more expensive if it was fee-simple."

"Fee-simple?" Allie said.

"The land comes with the house," Mr. Speer explained.

"Like real estate everywhere else on Earth," Allie muttered. "Who are we paying this land-rental to?"

"The Howland Trust, of course," Mr. Speer said. "They own most of the North Shore."

"My sister's marrying Travis Howland tomorrow."

"That's fortunate," Mr. Speer said. "Maybe they'll give you the land as a wedding present. Even if they don't, the lease is coming up for renewal, and you'll get a good deal."

"This sale happened so quickly," Jesse said. "I'm not ready to go to Japan yet."

"You can stay in the house for another week," Allie said. "Wendy and Travis will spend their honeymoon in the Piikoi Palace."

"And I have sell all that furniture."

"We'll buy it for another $20,000," Derek said. "If that's OK with you."

"Wonderful!"

Derek wrote her a check.

"Just take your personal things," Allie said.

"So many memories in that house!" Jesse said, her eyes tearing up. "I raised two wonderful sons. My oldest was married there."

Allie hugged her again.

"I'm paying a million and a half for a pile of lumber?" Derek muttered.

With a sly grin, Mrs. Murakami quoted the popular bumper-sticker, "Lucky you live Hawaii."

✳✳✳

At three, they met the plane in the General Aviation part of Honolulu Airport. Limos from the Piikoi Palace picked every-one up and took them there, where they checked in.

Then, everyone except for aunt Abigail walked the two blocks to the Ala Moana Mall — a sprawling two-story open air complex of department stores, restaurants, and specialty shops.

Derek and Allie took Wendy to Bloomingdale's. Wendy insisted on getting an elegant black and gold dress.

"Not really a wedding dress," Allie said.

"You wore brown at your wedding."

"This is true."

"Can we get camping supplies?" Wendy said. "Travis and I want to go hiking in Oz."

The clerk told them there was a store with camping supplies across Ala Moana Boulevard.

They summoned Travis and bought him a blue pinstripe suit.

✳✳✳

That evening, they all met at a hibachi steak house called Takashi's of Tokyo.

"This whole city's like a giant Chinese restaurant," Aunt Abigail muttered. "Foreigners everywhere."

"Don't put any strong foreign spices on my meat!" she snapped at the chef, who was juggling knives.

Kurt was visibly drunk.

"Could you recommend a place to hold the reception?" Derek asked him.

"I can but I won't. This wedding is fucking loony-tunes!"

"Kurt!" Grace said, her eyes tearing up. "How can you say that?"

"Cuss-words at the table!" Aunt Abigail muttered. "The Reverend Felcher would have something to say about that."

"They've known each other four fucking days, and they're getting married?"

"There's a wonderful Japanese department store called Shirokiya," Heidi said. "With a *whole street* from medieval Kyoto in it. You can buy crafts and foods from that place. It's fascinating."

"We know each other very well, dad," Travis said.

"This is your *practice* wedding," Kurt said. "I'll attend the *real* ones."

"Will you bring Leilani Kam to them?" Travis growled.

Kurt paled and fixed Travis in a grim stare. Then he stood and left.

"I'm sorry, mom," he said, putting his arm around his mother. "I saw him with ... a woman."

I read his mind, he wordlessly added, *He's been on the prowl for a new Mrs. Howland for a while. Leilani's Wendy's age.*

Grace started sobbing.

Although Heidi tried to lighten the mood several times, the dinner had died an unnatural death.

Grace and Travis left before it was over.

"Latter-day *alii,* my ass!" Derek muttered.

"Potty-language from you too, Derek?" Aunt Abigail said. "You weren't raised that way!"

✳✳✳

Back at the hotel, Derek, Allie, and Chloe cornered the Brocklesbys and gave them The Talk.

"What's the punch line?" Ed laughed.

"That's it," Allie said.

"It's why I've been so successful on Wall Street," Derek said.

Chapter 45

Travis's mother moved out of the Howland house into a room at the Piikoi Palace that Derek secured for her. After the wedding, she'd live with a sister on Maui until she got her bearings.

As they assembled in the hotel lobby before going to the chapel, Luther Howland presented Wendy with a prenuptial agreement. Today, he wore a new aloha-shirt, shorts, and leather sandals.

"Don't sign it, honey!" Travis snapped. "A prenup is like planning for a divorce from the beginning!"

"Then you're cut off from the Howland Trust," Luther sneered. "Good luck surviving on your own!"

The Evans party boarded a caravan of complimentary hotel limos for the twenty minute ride.

✳✳✳

The Punahou School occupied a lush park dotted with white stone buildings in the foothills of the Koolau mountains. Curtains of rain shrouded the campus, giving it the dreamlike aura of a Renoir painting.

The chapel was a avant-garde cube with colorful faux

stained-glass strips embedded in its walls, bordered on one side by a grassy field and on the other by a lily pond.

After the Reverend Teague administered their vows, Travis and Wendy kissed.

Annmarie and Jewel cheered loudly and hooted.

A smattering of Howlands occupied the chapel's right side, and the Evans guests — including Grace Howland — occupied the chapel's left side. Several of them glared at the girls from Boothbay Harbor.

True to his word, Kurt Howland had not shown up.

"I thought she was a *good* girl," Aunt Abigail softly sobbed after noting that Wendy's dress wasn't white.

✳✳✳

The reception was a small affair in the Piikoi hotel dining room.

"It was so touching!" Muriel Howland said to Thomas. "The way Wendy's aunt was sobbing at the wedding."

"Yes, it was very touching," he replied, not wanting to elaborate.

Luther Howland sat next to Derek and Allie.

"I still can't believe Travis turned his back on one of the oldest families in the islands," he said. "For *that girl*. Maybe you can talk some sense into them. She can still sign the prenup."

"I'm not going to tell them how to live their lives," Derek said.

"Let me motivate you," Luther said. "You bought a house yesterday. Wendy signs the prenup, and I'll give you the land it's on. That'll double its value. She doesn't sign, and I won't renew your lease. You'll have two weeks to move the house or demolish it."

"And to think I wasn't sure we'd get along. Thanks for clearing that up."

Luther Howland stood and left.

"What do we do?" Allie said.

"We move the house," Derek shrugged. "This sort of thing must come up from time to time."

"Let's move it to Oz!" Travis said, sitting beside Derek with Wendy.

"That would be *so awesome!*" Wendy said, clapping her hands.

✳✳✳

That evening, Travis and Wendy met Derek and Allie and the Brocklesbys in their hotel room.

"What are the sleeping bags for?" Ed Brocklesby said.

"We're camping out in Oz tonight," Wendy said.

"That place exists?" Ed replied.

"Yeah," Travis said. "We'll have a whole world to ourselves. And we going to scout locations. For the you-know-what..."

"Why aren't there any people?" Ed asked.

"That's a good question," Derek said.

"Be *careful,* you two!" Allie said. *"Scan everything!"*

"Yes, maw," Wendy said, and the two vanished — sleeping bags and all.

A slack-jawed Ed stared at the empty space they left.

"I paid for a honeymoon suite, and they'd rather sleep on sand," Derek muttered.

"What's wrong with kids these days?" Allie laughed.

"What's Oz like?" Ed asked.

"It's this world with no people," Derek said. "I landed in the New York City part of Oz, and it's pure wilderness. Wild bison roam Flushing, Queens. The Hawaii part of it is Hawaii *before* the Polynesians got here."

"Did something kill the people off?" Heidi said.

"I don't know," Derek said. "There are no signs people *ever* existed. No ruins, no nothing. It's disturbing as hell."

"Wendy and Travis want to spend their honeymoon hiking and planting stuff," Allie said.

"Sounds like fun," Ed replied.

"We can take you there," Derek said. "I think they want some privacy tonight."

They went to bed. Derek and Allie put Wendy and Travis's honeymoon suite to good use.

✳✳✳

At five in the morning, Derek floated near the ceiling of a conference room in Riker's Island where Ustinov conferred with his attorneys. It was ten, New York time.

"It would be *great* if telepathy existed," Henry Vandermonde said. "But it doesn't."

"Why would it be great?" Ustinov said.

"Probing your brain would violate your privacy rights," Vandermonde said. "I can make a case for that. That would negate a lot of the evidence against you. Fruit of the poisoned tree and all that."

"Well, it *does,* goddamn it! Talk to Mrs. Pembroke!"

"She won't speak to us," Vandermonde said.

"I researched the Pembrokes," Mark Rothko, his legal assistant said. "They're *incredibly* dirty. Unauthorized genetic experiments with at least one dead student. Dozens of missing street people."

Not to mention her own son.

"We may be able to twist her arm, "Rothko said.

"Get on it!" Vandermonde said. "If Evens *is* telepathic, we have to figure out a way to prove it in court. Or at least create reasonable doubt."

***

At the breakfast buffet, Derek, Allie, the newlyweds, and the Brocklesbys sat together.

"Oz is so incredible," Wendy said. "We flew to Derek and saw elephants!"

"Derek?" he said.

"We named North America Derek," Travis said. "And South America's called Alessandra."

"Oh come on," Allie laughed.

"You found elephants?" Ed asked. "Was there a zoo?"

"No," Wendy said. "Furry elephants with weird tusks that curve all over the place. There are herds of them all over the middle of ... uh, Derek. That does sound weird when you're right in front of me."

"Woolly mammoths!" Derek said. "They're extinct in our world. Paleolithic men hunted them out of existence."

"They *hunted* them?" Wendy said. "Those cave-men must've been heavy-duty dudes."

"That almost proves humans never evolved in Oz," Derek said. "Or something wiped them out a *long* time ago. Before they left Africa."

"How long ago was that?" Travis said.

"*Homo erectus* was supposed to have migrated more than a million years ago," Derek said. "And *homo sapiens,* about 200,000. That's what they thought in my anthropology class. I think there were times when the entire human population dwindled to less than two thousand. Like during a volcano eruption in Sumatra. In our world, they managed to barely hang on. Maybe in Oz, they weren't so lucky."

"You really studied this stuff!" Heidi said.

"No. I slept through a class at NYU, but remember every

word of it now — and every word of the textbook. An Indigo thing."

"Sure!" Wendy said, reading Ed's mind. "We'll take you guys with us. It'll be fun."

"Watch out for saber-tooth tigers," Derek said.

"Cool!" Wendy said.

"Be careful," Allie said.

"I know," Wendy said. "I'll do the teleporting, and Travis will spot me."

"Why does he need to spot you?" Ed asked.

"If my spirit-body doesn't engulf you, stuff gets left behind. Amputated."

"Oh, OK. I don't really need to see..."

"Don't worry! I'll be careful."

"We found the perfect place for the Murakami house," Travis said. "On Destiny Beach."

"I cleared and excavated it in *two seconds,*" Wendy laughed. "We don't need no stinking bulldozers!"

Derek realized she'd made her spirit-body take the shape of a large cube and teleported, carrying rock, soil, and palm trees with her — leaving a bare surface as smooth as a pane of glass.

It shocked him.

He almost felt nostalgic for the time when he and Allie had been the only Indigos, when they'd owned it. Wendy and Travis were spinning it off in strange new directions.

Where would it end?

***

Derek and Allie arrived at the General Aviation section of the Honolulu Airport at nine to find the place packed with news media. Holding court in their midst was Eldon Trask himself.

"Here's the man whose invention will change the world," Mr. Trask said, pointing to Derek. "It has kept a Joule Roadster running continuously for seventy-two hours, covering more than four thousand miles."

Cameras turned to them.

Luckily, Derek and Allie wore their brown contacts.

"Reginald Pincus invented it," Derek said. "I simply recognized his genius. His invention will change the world, however. Someday, houses will have these generators and not be dependent on power grids."

"Isn't it true your grandfather is the Mafia Don, Carlo Giancana?" a reporter asked Allie.

"Unfortunately," she growled.

"Isn't it also true that he's a major investor in your firm?" the reporter said.

"No," Derek said. "He hasn't invested a dime in it. The last time we spoke, he threatened to kill me."

This elicited a flurry of questions, to which Derek and Allie replied, "No comment."

✻✻✻

The interior of Mr. Trask's jet looked very different from that of the one they'd chartered. A high-end workstation with large screen and virtual-reality goggles filled one end, and piles of notebooks and papers with scribbled diagrams and equations cluttered a table and the three seats around it.

With a sweep of his arm, Mr. Trask cleared a space for them to sit.

"Sorry for the ambush," he said. "I seem to attract media wherever I go. Did her grandfather really threaten to kill you?"

"Every family has its ups and downs," Allie sighed. "Or so I've heard."

"Ah," Mr. Trask sighed. "I guess mine has had more than a few of those. Of course they don't have teams of gunmen working for them."

"Going public will probably sour things even more," Allie said. "Not that I care."

"You think he'll act on that threat?" Mr. Trask said.

"No," Derek said. "He's probably satisfied with sabotaging our security clearance. It killed off our fifty million dollar navy contract."

Mr. Trask whistled.

Derek realized he was sitting on something, stood, and pulled a circuit-board from under himself.

"Oh *that's* where that went," Mr. Trask said, taking the board. "A controller for a Shrike rocket fuel valve motor. Bridgeport Robotics charges a hundred thousand for it, when we can make our own for two thousand."

The next two hours consisted of a delightful discussion with Mr. Trask. They discussed the future of transportation, space exploration and a thousand other topics.

Mr. Trask wanted to crash-test the generators and wanted "ruggedized" versions for aerospace applications.

They concluded that Joule would buy Pincus Generators from Energistics rather than trying to license the technology. Mr. Trask would announce a "strategic partnership" with Energistics.

And you thought we'd be staring at clouds, Allie wordlessly said.

In California, Mr. Trask took them on a tour of his Space Ventures factory and they discussed the difficulty of protecting intellectual property that cannot be patented.

***

Wendy and Travis and the Brocklesbys stood on Destiny Beach.

"It's incredible," Heidi said. "Like swimming in a sea of pure energy. Life force."

"That's what the spirit world feels like to us," Wendy said.

"Hey where did the hotels go?" Ed laughed, pointing to Diamond Head and the empty beach.

"You have a whole world to yourselves?" Heidi said.

"I want to see elephants," Ed insisted. "Or mammoths or whatever they are."

"I'll try to locate some," Travis said, lying on the sand.

"He'll fly in his spirit body to Derek and look for a herd," Wendy said. "Then we'll teleport over."

"You really going to call North America *Derek?*" Ed laughed.

"He hates it so ... yeah."

Travis opened his eyes and said, "You teleport and I'll spot."

✳✳✳

They all found themselves in a copse of trees on a vast grassy plain. A herd of a thousand huge animals grazed in the long grass — they might have been elephants were it not for their long brown fur and unusually long front legs. Their tusks formed white corkscrews.

"It looks like Africa," Ed murmured.

"You were never in Africa," Heidi said.

"It's like *movies* of Africa, damn it," Ed muttered. "She's always correcting me!"

"Except for the fur," Wendy said.

An image flashed through her mind of deep snow banks and the mammoths pushing forward through it — thrashing their lowered heads from side to side, using their tusks as snow plows.

Wendy told them of it.

"You can read animal's minds?" Heidi said.

"Yeah," Travis said. "All animals think something. They're not *da kine* rocket scientists, but they think."

"Looks like we're in for rough weather," Heidi said, pointing to a black wall of clouds on the horizon.

The black wall raced toward them, spanning half the sky and roaring like a cheering stadium.

"It's alive!" Wendy said. "A huge consciousness made up of many small ones. Birds!"

The tsunami of birds — now in three visibly-distinct layers at least a hundred feet up — closed off the sky, turning day into twilight. A few separated from the flock and circled the people. In the dim light, they looked like slender gray or light brown pigeons. They rejoined their flock.

Bird droppings rained down like putrid sleet.

"Now I know what a cat box feels like," Ed muttered.

Wendy and Travis returned them to their hotel rooms.

✳✳✳

After they made love and Allie drifted off to sleep, Derek floated in his spirit-body above their bed.

"The common denominator is Derek Evans," a voice said. "Ustinov is claiming he's a telepath and Lee Kuan-Yu interviewed with him."

He floated near the ceiling of a conference room with four people sitting around a large table. The voice belonged to Renard Moreau, director of something called the National Clandestine Service.

This is in CIA headquarters!

"It's a coincidence," a woman named Susan Winkler said.

"I don't believe in them," Mr. Moreau said. "The Chinese intelligence service is in the throes of the biggest crisis in its history, and it's connected to Evans."

"If he's a telepath, he could be CIA's best asset ever," Ms. Winkler said.

"Or our worst nightmare," the fourth man — a case officer named Mitchel Wilkins — said.

"Go *deep* on Evans," Mr. Moreau said. "I want to know everything he's done and everyone he's spoken to over the past ten years."

Derek returned to his bed and fell asleep.

Chapter 46

The next morning, Mrs. Pincus handed Derek a sheaf of notes — requests for interviews from Forbes, the Wall Street Journal, and several local newspapers and TV talk shows.

"I saw your interview on TV," she said. "Reporters will be crawling out of the woodwork after your 'death threat' remark."

"I have a *big mouth*," he muttered.

"There's no such thing as bad publicity," she said.

Wendy flashed him a mental message that she and Travis had helped Mrs. Murakami pack and the house was now empty.

"We're moving!" she said in his mind.

Derek spoke to their new Research and Development Department — consisting of an electrical engineer named Ralph Mortenson — and asked him to develop a power-converter to produce a three-phase 240 volt electrical service suitable for a house.

A thirty-something woman appeared at the door.

"How do you respond to Ustinov's claim that you're a telepath?" she said. Derek realized she was a reporter from the Daily Mail. "His attorney says he can prove it."

330

"You're trespassing," he muttered.

"He claims you violated his privacy rights and is demanding the charges against him be dropped."

"He's a confessed murderer!" he replied, calling the security guard.

✳✳✳

The next surprise visitor to the Energistics headquarters was Cynthia.

"We had something so special together," she breathed, stroking his face. "Our love knows no bounds."

"We had nothing," Derek growled, pushing her hand away. "You dated me to make Berkowitz jealous, and now you're his corporate whore. The best thing I got from you was Norton."

How the hell did he find out? Cynthia wondered, stunned. *Does he have private investigators tailing me?*

She regained her composure and screamed, "You owe me big-time! I'm pregnant with your child."

"The father is Neville Wong, a visiting businessman from Hong Kong. You were doing a three-way with him and Berkowitz. When the baby's born, everyone will realize that two whites don't make a Wong."

"Motherfucker!"

✳✳✳

He went into his office and mentally contacted all Indigos in the world.

"What if they decide telepathy violates peoples' privacy rights?" Allie said. "They outlaw it?"

"Like outlawing *da kine* breathing," Travis said. "Can they outlaw *us?*"

"If we have to," Derek said. "We move to another timeline where they don't know about us."

"We told too many people," Renata said.

"No, mom. The people we told are *wonderful*. Our troubles are coming from assholes who knew all along."

They arrived at a consensus.

Derek spent the next hour making phone calls.

✳✳✳

At lunchtime, he went to Manhattan Bullion Merchants on 47th street and 5th Avenue and purchased 1400 one-kilo gold bars, issued by Credit Suisse. He wired a bit more than 50 millions dollars from his Continental Bank account. He also paid them to have an armored car deliver it to the Energistics headquarters.

✳✳✳

Mrs. Pincus watched, open-mouthed, as uniformed, armed guards came in carrying gold bars and stacked them on a wooden pallet in the back room.

"We don't have security for that much gold," the building's security guard said. "The floor probably can't handle that weight for any length of time."

"It won't be here long," Derek said.

When they were finished, Derek lay on the floor and tried to engulf the gold with his spirit-body. Allie appeared, spotting for him, and he teleported it all to Destiny Beach in Oz.

"What's that?" Travis said.

"Our treasury. If something goes wrong, we'll have some money to fall back on. Gold is valuable in any timeline with people in it."

"You going to leave it on the beach?"

"No. I want to find a flat spot in Diamond Head crater and move it there," Derek said.

"I'll do it," Travis said.

As he was about to return to the office, he spotted the Murakami house nestled in grove of palm trees. The house's concrete slab was perfectly situated on the area Wendy had cleared, with a foot-wide margin on all sides. Although the house had passed a termite-inspection, Derek felt better about having a barrier like that.

"Nice location!" he said. "Did the move go OK?"

"*Ono!* Wendy dug a cesspool and well. Ed told us how to put a water pump in the well and we connect the drain pipes to the cesspool. Just need electricity now. No *huhu,* bruddah!"

"Did you shut off the water in Hawaii before you moved the house?"

"*Auwe!*" Travis muttered and vanished.

✳✳✳

Derek returned to the office.

"What was that all about?" Mrs. Pincus said.

"Insurance, in case things go south. Our big secret might not be secret much longer."

"A problem for the company?"

"No, the company's going to do fine. Allie and I may have problems."

"You two *are* the company!"

"Don't worry. Nothing's gone wrong yet. Are you and Reginald free for dinner in your favorite restaurant at seven tonight?"

"That's short notice," Mrs. Pincus said.

"I'm sorry," Derek said. "Things are spinning out of control and I have to get ahead of them. I plan to make a big announcement."

"We'll be there!"

The afternoon was spent people and making calls.

One was to Renard Kolodny's secure phone at the CIA.

"Derek Evans here. You wanted to go deep on me. Here's your chance."

***

All the world's Indigos and those who knew them gathered in the banquet hall. Energistics employees sat together at a table in the center.

Eldon Trask participated via a video conference system.

"I'd like to thank you for attending this event," Derek said. "I'll get to the point. For the past two decades, the late Harry Pembroke conducted illicit experiments. He developed a DNA-altering virus and tested it on people without their knowledge or consent. As for why he did this, you have to ask his widow."

Mrs. Pembroke tearfully nodded.

"We are the fruit of these experiments," Derek said, indicating the other Indigos with a wave of his hand. "The now-dormant virus altered our DNA to the point where we are technically no longer human. You may ask Professor Fischer here about that. She and her colleagues will be studying us."

Professor Fischer stood, looked around, and awkwardly bowed.

Derek explained their experiences with the spirit-world, teleportation and other timelines, including Oz.

People ordered food and lined up at the open bar. A cluster of people surrounded Professor Fischer and Ian Roberts.

Finnbar and a twenty-something raven-haired beauty in a slinky black evening gown came up to Derek's table. Finnbar introduced her as his wife Fiona. Derek invited them to join him.

"Jesus boyo!" Finnbar said to Derek. "You could've kept quiet about telepathy!"

"Is it illegal?" Derek said.

334

"It will be. When this gets out, the SEC will bar you from coming within a hundred yards of a brokerage firm. Maybe we can close some quick deals before that?"

Wendy and Travis came to their table, thanked them for the dinner and vanished.

"These kids are on their honeymoon and spend it mucking about in Oz," Derek muttered.

"A truly amazing illusion!" Fiona said. "I'm a bit of an amateur magician myself. Those two were holographic images, right?"

"That would be one way to produce that effect," Allie chuckled.

"But their voices seemed to come *from* the images, and the lip-synchronization was *perfect.* Parabolic directional speakers, right?"

"If you really can teleport," Mr. Trask said. "Teleport to my location now."

Derek obliged.

***

Eldon Trask was in a conference room with two engineers at Space Ventures, and they nearly fainted as Derek materialized.

"That insane rant of yours was true?" Mr. Trask said.

"Every word of it. We feel our friends and business partners deserve to know."

"Can you travel to other planets?"

"Probably, but I'd need a spacesuit. I'd hate to go to Mars dressed like this."

They chuckled.

"The world as a whole doesn't know," Derek said. "Can you imagine what society will make of us when they do? People who can cross national boundaries at will? Who can get into anything, rob any bank? I can hack any computer account in the world, because I know everyone's password. I cringe at what lies ahead. We may have to flee this country ... or even this timeline."

"Then why come out with it now?"

"Some very nasty people have always known," Derek said, telling them of his war with the Ustinov gang. "Now that they're on trial, they'll compel me to prove it in court. And the CIA's investigating us."

"How do you explain teleportation?" Trask said. "It appears to violate a lot of physical laws. Like conservation of mass-energy and momentum."

"Angular momentum, too," Derek said, launching into his ideas about the spirit world and the universe being a kind of computer game.

"That isn't science, it's metaphysics!"

"Ideas of calculus grew out of questions like 'how many angels can stand on the head of a pin?'. Science hasn't caught up with the philosophy."

Mr. Trask stared out the window onto the factory floor.

"You need a spacesuit?" he finally said. "We may be able to fit you with one. We're developing a cool-looking one."

"You'd like to develop a machine that can do what I do," Derek said.

"Damn right."

"Since I don't know how it works, we should follow the biology."

"Professor Fischer?"

"And her group in Munich."

"OK, Mr. Evans," Mr. Trask said, standing. "I need to make some calls and become an expert on quantum mechanics. We will be in touch regarding the spacesuit. Or will you just know when we're ready?"

"I should get back to my guests."

They shook hands and Derek vanished.

***

That evening, Derek and Allie flew to Oz's version of the Caribbean sea.

The only animal life in the vicinity was a pod of humpback whales, frolicking and singing to each other. One of them breached, seeming to wave at them with its dorsal fin.

Under a cloudless sky, in water as calm and warm as a bath, they made love.

"We baptized this place," she laughed. "Now it's ours. The Caribbean's *perfect*."

"We should give it an Oz-name."

"The Sea of Desire ... between the continents of Derek and Alessandra."

Chapter 47

Derek teleported to the workshop without trying to hide — but no one noticed his arrival.

Vaughn Williams turned and slapped him on the back, saying, "That was a hell of a show last night!"

"Thanks! Have you guys been working on the power converter?"

"Done," Mr. Mortenson said. "I can get two hundred fifty amps out of it. Probably more when I refine it."

"Fantastic!" Derek said. "Let's install it in a test house."

"I'll get the pickup trick," Vaughn said.

"Not necessary," Derek said as Wendy and Travis appeared. They all teleported to the Murakami house.

Vaughn Williams and Mr. Mortenson stared in shock.

"Last night was not a magic show," Derek said.

"Where the hell are we?" Mr. Mortenson said. "It looks a little like Hawaii, but..."

"It's Oz, like I said last night," Derek said. A parallel universe that's like ours, except the Earth seems uninhabited."

"A parallel universe?" Vaughn silently mouthed.

"How do we hook this up?" Derek said.

"Huh?" Mr. Mortenson said. "Uh, just connect those three terminals to the house service."

Derek did this and activated the Pincus generator. The house-lights came on, the water-pump rumbled to life, and the gauge on the pressure-tank registered pressure rising until it reached 30psi.

"Some ono!" Travis shouted, hugging Mr. Mortenson. "Now we got running water and can do laundry."

"We can even take a *bath*," Wendy said.

"Yeah, God forbid you use your honeymoon suite," Derek said.

"We like having our own *whole world*," Wendy said.

A disheveled Annmarie and Jewel staggered out of the house.

"What?" Derek exclaimed.

"They got kicked out of their hotel room," Wendy said. "So I said they could crash here. They're sleeping on the sofa and the floor."

"We were in a wet tee-shirt contest," Annmarie said.

"I *won* a wet tee-shirt contest!" Jewel said. "And these cute boys were so generous and gave us wine and beer."

"You're under age!" Derek said.

"They said not in Hawaii," Jewel said.

"Yes in Hawaii," Derek said.

"We invited them to our room," Jewel said. "Then a bunch of other kids came with them and told Chloe to F-off when she asked them to leave."

"They were peeing off the balcony on people," Annmarie said. "It was so funny."

"They broke some furniture too," Jewel said.

"The cops came and arrested some of them," Annmarie said. "The hotel manager told us to just get the hell out."

"Chloe's super upset," Wendy said. "She's crying in her room now."

✳✳✳

Derek teleported to Chloe's room and knocked on the wall. She looked up, and he hugged her.

"I hate to be judgmental but those boys looked like total losers," she sobbed. "They made lewd jokes about Annmarie right in front of us. If this had been a horror movie, those two girls would've been the first ones to check out the growling sound from the creepy basement. I don't think I was *ever* as young and dumb as them."

"They're fine now. They're trapped in Oz."

He explained Oz to her and they teleported.

✳✳✳

Chloe looked around Destiny Beach in wonder and, when she saw Annmarie and Jewel, she said, "I'm *very* disappointed in you two."

"We're sorry," they both said.

"It's too bad there's one convention *kine* in Honolulu," Travis said. Can't find you another hotel room."

"Yep," Wendy chimed in. "You'll just have to stay here until it's time to go home."

"You're going to take us on safari, right?" Jewel said.

"You're taking them to the *mainland?*" Derek said.

"Yeah," Wendy said. "When Ed and Heidi can join us. We'll be *very careful.*"

"Safari?" Chloe said.

Derek explained.

"I wouldn't mind seeing woolly mammoths myself," Vaughn Williams said.

"Maybe Allie and I should go with you," he sighed. "More people to teleport out if things go south."

Derek ferried Vaughn Williams and Mr. Mortenson back to the workshop.

***

They all teleported to an area that would've been near Los Angeles on Earth. On Oz, it had a grassy plain with a herd of grazing mammoths.

They snapped pictures.

Wendy suggested another place to visit, a surprise.

They teleported and found themselves standing on the edge of a small island in the middle of a bay. An impenetrable forest covered the shoreline, and a chilly wind blew.

"Guess where we are!" she said.

"It looks familiar, somehow," Heidi said.

"Oh, my God!" Ed exclaimed. "This is Boothbay Harbor. We're on MacFarland Island. You know, that little island in the middle of the bay with a lighthouse."

"Oh, yeah!" Heidi said. "There's no lighthouse here."

"No boats, no piers, no nothing," Ed agreed.

"Look in the water," Wendy said.

Just below the waterline, they saw a six-foot long lobster, its claws easily able to sever one's arms.

"That's got to be a hundred pounds," Heidi said.

"We could walk across the bay on lobsters' backs," Wendy said.

As she said that, an enormous brown bear crashed through the forest line and scooped a four-foot long fish from the water. It looked like a salmon.

"OK," Wendy said. "I'm putting a teleport envelope around everyone. Half the island will come with us."

"Why?" Jewel said.

"Bears can swim."

An ear-splitting roar resounded in their chests like thunder and echoed off the hills around the bay.

The bear turned.

"A smilodon," Travis said. "Sabertooth cat. I looked it up."

The smilodon stood five feet tall — twice the size of any lion — with fangs that extended a foot below its jaw. Its fur was orange with black spots.

The bear reared up on its hind legs — standing a good nine feet tall — and faced off with the smilodon.

"The Oz movie had lions and tigers and bears," Heidi said.

"This Oz has things that *eat* lions and tigers and bears," Ed added.

"Cool!" Jewel and Annmarie both said, snapping pictures with their phones.

In an orange flash, the smilodon knocked the bear on its back and sank its fangs into it. Fountains of blood gushed from the bear's chest, pooling on the ground and staining the water.

"This is getting too real for me," Allie said.

"Oh come on!" Jewel whined. "I want to see him eat the bear."

They teleported back to Destiny Beach.

✳✳✳

The rest of the girls' stay in Oz was uneventful. At the end of the week, Wendy and Travis teleported them to the airport for the ride home, and Derek and Allie joined them.

As they said their goodbyes to the girls, Abigail, and the Brocklesbys, Annmarie cocked her head to one side and said, "Please, Mr. Evans. Please bite my neck."

"It's doesn't work that way, honey," Allie said.

"We're not vampires," Derek said.

"You guys are the coolest people in the world," Annmarie said. "We want to be like you."

They returned home with cell-phones full of pictures.

Wendy and Travis's honeymoon ended.

This, of course, didn't change their lives one iota. They continued exploring Oz and planting vegetable gardens.

They signed up to start their studies in the summer semester at the University of Hawaii. Course-offerings in the summer were limited so they could only take a single course each: Wendy signed up for A Survey of Astronomy and Travis for Introduction to Biology I.

Derek and Allie gave them the Murakami house.

Chapter 48

The next morning, Derek appeared at the Space Ventures plant at eight, local time.

"Like a genie from a bottle!" Eldon Trask laughed, shaking his hand. "Dr. Brunetti here is head of our space-suit development program."

The lab-coated middle-aged man standing beside Mr. Trask just stared at Derek with his mouth open.

Derek offered his hand.

Dr. Brunetti stared at Derek's hand for a moment — as though inspecting it for tumors or fungi. He came to his senses and shook it.

"We have made some major breakthroughs in space-suit technology," Mr. Trask said.

"Question!" Dr. Brunetti said. "Why wasn't there a sonic boom when you appeared?"

"Hmm," Mr. Trask said. "That *is* a good question."

"I've wondered that myself. I think *volumes* get swapped when I teleport."

"So every time you go to Oz..." Mr. Trask said.

"Oz air winds up here," Derek said.

"You could be contaminating our world with deadly bacteria!" Dr. Brunetti said.

"It doesn't seem to have been dangerous. Oz doesn't have humans so there aren't any bacteria adapted to infect us."

Dr. Brunetti led them into a walled-off section of the hangar, punching buttons on a keypad and looking into an retina-scanner.

They entered a shed with racks of what looked like enormous, brightly-colored garment-bags.

"Since NASA's heyday, space suits have had one *major* problem," Mr. Trask said. "They had to be custom-made for the person who wore them. We want generic space-suits *anyone* can wear."

Dr. Brunetti helped Derek step into one of the garment-bags, which turned out to have arms and legs, and zippered it up. It looked like a colorful burlap sack hanging over him.

"Now, press the red button," Dr. Brunetti said.

Derek did so, and the suit gave off a high-pitched hum and contracted until it fit him like a glove.

"It fits itself to your body contours," Dr. Brunetti said. "As if custom-made for you. The blue button causes it to relax into a loose sack again."

"That's fantastic! Does it have little motors in it?"

"Artificial muscle," Dr. Brunetti said. "A special polymer that contracts when electrical pulses are fed to it. We're using it in robots, too."

"The suit contains a shear-thickening fluid that hardens when shocked," Mr. Trask said. "Protecting you from micro-meteorites."

"It looks so cool!" Derek exclaimed, looking into a full-length mirror. "Like Commander Shepard in the *Mass Effect* games!"

"Legal tells us this is different enough to not infringe," Mr. Trask said.

Derek registered shock.

"Yeah," Mr. Trask said. "We wanted it to look cool."

Derek fastened and sealed the helmet to the suit and posed in front of the mirror.

"I'd like you to take this transmitter to Mars," Mr. Trask said, pointing to a two-foot tall device on the floor with a dish.

"Uh," Derek said. "Where is Mars? I mean, as the crow flies. Or as the soul flies."

"Ah, yes," Mr. Trask replied. "We have an mechanized arrow outside the factory pointing to the current position of Mars. At the moment it's about twenty degrees above the horizon and rising."

"Let's do this!"

"If your theory about volume-swapping is correct and you teleport to space," Dr. Brunetti said. "You'll be swapping your body for a vacuum. There's going to be a huge sonic-boom."

"We can use the vacuum chamber," Mr. Trask said, pointing to what looked like a bank-vault. They carried the transmitter into it, stepping over the door's high threshold. Derek entered the chamber and they closed and locked its door.

✳✳✳

As the pumps began to evacuate the chamber, the heads-up display in the spacesuit came alive and displayed the air pressure. The air-pumps' rumble faded as the pressure dropped. According to the heads-up display, the pressure inside the suit remained stable.

Finally, Derek stood alone in complete silence.

"Can you hear me?" Mr. Trask's voice boomed in the helmet.

"Yes. I'm going to try to get out of body."

"Don't let me disturb you."

Derek managed to get out of body and tried to engulf the transmitter with his spirit-body. Allie's spirit appeared and helped to spot him. He located the motorized arrow's faint image outside the factory and imagined an infinite line extending from it. He instantly saw a brilliant white line in the spirit-world extending into the distance.

It's like a cursor.

He raced along it until he encountered a huge object — a whole world — and hovered over its surface.

He materialized.

Derek stood under a pink sky on a rust-colored desert with the transmitter beside him. Orange and brown clouds of dust whipped around him with dust-devils hovering in the distance. He turned the transmitter on by pressing a button on it, and a flashing blue light rewarded him.

He returned to the vacuum chamber.

"OK, let the air back in," he said. "I'm done."

"When are you going to Mars?"

"I'm back from Mars or ... someplace."

Air roared into the chamber, the door opened, and Derek removed his helmet.

"Wherever you went, it wasn't Mars!" Mr. Trask said.

"How so?"

"You were gone less than a minute. It takes a radio signal *twelve minutes* to reach Mars. Traveling at the speed of light! A round-trip should've take almost half an hour."

"OK, I gave it a shot," Derek said, carefully taking off the spacesuit. "I love this thing. I could use it to explore the solar system in Oz. How about five million dollars for it?"

"It's a prototype," Mr. Trask said. "Not ready for prime-time. It's full of proprietary technology."

"Thumbnails coming in," Dr. Brunetti said. "From the transmitter."

"Thumbnails?" Mr. Trask said.

"It's been about twelve minutes," Derek said.

They went into the control room and watched the monitor. Tiny, grainy images covered it and then a high-resolution image formed — one excruciating scan-line at a time. When it had completely downloaded — forty-five minutes later — it showed Derek in the spacesuit with a rust-colored desert in the background and the Space Ventures logo at the bottom.

"Sure as hell looks like Mars," Mr. Trask murmured.

"See! I *told* you I went to Mars. I'll pay *ten* million for the spacesuit."

"It's yours, Trask mumbled. "Take it. No charge."

"You had to travel at least *thirty* times the speed of light," Dr. Brunetti said. "Maybe faster."

"We could experiment some more and measure it precisely," Derek said. "Want to do that?"

"I need to think," Mr. Trask mumbled. "Think everything through."

"I should get back to Energistics anyway. OK, if I take the space suit?"

"Sure."

Derek teleported to the Murakami house with the space suit and then the Energistics workshop.

That evening Derek, Allie, and Renata watched the news in

their Flushing apartment. The big story was the Space Ventures "secret space program" and a possible astronaut on Mars.

Ground stations all over the world had picked up Derek's image in the Martian desert. An astrophysicist from Jodrell Observatory in England said the image was genuine and appeared to be coming from the northern Cydonia region. The Russians called the picture of an astronaut was an "obvious hoax," although they admitted the signal came from a place on Mars where no previous probe had landed.

The news show featured a retired NASA engineer named Walt Maginnis who said Space Ventures had to have launched the rocket early last Spring. Oddly, no record existed of a launch then with enough power to reach Mars — so it must've been an "unauthorized launch."

Mr. Maginnis pointed out that an unauthorized launch would be illegal.

"It's necessary to reroute all air traffic away from the launch site."

"Surely," the TV anchor said. "Launching a rocket cannot go *completely unnoticed.*"

"He did some early launches from the Kwajalein Atoll in the Marshall Islands," Mr. Maginnis said. "A launch there wouldn't attract much attention."

Efforts to reach Trask had been unsuccessful.

"He should've left off the company logo," Derek said. "Then it would've just been an unsolved mystery."

"Not our problem," Allie said. "Want to go back to Mars?"

"No. The beaches are a lot better in Oz."

Chapter 49

The night of Allie's big opening arrived. New York's glitterati thronged Indigo East and chatted with Allie and a few of the artists she represented. Jessica Grey from the Times interviewed Allie.

Caterers served silver bowls of buttered popcorn and magnums of *Veuve Clicquot 'La Grande Dame'*.

That champagne occupied a special place in Allie's heart.

Derek joined them.

Allie had blown up Derek's photo of lava pouring into the ocean and put an elegant koa wood frame on it — with a brass plaque bearing the caption "Volcano Island in Oz."

"What is the significance of it?" one man said. "Does Oz represent the 'House on the Hill'? The perfect society without the flaws of ours?"

The man wore black leather pants, a red silk blouse and bright yellow sunglasses.

"I hope our Oz turns out like that."

"And the lava flowing into the ocean represents creative frenzy?"

"Uh, yeah."

The conversation ended when unexpected guests appeared on the scene: Carlo Giancana, Robert Accardo and four large men in suits.

Carlo came up to an astonished Derek and hugged him.

That's as much of an apology you'll ever get, Allie wordlessly said to him. *I'm amazed he went this far.*

Then Carlo hugged Allie and congratulated her on the gallery opening.

✳✳✳

After a magical evening, Derek and Allie went-out-of-body and floated home, preparing to teleport.

Four men awaited them in the apartment.

They teleported to the Tung-Bo restaurant and called the police.

A police car with two police arrived fifteen minutes later — a burly young man named Bob Kelly and a young black-haired woman named Marina Volkova — and Derek met them on the street outside the restaurant.

"We heard people talking in our apartment and it looks as if the door's been jimmied."

Derek accompanied them up to the apartment.

"Open up," Officer Kelly shouted, banging on the door. "It's the police."

Machine-gun fire erupted through the wooden door, knocking Kelly down. Derek and the Officer Volkova ducked around the corner. Derek ran to the door and took several hits while dragging Officer Kelly to safety, as Volkova frantically called for backup.

Derek reset.

As a man attempted to leave, Officer Volkova fired, wounding him, and sending him crawling back into the apartment.

When hallway doors opened and heads popped out, she told them to stay in their apartments.

Fifteen minutes later, two large black vans arrived and unloaded a SWAT team. They took up positions in the hallway and the back yard, as an ambulance took Officer Kelly away.

A half hour later, the four men surrendered. By then, Officer Kelly had died.

***

Derek and Allie spent the rest of the night answering detectives' questions at the 109th Precinct.

They told them everything.

"You two belong in a fucking psych ward," Detective Nolan said. "We're trying to solve a crime and you're stark raving mad."

At midnight, an officer came in and whispered something to Detective Nolan.

"He told you the four suspects are dead," Derek said.

"An officer named Greg Martinez slipped strychnine into their food," Allie said.

"What?"

"We're telepaths," Derek and Allie both said.

The door opened and two men in suits entered the interrogation room.

"The questioning ends now," one of them said, showing his FBI identification.

"Everything they told you is classified at the highest level," the other man said. "All records of this session are to be destroyed, and you are not to discuss it with anyone. To do so will incur a fine of up to one point five million dollars and up to twenty five years in a federal penitentiary."

"You've got to be shittin me!" Detective Nolan snapped.

352

"Tonight's meeting never happened," the second man said. "You were home in bed. Just ask your wife. We've already spoken to her."

Derek realized this man was named Antares Hoskins, and he worked for the CIA.

"Closing the barn door a week after the cows left," Derek muttered. "*I* was denied security clearance. Will you arrest me for what I know?"

They ushered Derek and Allie out of the police station into a waiting black van.

"Where does this leave us?" Allie said.

"We provide safe passage to a safe house," Antares said, as the van pulled into the street.

"Can't we just check in to the Plaza for the night?" Derek said.

"We're not budgeted for that," Antares said.

"We'll pay out of pocket, of course."

"I'm afraid that's…" A loud crash cut him off and rocked the van as a garbage truck impacted it. Men in black ski masks ripped open the van's doors and yanked Derek and Allie out. After cuffing their hands behind their backs, they stuffed them into another van.

As the second van lurched into motion, Derek and Allie teleported to the Champagne Bar at the Plaza, making no special effort to hide their arrival. Nobody noticed.

"Oh, shit!" Allie said, pointing to a severed hand clinging to Derek. They wrapped it in a newspaper someone had left on a table.

After champagne and popcorn, they checked into a Carnegie Suite, put the wrapped hand in the refrigerator, and passed out, exhausted.

✳✳✳

They had sugar-covered lox, eggs, and coffee for breakfast in the Palm Court, and contacted the others. Thugs had attempted to kidnap Derek's parents and Renata, but they'd easily escaped; Thomas and Liz, to the Murakami house, and Renata to her favorite hotel in Taormina, Sicily. A team had attacked Carlo Giancana, but his bodyguards had driven them off.

Others had the Howland house in Hawaii under surveillance but hadn't decided whether to act.

"Oh my God," Allie sighed, holding up a New York Times article entitled "Mafia Princess Opens Art Gallery."

"That's all that registered with those pea-brains?" Derek said.

"Maybe it'll help," she said. "Intellectuals and culture-vultures get a thrill out of hobnobbing with gangsters."

"May I join you?" Renard Moreau said, wincing at the sight of their breakfast.

"Be our guest," Derek said.

"You didn't have to check in under your own names," Renard said. "We would've found you."

"I think we'll decline your kind offer of a safe house," Allie said. "I hope your people weren't harmed."

"Severely wounded egos," Renard said. "I know, it was pathetic on our part. Greg Martinez has told us what little he knows. We think this was a Chinese operation but we can't be sure."

"One of the people who snatched us left something behind," Derek said, handing Renard the newspaper-wrapped severed hand. "You might be able to pull prints from it."

Renard's eyebrows shot up.

"He was gripping my arm when we teleported."

"To answer your question, yes," Allie said. "We're willing to work as *occasional* consultants to the CIA."

***

They returned to Allie's apartment in Flushing, fed Norton, and cleaned up. The four men had ripped their furniture to pieces, searching for God knows what.

Derek called Praetorian Security. A half hour later, Royce Watkins showed up.

"I can't take it anymore," Allie sobbed. "They'll never stop coming after us. We'll never be safe."

Derek hugged her.

"We'll get a beautiful home," Derek said. "With a nice studio for you. And it'll be in a *totally* safe place."

"I don't know what to say," Royce said. "They were pros, I mean the best of the best. They used a mainframe to hack the door controls."

Derek scanned the Energistics workshop and headquarters. Their headquarters had been pillaged, and Mrs. Pincus and her staff were cleaning up. The workshop was intact because the security guard had called the police, and they'd arrived in time to stop the break-in.

They'd left Indigo East alone.

Derek and Allie ferried her remaining paintings and easel to a storage room at Indigo East, and then took Norton to the Murakami house. Derek pulled a printout from the Pincus Generator for Vaughn Williams and Mr. Mortenson to analyze.

"Maybe we should take Renard up on his offer of a safe house," Derek said.

"I know," Allie said. "We're putting people in danger just by living in an apartment."

"As Travis would say, I just had *one idea kine*," Derek said.

"You're a certifiable fucking genius!" she said, hugging him.

Derek dropped the printout off at the workshop, dropped Norton off at the Murakami house, and rejoined Allie.

✳✳✳

Derek and Allie stood outside the *Ristorante Alberto.* A sign on the door said "Closed Mondays."

"Ready?" Derek said.

Allie shook her head, closed her eyes, gulped, and then said, "OK."

They teleported into the restaurant — and ran into Allie.

They stared at each other for a moment.

"If this is a bad time, we can leave," Indigo Allie said.

"N...n...no!" the other Allie said. "Derek! Come out here!"

Derek emerged from the kitchen, stared at them, and hugged them.

They all sat and had a long talk. After comparing dates, they realized that travel from their original timeline to the one with Culinary Derek and Allie seemed to move them five years into the future.

Culinary Derek and Allie told them about their children, Tony and Loretta.

Indigo Derek and Allie told them about their battle with the Ustinov gang, their trips to Hawaii, and Energistics Corporation.

"Your lives are so *goddamn* exciting!" Culinary Allie said.

"Too exciting!" Indigo Allie muttered.

"I wish I'd taken that red pill," Culinary Derek sighed.

"Most timelines have us getting murdered after taking it," Indigo Derek said. "I was just lucky. And you wouldn't have met Allie."

"So you guys want to ...crash here for a while?" Culinary Allie said. "We can't loan you much money. Business hasn't been good lately."

"We don't need money," Indigo Allie said. "Indigos are

356

good at making money, *shitloads* of it. We have lots of money at home, which we probably shouldn't use here."

Culinary Allie's face lit up.

"Just look into the future and see tonight's lottery numbers," Culinary Derek said. "The MaxiMillion Lottery is up to a half billion dollars."

"No," Indigo Derek said. "There's no such thing as *the* future. There are an infinite number of possible futures and I see all of them. For instance, if I look up tonight's numbers... oh shit!"

"*What?*" the other three said.

"I see the numbers 3, 17, 21, 22, 53, with a maxi-ball of 25."

"That's impossible," Indigo Allie said.

"There's only one way something like this is possible. Tonight's drawing is *fixed.*"

"Who?" Culinary Allie said.

"I don't know. I can't even imagine how you would go *about* fixing the lottery. The security must be incredible."

"I'm guaranteed to win if I use those numbers?" Culinary Derek said.

"Yeah," Indigo Derek said. "For some reason, those are the only numbers that can *possibly* come up. You'll have to split the pot with at least one other winner — the person who fixed it."

"I don't know," Indigo Allie said. "These people may be really nasty, mobsters. You guys have kids to think of."

"Even if they fixed the drawing," Culinary Derek said. "That doesn't mean someone else couldn't accidentally pick the same numbers, does it?"

"I guess not."

"Why don't you guys spend the night in our guest room, and we'll watch the drawing on TV?" Culinary Allie said. "We'll split a great bottle of Prosecco."

"That sounds wonderful," Indigo Allie sighed. "How do you explain us to your kids and mom?"

"We'll think of something," Culinary Allie said.

✳✳✳

Culinary Allie introduced them to Renata and the children as Hannibal and Clarice of the Doppelganger's Club.

"Everyone has a double somewhere in the world," Culinary Allie said. "We submitted our photos and here they are."

"The resemblance is uncanny," Renata said. "How well do you know these people?"

"We feel we've known them all our lives," Culinary Derek said.

"Well, have fun," Renata said, leaving.

"Silence of the Lambs?" Indigo Allie said.

"A brain fart. Sorry!"

"You know, mom didn't believe you for a minute."

Culinary Allie introduced them to the children, Tony and Loretta.

Tony was a sandy-haired four-year old and Loretta was a cute three-year-old with long black braids.

Culinary Derek whipped up veal scallopini for the adults and macaroni and cheese for the children.

The adults shared a fine bottle of red wine, a Barbaresco from the Capello vinyard.

"We know the Capellos," Culinary Allie said. "We spent a week at their winery last summer. Barbaresco's such a cute little town!"

"The wine's magnificent!" Derek said.

After dinner, Culinary Allie put the kids to bed and Culinary Derek popped the cork on a bottle of Prosecco. They toasted and Indigo Derek talked about Musical Allie, and Nun Allie.

"Souls are so vast," Derek said. "Their abilities can't be expressed in any one life or timeline so they split off portions of themselves, they specialize. When I was a kid, I loved cooking things occasionally, and you became a master chef."

"History is so strange," Allie said. "I found a timeline where neither world war happened, kind of a steampunk world. The most powerful nation is the British Empire, and America is called the United States of Columbia. Named after Christopher Columbus."

"I had enough trouble passing *our* American history," Culinary Derek said.

✳✳✳

At eleven, they turned on the TV and watched the drawing.

Culinary Derek and Allie shouted out each number as the balls were selected and, at the end, they hugged each other and cried.

"You're our guardian angels!" Culinary Allie sobbed, hugging the Indigos.

"This is almost as wonderful as the day we met," Culinary Derek said.

"I told you my name," she sobbed. "And you said *Alessandra Giancana* was the most beautiful poem you ever heard."

The Culinary couple shared a long, passionate kiss.

"You never said that to me," Allie whispered. "You felt it. Culinary Derek seems to express his feelings better."

They spent another hour discussing how they'd use the money but promised not to cash in the ticket until Derek had checked out the other winner.

They all went to bed.

Chapter 50

At breakfast, Loretta asked Derek and Allie whether they were angels.

"You're so sparkly!" Loressa said. "Like a sparkly mommy and daddy!"

"No, sweety," Indigo Allie smiled. "But you're a little angel."

"There was another winner," Culinary Derek said showing them a picture in the morning paper. "An unemployed hairdresser."

"I'll scan her when I get a chance," Indigo Derek said. "I've got to check in at Energistics."

Culinary Allie looked at Indigo Allie quizzically.

"Of course," she said. "I'll take you and the kids to my gallery. First I have to check that the coast is clear."

"Why?"

"The people who know about our abilities are the ones we don't want to know. Intelligence services who want to force us to work for them. They tried to kidnap us in our apartment in Flushing."

"I lived in Flushing for a while," Culinary Allie said.

"I'm sure it's the same place! There was a shootout in the hallway that killed a police officer and could've killed other tenants."

"What are you saying?" Culinary Derek said.

"I'm afraid our timeline might become toxic to us," Indigo Allie said. "Oz is safe, but too primitive for my liking. I'm a city girl."

"Move here!"

"We're 'extras' here. When you cash in your lottery ticket, you'll be under a microscope and someone will notice us. We're hoping to live here a few months and buy houses we can transport to Oz. Then we'll look for another timeline to live in."

"We'll be sorry to see you go," Culinary Allie said.

"We love you guys, and we'll always stay in touch. I don't why we feel closer to you two than the thousands of other Allies and Dereks in other timelines but we do. I bet your kids would love Destiny beach in Oz."

"I've got to prep for this evening," Culinary Derek sighed and left.

"Shit!" Indigo Allie muttered, shutting her eyes. "A man from the Russian SVR named Igor Raskolnikov is watching the place and a Worldwide Moving van is waiting to cart me away if I show up. He already asked my interns when I'll arrive."

"I have to make some calls," she added, pulling out her phone.

She vanished.

✳✳✳

In a coffee shop across the street from Indigo East, Allie called Renard.

"Where the hell were you?" Renard said. "It's like you dropped off the face of the Earth."

"We dropped off the face of the Earth."

She told him about the Russian agents, and Renard said he'd contact the FBI's Counterespionage group.

Then she called her intern, Beth, and said she'd be by the gallery in the next fifteen minutes.

She bought a newspaper.

∗∗∗

Back in Culinary Allie's kitchen, she said, "I called the FBI on them."

"You're crying!" Culinary Allie said.

"I am?" she said, wiping the tears from her face. "The day before yesterday, I had my gallery's grand opening, and now I may have to close it. Those sweet girls working for me had to deal with spies who'd kill them as soon as look at them."

Culinary Allie hugged her and murmured, "Not to mention the danger to you and Derek."

"We're practically invulnerable, my dear. God, it's weird saying 'my dear' to myself."

"I'm not you. Not exactly."

"True. Anyway, when we battled Ustinov, Derek took a bullet *through his heart* and shrugged it off. I guess an atomic bomb could mess us up. That's what it would take."

Culinary Allie looked shocked.

"Pembroke set out to create a master race, and it seems he succeeded."

"He knew how to *do* that?"

"No. His widow was as shocked as you are ... as *we* are. Pembroke tried to create telepaths and stumbled onto ... us. Like so many scientific discoveries, it was an accident."

"Could the bad guys follow you here?"

"No. We come here by tunneling through the *spirit-world*. I don't know of a single scientist, including Pembroke, who wouldn't sneer at the whole *idea* of a spirit-world. Even among those who believe timelines exist. Here's a newspaper from our world."

Culinary Allie examined it — especially the article about the gallery opening.

"So grandpa embraced your Derek?"

"Yeah."

"After papa opened the restaurant, grandpa sent all his goombahs and *soldati* to eat here," Culinary Allie said. "It was creepy but the money just rolled in. The wait-staff loved them, too."

"Big tippers?"

"Yeah, it was a macho thing, or they were trying to impress grandpa. When papa died, it tapered off and, when I married Derek, it stopped cold. It's ironic because Derek's a better chef than papa was, even for Italian food. His spinach gnocchis are lighter than air. In an Alfredo sauce, they are heavenly."

"Grandpa forbade his people from eating there?"

"He never said so. Actually he never spoke to us again. Is the coast clear at the gallery, now?"

"In a few minutes. They're arresting the Russian spies now. Unfortunately, they haven't broken any laws except for stealing the moving van. Do you guys have bathing suits? Maybe the kids would rather go to a beach."

***

"I've never been to Hawaii, but I've seen pictures of Waikiki beach," Culinary Allie said. "That's Diamond Head, right?"

"In our world it would be," Allie said. "There would also be a solid wall of hotels along the beach. We have to give the crater an Oz name."

"What's that?" Allie said, pointing to a shed next to the Murakami house.

"Old Man Milnor's chicken coop," Wendy said. "He was selling his farm in Wiscasset to developers, and we offered him a thousand dollars for it. Just take it, he said, no charge. So we did."

Like clouds of white and brown, chickens gracefully strolled the beach.

"Can we pet them?" Tony and Loretta shouted.

"Sure!" Wendy said.

"I told Norton they're part of our family," Wendy said. "I think he understands."

Culinary Allie and the children changed into bathing suits at the Murakami house, and Wendy excavated a shallow wading pool and channel for the kids. Waves washed into the channel and filled the pool.

"I just don't understand how you guys can live like this," Allie said. "In such isolation."

"People who can teleport are never isolated," Wendy said. "We like coming home to Oz. Our own world."

"Hey, we went to a Broadway show last night," Travis said. "Something called *The Getting of Wisdom.*"

"I loved it," Wendy said.

"You show up when the box office opens and if they have any cancellations, you get tickets."

"This is Allie from the Culinary timeline," Allie said. "And her wonderful children."

"Aloha!" Wendy and Travis said.

"We're going to build a few more houses and bring them here," Allie said.

Tony and Loretta splashed in the wading pool and made sand castles. Travis persuaded some of the dolphins to give rides to them and Culinary Allie, and they all had the time of their lives.

Then Travis introduced them to Norton.

"We had a cat named Norton," Culinary Allie said. "Before you kids were born."

"Oh my god!" Allie moaned. "Is Wendy going to be a widow before her first anniversary?"

"What?" Culinary Allie said.

"A great white shark bit my leg yesterday," Travis muttered. "The dolphins screamed at me to stay out of the water, but I didn't listen. I teleported to the beach and took the shark's head with me. Then my leg came off and I had to reset. Now the dolphins think we're the biggest badasses on the planet."

"Are there any sharks there now?"

"No," Allie said. "Dolphins are good at fighting sharks, but not one-on-one. Where are the remains?"

"I teleported with them to a mile above the volcano on Volcano Island and let em fall in."

"You're a wild man! You could've fallen in yourself!"

"I always get away in time. That's how I dump our trash."

As he said this, Derek appeared with a pile of gold bars.

"What?" Culinary Allie said.

"Another fifty million dollars worth of gold," Derek explained. "From our timeline. It's our Indigo treasury."

"I'll put it in *da kine* crater," Travis said. "We should call it Treasury Head. Or Money Head."

"You might as well call it Black Head," Allie muttered.

Wendy gave them a tour of her many gardens: areas growing carrots, onions, potatos, garlic, and mangoes.

"I had a garlic bulb that started sprouting," she said. "So I pushed it into the ground, and it's got more than a hundred plants now. We're also planting coffee and chocolate."

✳✳✳

They returned to Culinary Derek and Allie's apartment as Renata arrive to look after the children.

"We took rides on *fish, grandma!*" Tony shouted, as Loretta jumped up and down. "And we *petted chickens!*"

"You children have sunburns," Renata said. "There aren't any beaches open around here."

"We went to *another world*," Culinary Allie said.

"Sparkly auntie Wendy made us a *swimming pool!*" Loretta said. "Using magic!"

Derek tried to explain the nature of timelines to Renata but she said, "I liked it better when you were dopplegangers."

"Wait until you meet Indigo Renata," Derek said. "Incidentally, I think it's OK to cash in your lottery ticket."

"So it wasn't fixed after all?" Culinary Allie said.

"Oh it was fixed alright. The man responsible, a Jonas Nakatomi, is a financial planner who came up with a clever scheme to control which numbers come up."

"Why doesn't he make himself win?" Culinary Allie said.

"He'd come under too much scrutiny, and they'd figure out how he does it. So he recruits someone to win *for* him."

"Then he takes their money?"

"*No.* A lottery winner can't just give away a big chunk of money without it looking suspicious. So they do the wise thing and pick him as their *money manager.* He gives them an allowance of fifty thousand a month and collects millions in fees and interest. Eventually they get all their money back."

"So he's not greedy?" Culinary Allie said.

"He's playing the long game. Nakatomi is managing money for the last five winners. One double-crossed him, blew the money, and Nakatomi had him killed."

"Shit!" Culinary Allie muttered.

"He's a murderer," Derek agreed. "But he thinks your win is dumb luck."

***

While Renata watched the children, the two Dereks and Allies gathered in the Ristorante Alberto after closing time.

Culinary Derek served a wonderful dinner of Sole *Meuniere* and they talked.

"So cash in your lottery ticket," Indigo Derek said.

"And give you half."

"No. People will notice. You'll be living under a microscope. You'll be expected to invest the money, so I suggest you buy ten million dollars worth of gold from me. Then we'll have ten millions dollars of money from this world we can use to pay rent and purchase houses that we take to Oz."

"We owe you half of that money!" Culinary Derek said.

"You do and you don't," Indigo Allie said. "After all, you're *us* if our lives had turned out a little differently. If it makes you feel better, give us back the gold when the dust settles. Probably years later."

"What happens now?" Culinary Allie said.

"We spend a few months here, order prefabricated houses, and move them to Oz."

"Then we never *see* you again?"

"We'll *always* be in your lives," Allie said, hugging her. "You're our friends and you can't get rid of us."

Part IV

Exile

Chapter 51

At the Energistics headquarters, Mrs. Pincus said she had the feeling she was being followed.

"You are," Derek said. "By members of the Russian SVR and the Chinese intelligence service."

"What do we do about it?" Allie said.

"This," Derek said, pulling up a thick sheaf of paper. "It's a list of all SVR field agents with their names, locations, current assignments, and aliases."

Mrs. Pincus let out a low whistle.

"Either I give it to the CIA and FBI, or I give it to the SVR and *threaten* to publicize it. I have a similar list for the Chinese intelligence service."

"Give the Russian list to the CIA," Allie said. "Those bastards already attacked us."

***

Derek teleported into a restroom at CIA headquarters and strolled into a room where a meeting was taking place.

Renard Moreau, Susan Winkler, and Mitchel Wilkins sat around a conference table.

"Ah, you weren't invited," Renard said. "But sit anyway. We've decided the attack on your apartment came from the Russian intelligence service. Apparently Ustinov has contacts with them and told them about your abilities."

"Here's a belated Christmas present," Derek said, passing printouts to all in attendance.

They examined the printouts and their eyes widened.

"This is the holy grail," Renard whispered.

"The couple at the bottom of the list are still in Moscow, but will fly to Seattle tomorrow," Derek said. "To infiltrate Boeing."

"What are your demands?" Renard said.

"Demands? Get these people off the street. They trashed our apartment, killed a police officer, upset employees at Allie's art gallery, and are tailing Energistics employees. We're getting pissed off."

***

Derek went to the Murakami house, lay in a guest bed, and scanned the CIA meeting.

"Do we call local police or the FBI?" Susan Winkler said.

"Neither," Renard said. "We *turn* as many of these agents as possible. Leave their network in place."

"What about the one *at* CIA?" she said.

"We *firewall* him and feed him disinformation."

"What about people tailing the Evans people?" she said.

"Obviously, we don't interfere, and block the police from doing so."

"Isn't this going to piss off Evans?" she said.

"Civilians don't dictate our policies," Renard said. "And we're not law-enforcement."

"With all due respect, sir," Susan said. "These are not ordinary civilians."

"I'm *painfully* aware of that," Renard said. "They're transferring gold . . . somewhere, and I want to know where."

"We trace it to Energistics corporation," Susan said. "Then Mrs. Pincus said it went to another dimension. A place they call Oz."

"Of course they teleported it out of there," Renard said. "But not over the goddamn rainbow. They're stocking an offshore bolt-hole."

"If we piss them off, will they give Moscow and Beijing lists like this?" Susan said, holding up the printout Derek gave her.

"That's what worries me," Renard said. "We need *leverage* over them dammit! I need *suggestions, people!*"

"They're a boy-scout troop," Susan said. "Except for Mrs. Pembroke. She's got a mountain of skeletons in her closet. There are the twenty people she and her husband murdered — that we *know* of. Including one of her own children."

"We don't care!" Renard said. "She's no use to us. We'll have to get ugly!"

"That will probably violate our charter," Susan said.

"That ship sailed a long time ago," Renard said, thinking of how the CIA kept key senators under close surveillance. "Violating foreign laws is our business. Is it that big a stretch to pretend the US is a foreign country?"

✳✳✳

Derek, Allie, and the Pincuses held a "stockholder's meeting" at the the Han Joo Chik Wine Bar.

"Building a network of double agents makes sense," Derek said. "I guess."

"In one *afternoon,*" Allie said. "You could learn more Russian secrets than their stupid network could in a *fucking year.* They could replace the whole goddamn CIA with *you.*"

"Maybe that's what bothers them," Mrs. Pincus said.

"No," Allie said. "They're paranoid assholes who don't trust anyone they can't control."

"I can fight the mafia but not governments," Derek sighed. "Including *our own!*"

"I knew having an art gallery was too good to be true," Allie groaned. "I'll sell Indigo East."

"Where does that leave us?" Mrs. Pincus moaned.

"Don't sell it Allie!" Derek said. "We haven't broken *any laws!* We're law-abiding American citizens."

"The CIA doesn't give a shit about laws," Allie said.

"They can't conduct operations on American soil," Derek said.

"I repeat my previous statement."

"Then they're in for a shock. We have our own laws and enforcement."

"Are we going to be in a tit-for-tat war that never ends?"

"We'll build homes on Destiny Bay, honey," Derek said. "Every night we'll go home to a place where they can't touch us."

"It would be nice to see the ocean from my living room. To hear the pounding surf as I sip my morning coffee."

"I'll double the security on you two," Derek said, making a call.

They ate dinner.

✲✲✲

They spent the night at the Plaza Hotel in Culinary Derek's timeline, and visited Culinary Derek and Allie the next morning.

Culinary Derek had announced his winning lottery numbers and had an appointment to visit the State Lottery Commission that afternoon. The restaurant would be closed that day.

Indigo Allie explored some new art prospects in hers and Derek's timeline while Culinary Allie stayed behind with Renata.

"I can take you on a tour of the art gallery," Indigo Derek said.

With Wendy spotting in her spirit-body, Indigo Derek teleported himself and Culinary Allie to Indigo East, while Renata looked after the children.

***

"They're going to think you're her, so just nod and say OK," Derek said.

"This is fun," Culinary Allie said.

They stepped out into the gallery.

"I thought you'd be out this afternoon," Beth said, staring Culinary Allie's pregnant belly.

"I need to do some inventory first," Culinary Allie said.

"Nice catch," Derek whispered in her ear.

"The *Mote in God's Eye*," Derek said, pointing.

"Yes, it takes up six square feet, at least," Allied said, and whispered in Derek's ear, "Wow! It's beautiful!"

They strolled through the gallery and the various installations stunned Allie.

"She's thinking of opening a gallery in *your* timeline and turning it over to you when we leave. What do you think?"

"That would be fantastic, but ... I don't know anything about running an art gallery."

"Oh well. It's something to keep in mind. Oh, my God!"

"What?"

"I shouldn't have brought you here. Please don't say anything."

Renard Moreau entered the room.

"If it isn't the head of the CIA's Clandestine Service. I didn't know you were into art."

Wendy! Teleport behind that sculpture and record this on your phone.

No problem.

"Great thing about dealing with telepaths," Renard said. "I don't have to say a word."

"You don't have the *balls* to admit your criminal acts," Derek said.

"We swept this place and disabled your security cameras," Renard shrugged, staring at Culinary Allie's belly. "OK, we disappeared the Pincuses."

"We put state of the art security on them!" Derek said.

"They were good," Renard admitted, never taking his eyes off Culinary Allie. "Even the best rent-a-cop realizes he can't spend his salary dead. The quality of the Pincus's lives — the *length* of their lives depends on how well you two obey orders."

Something's different about Allie, Renard thought. *What the hell is it?*

"They never even so much as jaywalked!"

"That's good. I'd hate to think we had *criminals* in our CIA prisons."

"We are patriotic Americans and gave you the names of all the Russian agents in this country!"

"More than anything else, that convinced me we need to keep you on a short leash. A *very* short leash."

"If kidnapping the Pincuses doesn't do it..."

"I'll put the whole goddamn town of Boothbay Harbor into Guantanamo if I have to!"

Derek hugged Culinary Allie and teleported them back to her apartment.

✳✳✳

They stood on a thin sheet of the gallery's parquet floor.

"I made my envelope large to be sure to bring all of you," Derek said.

"What?"

"When the teleport-envelope's too small, parts of people come along, but not everything. Amputations happen..."

Allie registered shock.

"I'm sorry, but I've got to rescue our people."

He vanished.

***

Derek and Allie traced the Pincuses to an old warehouse in New York's Garment District.

Derek called the Detective Roberts, said the Pincuses had been kidnapped by heavily armed strangers, and gave him the address. Then he scanned Renard.

Renard sat in the rear seat of an armored car being driven on Route 95 by two agents in the front seat.

He followed them in his spirit-body.

They stopped at a rest area outside Baltimore, and Renard went to the Men's Room. His phone rang and he answered.

"Hang tight," he said. "I'll get the police off your backs."

Derek appeared next to him, hit him with a stun-gun, and teleported him.

***

They materialized in a dense rain-forest on a hill overlooking an enormous valley with a mountain in the distance. Down the hill, a pounding surf crashed into the beach, roaring like distant thunder. The hot, humid air smelled of orchids and wild onions.

"You just committed a *felony!*"

"You're one to talk!"

"I have a GPS tracker on me, and CIA's going to rain an ocean of shit down on you and your family."

"I'm pretty sure GPS signals don't cross dimensions."

"This is Maui, you idiot," Renard said. "My wife and I vacation here every August. That mountain is Haleakala, and the town of Lahaina is right down that hill. We stay at the Beachcomber Spa there."

"If you say so."

"One phone call and you're toast," Renard said, whipping out his phone.

"I'd be shocked if you got any bars on that."

Renard shut off his phone and slowly scanned his surroundings.

"Wendy set up a utility shed on the beach with a cot and food and bottled water. She'll drop off more stuff every day."

"How long will you keep me here?"

"A day or two."

"Then you go to prison."

"Then we leave your putrid pustule of a world forever."

***

After a initial shootout that killed a police officer and a forty-five minute standoff, the four men operating the CIA's "black prison" surrendered and released their prisoners: the Pincuses.

Derek visited them at the police station.

"They refused to tell us anything," Detective Roberts said. "Even their names. They haven't asked for lawyers either. Odd behavior for people charged with kidnapping and murder. Their fingerprints are not on file anywhere."

"They work for the CIA," Derek said. "If I meet them, I can tell you their names."

"What does the CIA have against the Pincuses?"

"They wanted the Pincuses as leverage on us."

"Kidnapping is a federal felony," Detective Roberts said.

"Murder is a state felony. Hell, doing *anything* on American soil violates the CIA charter."

"That's why they'll let your prisoners rot."

"Why does the CIA have against you guys?"

"We agreed to work with them, and they won't take yes for an answer."

Derek's took a call. It was the director of Praetorian Security.

"We can't offer our services to you anymore," the Director said. "Our best man on the Pincuses detail was a former Navy SEAL."

"Was?"

"He died. The people who are after you guys are beyond our competence-level. I'm not taking any more of your money when we can't protect you."

"Want to meet them?" Detective Roberts said.

"Want to?" Derek said. "No. But I will."

✻✻✻

Detective Roberts led him to the lock-up facility in the basement. They walked past several empty cells until they reached four cells with prisoners in them.

The prisoners had shaved heads and wore prison jumpsuits. One was doing single-armed pull-ups from a pipe near the ceiling, switching arms every ten repetitions.

"Someone I want you to meet," Detective Roberts said. "He's going to tell us all about you."

They ignored him.

"OK," Derek said. "This one killed your officer. His name is Dalton Ridgefield."

Ridgefield flinched and glared at Derek.

"Former Army Ranger. Works for the National Clandestine Service. Did three black ops in Chechnya and Abkhazia. His supervisor at the CIA is named Wally Combs."

"Who the *hell* are you?" Ridgefield growled.

"A mind-reader."

"This man is Trey Mainwaring," Derek continued, pointing to a ruddy-complected man in the next cell who stopped his pull-ups and dropped to the floor. "He's former SEAL Team-six, and his most notable achievement is taking out the ISIS number two man in Syria."

Derek named the other two men and gave brief bios.

"The couple you guys kidnapped were the most law-abiding people I've ever known," Derek said.

"They were terrorists," Ridgefield muttered.

"They were innocent hostages. And you guys are nothing but goons, kidnapping people you're supposed to protect. So the CIA can control me."

***

"I'm afraid to go home," Mrs. Pincus sobbed. "We're not safe anywhere."

"There's a place where you'll be totally safe," Allie said. "We'll take you there."

They teleported to a street in front of the *Ristorante Alberto.*

"We're in Astoria, Queens," Derek said.

"The CIA will find us!" Mrs. Pincus said.

Allie bought a newspaper at a grocery store and showed it to the Pincuses.

"Did you teleport us five years into the future?" Mrs. Pincus said.

"No," Reginald Pincus said. "It's another timeline that's five years out of sync with ours."

"Bingo!" Derek said. "Here, the CIA doesn't know you exist."

They entered the restaurant and the Pincuses got another shock.

They all went to Culinary Allie and Derek's apartment for dinner.

Chapter 52

They all watched a grinning Culinary Derek on TV accept a four-foot-long check for $171 million dollars from the New York State Lottery Commissioner.

"We'll set up a ten million dollar checking account for you guys," Culinary Allie said. "Just pose as us and write checks. We'll find an investment advisor for the rest."

"Ask your grandfather to recommend someone," Derek said. "Mr. Nakatomi will offer his services. You need to have someone else lined up."

They found rooms for Derek, Allie and the Pincuses at the Astoria Grand Hotel.

❊❊❊

Derek took a copy of Wendy's recording and teleported to Eldon Trask's office, almost giving him a heart attack.

"This is what we're up against," he said, showing him the video.

"Are the Pincuses, OK?"

"Yes, we called a SWAT team to rescue them, and their kidnappers are in jail. Your association with us could put you in grave danger."

"I know several senators who'd *love* to see this video."

"If we have to leave this timeline, we may have to take the Pincuses with us."

"*Flee?*" Mr. Trask bellowed. "That's the most ridiculous thing I ever heard! We're building something here that'll change the world. I'll order security for the Pincuses and your gallery."

"We had security but they bugged out."

"Mine is better! The more I think of this the angrier I get."

He made a call and messaged the video clip to someone.

"Senator Mary Rubinstein," he explained. "Head of the Senate Select Committee on Intelligence."

"That video clip was taken at an art gallery in New York belonging to my partners," he said into the phone. "What do you *mean* what video clip? I just messaged it to you. I'll send it again."

He sent it again and called Senator Rubinstein back.

"Still didn't get it? I'll *hand-carry* it to you. Five hours from now, you'll get the shock of your life."

Then he called his security firm and pilot. He told his pilot to prepare the plane to fly to Washington DC with a security detail.

"I can teleport you there in seconds," Derek said.

"You're on!"

Mr. Trask called his pilot back and told him he would use alternate transportation to Washington but the pilot was to fly there anyway — he'd take the plane back.

Derek asked Wendy to spot for her and they teleported to an empty corridor in the Senate Office Building.

"That was the most incredible experience of my life."

"That's the spirit-world for you," Derek said. "I think Rubinstein is in her office."

She knocked on a door and a gray-haired woman answered.
"How did you get here?" she said.
"My new technology," Mr. Trask said. "It got a man to Mars."
He showed her the video clip.
"I've met that man," Senator Rubinstein said, tapping her finger on the phone's screen. "Renard Moreau."
"Your phones are tapped, senator," Derek said. "They intercepted Trask's video messages. Your office is probably bugged too."
"Let's get out of here," she said, leading them out of the office and the building.
A black Lincoln limousine with government plates pulled up, and they all piled into its roomy back seat. A glass partition separated the driver from the passengers.
"Take us to the Blue Bird, Morton," Senator Rubinstein said into a microphone on the partition.
"Sure thing, senator."
During the fifteen-minute drive, Derek tried to explain Indigos to the senator.
The car pulled up to the Ambassador Hotel, an elegant art-deco building on M street. A fenced-off area to the right of the main entrance had many stacked chairs and tables.

✳✳✳

The hotel lobby had comfortable chairs and sofas arranged around a TV featuring a talk show.
They crossed the lobby and entered a dimly-lit restaurant and bar. Shiny black bricks lined its walls, except for the one facing M street, which was glass. It looked out on what must've been the place's outdoor dining area in summertime.
Ceiling-mounted spotlights illuminated tables in the dimly-it interior — making them seem to hover in the air.

"Hello Armando," Senator Rubinstein said to the matre d'. "A table by the window, please."

"Right this way, senator."

"If you're a regular here, they might have this place bugged too."

"We don't even know for sure that my office is bugged!"

Armando seated them.

After glancing at the menu, the senator ordered a chef salad, Derek ordered Dover Sole meunière, and Trask ordered filet mignon.

"I'm going to call a meeting of the Senate Select Committee on Intelligence and subpoena Renard."

Senator Rubinstein pulled out her phone and made a call.

"Yeah, just look at this video," she said. "What do you mean *what* video?"

She made three other calls that didn't go through.

"I saw Senator Baker in his office, but calls just go to voice-mail."

Their food arrived.

As they ate, Senator Rubinstein muttered, "I'm getting very pissed off. Maybe I'll just take this video to the Washington Post."

After they finished, Derek offered to pay but Senator Rubinstein signed for it.

They left.

As they crossed the hotel lobby, breaking news interrupted regular TV programming: Trask's private jet had exploded on takeoff from Los Angeles. He was believed to be dead along with with a security detail of ten.

Trask and Senator Rubunstein stared at the screen in shocked disbelief.

"They must've had people in place," Derek said. "Maybe

some of your security people work for them. I told you your association with me might be dangerous."

"My pilot was a friend," Mr. Trask moaned. "I met his family."

"Don't call your car, senator," Derek said. "Your driver just reported to the CIA that Trask is still alive."

"Morton has driven me for years!" she snapped, calling the car on her phone. "He's practically family."

"You should listen to him, senator," Mr. Trask said. "He's a telepath."

The car arrived and the senator slid into the back seat.

"Let's join her," Derek said.

"Why?"

"So I can rescue her."

They slid in beside her and the car left.

"Please take us to the Washington Post, Morton," Senator Rubinstein said.

"Sure thing, ma'am."

The car drove several blocks and entered the Washington Beltway — the highway circling the city. After a while, the car took an exit heading for Maryland.

"Wait a minute, Morton," Senator Rubinstein said. "We're heading out of town!"

The door-locks snapped into place.

"I'm sorry ma'am. My orders are to bring you in for questioning."

"Your *orders?* You work for me! You've been like *family.*"

"I never really worked for you ma'am. I hoped and prayed it would never come to this. I'm very sorry."

"You're committing a felony!"

"Just give them the video and answer their questions! They'll probably let you go. Maybe not the other two."

"Feel free to rescue us, Derek," Mr. Trask said. "Anytime." In her spirit-body Wendy carefully inspected them and said, *You've got them covered.*

✳✳✳

They teleported to Destiny Beach, landing on a sand dune — still sitting on part of the car seat.

Senator Rubinstein screamed. Then the heat and humidity struck her and she stood with the help of Derek and Mr. Trask. She looked around in a daze.

"It's like a dream... Where the *hell* are we? How did we get here?"

"Derek Evans teleported us."

"*Teleported us?*"

"I *told* you I could that," Derek said.

"Wait, I *know* where this is!" Senator Rubinstein said. "I attended a conference on Inner City Entrepreneurs at the Hilton Hawaiian Village... over... there..."

Her voice trailed off as she realized she was pointing to a grove of palm trees.

"This is an alternate parallel universe we call Oz."

"It's a *what?*"

"Who ... or what is that?" Mr. Trask said, pointing.

Wendy and Travis were playing an odd game over the ocean. One would throw a ball and the other would teleport into its path and throw it back. Gravity was their other, hidden opponent, pulling them down so they had to teleport to higher altitudes to avoid falling into the ocean. On the rare occasions the ball hit the water dolphins popped it back up into the air.

Below them, the entire pod of dolphins watched, chattering and squealing their encouragement.

"That's my crazy sister and her crazier husband," Derek said. "Hey! Come on over and meet your guests."

The senator yelped as Allie popped into view.

"Howzit?" Travis said, appearing beside her.

They went to the Murakami house, and Derek explained the whole story to Senator Rubinstein.

"I understand why the CIA wants to put a tight leash on you people," she said. "Their methods are monstrous and illegal. But the very *idea* of people ... with your abilities. It's ... it's a nightmare."

"Every time you drive a car," Allie said. "You could go bonkers and mow down fifty people. In *theory,* right?"

"I suppose in *theory,*" Senator Rubinstein said. "But it's never going to happen."

"Since it's *theoretically possible,* maybe you shouldn't be allowed to drive. Maybe you should be punished as if you'd *already* committed that crime."

"That analogy is nonsensical," Senator Rubinstein said. "There's no equivalence between killing fifty people and possibly killing millions."

"We don't have atomic weapons," Allie said.

"You could steal one from a military base. With your abilities, that would be easy. I'm surprised you haven't already done it."

"Thanks for that helpful suggestion," Derek said. "You win. We'll send you home. Tell the CIA you support kidnapping innocent American citizens, murdering them, and trying to murder Mr. Trask. As your driver said, *maybe* they'll let you go."

"I *don't* approve, damn it! I *will* go after the CIA."

"But you won't help us beyond that," Allie said. "OK, we get that."

"I have an idea," Derek said. "Put the video on YouTube and some other video sites, and *then* tell the press about it."

"We can drop you off at the Washington Post," Allie said. "As soon as we figure out where it is."

"Look up the address," Senator Rubinstein said. "It's somewhere on K street."

"We can't read addresses in the spirit-world," Derek said.

After a lengthy session of scanning downtown Washington in her spirit-body Allie located the Washington Post main building.

"They have people watching the entrances and three inside the building," Allie said.

"Maybe the New York Times would be better," Derek said. "I can go to World Wide Wired and post our copy of the video."

And they did.

***

Over the next two days, Derek, Allie and the Pincuses stayed at the Astoria Grand Hotel in the Culinary timeline, did apartment-hunting, and commuted to Origin — the name they'd finally given to their home timeline.

Reginald Pincus looked up his counterpart in this timeline and learned that he'd committed suicide, three years ago. Joyce had died of a heart-attack a year later.

Eldon Trask remained in Origin under massive security.

Derek set up an assembly line for Pincus generators and purchased five more generators that he stored in Oz.

Senator Rubinstein convened the Senate Select Committee on Intelligence.

***

Derek teleported to Kolodny's prison island in Oz.

He found Moreau body-surfing nude off what would've been Launiupoko Beach in Origin. In Oz, it had no name.

When Moreau spotted Derek, he staggered out of the water.

"What's up?"

"Time to go home," Derek said.

After Moreau got dressed, Derek teleported him to his office at the CIA. The building had shower facilities and a change of clothing.

∗∗∗

The Senate Select Committee on Intelligence held its closed-door hearing in a cavernous conference hall in the Senate Office Building. The room was dimly-lit except for spotlights directed at a long table with grim-faced CIA directors seated at it and a wooden stage with a blue curtain behind it where the committee sat.

It was said President Eakins monitored the hearing via closed-circuit television.

Derek still hadn't been arrested.

One by one, they questioned all of people relevant to the Indigo phenomena: Mrs. Pembroke, Dr. Fischer, Derek and Mr. Trask.

"You confess to assaulting, Renard Kolondy?" Senator Rubinstein said. "And imprisoning him?"

"Yes, senator," Derek said. "To prevent him from blocking the Pincuses' rescue. Imprisoning is a harsh word. I left him on a beach in Oz with supplies. It was for two days."

He explained the nature of timelines, and Mr. Trask and Senator Rubinstein testified to having been in Oz.

Mr. Ehrehreich, the CIA Directorate of Science and Technology's chief, insisted that the Many Worlds Interpretation of Quantum Mechanics was "utter nonsense."

"Where would you put all those worlds?" he sneered.

"Isn't it true that about thirty percent of the physics community subscribes to it or a theory like it?" Senator Rubinstein said. "I asked people at Georgetown University."

"I suppose," he admitted.

"How do you explain people's experiences in Oz?" Senator Rubinstein said.

"They were obviously dosed with a psycho-active drug and hallucinated their experiences. Derek teleported you somewhere, senator, but not another dimension. Probably an abandoned warehouse."

Chloe Teague tearfully testified that Derek and Allie had risked their lives to legitimatize their marriage, calling them "the most spiritual people I ever met."

After six hours of testimony without a break, the witnesses were asked to leave.

✳✳✳

In the hallway, Detective Roberts hugged Birgit Fischer.

"What's happening?" Eldon Trask asked Derek as Mrs. Pembroke fixed him in a pointed stare.

"I'll scan them."

"OK," Derek added, after a few minutes. "President Eakins has halted the hearing in the interest of national security. He ordered the CIA people and committee members to meet him at the White House in ninety minutes."

"Why?" Mrs. Pembroke said.

"I think he's going to make a decision. I can't scan him because I've never met him or anyone he's met. That'll change in ninety minutes."

"We should all go somewhere quiet," Detective Roberts. "So you can eavesdrop on them."

"How about Oz?" Derek said. "The hallucinogenic warehouse."

"Yes!" they all replied.

Allie, Wendy, and Liz helped to ferry people over.

✳✳✳

"What a glorious hallucination!" Chloe breathed, twirling on one foot.

"We can loan you swim suits," Allie said. "Won't fit very well. Unless you want to skinny-dip."

"I've had a dream about Oz last night," Wendy murmured, staring into space. "A mighty spirit lives here. She called out to the universe. You are the only one who heard her, Derek."

"I've sensed a presence here," Derek said.

"Like Gaia?" Allie said.

"What does she want?" Derek said.

"She needs us," Wendy whispered. "If we love this place, it will love us back. That's why Travis and I enjoy spending time here."

"Interesting!" he sighed. "I wish we could pursue this, but I've got to scan the president."

✳✳✳

Derek lay in the guest bedroom, drifted out-of-body, and thought of Senator Rubinstein.

She sat in the back seat of a limousine muttering, "He had some nerve canceling our meeting! We were getting to the bottom of things."

"Yes, senator," her driver said.

"Don't dare speak to me Morton! I was talking to myself."

Derek followed them in his spirit-body as the car drove under the White House's West Portico.

✳✳✳

They convened in the Oval Office.

"Let me summarize the CIA Charter for you," President Eakins said. *"Don't shit where you live!"*

"Yes, Mr. President," Renard said.

"You laid a mountain-sized turd on the kitchen floor, and I have to clean it up. And I *will* clean it up, but you will owe me like you've never owed anyone before in your life."

"Yes, Mr. President."

"If I ever say jump, and you don't ask how high, I'll hang you by your fucking balls! Am I clear?"

"Very, Mr. President."

"Did you try to recruit these two?" President Eakins.

"They agreed to work for us," Renard said. "But we couldn't trust them without a big stick to hold over their heads."

"Failing that, you want them dead."

"They represent a potential threat to this country that *cannot* be countered. They could plant atomic weapons in our cities and there would be no defense."

"I'll develop a narrative that will justify that. None of you may contradict one iota of it."

"These are law-abiding American citizens!" Senator Rubinstein shouted.

"They're not even human. My narrative will be extreme and consistent. God, I just love wars. They are fantastic — we couldn't function without them. They free us from so much legalistic bullshit. World war two allowed us to intern the Japanese, the war on drugs allowed us to confiscate peoples' houses. The war on terror allowed us to lock people up at gitmo with without that habeas corpus crap."

"Internment of the Japanese was after an *actual attack*," Senator Rubinstein said. "The war on terror occurred after an attack too. The Indigos haven't attacked us *in any way* or even threatened to do so!"

✳✳✳

"I never had a barbecued lobster steak before," Chloe said.

"Two hundred pound lobsters aren't as tender as the ones we're used to," Liz said.

"I'll take the leftovers to Derek," Travis said.

"What'll Derek do with them?" Chloe said.

"I mean I take them to *da kine* mainland, for animals to eat." Derek came out of the Murakami house and described the meeting he'd overheard.

"I don't believe it," Mr. Trask said. "That's the most insane story I've ever heard."

"You don't have to believe a word I said," Derek said. "The president is making a speech from the Oval Office. Seven o'clock, Eastern."

"Let's watch from my place in LA," Eldon Trask said. "You're all invited."

"If I'm telling the truth, you don't want go home," Derek said.

Mr. Trask frowned.

***

They watched the President's speech from the Willis Hotel's lobby in Chicago. They had the place to themselves and arranged themselves on sofas around the TV.

A quiz show played.

At five minutes to six, a special broadcast interrupted the show's final showcase question.

"This is going to be historic," Allie said, picking up her phone and recording.

President Eakins finally came on.

"Greeting my fellow Americans," he said, with a grim expression. "Tonight, I speak to you with a heavy heart. America faces the greatest threat to its existence in its more than two-hundred-year history. Make no mistake: we are at war. Intelligent alien life exists, creatures from another galaxy bent on exterminating the human race. And they are among us, with their traitorous human collaborators."

"Another *galaxy?*" Trask muttered. "That's the most asinine thing I ever heard! The nearest other galaxy is *millions* of light years away. He could've said another planet or star system."

"His advisors agree," Derek said. "He's playing to his base. He's calling us space aliens because 'Earth aliens' is just too subtle and complicated for his target audience."

"This speech is a steaming pile of shit!" Trask said.

"He knows that," Derek said. "He just wants it to be an *effective* steaming pile."

"No foreign government will believe it," Trask said.

"Of course they won't. He'll get WTF phone calls from all over the world."

The TV showed pictures of Derek and Allie.

"These creatures look human," President Eakins continued. "They sound human. They even act human, but make no mistake. They're *monsters.*"

"I have assembled a special task force from the CIA to hunt these monsters down and protect America. This is not easy and my task force has been forced to *technically* break a few laws."

"Killing a cop and kidnapping people," Derek muttered.

"I hereby issue a full and complete Presidential pardon for all crimes they *have* committed and *will* commit in the future."

"Holy shit!" Liz said.

"Crimes they *will* commit?" Mr. Trask said.

"He'll accuse his rivals and enemies of supporting us," Derek said. "Basically anyone who doesn't obey him."

"These monsters have the power to brainwash humans into doing their bidding," President Eakins continued. "Their first victim was Eldon Trask who built them a base on Mars from which they'll launch attacks on Earth."

"*What?*" Mr. Trask roared, standing.

"Quiet," Allie said. "You're attracting attention."

"His task force plans to kidnap people and lock them in psych wards until they come around to the official narrative," Derek said. "No contact with legal counsel or anything. They'll do that to you, Eldon."

"Oh shit!" Allie muttered. "Senator Rubinstein had second thoughts. Now she's is in the criminally insane ward in Georgetown General Hospital. She'll stay there until she publicly supports the president's actions. After a hundred electroshocks, her brain will be *guacamole* — a tragic victim of our brainwashing."

"I can't believe I'm saying this, Derek," Mr. Trask said. "This is actually *worse* than what you told us."

"He kicked his speech up a notch since I scanned him."

"Let me put the entire world on notice," President Eakins continued. "If any nation offers sanctuary to these monsters, we will regard that as an act of war against the United States. All of our arsenal is on the table, including nuclear weapons."

"That's his answer to foreign governments' WTFs," Derek said.

"This is too depressing," Liz moaned, covering her eyes.

"America's first line of defense has always been a well-armed citizenry. Any private citizen who kills these monsters or their traitorous supporters will receive a full and complete presidential pardon — and the thanks of a grateful nation."

"Idiots will be blasting away at anything that moves!" Chloe said.

"Tell me this, Derek," Mr. Trask growled. "Is there any life you've touched you haven't *completely ruined?*"

"No," he muttered.

"My late husband and I ruined your lives," Mrs. Pembroke said. "Not these two."

"We're just trying to survive in an insane world," Allie said, hugging Derek.

"Where do we go from here?" Mr. Trask said. "I don't want to spend the rest of my life camping out on a fucking beach!"

Epilogue

The Indigos ferried everyone except Mrs. Pembroke to the Culinary timeline. Although she was the only real criminal in the group, the authorities had no interest in her. She returned to her old life.

They teleported Birgit Fischer and Ian Roberts to Munich in Origin where she'd try to resume her career at the *Ludwig-Maximillian Universität*.

The Brocklesbys also stayed in Origin, apparently under the radar. They were frequent visitors to Oz.

***

When Allie showed Culinary Derek and Allie the recording on her phone, Culinary Allie said, "Eakins is *president?* No *wonder* your world is so fucked up."

Derek sold them twenty million dollars worth of gold, bought a lot on Staten Island, and ordered six prefab houses and a workshop to be built on it.

They found apartments for everyone in Brooklyn and Queens.

Eldon Trask looked up his counterpart in the Culinary timeline and contacted him. Culinary Trask was in the throes of launching his new Heavy-Lift Vehicle to send a habitat to Mars. He refused to meet with Trask.

"I'm such a driven prick in this timeline," Eldon said. "I guess I was in mine too. I'm kinda proud that his Mars program is way ahead of schedule."

***

Chloe signed up to Facebook under a phony name and befriended her counterpart. After a crisis of faith, Culinary Chloe had left the ministry and moved to Portland, Oregon, where she lived with her husband and two children.

"I could get my old church back in Boothbay Harbor," she said. "I'd have to go to divinity school again to get credentials."

"I'll cover the expenses," Derek said.

"I don't know... If *that* Chloe had a crisis of faith, I'll definitely have one. Especially, after what I've seen of the spirit world. It's not that Christianity is wrong, it's just ... there's so much more going on. I love Jesus and his teachings, but if he ever returns to Earth, he'll have a lot more to say."

"Take all the time you need, Chloe. We'll always support you."

***

As the prefab houses were finished, Wendy and Travis transported them to lots on Destiny Beach. They hooked up water pumps, sewer facilities, and a Pincus generator to each house.

The Pincuses loved theirs.

"At my age, I've had enough of the Big City," Joyce Pincus said. "It's so beautiful and peaceful here. Reginald feels better too. He even skips his meds, sometimes, without any dire effects. He has even taken up hiking."

***

Liz and Thomas found a timeline in which the Evans family had never moved to Boothbay Harbor. They used Indigo gold to buy a house there and tried to convince themselves they were "home" again.

This didn't work out very well.

Although the Happy Cormorant existed there, Thomas's cronies didn't and — if they had — he wouldn't have been able to recount his greatest adventures without them thinking him insane.

You can't go home again.

✳✳✳

Derek contacted Vaughn Williams.

"Get away from me, man!" Vaughn muttered. "They almost shot us just for *working* for Energistics. They're shooting people in the streets! I don't know if you are monsters like Eakins said. I do know you can get us killed."

"I can take you to Oz. Remember Oz?"

"Can you take my wife, my extended family, and hers? Hundreds of people. Most of them wouldn't even be *willing* to go! Just leave us alone! Things might cool off if they manage to impeach Eakins."

✳✳✳

Wendy and Travis enrolled in the University of Hawaii in the Culinary timeline. Their fears someone would recognize him on campus seemed to be unfounded.

Over the next four months, Allie, Wendy and Liz became visibly pregnant.

Allie designed an "Oz Passport" with an elegant O with inscribed Z on the cover. Its interior pages featured faintly engraved images of woolly mammoths and smilodons — and had a printing firm in the Culinary timeline make a hundred of them.

Allie got her house on the beach with a concert grand piano in the living room. Over a week the Brocklesbys helped Derek built her a deck facing the sea — the old-fashioned way, using hammers, saws, nails, lumber, and sweat.

Allie could drink coffee each morning and go for a swim.

She and Derek went to two Broadway shows in the Culinary timeline and spent a week in London, taking in a show in London's West End and visiting the British Museum.

It had an extensive Ancient Egypt section.

"He looks so distinguished," Allie said, of a bust of Pharaoh Senusret I.

***

In June, the CIA tried to kidnap Professor Fischer in Munich, and she barely escaped. Derek and Allie transported her and Ian Roberts to Oz and gave them a house.

Birgit Fischer rejected the idea of trying to establish herself in the Culinary timeline.

"Everyone knows who I am," she said.

"You're world-famous?" Allie said.

"In a tiny world, yes. There are, maybe, forty people working in my area of biology on Earth. I know all of them. I've even met most of them at conferences. My counterpart there is retiring, and those people know it."

"I have one idea *kine*," Travis said.

"Oh no," Birgit Fischer chuckled.

"It is one *ono* idea," Travis laughed. "Tell your counterpart *not* to retire. She can party at home while you teach her classes and do her work."

Professor Fischer laughed.

"We'll greet you with a hot meal every evening, honey," Ian laughed.

"That sounds so ... tempting, but I don't think so."

"Study *Oz!*" Derek said. "It's not every biologist who gets a whole new world to explore."

"I can't publish."

"Publish *here.* Oz is a place, or it will be someday. You'll be the legendary Sage who founded science here."

✳✳✳

In September, Culinary Renata, Derek and Allie and their children spent two weeks in Oz, swimming, hiking, and going on safari.

Culinary Renata stayed in her counterpart's guest room, and the two of them spent hours comparing their divergent lives. Culinary Derek, Allie and the kids stayed with Derek and Allie, in their house's spacious guest quarters.

Every morning, Loretta and Tony made a mad dash to the chicken coop, petted chickens, and gathered eggs for breakfast. Some of the eggs even made it back to the house intact. After breakfast, they'd feed scraps to the chickens.

✳✳✳

At the end of this vacation, Derek invited everyone for a celebration and feast. They ferried Eldon Trask, Chloe, and the Brocklesbys to Oz and, after many bottles of fine wine and champagne, popcorn, and lobster steaks — Allie handed out Oz passports to everyone.

They deserved them.

"I have a proposition for you all," Derek said. "Take your time and think it over because it will change your lives forever. *Who wants to become an Indigo?* You'll always be welcome here whatever you decide."

Minutes of stunned silence followed.

"Are you getting sick again?" Wendy said.

"No. I know where we can get all the red pills we need."

The End

Some Pidgin Kine

Some of the Hawaiian characters — i.e. Travis Howland speak Pidgin, sometimes.

"Alii," pronounced "al-*lee*-ee" were the nobility under the old Hawaiian monarchy.

"Auwe," pronounced "ow-*way"* is an expletive meaning "Oh no!" or "Damn!"

One of the most common phrases is *"da kine,"* meaning "that kind of" or "something like that." Generally this refers to something vaguely similar to something else that the speaker doesn't want to nail down.

Often speakers like to be vague about things that are actually specific. For instance Travis might say "I have one idea *kine"* meaning I have something *like* an idea, when in fact he has *precisely* an idea.

"kama'aina" means someone who has lived in Hawaii a long time.

"No huhu" means "no problem" or "no worries."

"Not!" by itself means "it can't be" or "no way".

"one" is often used in place of "a".

"ono" means "good" and "some ono" means "fantastic."

"talk story" means "have a conversation" or "chew the fat."

Acknowledgments.

About a year ago, I heard of a stage-3 clinical trial at the Perelman School of Medicine at the University of Pennsylvania and the Children's Hospital of Pennsylvania of a virus that cures certain types of blindness by altering genes.

This inspired the novel.

The images of the spirit-world were based on a profoundly inspiring out-of-body experience I had about twenty years ago. The novel's world-view owes a great deal to the system of metaphysics collectively known as the Seth Material — developed in a series of fourteen books by Jane Roberts and Robert Butts.

I'd like to thank Eva Thury for reading and editing an early version of this manuscript and making many very helpful suggestions.

I am grateful to Ed Brocklesby (completely unrelated to the character by that name!) for reading an early version of this book.

The scenes where the CIA spied on members of congress, were inspired by the 2014 incident where Senator Feinstein accused the CIA of spying on her and other members of congress, removing files from their computers, and intimidating congressional investigators.

An early version of the novel had a courtroom-drama that I cut later (it may reappear in a sequel). I would like to thank

Laura A. Fox, Esquire, and Professor David Cohen of the Drexel School of Law for interesting and informative discussions on legal matters. I'd also like to thank Tom and Karen Devlin for helpful legal suggestions.

Made in the USA
Middletown, DE
27 March 2016